Java Spider

ALSO BY GEOFFREY ARCHER

Skydancer
Shadowhunter
Eagletrap
Scorpion Trail

JAVA SPIDER

Geoffrey Archer

CENTURY

Published by Century Books in 1997

1 3 5 7 9 10 8 6 4 2

Copyright © Geoffrey Archer 1997

Geoffrey Archer has asserted his right under the Copyright, Designs and Patents Act, 1988 to be identified as the author of this work.

Century Books,
Random House UK Limited
20 Vauxhall Bridge Road, London, SW1V 2SA

Random House Australia (Pty) Limited
20 Alfred Street, Milsons Point, Sydney,
New South Wales 2061, Australia

Random House New Zealand Limited
18 Poland Road, Glenfield
Auckland 10, New Zealand

Random House South Africa (Pty) Limited
Endulini, 5a Jubilee Road, Parktown 2193, South Africa

Random House UK Limited Reg. No. 954009

A CIP catalogue record for this book is available from the British Library

Papers used by Random House UK Limited are natural, recyclable products made from wood grown in sustainable forests. The manufacturing processes conform to the environmental regulations of the country of origin.

ISBN 0 71 267504 3

Typeset by Deltatype Ltd, Birkenhead, Merseyside
Printed and bound in Great Britain by
Mackays of Chatham, Plc, Chatham, Kent

Author's Note

The island of Kutu doesn't exist. However, the events that take place there in this story will be familiar to islanders in some parts of the Indonesian archipelago, particularly in East Timor and Irian Jaya.

All of the characters and some of the companies in this work of fiction are invented. Any resemblance to actual persons or companies is purely coincidental.

*To Eva, Alison
and James*

I

STEPHEN BOWEN DREW back the curtains of his tenth-floor hotel room. The dawn sun sat on the city's concrete horizon, the colour of a ripe guava, staining the city's pollution haze a murky pink.

The Indonesian day began early. Already across the street he saw brown-backed men bolting the steel frame for another new bank. By midday the blazing sun would make such work impossible. By mid afternoon it would be raining – tropical torrents, silver rods of water bringing street life to a halt.

Bowen slid open the glass door and stepped on to the small, tiled balcony. From the road below came the putter of two-stroke *bajaj* tricycles, weaving their smelly way through the commuter traffic. Already the sun felt hot on his face.

He had patrician good looks, with peppery hair combed in lines neat as plough furrows. A man in control. His appearance had served him well. Politics, business, women – his looks had helped.

He leaned on the steel rail and gazed down at the crush of traffic. The country's population was growing at two million a year, Jakarta almost choking with bodies. A tough place for foreigners, although many lived here, oiling the wheels to create business for their companies back home.

This was his fourth visit to Indonesia. He loved the place in the way he loved casinos. Men living by their wits, playing their cards right and winning big. The place smelled of banknotes.

His first two trips to the south Pacific had been as a backbencher, free to explore his own business interests. The third and this one had been official. Straitjacketed by being a minister of Her Majesty's government. Publicly, at least.

He heard the door chime and let in the room-service waiter. The

I

dowdily-dressed, brown-faced Javan eyed Bowen's maroon silk pyjamas, set down the tray and grinned. Fruit, coffee and fried rice. Bowen gave him a thousand rupiah note. Big money here, thirty pence back home.

The waiter bowed, but his eyes mocked. Bowen closed the door and locked it. Always the eyes that gave away the Javans contempt for the pink-faced Europeans who'd once been their masters.

Bowen drank the fresh-pressed juice. Half an hour to go before the car came. Half an hour in which to be washed, dressed and checked out of this middle-ranking, characterless hotel. His case lay on the second bed, almost packed. He'd done it last night, several hours and a change of hotels after the final handshakes that had concluded his official visit.

The trip had been a success. The Memorandum of Understanding he'd signed meant the two governments were now firmly locked into the arms deal, with final terms to be settled between the British manufacturers and ABRI, the Indonesian military. The contract had been hard fought – they'd beaten the French by a whisker. Although the donkey work had been done by the UK consortium DefenceCo p.l.c., the clincher had come from him. A touch on the political rudder, a twisting of arms, and a high-stakes gamble that was set to pay out in style.

Bowen sat at the low table and ate the slices of pineapple and mango but rejected the *nasi goreng*. Greasy chicken-fried-rice was not his idea of a breakfast. He downed some coffee then removed his pyjamas and packed them, before stepping into the shower.

For a man of nearly fifty the Rt Hon Stephen Bowen MP, Minister of State for Foreign Affairs, was fit, his muscles toned regularly in a Westminster gym. A mat of dark hair extended from chest to groin. As the water pricked his skin he felt a shiver of anticipation, like when entering a casino – the thrill of risk, the buzz that came with abandoning life's safe zone. What he was about to do was, he knew, distinctly unwise – but it would taste like nectar.

Twenty-four hours ago he'd received a guarded invitation from an Indonesian friend, a lavish offer of hospitality. A child could have seen that accepting it would rate as ministerial impropriety if it became public knowledge back home – the personal bank account of his host was to benefit handsomely from the arms deal he'd just signed. If the London papers found out they'd chew him to pulp.

Stephen Bowen, however, was a man facing his second half-century, a man whose marriage survived in name only. What he'd been offered, few in his situation could resist – the promise of a few days on a luxury yacht and the intimate company of an exceptionally pretty woman half his age.

He'd convinced himself no one back home would ever know. Total privacy had been guaranteed by his host. He'd cut free from his Foreign Office minders in Jakarta, moving from the plush suite in a five-star tower where he'd spent the past few days into this more anonymous hotel. And he'd ignored the Ambassador's demands to know where he was going for his 'few days' leave'.

He turned in the shower, letting the spray play on his chest and stomach.

Selina was her name. Working for the Indonesian Ministry for Foreign Affairs, she'd acted as social secretary for his visit. Only ever seen her in a smart business suit.

As he towelled himself down, he felt a moment's guilt about Sally. Always did in the hours before an indiscretion. A twitch of regret at not having made a better fist of his marriage. His fault entirely, but too late to change.

He dressed quickly in clean, blue sports-shirt and buff, cotton trousers. Three days of bacchanalian pleasure on the big man's motor yacht, a little light gambling – and Selina . . . Didn't even know her second name. Knew her smile though, and her submissive eyes. Every man did in his dreams. And now the dream was being made flesh. A little thank you, a little *quid pro quo* for the way he'd fixed the arms deal.

And what a deal. Good for Britain, but above all good for *him*. As Bowen closed his Samsonite bag, he felt the thrill of the tightrope. One slip and he'd be finished. Never before had he staked so much. Never before had he *had* to. The arms deal he'd signed would not only benefit the nation he served, it would save him from bankruptcy. Unless he got found out . . .

He checked his watch. Time to go. Seven hours ahead of London. Still Tuesday there. He grabbed his briefcase, did a final check round the room, then wheeled his bag into the corridor and let the door click behind him.

Indonesia was another world from the one he'd cut his teeth in. Normal politics, normal business practice didn't exist in a nation controlled by a single man, his family and his cronies. The key to business here was simple yet complex – knowing who to bribe. Dozens of Indonesians in the military and in government would benefit personally from the deal he'd just signed.

Bowen knew little of the details. DefenceCo handled it. In the company accounts the money would be listed as commission, a lump sum to a single agent, which would cascade down to the other beneficiaries. The choice of agent was crucial. DefenceCo's man could not have been better placed.

Bowen emerged from the rattly lift and strode across the lobby to the cashier. Even at this early hour there was a check-out queue. He waited in the air-conditioned chill for a couple of minutes, glancing towards the swing doors for the limousine. Then he passed his Visa card to the smiling clerk and checked his bill. One night only, supper in the room, no phone calls.

'You use minibar?'

He shook his head and signed the slip. Pocketing the receipt and his card, he turned – and almost collided with her.

'Good morning, Mr Bowen!'

Selina. White T-shirt today, blue denim skirt, eyes as black as her hair, a face the shape of a heart and a smile as shy as a virgin's.

'Oh, hello! Hi . . .' he floundered, his throat dry suddenly. 'I . . . I didn't realise *you* were picking me up. I was expecting some ugly driver.'

Heart pounding, he fell in love.

'I the ugly driver,' she grinned. 'You ready?'

'Ready, willing and able,' he purred, stupidly.

The City of London – a few hours earlier
Tuesday 19.35 hrs

An autumn nip in the air. A London night black with gloom.

Nick Randall hated murder cases. They gave him a knot in the stomach and a feeling of guilt. Not to mention revulsion – particularly when the weapon was Semtex. No limit to the number of ways it knew to smash up bodies.

He stared broodily through the car window as the siren wailed them out of the Blackfriars underpass and into the clog of traffic the explosion had caused.

'Damn!'

Every lane solid. Nothing moving. He leaned forward.

'Turn that frigging siren off,' he told the driver. 'No way we can get through this, short of flying.' He settled back in the seat, waiting for the jam to clear.

The attacks had begun in the summer. Crimes of *envy* the government called them. The targets until now had been the super-rich

– company executives pilloried in the press for corporate greed. The terrorists had escaped detection so far, unknowns, cleanskins. They'd begun low key with a break-in at a rich man's home – then graduated to arson and letter-bombs. And now an explosion in a City bar.

Randall was a detective-sergeant, known by his peers in Special Branch as an easy-going bloke, except when the 'media' got on their high heels, howling about the police's failure to catch the terrorists. Tomorrow's papers would be another uncomfortable read.

'What gets me is the way they always demand resignations,' the driver complained, as if reading his mind. 'If we can't find the buggers with the men we've got, how're we goin' to do it with fewer?'

Randall grunted. Not enough hours in the day. Earlier he'd rung home to tell his girlfriend Debbie he was going for a quick drink with the lads but would be back by eight. Ten minutes later he'd had to phone again.

The traffic crawled. Near the Bank of England, the Mondeo cut free and the driver banged on the siren again. Blue lights everywhere. Fire pumps, ambulances. Havoc, just when the City had been winding down for the evening.

Wag's Bar. What a name. Conjured up a picture of smug young traders drinking the cream off their money-market profits. That's how the wannabe revolutionaries with the Semtex must have seen them. Not fat cats *yet*, but heading that way.

The rich getting richer and the poor poorer – a symptom of the times. Randall was as envious as the next man of six-figure salaries, but drew the line at killing people over them. The terrorists, however, had uncovered a vein of public sympathy for their crimes, which had curbed the information flow. No mean feat. Usually took a war for people to sanction murder.

A hundred metres ahead, a uniformed City constable pushed back gawpers and cameramen to let the Mondeo into the narrow street of banks and brokerages. The car stopped. Fluttering tape sealed an alley. Randall waited a moment, reluctant to leave the vehicle's warm, friendly smell. Outside on the alley's cobbles he could see the litter of terror. Splintered timber, shards of glass and thick, dark smears of blood.

Hooligans. Mad buggers. That's what they were. Yet when the attacks began, people had called them Robin Hoods. On the first raid, a domestic break-in, nothing had been stolen. Just a fine emulsion of human excreta sprayed over the soft furnishings. Tabloids had loved it.

Two more raids like that, then they'd got nasty. A north London mansion burned to the ground. The millionaire owner and his wife unharmed, but not their twelve-year-old daughter, asleep upstairs. Arson, and murder. That's when the case had become one for the Yard.

The car's fan sucked in smoke.

'All right, constable,' Randall growled. 'Tell me to move my arse.'

'Move your arse . . . *sir*.'

Randall had lived with terrorism for six years, mostly IRA. This lot had seemed different – anarchists, social revolutionaries or whatever – but now they were into Semtex he'd begun to wonder. Not the sort of stuff you could pick up at a chemist's. And he knew the Provisionals still had tons of it.

He closed the car door and sniffed the air. Damp from the doused fire, and acrid with burned plastic. His soles crunched glass as he stepped over the fat snakes of hoses. 5' 10", with thick, brown hair and a body useful in a scrum, he picked his way forward.

He ducked under the incident tape and, approached the gaping, smoke-blackened cavern, all that was left of the bar. Bomb Squad were inside. So were paramedics checking none of the remaining bits of human tissue could be sewn back to life.

A uniformed City sergeant checked who he was then told him there were eight dead.

'That's from a count of the heads,' he added ghoulishly. 'And there's about thirty injured.'

'Witnesses?' Nick shivered and tugged up the zip of his dark green Berghaus.

'Anyone who was inside and *lived* is down at the hospital.'

Nick sniffed the bitter, black smoke. A foam fire. Furnishings had burned but not much else. Ceilings down, fittings smashed. Just a few ounces of plastic would have been enough. He imagined the place. Young people, mostly men, crowding in after work, their gym-hardened bodies pulped by the blast.

One of them must have seen something.

'Which hospital?'

'Southwark.'

'Thanks.'

He stared into the wreckage. Eight lives gone here tonight. Eight families pole-axed. Not right, no matter how unjust the world.

'World's gone mad,' he muttered.

Out there somewhere, were the handful of people who'd done this, but Randall's team had no clue who they were. Heavy surveillance of PIRA regulars and of known subversives had produced nothing. The group called itself the Revenue Men, acting to stamp out graft and corruption according to a statement posted to the media two weeks ago.

Levying a *tax of suffering* on their victims was the way they'd put it. Somebody with a sick sense of humour.

From the charred shell of Wag's Bar a woman from Forensic emerged, carrying a heavy plastic sack. Nick knew her a little, having chatted her up once in the canteen. Married, he remembered. They exchanged grimaces but said nothing. Then he returned to the car, avoiding the larger shards of glass. The back seat was still warm. Comforting.

'Bastards,' he mumbled. 'How do they sleep at night after doing something like that?'

Randall picked up the folder containing photos combed from the files at the Yard and the Security Service, MI5. Any suspect with a remote chance of being involved. What he needed was a break. For a witness to recognise someone.

'Southwark,' he told the driver. 'The hospital.'

Away from the incident scene the traffic soon thinned. London was strangely nervy these days, more so than when the IRA did their worst. In the canteen at the Yard the reasons for this were the subject of speculation. The chaps with university educations said because the Irish were *foreign*, the Brits had stood up to them. But the Revenue Men were *Brits*, part of *us* – a sort of enemy within. It made people anxious. Made them wonder where they'd stand if the barricades went up.

All fanciful crap as far as Randall was concerned. More evidence of the futility of having letters after your name.

The driver stopped at a road block. A random check. Traffic Branch threw them up all over the place. Groping in the dark, the press called it. The driver flipped his warrant card and they were through.

Groping in the dark? Or leaving no stone unturned . . . Earlier that afternoon, Randall had slung the Nikons round his neck, stuffed the press pass in his pocket and slipped in amongst the hacks to take a look at a group of women picketing parliament. Anti-arms-trade. Not a shred of evidence linking them with the Revenue Men. But it was faces. Faces to add to the collection that one day might ring a bell.

The Southwark hospital had been new, twenty years ago, but looked ready for demolition now. At casualty reception normal patients were being turned away. The City bombing had swamped facilities here.

Nick showed his ID and was taken inside. Twenty minutes since the last bomb victim was admitted, he guessed. The most serious were already in theatre. Treatment bays lined the walls of the department, all full. Some victims lay motionless, wounds covered with bloodstained dressings. In others staff worked on their patients.

7

A harassed casualty officer brushed past, her pager bleeping. Young-looking but in charge. Nick touched her arm.

'Any fit enough to talk?' he asked. 'I'm police.' He showed his ID.

She took in his face then noted the cord trousers and pullover under his coat. Preferred her policemen in uniform probably, Randall guessed.

'Just a moment. I'm being beeped.' She grabbed a wall phone, dialled a number, gave her name and listened.

Her face was English and cultured. Well-bred, well-educated and good-looking. Like the crowd he'd been brought up with as a child and then rejected in his teens. She harangued the caller with words all the more cutting for their omission of obscenities. Finally she slammed down the receiver.

'If they want miracles they should phone a priest,' she snapped, turning back to him. 'Now ... you're looking for witnesses?'

'That's the idea.'

'Well, there's a man over there. I think he worked behind the bar. Minor cuts and burns. And shock, so take it easy.'

She led him to a bay with its curtains closed, then abandoned him as her pager trilled again. Nick peered inside. The man was in his thirties, his face red. Flash burn, he guessed.

'Hello. Can I talk to you? I'm police.'

A blank stare. 'Why?' The man's voice trembled.

'Just a chat.'

'No,' he moaned. 'I mean why'd they do it?' Angry now, as if it were Nick's fault.

'That's what we're trying to find out. Maybe you can help.'

'Bit bloody late ...'

'I don't think so. You worked there, is that right?'

'*Worked* there? It was my sodding bar.' His face twisted with the shock of his loss.

'I'm sorry. You must've known everybody in there, then?'

The man turned away, mouth trembling. Nick left it for a few moments.

'I wonder if you'd look at a couple of pictures?' he asked after a while. 'No rush.'

He leaned through the curtains, spotted a chair and retrieved it. He placed it beside the bed and sat down.

'OK now?' he checked. The man nodded. 'Sorry to press. Any strangers in the bar tonight?'

'Always a few I don't know. Mixed up amongst the regulars.' His eyes were remembering what he'd seen.

'Nothing special you noticed? Someone acting strangely, differently?'

The man thought, but couldn't get his brain past the images of shattered flesh. He shook his head. Nick took out the photos from the folder.

'Who's this, then? Are these the ones,' the bar owner asked.

'Just wondered if you've ever seen any of them.'

The man took the prints from him, but his hands couldn't hold them still.

'Here. Let me.'

Nick watched the bar owner's eyes as he shuffled the prints. Nothing. The man shook his head again, which made him wince this time. He put a hand to the small dressing on his neck. A glass-splinter cut.

'Can I take your name and address in case I want to contact you once more?'

Randall wrote it down.

'You bloody nail them, right?' Angry again. 'Those were my *friends* . . .'

'Don't worry. We'll get 'em.' He pushed through the curtain, wishing he believed it.

The young casualty officer was on the phone again, close to losing control. She really was a very pretty girl, he decided. Pale, creamy skin with heat blotches on her cheeks. When she put the receiver down, she looked close to tears. He wanted to hug her.

'Any luck?' she asked, dabbing her nose with a tissue.

'No. He couldn't help. Got any more?'

'There's two others able to talk. But they're confused . . . Still, if you're gentle . . .'

'I'm always gentle.' He gave her the smile that had got him in deep water several times too often and watched her blush.

West End of London
22.45 hrs

Charlotte Cavendish pushed through the glass door, paused on the step and turned up the collar of her fawn coat against the cold. It had been a long day, made longer by the Wag's Bar bomb. She should have gone off shift at seven, but at the thinly-staffed News Channel when something big happened it was all hands to the pump.

'Got 'ny change?'

9

She jumped. Hadn't noticed the vagrant huddled in the entrance. She peered left and right for the lights of a taxi.

'I *said* can you spare some change, please?'

More of a threat than a request. She pulled the black leather purse from her pocket and gave him a pound.

'Thanks, miss.'

'For something to *eat*, right?'

She wished she hadn't said that. Made her sound like her own mother.

'Yes, miss. I'll go to the caff,' he mocked, lifting a lager can to his lips.

Charlotte stepped on to the pavement as a taxi turned into the street, its lamp like Florence Nightingale's. She crossed to the kerb, arm outstretched.

Inside the cab, she flicked on the heater and hugged herself for warmth. She looked for the usual sign saying THANK YOU FOR NOT SMOKING. None there, so she lit up. Her nicotine levels felt uncomfortably low. The News Channel was a non-smoking office.

Charlotte pushed her free hand through her blonde hair and squeezed the tension from the back of her neck. Aged twenty-nine, she was a video-journalist with a new, low-cost television news station broadcasting on cable and satellite where *everyone* abbreviated her name to Charlie. She was ambitious – chief reporter at the BBC was where she'd set her sights. Meanwhile, as a humble VJ for now, she was jack of all trades – on-screen reporter, off-screen writer of scripts for the studio, and occasional camera operator.

The wine bar bomb had squeezed out her earlier report on the arms contract with Indonesia – submarines, patrol boats and aircraft upgrades, worth half a billion pounds. Lots of jobs – and votes for the beleaguered government. In the afternoon she'd filmed the small crowd outside Downing Street, anti-arms trade activists protesting that the weapons were for a regime that ruled by torture and murder.

In truth she knew little about Indonesia. Had to look up the Times Atlas to find where it was. Foreign news wasn't high on the News Channel's agenda anyway, so when Wag's Bar flashed they'd switched her to the bomb story.

A News Channel cameraman had been one of the first at the scene. She'd edited and voiced his tape from the studio. Horrific footage. When another reporter was sent to do the live spots there she'd been glad it wasn't her.

The taxi stopped at red lights, the third in a row. The driver was black. She didn't see herself as socially or racially prejudiced, but the

Revenue Men bombings had divided people. Haves and have-nots. Irrational fears had crept into her head.

She glimpsed a flash of white in the mirror – his eyes watching her. She shifted across to be out of his sight, then felt bad about it. The driver slid the glass partition. Charlotte shivered. No conversation please. Just get me home.

'D'you mind openin' the window if you're goin' to smoke?' he asked.

She smiled weakly. Why did *everyone* make her feel bad about her habit?

'Sure.' She took a last deep drag, opened the window a crack to throw out the butt, then closed it. Better to die of nicotine starvation than of cold.

She'd been with the News Channel for a year. Joined when it started, after training and working at the BBC for four years. The Channel wasn't her style – a downmarket mix of hard news and soft porn financed by a tabloid paper – but it *had* given her the chance to be a reporter. She knew she had the looks to make it up the ladder and hoped she had the talent. All she needed were the breaks.

The taxi's brakes squealed. Ahead stretched red tail lights. A jam that seemed to go on for ever. The driver slid back the glass again.

'Sorry 'bout this. Didn't see it in time. Could've taken the back doubles if I'd realised . . .'

'What's up, can you tell?'

'No. It's way ahead. But there's blue lights. P'lice. They keep doin' this. Road blocks. Lookin' for the bombers . . . Haven't a clue, have they?'

They were stuck. No way to turn or move forward.

'Nothin' I can do. Sorry.'

'Don't worry,' she told him. 'At least it's warm in here.'

'Yeah . . .' The driver hugged himself. 'If we're stuck here long enough, I might get in the back there with you!'

All she could see in the mirror was his grinning teeth.

'Don't even think it . . .'

The words slipped out before she could check herself. The driver turned away and hunched his shoulders. Damn! Rich white bitch – that's what he'd think.

Charlotte bit her lip. Oh for the knack of never saying the wrong thing – particularly to men. She would turn thirty next year. Always thought she'd be married by that age, but the long hours and the frequent need to drop everything for the job didn't sit well with relationships.

There *had* been affairs, mostly short-lived. Men lost interest when they came second to a career. She did have dates occasionally – men she met in the course of her work. Businessmen, politicians, powerful men turned on by a woman they'd seen on TV.

From the start at the News Channel she'd made a rule not to go with men from the office. Then, two weeks ago loneliness and fear had got the better of her.

Heading home late after a gruelling day, she'd gone for a drink with the video technician she'd been working with. Jeremy was pleasant enough, but a boy – a diffident, fair-haired lad who browsed computer magazines in his meal breaks and tended to blush when he talked to her. She'd babbled to him about how frightening London had become and he'd suddenly turned grown-up and protective. Insisted on escorting her home and she hadn't objected. Slept on the sofa that night. The next night, however, he'd shared her bed.

The taxi driver slipped his cab into gear. The tail lights were moving again. He wound up the volume on his radio. A talk show. The topic – the Revenue Men and the Wag's Bar bomb. Charlotte pricked up her ears. Some of the callers were *supporting* the terrorists.

The highway to the west rose up on to its elevated section. The taxi picked up speed. Five more minutes to the cosy, ground-floor flat in Shepherd's Bush which she'd bought three years earlier on a mortgage she couldn't afford.

The driver slid the glass again and switched off the radio.

'Down here somewhere?' He'd turned left off the highway.

'Third on the right, then second left.' She'd felt safe in this neighbourhood, until a recent spate of burglaries. 'Just before the next lamppost, please.'

She reached in her bag for her purse. Out on the pavement, she handed him a ten-pound note.

'I didn't mean that, you know. About gettin' in the back,' he whined, giving her some change. 'No offence.'

'I know. And I didn't mean to sound like a racist bitch. It's been a long day.' She gave him an extra pound.

A four-storey Edwardian house converted into flats in the sixties, Charlotte had picked the ground floor apartment for its neat rear garden. No worries then about intruders.

She undid the mortice lock, then slipped in the Yale key. The light was on inside, just as she'd left it that morning. Stepping into the tiny hall, the warmth welcomed her. Ten seconds to de-activate the alarm. She tapped a code on the small wall panel installed just days ago at Jeremy's suggestion.

She hung her coat by the door, then checked her face in the gilt-framed mirror next to it. Brown, almond-shaped eyes, high cheek bones and a mouth that men liked kissing. A complexion that got puffy when tired. She straightened her hair. Hell! Forgotten to book an appointment to get her roots done.

From behind the closed kitchen door she heard a muffled mewing. Since the alarm was installed the cat had been banned from the run of the house. She opened the door.

'Hello Rudolf,' she whispered, stroking the fluffy grey creature that pirouetted at her feet. 'Are you a hungry puss?'

She flicked on the kitchen light and searched the cupboard for cat food. The last tin – the type the cat disliked. Have to buy more in the morning. Silence, apart from the relentless tick of the wall clock. The place felt so empty.

She opened the can and forked tuna into the cat bowl. The animal sniffed it once, gave a look of bitter resentment, then pushed through the catflap into the garden.

'Sodding animal!' Charlotte hissed. 'I'll bloody give you to Oxfam if you don't watch it . . .' She left the spurned food in the bowl. Stupid name for a cat, Rudolf. As a kitten he'd looked like Nureyev.

She opened the door to the living room. A folding metal grille covered the French windows to the garden. Hideous, but she slept better knowing it was there. Her furniture was a jumble, acquired during the past four years. A squashy velvet sofa, a dining set in chrome and a sideboard with glasses and a bottle of Stolichnaya. Beside it was the answerphone. She checked. No messages.

She was glad Jeremy hadn't rung. Their relationship which she'd drifted into for reasons of self-interest was getting out of control. Her fault for encouraging him. Yesterday she'd even asked him to take her to Devon at the weekend. A visit to her *parents*. Madness. Her mother would get the wrong idea, her father hated visitors and, anyway, had been extremely ill, and Jeremy would think she was serious about him.

She ran a bath, dropping her clothes on the floor. Breasts smaller than she would have liked, hips bigger than she wanted. She sprinkled Badedas under the running tap and fluffed up the foam.

Jeremy had a car and she didn't. That was the point. That's why she'd asked him to take her to Devon. To save her a train ride. Pretty selfish really. But then, she assured herself, the relationship wasn't *entirely* one-sided. Sex for him was no longer a *solitary* activity, she thought bitchily. And he was doing it with someone famous, to boot.

But not for much longer. Not if her horoscope was to be believed. Much talk of a new man in her life.

She smelled of lilies and musk, sitting just inches from him, but he couldn't risk touching her. It was too soon. The invisible barrier between them had still to be broken and it wouldn't be while they remained jammed in the traffic. Stephen Bowen tapped his head against the window in frustration. Gridlock, time and again in their escape from the city.

Outside, an arm's length away, skinny youths hung from buses, staring and grinning, nudging each another about the middle-aged European with his pretty young Indonesian girl. That his intentions should be so plain to these yobbos needled him. Where was the privacy he'd been promised?

She'd probably done this before, he decided. Paid by the big man to sleep with useful foreigners. How else could a low-salary government employee afford a brand new Toyota?

Yet he wasn't sure. For the first few minutes of the drive she'd been chatty and smiley, still the professional from the protocol department, but beneath the mask there was a tension which suggested that perhaps she *wasn't* so experienced at this sort of thing.

He cleared his head, concentrating on the game. Whatever she'd done before, whoever she'd done it with, it didn't matter. For the next three days she was there for *him*, and by God was he going to make the most of it.

Suddenly the traffic unblocked and they turned on to a toll road that sliced through the city's overcrowded suburbs towards the airport.

'This road owned by president daughter,' Selina announced, back in tour-guide mode. 'She make us pay big price to use it. You know how we say *expensive* in Indonesia?' she asked, laughing.

'Nope.'

'*Mahal*. India has *Taj* Mahal, but we have *Toll* Mahal!' She laughed again.

Bowen chuckled. 'Very good . . .' He longed to touch her.

'You're very lovely, Selina,' he growled, relaxing slightly. 'Makes my heart go boom-badi-boom-badi-boom-badi-boom! Remember that film? Peter Sellers?'

She frowned, not understanding. 'You think I *lovely*?' she asked coyly.

'Oh yes. And how . . . You've got ebony eyes, velvet skin, the body of an angel . . .'

'Ohhh . . .' she giggled, blushing. 'You make me embarrass, Mr Bowen.'

'Stephen,' he beamed. 'Steve if you like.'

After thirty minutes the car turned into Soekarno-Hatta Airport. Skirting the taxi-choked terminal, Selina took a road parallel to a chainlink fence, then halted at a red and white pole. Beyond, executive jets were parked. She gave the gate guard two thousand rupiahs and he let them in.

Bribes at every level. Without them the country couldn't function. Big commissions at the top, a pittance at the bottom to oil the wheels of even the simplest service.

The General Aviation terminal was old and drab.

'He's meeting us here?' Bowen checked. His host had been vague about the travel arrangements.

Her face clouded.

'No. He er . . . he meet us in Singapore.'

'*Singapore?*' he exclaimed. 'He told me yesterday his boat's in Bali.'

'Yeh. Bali where boat is. But *he* have to go Singapore last night for business dinner.' Her smile had gone, replaced by that tension he'd seen earlier. 'We go Singapore first, pick him up. *Then* we go Bali.'

She looked acutely uncomfortable. Javans hated giving bad news, he'd been told. She was expecting him to be angry.

'That's going to take some time,' he remarked gently.

'Maybe two hours more. Not long. And airplane very comfortable. You like champagne?'

'What kind of plane is it?' He had a terror of small aircraft. Claustrophobia.

'Is British!' The smile was back. 'One-two-five. Very nice. Big so-fa.' She flickered her eyebrows flirtatiously.

'Now you're talking . . .'

Inside the scruffy terminal a small, empty executive suite was furnished with sticky, vinyl-covered armchairs. Selina left him there with a cup of coffee and took his passport to be stamped.

Bowen picked up the *Jakarta Post* to see if his picture was in it. Certain to be. When the president met a visiting minister, no paper here dared ignore it. The photo was on page two. Full face of the president, but just the back of his head. He read the copy.

President supports 1750 Billion Rupiah arms deal for ABRI. Britain will supply two ex-Royal Navy submarines and four new-build corvettes, together with special equipment to upgrade the Hawk fighter jets delivered in the 1980s.

British Foreign Minister Stephen Bowen was yesterday honoured by a reception at the Presidential palace.

An honour indeed for a *junior* minister like him, but Bowen knew the reason. The DefenceCo agent for the arms deal was a *very* close associate of the president. Bowen had been given a hint the old man himself might be on a percentage.

He smiled. This was the most extraordinary country. Conventional economics didn't apply here. Contracts went not to the *lowest* bidder, but to the *highest*, to ensure the price included a commission big enough to line the dozens of pockets involved.

The door burst open.

'Come quick! They wait for us.' Selina was flushed from running.

'Right. Where's my suitcase?'

'They load already. Come quick.'

He pursued her on to the tarmac where a uniformed official hustled them to the jet fifty metres away. The air was thick and hot, the humidity rising.

'Why the sudden panic?' he panted.

'I don' know. Control tower, maybe.'

Air traffic. Always air traffic. He looked at the HS-125 and shivered. Why did they make those planes so darned small?

Ducking, he climbed inside, fighting his terrors. His eardrums popped as the door closed. When the engines began their whine, he felt he was being buried alive.

Cream leather. Two large armchairs and a long, soft bench which he eyed with interest. Selina strapped herself in on the other side of the narrow aisle.

'Nice plane, yes?' she smiled, eager to please.

'I rather prefer jumbos,' he confessed.

The aircraft swung towards the runway. He knew he'd feel better once airborne. He sank back into the soft leather and closed his eyes. He kept them closed until the plane had climbed above the early morning turbulence. Then he looked through the glass and saw the capital spread out below under its shroud of pollution. Six hundred square kilometres of urban sprawl – in the centre a golden triangle of corruption and wealth, but around it slums.

When he turned to look at the girl, she was gone. He unclipped his belt and glanced behind. She was leaning into the cockpit, talking to the co-pilot. The hem of her T-shirt rode up, exposing the ridge of her spine, her skin the colour of dark honey. The thin denim of her skirt was tight across her small, firm behind. Bowen began to feel better.

'Now where's this champagne you promised me?' he chuckled as she sat down again.

'You want I look in the ice-box?' The refreshment cabinet was on the floor behind her seat.

A waft of lilies again as she crouched beside him. He'd explode if he didn't have her soon.

Suddenly the plane banked to the right. Bowen looked out. They were in a long, steady turn. He frowned. They were changing course, heading east, along the Javan coast. Singapore was northwest.

'What's going on, Selina? We're heading east.'

'Ye-eh,' she laughed. Her eyes betrayed her nerves, but all Stephen Bowen could see was her soft mouth and her perfect, perfect teeth. 'Yeh, it all change again. He just call pilot from Singapore to say he take Garuda flight to Bali. We meet him there after all.'

'Good. Straight to Bali, then,' he smiled. Ninety minutes flying time. Ninety minutes alone with her.

'Yes,' she purred, lips parted. Her eyes spoke to him – *fuck me now if you want.*

He reached out and slipped his hand round the back of her silky neck. He glanced towards the cockpit to check the door was closed.

She laughed again and shook herself free from his fingers.

'First, we drink champagne.' She held out the bottle for him to open.

As he picked at the foil and untwisted the wire, the skin crawled on the back of his neck. In a flash of insight he saw Selina and himself as performers in some play. The trouble was *she* seemed to have seen the script, but *he* hadn't.

2

South Devon
Sunday 12.35 hrs

THE FIRM ESTUARY sand exposed by the retreating tide crunched under their bare feet like meringue. The river itself had shrunk to a stream. They waded it to reach the broad bank beyond, which curved like a brown belly towards the open sea half a mile away.

Charlotte Cavendish watched gulls squabble over mussels in the autumn light, but hardly saw them, her mind a blur since yesterday when her mother had revealed that her father was dying. The tumour operated on a year ago was no longer in remission. The consultant talked of months, or even weeks.

Charlie walked in front, Jeremy a pace behind. She felt bad about bringing him. Crises turned families inwards and against outsiders. Jeremy had offered to leave, but her mother wouldn't hear of it. He was a guest, her daughter's friend. More than a friend maybe. Hospitality was due, whatever the circumstances. She'd made a bed for him in a room on his own. During the night however, he'd come into Charlie's room to comfort her.

She stopped and scraped at the sand with her toes. They'd walked far enough. Jeremy slipped his arm round her waist. Yes, he'd been sweet to her. A support she badly needed. She was an only child and he felt like the brother she'd always wanted.

The October air was much milder down here than in London. She wore a dress of white cotton, which a gust of wind flattened against her stomach. In the distance a curlew mewed. She stooped to pick up a baby crab left high and dry by the tide. She loved this place for its tranquillity, but hated it for what it signified.

'Y'know, it's fantastic that old pile,' Jeremy breathed, looking back at the house. 'People would pay a fortune for it today.'

'Not for sale. Belongs to the estate. The one my father managed.'

Sandpiper Cottage was the only building for half a mile. Almost a mansion, it stood rooted to rocks just above the high tide mark. Solid grey stone, a steep pitched roof and a tall, red-brick chimney for the fires which kept the inside snug. Her father's fortress. For twelve years they'd lived here, the house being part of his pension.

He was a recluse, a man dogged by a past he could never discuss. This was his hide-out, a cave where he'd withdrawn from the world to keep his secrets safe until he could take them with him to his grave. And now he was about to.

He'd been a colonel in the army. Forty-seven when Charlie was born, he might never have married if it hadn't been for the persistence of her mother, a brigadier's daughter twelve years his junior.

Ambrose Cavendish had served in the Second World War as a second lieutenant, but for some unexplained reason wouldn't talk about it. Only once had Charlotte asked why, when she was fourteen, a day engraved in her memory. The blood had drained from his face, he'd shut himself in his bedroom and not spoken to her for days. Only then had her mother revealed he'd been a prisoner of the Japanese.

It had shocked her. Not the imprisonment itself, but the fact that she'd never been told about it.

Across the estuary she saw her father walk from the house to the terrace. She waved, but he couldn't have been looking. Her mother would lose Sandpiper Cottage when Ambrose died, she realised. She'd have to move. But not in with her. Not at any price.

'We'd better go back,' Charlotte murmured. 'Verity'll be wanting sherry and won't dare start without us.' She headed for the bank on which oaks and beeches bore the first specks of autumn gold.

'Just time for a ciggy,' she said, stopping again. Her mother didn't allow smoking in the house. Jeremy reached into his trousers for her Silk Cut, gave her one and took another for himself.

They turned at the sound of feathers on water, a pair of swans struggling into the air. They watched the birds pass low overhead, wings sighing like harmonica reeds, then waded back across the stream.

They entered the house through a fragrant conservatory stuffed with chrysanthemums. In the pine kitchen Verity was pulling the joint from the oven to baste it.

'Hmm, smells good,' Charlotte hummed. She rested an arm on her mother's shoulder.

'Lamb. It *is* Sunday,' her mother said.

Verity had spent her life suppressing her feelings, but this crisis over her husband's illness had all but defeated her. She slipped the meat dish back in the oven and closed the glass door with a bang.

'Another quarter of an hour . . .' she gulped, removing her apron and looking away to hide her face. 'Time for a sherry, don't you think?'

Charlie could see her mother needed to talk. 'Jer?' She touched Jeremy on the arm. 'Know anything about cricket?'

'Oh yes.' His face lit up. 'Everything.'

'Good. Go and pour my father a drink – the decanter's on the sideboard – then talk to him about stumps or silly-mid-whatsit.'

'Aren't *you* coming in?' he asked uncomfortably.

'Soon, yes. Just want to help my mum a bit.'

'But everything's done, dear,' Verity protested.

'Then we can *chat* instead, can't we?'

Charlie jerked her head towards the living room. Jeremy fixed a smile and left the kitchen.

'What's there to chat about?'

'Oh, I . . . I don't know. Everything, I suppose.' Where to start, that was the problem. 'How . . . how do you think he is?'

'Your friend, you mean?'

'No, mother. Your husband. My father. How's he coping? Has he talked to you about . . .' Still hard to say it. 'About dying?'

'Of course not . . .' Verity flopped on to a wheelback chair at the kitchen table. Hair almost snow-white, eyes a watery grey, she looked defeated. '*I* want a sherry, even if you don't. There's a bottle in that cupboard.' She pointed to the right of the cooker. Charlie filled two small tumblers.

'He's not said a word about . . . about what's going to happen?' Charlie queried, hardly surprised. Not easy for a man to unbutton his feelings after a lifetime of keeping them private. So much she didn't know about him. In fact, the more she thought, the more she realised there was almost nothing she *did* know.

Verity was on the verge of tears.

'Let it out, Mum,' Charlie coaxed, touching her hot cheek. 'It's good for you.'

'I can't,' Verity wailed, pulling away. 'If I do I might never stop.' She bit her lip.

Charlotte turned towards the living room. She heard a rumble of voices. The men had clicked at last. The key for them had been easy – the freemasonry of cricket. If only *she* could find such a route to her father's heart, she might yet free him from his nightmares and let him die in peace.

'What happened to him, Mum?'

20

Verity didn't understand.

'In the war. In the Japanese POW camp. He must've told you *something*.'

'No. Nothing. Nothing at all,' she whispered. 'You see it was understood from the moment we were first introduced that he'd had a dreadful time and couldn't talk about it. And, well, I knew I wanted to marry him from the moment I set eyes on him, so there was a sort of unspoken agreement that I would never ask about it. He knew that and trusted me because of it.'

'But since?'

Verity shook her head. 'It was up to him, wasn't it? If he'd wanted to tell me about it he would have done,' she said defensively. 'In those days there were lots of things people simply *didn't* talk about. Not like now when you get *counselled* for everything.'

'What if *I* were to ask him about it?' Charlie pressed.

'No!'

'Why not?'

'How can you say *why not*?' she gasped. 'You know perfectly well what the reaction was last time.'

'I'm *going* to ask. After lunch I'll sit with him on the terrace. He *needs* to tell someone before he dies, Mother.'

'I forbid you!'

'Don't be ridiculous, Mother. I'm nearly thirty.'

'I don't care how old you are you *must not ask him about it!*'

Charlie trembled. She'd never seen her mother so animated, the pale eyes awash with fear, the lines round her mouth drawn tight.

'You *know*, don't you, Mum? You know what happened to him?'

Verity shuttled her head.

'No I do not. But . . .' she dithered, wondering whether what she was about to say could be construed as betrayal. 'I . . . I do know your father well enough to realise that whatever it was, it's something he is deeply, deeply ashamed of. To bully him into talking about it *now* would be an act of the utmost unforgivable cruelty.'

Charlie felt a lump in her throat big enough to choke on. Her eyes filled with tears, not because of the reprimand but because she saw for the first time that her mother's unswerving loyalty to her father had done nothing to help him, but had simply reinforced the bolts on his prison.

A shrill beep pierced the stillness of the house.

'Good Lord! What's that?' Verity clutched at her chest.

'My pager, Mother,' Charlie explained. 'Jeremy's got it. The office is sending me a message.'

She scraped the chair legs on the terracotta tiles as she stood, then collided with Jeremy in the hall. She read the display on the messager.

Need you in soonest. Please ring. Mandy.

'Damn!'

'What's happened?' her mother called from the kitchen.

'I don't know. Can I use the phone?'

'Of course.'

Jeremy hovered as she dialled the News Channel newsdesk.

'Mandy? Charlie here. What's the prob . . .'

'*Oh, thanks for ringing, love. Look there's a story brewing. Could be big. I know it's your weekend off but we're desperately short. Ted's specially asked if I could track you down.*'

Ted Sankey. The editor.

'What's the story?'

'*That's the trouble, love, we're not quite sure. Could be another political sex scandal.*'

'Uh-huh.' Any story involving sex got priority on the News Channel. 'What d'you mean you're not sure?'

'*We got this odd call from a stringer in Warwickshire. He said Foreign Minister Stephen Bowen's gone missing. Should've turned up in his constituency on Saturday – a weekend with the family, local surgery, all the usual. But he never arrived.*'

'You've confirmed this?'

'*Oh yeah. It's straight. Wouldn't have buzzed you if it wasn't, would I, luvvie?*'

'No. I don't suppose you would.'

Mandy was a temperamental news editor not famed for her reliability, but whom it was best not to cross.

'*Yeah, I've spoken to his agent. A real prat. No comment of course. But he did confirm he'd had to cancel the surgery. And I've tried Bowen's wife but I think she's taken the phone off the hook.*'

'Bowen was in Indonesia a few days ago,' Charlie frowned. 'For that arms deal. There were Reuters pictures of him signing.'

'*You've got it. But it's extraordinary! Nobody seems to know if he ever came back.*'

'The Foreign Office?'

'*Well, if they know, they're not telling us. Said they were still expecting him in on Monday.*'

'And the police?'

'*Not involved, they say. A family matter. Which could be the giveaway.*'

22

Down at the Commons they say Bowen's a bit of an old lech. He also likes gambling. Has all the makings for a good scandal, don't you think?'

'Well, yes. Are we running it?'

'Not yet. Ted's trying to get something firmer from his mate at Downing Street. The point is we need you in to work on it. When can you get here?'

'I'm down in Devon, Mandy. It'd be hours, and frankly I've got family problems of my own at the moment. Isn't there anybody else . . .'

'Devon? And of course you don't drive, do you? Hang on a minute. There's someone else down there this weekend . . .'

At the other end Charlie heard Mandy shout across the newsroom. Her heart sank.

'Jeremy,' Mandy came back. *'Jeremy Maitland's down there somewhere. You know . . . the video-editor?'*

Charlie glared up at him. And she'd thought him discreet. 'Yes,' she said. 'I know who you mean . . .'

'Tell you what. We could do with him in too. If we can find out where he is, maybe he can give you a lift. Not seen him by any chance, have you?' she asked facetiously.

'Ummm . . .' Telling lies, even little white ones, was something Charlie had always found absurdly hard to do.

'Not with you by some chance, is he?' Mandy mocked.

'Ummm . . .'

'Hey! You're not serious?'

'Well it just so happens . . .'

'My God! Since when? You dirty little devils. I had no idea. Well put your knickers back on and get in that bloody car of his. See you here in about three hours, OK?'

'Mandy!' Charlie felt herself blushing. 'I'm at my parents'. My dad's ill. I can't leave just like that.'

'Really?' Disbelief. *'Look, there'll be big gold stars from Sankey if you can get back quick. Let me know when you're on your way, OK?'*

'Sod you, Mandy. All right.' Deflated, she hung the phone back on the kitchen wall. 'Big mouth,' she snapped at Jeremy, then marched into the living room.

'What's up?' he asked, his face a picture of offended innocence.

Her father stood in the big window bay overlooking the estuary. Tall but somewhat stooped, with a thin, angular face and silver hair, the soft brown eyes which Charlie had inherited unable to hide their fear.

'Why do they want you?' he asked, his voice like a rake on gravel. 'Another bomb?'

'No, Papa. It's a politician gone missing. Stephen Bowen – he's a

23

junior minister at the Foreign Office. The newshounds have caught the whiff of scandal.'

Ambrose gave her the disdainful look he reserved for politicians and the gutter press.

'Ignore it, is my advice. Politicians are like children. Always seeking attention.'

'Can't ignore it, Papa. It's news.'

'Well if it's his private life you're talking about it shouldn't be . . .'

He'd never approved of her work. She was relieved they didn't have cable down here and couldn't see how downmarket the News Channel was.

'Unfortunately, Jer and I are going to have to leave. Pretty soon . . . I'm sorry.'

'Charlotte . . .' Verity whispered, tilting her head towards Ambrose. 'You can't . . .'

Charlie felt horribly torn. She knew in circumstances like these family should come first. But then, if she couldn't talk to her father about anything that mattered . . .

'It's the job. Always on call, you know that, Mum.'

'You'll stay for lunch at least.'

'Of course.'

'I'd better see if it's ready.' Verity padded back to the kitchen.

'They want me in too?' Jeremy asked meekly.

'Yes.'

Charlotte didn't look at him. The thought that he'd traipsed round the office dropping hints that he was seeing her made her seethe.

Halfway through lunch Charlie's bleeper trilled again.

'How can you *live* with that thing . . .' Verity gasped.

Charlie checked the display. *Ted asks are you on your way yet? Mandy.* She pushed the remains of her food away.

'I'm sorry. We really do have to go.'

Her mother cried openly when they said goodbye in the hall. Charlie cried too.

'I'll come again soon,' she assured her. 'And *ring* me!'

Verity thought long-distance calls extravagant.

Charlotte returned one last time to the dining table where her father sat surrounded by the debris of lunch. He stood up stiffly and gave her a hug.

Hadn't done that since she was a child, she realised.

She shivered. For a split second it had felt as if he sensed she wouldn't see him alive again.

A tall woman with yellow-blonde hair, Sally Bowen put down the trowel and looked at her watch. The chief constable had said he'd have someone round within half an hour. The flower-bed hardly needed weeding, but it kept her busy and away from the temptation to put the phone back on the hook.

There'd been two calls from the media before she'd decided to ring the police. The chief constable was a friend from the cocktail circuit. Should've rung sooner, he'd said, but then he didn't know how used she was to covering for Stephen's absences.

She removed her gardening gloves and pushed at her hair with elegant fingers. The sky was azure but rain was forecast. She turned to the eighteenth-century stone farmhouse which had been in her family for four generations. The long-case clock in the hall said nearly three. Too early for tea, but she would put the kettle on anyway. Aged forty-two, she looked fifty today in the pine-framed kitchen mirror. Bloody Stephen!

Being married to an MP was everything people said. All the shades of hell. Inconvenience, suspicion, the feeding of the bloody man's ego. She'd had more than enough in the past eighteen years.

Stephen had been due in Warwickshire on Saturday morning. Phoned last Tuesday from Jakarta in typical self-congratulatory mood, to say he was having a couple of days sightseeing before flying home on Friday. Told her to confirm with his agent he'd be at the weekend 'surgery'. Since then, not a word.

Reliability had never been a byword in their marriage. On countless occasions he'd broken promises and changed arrangements without telling her. So when he'd failed to appear on Saturday it was just typical Stephen. Then she'd begun to worry, checking the teletext for disasters in Indonesia.

At eleven on Saturday the agent had rung. She'd put off phoning *him*, for fear of finding that Stephen was *there* already and hadn't told her.

'Christ, Sally, there's a huge list of people to see him.' The agent had sounded exasperated. 'Was he on the early train?'

'I don't know,' she'd replied. 'He was supposed to be coming back from Indonesia on Friday. The Foreign Office say he was making his own travel plans, and they're still expecting him in on Monday.'

'Not at the Westminster flat last night?'

'I rang twice. Just the machine each time. What should I do?'

'Maybe best to leave it a while. There's probably some perfectly rational explanation . . .'

They both knew what. Another woman, or a game of cards . . .

It had been after midnight when she'd gone to bed. With the children both at boarding school she was alone in the house. In the dark silence of the countryside her imagination had run riot.

For Stephen, an evening in a casino could drag on interminably, his sense of time erased as he struggled to stem his losses. She guessed too that on the few occasions he won, a pearly smile and a trim bottom could turn his head and part him from his money. Sometimes she thought he had the hormones and sophistication of a pubertal teenager.

Twenty-eight minutes ago the chief constable had told her to leave the phone off the hook so she wouldn't have to speak to journalists. But she worried suddenly that Stephen might be trying to ring and replaced it.

She crossed to the huge sash window that faced the drive. She loved their home. The house belonged to *her* not Stephen. And the money she and the children lived on was *hers* from a family trust, not his. As far as she knew, every penny he earned as a minister went on gambling.

Why the prime minister tolerated him she'd never understood. They must all *know* what he was like. Perhaps they didn't. Maybe the screen of respectability *she* had provided had worked too well.

At times she'd been close to walking out on him, but had never had the courage. Maybe this little indiscretion would be the final straw.

She heard tyres on gravel and looked up the drive. A plain blue car but the two men inside were unmistakably police.

One turned out to be a flat-chested woman, in a mannish jacket. They introduced themselves as Special Branch.

She gave them tea and filled them in on her husband's vague travel plans. From the look on their faces she guessed the chief constable had told them what Stephen was like.

'Was he er . . . on his own for this sightseeing?' the male officer asked, awkwardly.

'I really don't know. He didn't say. But I doubt it.'

The man and woman glanced at one another.

'Look, Mrs Bowen . . . we need to ask some personal questions. D'you mind?' the man asked. 'I can leave it to my colleague here if you'd rather just talk to a woman. I can take a stroll round your lovely garden.'

'No. That's sweet and old-fashioned of you, but let's get on with it.'

'Then, first off,' the woman began, 'how would you characterise your relationship with your husband?'

'My relationship?' Sally swallowed. 'Umm ... formal, I suppose would be the word. What I mean is ... we don't have a *personal* relationship any more. In other words ... no sex.'

Her frankness made the male officer's eyelids flicker.

'Our marriage is a convenience. He needs me for his image as a family man ... and that's vital for an MP around here. And *I* don't want our children to come from a broken home.'

'But he does live here some of the time?'

'Weekends when he has a surgery. And in the parliamentary recess when the children are home from school. He's fond of them in his own way.'

'And the flat in London?'

Sally understood the question.

'Does he have another woman there, you mean? I simply don't know. I'm told men can't go without sex for long. But whether it's call-girls or secretaries at the Commons, I have no idea.'

'There's never been an affair that you've known about?'

'No. But then I've never asked.'

'So you've no idea if there's a woman with him in Indonesia?'

'You really should put that question to the Foreign Office. Maybe they'll communicate more with *you* than they do with me. To them I'm just the minister's boring wife, who refuses to come up from the country for Whitehall cocktail parties.'

The phone rang. The one in the kitchen was cordless and emitted a shrill warble.

'Shall I answer that for you, Mrs Bowen?' The woman officer was on her feet. 'If it's press, you're not wanting to speak to them, is that right?'

'Yes. That's right.'

'Hello?'

A female voice at the other end.

'No. I'm sorry she's not available.'

More jabber in the earpiece.

'Well, if she ever does want to talk to you, I'm sure she'll find your number. Goodbye.'

'Who was it?' asked Sally.

'The News Channel. That's the new one on cable,' the woman replied. 'Don't suppose you get it here.'

Sally shook her head. It was hard enough already limiting the amount of TV the children watched in the holidays.

'Now, Mrs Bowen, I have to ask about money,' the male officer continued. 'Did your husband have any financial problems? I understand he gambles a little ...'

27

'A little? He's an addict. Unfortunately he usually loses. Several years ago he got into serious debt. Over a hundred thousand pounds. Tried to get me to bail him out. I have my own money from family trusts, you see – and this house. Stephen asked me to mortgage it to pay his debts. Well, I refused.'

'And his financial situation at the moment?' the man asked.

'No idea. He knows I won't help, so even if he was in trouble he wouldn't tell me.'

The police sat back and looked at one another.

'Can I speak frankly?' the man asked.

'Of course. *I* have.'

'Well, if your husband's just been a naughty boy, but turns up at the Foreign Office tomorrow, then it'll probably be best if there hasn't been a great hue and cry. See what I mean?'

She did. But doing nothing didn't seem right.

'Can't you make a few discreet enquiries? What about the ambassador in Jakarta? He might know something.'

'Of course. Scotland Yard will deal with that. But what say we just keep an eye on things for the next twenty-four hours, yes? Give us a ring if you hear anything, right? Day or night. Or if you just want to talk . . .' He gave her a card.

Sally stood in the porch until the blue car had gone. Then she heard the trill of the phone again and ran inside.

'Hello?' She tried to sound like her fourteen-year-old daughter.

'Sally?' The caller wasn't fooled.

'Peter.' Stephen's agent.

'You all right?'

'Yes. Just had the police here.'

'Ah. What do they know?'

'Nothing. They asked a lot of questions.'

'And what are they going to do?'

'Wait, basically. Until tomorrow. See if he turns up.'

'Hmm. Have you had the press on?'

'Non-stop. Can't someone ring their editors? I mean, you know as well as I do what's probably behind all this.'

'Yes.' His voice betrayed his weariness of nearly two decades of coping with Stephen Bowen. 'I just think it's ridiculous they allowed a government minister to be completely out of touch for five whole days.'

'He was owed leave,' she explained.

'Even so. I'll speak to the big boys in London about the media. Talk to you tomorrow, Sally.'

'Thanks Peter.'

In the centre of the room was a low mahogany table. She picked up the silver photo frame that stood on it. She and Stephen on their wedding day eighteen years ago, a couple of months after he was elected to the seat. He was terribly good looking then. Still was.

And now someone else was getting her kicks from him. Sally flopped on to the cream, damask sofa, straightened her long, navy-blue cotton skirt and laid the photo face down on the table.

Good luck to her, whoever she was. And she would need luck. Because it would end in tears. With Stephen everything always did.

Northwest London
15.25 hrs

For Detective Sergeant Nick Randall this Sunday was special. A guaranteed day off. No interruptions, no demands to do an extra shift on overtime. All so he could see his daughter.

He'd not often put family first in his life – one reason he was now divorced. But Sandra was fifteen years old and very special to him. She lived with her mother. Lindy had rung last night to check he was coming, and to tell him there was trouble brewing. She'd found pills in Sandra's room. Contraceptives and something else she thought was Ecstasy.

Randall turned the car into the grid of rundown suburban streets where they lived – red-brick semis with dead Vauxhalls in the paved front gardens. Not the sort of neighbourhood he wanted his daughter brought up in, but there was no choice.

He stamped on the brake. A football had rolled between parked cars. A small, brown face peeked out to check it was safe. Nick beckoned the boy on and waited until he was clear. Every other family here was Asian.

He'd been wet behind the ears when he married. A dropout from the comfortable middle-class home of his adoptive parents, he'd ended up in the army. At twenty-one as a lance-corporal in the Redcaps, Lindy had swum into his field of vision, a nubile tease of a girl, a squaddie's wet dream. She was just seventeen, with a company sergeant major for a father who had the charm of a puff-adder.

Randall had been smitten. Blinded. All he knew was that he had to have her. Not easy with the CSM on the prowl. But he'd found a way.

Four months later she'd announced she was pregnant. The CSM had told him to marry her or get his neck broken.

It was eight years after that when he bought the little house in Wembley. He'd just left the army after two years unaccompanied in Hong Kong. The marriage was in trouble and he'd signed with the police in the half-witted belief he would spend more time at home. He and Lindy had stuck it for another year.

Sandra had been eight when he moved out, her face a tight button of bewilderment. And now she was fifteen, on the pill and doing drugs like every other teenager in the nineteen nineties. On the back seat he'd brought a horror pack. Police photos to show her. Morgue shots of dead junkies.

He turned into the crescent and found a parking space two doors from the house, recognisable by its peeling front door and the old bath left in the garden by a lodger who'd done Lindy a plumbing job in lieu of rent.

He switched off the engine, then his mobile phone rang.

'Fuck!' He reached into his briefcase. 'Yes?'

'Nick? Chris here. In the Ops Room. Where are you?'

'Wembley.'

'Right . . .' Hesitation in the voice. 'Summat's come up. We need you in.'

'Chris I can't. Not today. I told you why on Friday. In the pub.'

'Sorry. Boss's orders. He needs someone and you're it.'

'Look, at least give me a couple of hours.'

'Can't.'

'Fuck you, Chris!'

'It's tough at the top, chum. Here in half an hour?'

'You'll be lucky.'

The Security Group Operations Room on the sixteenth floor of Scotland Yard's Westminster headquarters was the combined nerve centre for Special Branch and the Anti-Terrorist Branch, a long, narrow room full of VDUs, with a panoramic view across northwest London.

On the back wall behind the duty sergeant's desk hung the roster list known as the 'chuff board', so called because when a policeman got a day off he was 'chuffed'. This being a Sunday, the list of those off duty should have been long, but following the City bomb, the surveillance net had been widened. Manpower was stretched.

Four men were in the Ops Room when Randall walked in. Two looked up and nodded. Chris, the duty sergeant, studied his watch pointedly. Just thirty-five minutes since he'd rung.

'What kept you?' he needled.

'Fuck off.' Randall wasn't in the mood.

'Look, sorry to drag you in, mate,' Chris said, softening. 'I did try to tell him. He's waiting for you.' He pointed to the SIO's office at the far end, separated by a glass partition.

The senior investigating officer, Detective Chief Inspector Terry Mostyn, was an old hand from the Irish Squad with a face like a large, lumpy potato and the look of a man who'd just emerged from under a car. He saw Nick coming and opened the door.

'Sorry, 'bout this, old son,' he mumbled. Mostyn was from Birmingham and sounded it. 'I know today was sacred. Your kid, isn't it?'

'Yes sir. My daughter Sandra. Only see her once a month.'

'Sorry. Couldn't be helped. We're down to the sodding bone.'

'So, what's up, sir?'

'I'm taking you off the Revenue Men. For the time being, anyway.'

Nick gulped. Didn't make sense. He knew as much about the case as anybody.

'I've no alternative, son. I need someone experienced. There's a government minister gone missing.' Mostyn handed him a single sheet of typed paper.

Randall read the name Stephen Bowen.

'Number two at the Foreign Office,' Mostyn droned on. 'Should've been in Warwickshire at the weekend but never turned up. Spent last week in Indonesia – that arms deal?'

Randall nodded, scanning the biog while listening. 'I know the one you mean.' The protesters he'd photographed at Downing Street.

'At the end of his official visit, he took a few days leave, saying he'd travel back Friday. No one's sure if he did. Could be woman trouble. Could be money. The Right Honourable Gentleman's second home is a casino apparently.'

'Sounds a natural for high office . . .' Randall quipped.

'The Foreign Office lost track of him, so Downing Street's got the jitters. We're being asked to start the ball rolling in case he's still missing tomorrow morning, but to keep it discreet. The media's been sniffing around apparently; the PM's spin doctor has told them it's just domestic.'

'Want me to go to his flat?'

'Yes. In case it's something simple like he got back from the far east and collapsed with food poisoning. I've spoken to his wife. She's agreed we can break in if we have to but she thinks there's a neighbour with a key. Just a quick look, right? No turning the place over. Not yet.'

Wesley Street, Westminster was less than five minutes away. A light drizzle fell as Randall crossed the road from where he'd parked.

Mansion flats. Nineteenth-century. Four storeys, with iron grilles on the windows. Most of the apartments would be homes for MPs, their occupants increasingly concerned the Revenue Men might turn their attention to *them*.

He studied the bell-pushes. Eight flats with a common entrance. He pressed the one marked Bowen in case the man was up there watching 'Rugby Special'.

No response. He glanced along the street. Two men in a car watching him, newspaper snappers on a stake-out. The tabloids had another victim in their sights.

He was about to check if there was a bell for a caretaker when he heard the lock click. As the door swung open, a small terrier sprang at him, yapping.

Its owner was female, late seventies and expensively preserved. She tugged on the leash. 'I'm *so* sorry.'

'Quite all right,' Nick smiled reassuringly.

'Were you coming in?' She stood to one side, then looked at him with suspicion. 'Who did you want?'

'Mr Bowen.'

'Oh . . . I don't think he's in. I'm next door you see. I heard his bell just a moment ago. It's been going on and off all afternoon.'

'That was me. Just now anyway. Tell me, is there a caretaker for these flats?'

'Yes, but today's Sunday so he's not here.'

'Madam, I'm a police officer.' He turned his back towards the press photographers and showed her his warrant card. 'Can we step inside a moment?'

She wound the dog's lead round her wrist, then put on half-moon glasses to check his ID.

'Do you by any chance have a key to his flat?' he asked. 'It's because of the bombs. We're checking the homes of MPs who've been away for a few days. Just in case . . . you know?'

She looked a little doubtful but led the way to the second floor, dragging her protesting animal. She went into her own flat briefly and re-emerged with a key.

Inside Bowen's flat, the first door was the kitchen. Next, a small bathroom. At the end of the hall a living room on the left and bedroom on the right. Bed made. All neat and tidy.

'Everything all right?' the woman called from the stairwell.

'So far, yes.'

The living room was chintzy sofas, and repro antiques. No bodies on the floor, no sign of trouble. On a rosewood card table by the door, a fax and answerphone. He touched the replay. A woman's voice, decidedly 'county', was coldly telling him to ring. The wife probably. Then a second message which caught his interest.

'*Greenfield here, Mr Bowen. Ringing at four thirty on Saturday.*'

The voice sounded north London Jewish.

'*I know you've been away this week, but I need to remind you that you've missed your payment deadline again. This really can't go on. I don't want to go public, but you're forcing my hand, Mr Bowen. We're not a charity. We've got to have our money. I'd be obliged if you'd call me first thing Monday. Please don't make me have to ring you at the House or the Foreign Office.*'

Money problems it was, then. Pity. Sex would have been more interesting.

One more message from the wife, concerned this time rather than angry. Then two from lobby journalists asking Bowen to call. Randall spooled back the tape and played it again, taking a verbatim note.

As he reappeared at the front door, the woman looked relieved his arms weren't full of stolen silver.

'Thanks for your help, ma'am. Everything's in order.'

Out in the street he was eyed with curiosity by the snappers. Back in his car he called DCI Mostyn's direct line on his mobile and told him what he'd learned.

'Well that's something,' the Midlander mumbled. 'Gives us somewhere to start if he's not turned up by tomorrow morning. Better get yourself back in here and draw up an action plan.'

Nick checked his watch. A quarter to five. He could see this dragging on all evening.

He dialled his home in Wimbledon. The voice that answered sounded sleepy.

'It's me, Debs. Were you snoozing?'

'Mmm . . . Just a little lie down.' They'd been living together for the past two years. Debbie worked in personnel at a local police station. 'What's up?'

'I've been caught for duty.'

'Oh yeah?' Always a little suspicious of him when he went to his ex-wife's house. 'How was Sandra?'

'Never saw her. They rang when I was parking. Had to phone the house from the car to say I couldn't make it.'

'Oh no . . . So when are you coming home?' Her voice sounded flat.

'No idea, chuck. You know what it's like.'

'No peace for the wicked, eh?'

33

'Something like that. See you later. OK?'

'OK.'

He rang off and turned on the ignition.

Debbie was a divorcee too. No kids though. She was good for him. Easy-going like himself, never nagging about where they were heading as a couple, never getting into a paddy over anything. Above all, she let him be himself. Women sucked blood, given half a chance, and he wasn't a willing donor.

M4 motorway
16.55 hrs

Traffic on the motorway into London was dense with country-weekenders returning home. Charlotte had spoken little on the long, fast drive from Devon. She hated her personal life being newsroom gossip, particularly when the man in question wasn't going to last.

They'd passed the airport and were approaching Chiswick when the pager went off again. A message to call the editor on his direct line. She used Jeremy's carphone.

'Ted! Hi. It's Charlotte here.'

'*Great, girl. Where are you?*'

'West London.'

'*Ah . . . Sorry, girl. Think I've dragged you back unnecessarily.*'

'Oh. Bowen's turned up?'

'*Not exactly . . . Just had my arm wrenched up between my shoulder blades, that's all. Downing Street's been on to all the editors. TV and press. They're saying it's a storm in a teacup. Marital hiccup. Asking us to leave him and his missus in peace so they can sort it out.*'

'Leave Bowen in peace? So they know where he is, then?'

'*That's the implication. Not said in so many words. Anyway I've talked with the competition and we've agreed to give them the benefit of the doubt – until tomorrow anyway.*'

'I see. So you don't want me in?'

'*No. We don't need Jeremy either. Will you tell him?*'

'Umm . . . yes I will.'

'*Sorry to spoil your er . . . cosy weekend together.*'

Charlotte could see his smirk as clearly as if it were a video phone. She took a deep breath, counted to three, then replied.

34

'We were visiting my parents, actually, Ted. My dad's dying. He's got a brain tumour.'

'*Oh fuck! You serious?*'

'Yes. Unfortunately. Jeremy was good enough to drive me down.' Silence for a few seconds.

'*I see. I'm sorry, girl. Very sorry.*'

'But that's private, Ted, about my dad. Don't want everyone knowing about *that* too.'

'*Point taken. Lips sealed. Now, Mandy tells me you're on the breakfast shift tomorrow.*'

'That's right. In at 4 a.m.'

'*Perfick. If there's an early break on Bowen, you can get stuck straight in.*'

'No problem. See you tomorrow, then.'

She clicked the phone back in its holder.

'The flap's over?' Jeremy checked.

'For now. Sankey's running scared. You know what he's like. Desperate for the Channel to appear respectable so the licence'll be renewed. And everyone in the media's scared of what'll be in the government's new Privacy Bill. So – good behaviour all round.'

She turned to look at him. Straight, fair hair, green eyes, fancy driving gloves, leather steering wheel, compass on the windscreen – he just wasn't her type. But he meant well. And he'd been kind. But it was time to ditch him before he thought he owned her. The trick was to do it kindly. She reached out and rested her hand on his shoulder.

'Will you drop me at my place?'

'Drop you?' He half-turned, eyebrow raised.

'Yes. I've got to be up again at three. And I want to be on my own for a while. You understand.'

He had the bruised look of a child parted from his teddy.

'Fine.' He shrugged.

'But thank you for driving me to Devon. You've been sweet. You really have.'

Sweet. Jeremy winced.

3

Monday 03.30 hrs

CHARLIE WAS STILL half-asleep as she fell into the back of the minicab, tugging at the hem of her short skirt. She was dressed in a red two-piece under her open fawn coat. The smell of the car's air-freshener reminded her of public lavatories.

'Early start then?' the driver asked, ogling her in the mirror. She'd always suspected there was something seriously wrong with men who spent their nights driving.

'Gosh! So it is,' she replied, pretending she'd only just noticed the time. The driver crunched the gear and shot off.

She'd heard the radio news at three. Of Stephen Bowen there'd been no mention. Probably turned up late last night with his tail between his legs. Or whatever.

The empty streets were bathed in sodium light. She liked the feeling of Londoners sleeping peacefully all around her while she set off to bring them up to date with the world when they awoke. But above all she liked the clear roads. Within fifteen minutes they were at Wendover Street. Tucked to one side of the News Channel entrance was the long sausage of the down-and-out in his sleeping bag.

The newsroom on the first floor was open-plan with a low ceiling, cream walls and small work-spaces cluttered by screens and keyboards. A dozen or so bodies at work, most having been on all night, looking forward by now to the end of their shift.

'Morning Charlie!'

The shout came from Tom Marples, producer of the morning show, a gaunt, swarthy man who was old-fashionedly coy about his gayness.

'Morning Tom.'

She hung her fawn coat on the wall hook behind her desk, then logged on to her terminal. The prompt flashed – *Mail.* Two service messages – an invitation to a leaving party for one of the VJs, and a style

36

advisory from Ted Sankey on the need to avoid clichés. Then a third message which made her squirm.

Charlie! How could you? The guy's a trainspotter. My dick's twice the size of his. Fancy a nibble?

Charlotte felt the blood rush to her face, sensing everyone in the newsroom watching. A glance up, then down. No one looking. All too busy.

The log-in for the message was *newsroom* – a code made available for temps. Anyone could use it. No way of tracing the author.

It was that bloody cow Mandy, she decided.

'Charlie!' Tom again, calling to her. 'Can we have words?'

She picked up a notepad and crossed to the producer's desk.

'Nice weekend, hun?'

She checked his eyes. The question was innocent. Marples was outside Mandy's knitting circle.

'Fine thanks.'

'OK . . . For the headlines at six, we have three minutes. Top story – today's health debate in the Commons. Not sexy, but important, and we'll be taking a "live" later in the prog – Angus at the Wickleigh Hospital with a bunch of nurses.'

Charlie jotted a note. It would be her job to write the stories.

'Then there's super pics of floods in Kansas that came on the overnight CBS bird. There was a shooting in Belfast, and finally a real treat from Australia. A cycling kangaroo . . . It's a hoot.'

'Can't wait. Nothing new on the missing minister?'

'No. What *is* that about? There's a weird note from Mandy saying you're *on top* of things.'

Charlie winced. How long before the bitch got tired of her innuendoes?

'Stephen Bowen,' she explained. 'Number two at the Foreign Office. Didn't turn up where he should've done at the weekend. Had a tiff with his wife, according to Downing Street. The big test is whether he arrives for work this morning. If he doesn't that's when we start ringing bells.'

'Sca-andal! Whoopee. But too late for the breakfast show, yup?'

Charlie nodded. 'Probably.'

'Pity. I'll put it down as a watch.'

'I'll start bashing the phones around eight, just in case,' Charlie told him. 'And I'll pull together some library shots of him.'

4.25 a.m. On air in ninety minutes.

Stephen Bowen's failure to return to England was a problem Harry Maxwell was determined he should not have to embrace. As Britain's official MI6 representative in Indonesia, he was meant to be concerned with the minister's security for as long as the man was in the country. But from the moment Bowen checked out of the hotel next to the embassy, telling the ambassador to mind 'his own fucking business' when asked where he was going, Maxwell had felt relieved of any responsibility towards him. His department head at Vauxhall Cross, however, who'd phoned him at home on Saturday night, hadn't seen the matter in quite such black-and-white terms.

Maxwell was overweight and sweated a lot. He loathed the humid heat of the tropics. He'd been here a year, listed as a political counsellor at the embassy. Another two years on station and he'd be moved somewhere cooler, he hoped.

He pressed his damp forehead to the warm side-window of the taxi and eyed the glass and concrete monoliths, which were the phallic symbols of Asia's 'tiger' economies. Alongside the taxi a *bajaj* motorised rickshaw waited in the jam, belching two-stroke fumes, it's sweaty rider looking with ill-concealed envy into the air-conditioned car.

Stephen Bowen was the sort of politician Maxwell automatically suspected of malpractice. Last Tuesday he'd sat in on Bowen's arms-deal press conference and concluded this was a man who found it easy to lie.

'No bribes were paid to get this contract,' Bowen had insisted, poker-faced.

'Commissions then . . .?'

'Normal practice. Matter for the companies concerned, not for politicians.'

Bowen's look had been too smug to be honest.

It was a British journalist who'd posed the question. Few Indonesian reporters had shown up. Most demanded cash payments to attend embassy press conferences, an aspect of the local culture which Maxwell's ambassador refused to go along with.

Bribery not a matter for politicians? In this country politicians were in the thick of it, but to say so in print was a crime. Maxwell was on his way to court, to watch the trial of a young journalist who'd written an article saying the commission on the arms deal with Britain amounted to £45 million and was going to a close crony of the president. For diplomatic reasons the hearing had been postponed until after Bowen's visit.

The car stopped outside the court. The driver took his money with a grunt. Maxwell got out. After the artificial chill of the taxi, the heat smothered him like a wet pillow.

The facia of the court house was Dutch colonial, its grandeur downgraded by the opening of a McDonald's next door. Maxwell wore a pale-blue shirt and light-grey slacks. He heaved his bulk up the steps to the portico, a handkerchief to his forehead.

The air in the lobby was heavy with the sweet, clove-scent of *kretek* cigarettes, a last chance for smokers, because inside the courtroom smoking was banned. In large letters above the entrance to the chambers a sign read PANCASILA, the acronym for the five principles upon which the nation of Indonesia had been founded. *Social justice for all* was one of them. Maxwell had a sneaking suspicion that the half-million or more people whose murder had been prompted by the nation's leaders in the past thirty years might have been short-changed.

He joined the swell of bodies, mostly younger than him, squeezing into the chamber, and craned his neck for somewhere to sit. His eye was caught by a young Javan grinning at him. There was a space beside him. The twenty-six-year-old journalist had a slim, almost boyish frame, and an alert face with a broad nose and thick lips. Abdul was one of what Maxwell described as his intelligence sources. A member of the semi-proscribed Association of Free Journalists, they usually met in quiet, un-public places. There'd be many young scribes here today, since one of their own was on trial.

'Thanks my friend,' Maxwell wheezed, easing his corpulence into the small space. 'How's things?'

'Busy. Busy. This should be quite a show.' Abdul tilted his head to the rows behind. Fifty or sixty young men and women in their twenties and thirties, friends and supporters of the accused. 'Why you here, Harry? Come to defend your country's reputation?'

Maxwell resisted the goad. 'Curious, that's all. Came for my education.'

The clerk called for silence. The air was electric. From a door at the far end of the white-walled court three black-robed judges entered, their faces like masks.

Then from a side entrance came the accused, escorted by a policeman in knife-sharp trousers. Aged twenty-five, black hair shiny with oil, street-wise face alive with excitement, he took his place at a table beside his defence counsel.

The accused's bribes story had not been published. No editor dared print such stuff if he wanted to retain his licence and liberty. The journalist's crime was to have *tried* to disseminate his heresy.

Maxwell's knowledge of the local language *Bahasa Indonesia* was insufficient for him to follow the proceedings. The outcome, however, was not in doubt. The accused would be gaoled for 'sowing hate', a catch-all law that made insulting the president a crime that could lead to seven years in gaol.

Suddenly the prosecutor branded the young journalist a communist, which prompted the rear of the court to stir like a wasp's nest. The bench called for order but the shout was ignored. The handful of police, there to protect the judges, eyed the crowd uneasily, knowing they hadn't the numbers to stop the protests.

'I don't understand your country,' Maxwell whispered.

'Nor do I, and I'm Indonesian,' Abdul grinned.

'We're in a police state, right? They're going to gaol your friend to silence him, yet these guys behind us can come in here, shout the same stuff that he was writing, and get away with it! Make any sense to you?'

'Easy. They want us to – how you say – let off steam?' Abdul answered. His voice was almost girlish. 'In this room we harmless, because no one dare report what we say *outside* the court.'

On the wall behind the judges hung a photograph of the president who'd had his way with this nation for over thirty years. Supported by the West as a bastion against communism, a man who'd used the development of the nation's economy to fill his family's coffers, Maxwell thought he saw a twinkle of amusement in those monochrome eyes. *Let them shout,* they seemed to say. *Words can't harm me.*

'What's the point of all this, then?' he asked, putting his mouth close to Abdul's delicately formed ear. 'Why do you guys bother to try to print stuff that'll get you locked up?'

The noise in the packed chamber rose. The soft Malay-based language hardened into a bark. 'Free the press! Free the press! No more gags!'

'You won't change things while *he*'s around,' Maxwell bellowed, pointing at the picture of the president. 'The man's got a skin as thick as an elephant.'

Abdul held up a finger to stop him.

'Yes . . .' he shouted back. 'But if you inject an elephant with a little poison each day, even *he* will become weak in the end . . .'

Maxwell smiled. It'd take a bigger syringe than the one these boys had. Yet he knew they were part of something bigger, a diffuse, disorganised democracy movement that was marshalling itself for the time when the ageing president gave up his hold on power. The regime was doing all it could to crush it. Hence this trial.

The sallow faces of the judges had the uneasy eyes of men

administering laws they didn't support. The accused was on his feet defending himself.

'Free-dom! Free-dom!' A new chant from the back of the court.

Maxwell saw strain on the judges' faces, caught the uneasy glances between them. Not long now, he thought. The verdict came within minutes. Guilty. The sentence – two-and-a-half years. Long enough to stifle a voice of protest, short enough to limit the anger of the mob.

The court erupted. The judges slunk away.

Maxwell knew his own masters would be pleased with the outcome. Trade with this country would flourish best if little was said about the means by which it was secured.

'Bad luck,' he murmured, his mouth close to Abdul's ear. 'Lost another battle, but you can still win the war.'

Important to keep the boy sweet. Abdul was useful.

London – the News Channel newsroom
06.55 hrs

'The re-write on the hospital . . . where the fuck is it?'

Tom Marples yelling, back from the gallery during a commercial break and haunted by the nightmare of a hole in his programme.

'Shit! Sorry! It's there! It's there!'

Charlotte hammered her keyboard. She'd written the item but forgotten to save it.

Down at the Wickleigh Hospital, linked by satellite, political reporter Angus Addy was waiting to do his live-spot before interviewing nurses. Her script was the intro for the studio presenter.

Inside the narrow control gallery packed with monitors, Marples sat beside the technical director. Charlotte squeezed in behind them.

'No probs?' Marples checked.

'Not yet,' replied the director. 'The Wickleigh bird's up.' He pointed to the monitor for Line 6 – Angus's face in close-up, mouthing silently as he rehearsed his words.

Tom keyed the talkback override.

'Hi, Angus. Hearing us OK?'

'Hi, Tom. Yup. No worries.' He pushed his earpiece in deeper. 'I've got three interviewees beside me.' The camera pulled out to show two middle-aged women and a young Asian man.

'Great. We open on tape, then come to you live at about five minutes in.'

'Fine.'

'Thirty seconds!' The director's hands hovered over the start buttons for the tape machines.

Charlie found live-spots terrifying, whether out there as the reporter or here in the gallery. Always the risk of the link failing or a mind going blank.

'Back on air!'

The title music rolled with the animated graphic of the station logo.

'*Good Morning. Welcome to Breakfast News . . .!*'

In the studio two presenters, one male one female, chosen for their sexual chemistry, perched on stools at a fake breakfast bar.

'*First the main news stories . . .*'

Little change from the last newsbelt half an hour before, except for a longer package on the health cuts.

'Coming to you next, Angus,' Marples warned.

'*And now for more on the health service cuts.*' The male presenter back in vision. '*Our reporter Angus Addy is live at the Wickleigh Hospital in south London.*'

'*Good morning . . .*'

Addy was safely on air. Relief. Charlie watched his lips move, heard his soft lowlands drone, but didn't take in his words. Angus was married with two young kids, but it didn't stop her fancying him. Most men she fancied turned out to be married.

The director tapped her arm and she checked the interview captions on a preview monitor. She was impatient for the item to be over. Her stomach needed food and she wanted to start badgering the Foreign Office about their wandering minister.

Addy's interview droned on. None of the nurses was strong.

'Wind them up, Angus,' said Tom Marples eventually.

Back to the breakfast bar. A suggestive line from the presenters linked into a long recorded item on swimsuits.

On the satfeed monitor Addy could be seen puffing his cheeks, relieved it was over. Charlie tried to guess from his face whether he'd had sex last night, a schoolgirl habit she'd never quite shaken off. Then the picture flickered and turned to 'snow'. The circuit was cut.

Marples stood up and stretched.

'Tit and bum time for our dear viewers,' he announced. '*Coffee* time for me. Thanks Charlie.'

He squeezed past her into the corridor.

'If it was men in Y-fronts he'd still be watching,' quipped the director when Marples was gone.

'Bitch,' said Charlotte. She was about to follow Marples out when the line six satellite monitor began to flicker. The 'snow' had gone. Instead, colour-bars and a caption.

'What the hell's that?' the director snapped.

Words on the screen. Flashing.

URGENT TO NEWS CHANNEL – ROLL TO RECORD.

'We're not expecting another feed, are we?'

'No . . . no we're not,' Charlie answered, puzzled. Then she shivered. A weird feeling that something was about to happen. 'Get a tape across it, quick!'

'Must be a mistake . . .'

'Or not. Get a tape running. Record the bloody thing!' she yelled, angry at his inaction.

'Tech Centre!'

'Seen it. We're recording line six.'

'Good man.'

For thirty seconds the caption continued to flash, then the screen went to black. Two seconds later it was filled by a face. In the control room there was a communal gasp.

'My God!' Charlie choked. 'It's *him*! What's happened?'

Stephen Bowen. A purple swelling on the left cheek. A cut on the jutting chin. Defeat in the usually confident eyes. Hair tousled, pale-blue shirt stained with blood. The minister opened his mouth to speak, flinching as if it hurt to do so.

Charlie reached for the intercom.

'Tom!' Voice taut as a violin string.

'Yes?'

'Are you watching line six?'

A pause.

'Am now. Who the fuck is it?'

'Stephen Bowen!'

'Chri-ist! Are you recording?'

'Yes. Hang on, he's saying something . . .'

'*I'm a prisoner. The people who have me say I'll never be free again unless the British government stops selling weapons to Indonesia.*'

Voice weak and stilted.

'*They say the equipment Britain's selling will be used against people on the island of Kutu, who are being murdered and tortured by the Indonesian army, so that their homeland can be dug up for gold and copper.*'

Not his, the words. Memorised and recited.

'*I will not be harmed so long as the British government tears up the arms contract that I signed last week and gets the United Nations to demand the full implementation of human rights in Indonesia.*'

Bowen's eyes flicked sideways as if for fresh instructions. Then he picked up a placard and held it across his chest.

STOP ARMS SALES TO THE INDONESIAN MURDERES it read. Then the picture went to snow.

'Tom!' Charlie screaming into the intercom. 'You're going to run that now, right?'

A moment's pause. 'Have to check it out first.'

'What's there to check?' she seethed.

Marples was scared. Terrified of taking decisions. Always sought Sankey's approval.

'Tom, we've got this on our own. It's a scoop! It's news! We *have* to break into this swimsuit crap.'

On the station output a Baywatch blonde was removing the top half of her bikini.

'*Now,* Tom!' Charlie screamed. 'I *know* the story. I'll ad-lib it.'

'OK,' he conceded tensely. 'I'm on my way. Get in the studio, Charlie.'

'Tech centre!' the director bellowed.

'Cue it again from the top?'

'You got it.'

'And line up that clip reel I cut,' said Charlie, turning in the doorway. 'Listen for my words. I'll make the cue clear.'

She sprinted through the newsroom, checking her top was free of coffee spills.

Mandy, bleary-eyed, was taking her coat off at the newsdesk, having arrived for the day shift. 'Ring PA,' Charlie shouted to her. 'Tell them we've got an exclusive on Bowen and to watch us.'

She pushed through the thick door to the studio, trying to write a script in her head. She was handed an earpiece. Through it she heard Marples brief the presenters.

'Coming to you in ten seconds, Charlie.'

She gave a thumbs up.

'Tell us all you know! And good luck.'

The presenters took their cue.

'We're sorry to break into that swimsuit feature, just when things were getting interesting,' the young man grinned, unable to change his style, 'but we've got some fast breaking news that's pretty sensational. The News Channel has just learned that the Foreign Office minister Stephen Bowen has been kidnapped. We've just received the first exclusive pictures of him, filmed by his captors. Our reporter Charlotte Cavendish is here to explain. She's been following the story. Charlie? What can you tell us?'

She took her cue from the light on the camera.

'For the past twenty-four hours there's been a mystery about the whereabouts of Foreign Minister Stephen Bowen,' she began, too excited to be nervous. 'He didn't return home at the weekend after a visit to Jakarta, where as these pictures show,' – she glanced down at the monitor to check her clip reel was rolling – 'he signed an agreement for Britain to sell Indonesia half a billion pounds' worth of ships and submarines. He was due back in England at the end of last week, but he failed to turn up in his constituency for weekend meetings. The News Channel along with other media was asked by 10 Downing Street not to report the matter because, they said, his absence was due to *personal* problems. Well, just a few minutes ago, we discovered the real reason. Mr Bowen has been taken prisoner. His kidnappers have sent us these pictures of him by satellite.'

She heard the director cue the new tape.

'As you can see, Mr Bowen has received facial injuries,' she ad-libbed. 'It appears he was forced to read this message from his captors.'

She stopped talking to let Bowen's words come through.

'*Perfect.*' Marples' voice in her ear. '*We'll come back to you out of the video for a comment on what you think it's all about.*'

Charlotte grimaced. What she knew about the human rights situation in Indonesia could be written on a postage stamp.

'*Cue Charlotte . . .*'

'As I said, the story has only *just* broken . . . We've no details yet as to how this happened . . . or where Mr Bowen's being held . . .' Her throat was beginning to dry. So was her mind. 'But . . . British arms sales to Indonesia have provoked protests in this country and abroad for many years . . .' she was floundering, 'and last week demonstrators paraded outside Downing Street.'

'*Wind up, Charlie.*'

'We've no idea who's responsible for the kidnap at this stage. It's not clear the government knows either. A statement from the prime minister is expected soon. This is Charlotte Cavendish for the News Channel.'

The last line had been a guess. No idea what the PM would do. She turned to the presenter, who linked into the next item – Hollywood Diary.

She began to shake. The technician took her earpiece from her.

'Terrific, doll,' he mouthed.

Back in the newsroom – pandemonium. Mandy had a phone to each ear, puffy face taut and bewildered.

'PA missed the start of the tape,' she yelled, spotting Tom Marples racing in from the control gallery. 'When are we running it again?'

'In ten minutes. On the half hour.'

'They're asking can we give them a transcript?'

'Oh *yes*,' Marples mocked. 'This place is crawling with bloody typists looking for something to do.' He swept an arm round the still largely empty newsroom.

Charlie perched on his desk, scribbling notes.

'We'll do it as a sandwich again,' he told her. 'Top and tail in vision, but edit together the file footage and the kidnap stuff. Got time? Eight mins before you're on air again.'

'Can but try.' She sprang to her feet.

'Ad-lib the script again. You were brilliant.'

She sprinted for the booth, hoping a video-editor would be waiting with the tapes.

Jeremy was.

'I thought you were doing the late shift today,' she needled.

'I am. But I knew you'd be here so I came in early.'

His doe-like gaze made her shudder.

'Fine. Have you got the tapes?'

'Clip reel and the hostage stuff.'

'Stick down fifteen seconds of Bowen in Jakarta, and about ten of him with his wife. There's pics from the last election. Then the kidnap shots. The whole thing.'

Jeremy started spooling. Charlotte grabbed the phone.

'Mandy? Charlotte here. Who've you rung so far?'

'No one. They've been ringing *us*. Foreign Office, police. The BBC, SKY and ITN. And Sankey on his car phone. He's negotiating to let the opposition have the pics . . .'

'But you've not rung the wife?' Charlotte interrupted.

'No.'

'OK. I'll do it.' She rang off and scrabbled for the number, then dialled again.

Engaged. 'Damn!' Should have rung her immediately. Not enough hands, that was the News Channel's problem. She dialled again. Still busy.

She logged on to the edit-booth terminal and checked the PA wires. Still in the 'flash' phase – one-liners updating the story as it unravelled.

She checked her watch. On air in three minutes.

'Three mins, Jer.'

'It'll be there.'

The computer beeped to warn of a new PA flash. She hit the keys.

News of the minister's kidnap was broken to his wife by the Press Association. Mrs Sally Bowen, aged 42, said she was deeply shocked. She'd not seen the TV pictures which so far have only been shown on the News Channel cable network. 'My husband's been missing since the end of last week,' she said, 'but as far as I know, neither the police nor the government had any idea he'd been kidnapped.'

'Great!' said Charlotte. Another line for her piece. 'I'm going to the studio. Tape ready?'

'No prob.' Jeremy pressed the eject key.

As she pushed into the studio, she saw Ted Sankey, red-faced with excitement, march into the newsroom in his white trench coat, his mobile phone to his ear.

4

WHEN NICK RANDALL arrived in the almost empty Ops Room, the phones were flashing like Christmas, the duty manager struggling to answer them. Randall had just spent forty minutes on the tube from Wimbledon, unaware of what had happened.

Chris jabbed a finger towards the SIO's office. Mostyn's door was open. Randall barged straight in.

'What's up, sir?'

'Just missed it. Video of him.' He pointed at a TV in the corner. On it a keep-fit girl was doing hip bends.

'Video of who?'

'Of a duffed-up Stephen Bowen. On the News Channel.'

'Christ!'

'The effin' wheels have come right off this one, son. Kidnapped.'

'I don't believe it . . .'

Nick gawped at the set as Mostyn filled him in. A caption flashed at the bottom of the screen – *Next news update in four minutes*. Mostyn pushed heavy-framed reading glasses on to his nose to decipher a phone number.

'The duty sergeant's rung the TV company,' he said, 'but it was all hysterical girls. Goin' to see if *I* can find someone sensible.'

He dialled the News Channel.

Randall's mind, never at its best first thing, began to think of lines of investigation. He remembered the well-meaning types he'd photographed protesting outside Downing Street last week. The worst any of *them* had done was break into an aircraft factory and smash up a fighter bound for Indonesia. It'd be a quantum leap to go in for kidnapping. Need to check his photos though. In case he'd missed some tougher nuts.

'Who's in charge, love?' Mostyn asked, when the operator answered. 'Scotland Yard Security Group here.'

Nick looked at the DCI's polyester tie. Worn the same one every day since he could remember, dark and greasy round the knot.

'Mr Sankey? Detective Chief Inspector Mostyn here, Scotland Yard.' Suddenly Mostyn bristled. 'Well, I suppose you *could* say we've been caught a bit on the hop, yes – but, er, that's certainly off the record. Now, where'd these pictures of Minister Bowen come from?'

Mostyn frowned in concentration as Sankey explained.

'Got any idea where it was being beamed from?' He listened. 'Europe . . . Couldn't be Indonesia?'

More explanations. He shook his head.

Randall glanced back at the screen. Pelvic thrusts for a better sex life. He had cable at home and was familiar with the News Channel's style.

'Tell you what,' said Mostyn, 'if I send one of my blokes round, can you give him a copy of the tape and answer his questions?'

Mostyn pointed at Nick.

'Wendover Street? Fine. It's a Detective Sergeant Randall. Round in twenty minutes. Thank you, Mr Sankey.'

He banged down the phone.

'Cocky bugger,' he growled. 'Says the pictures of Bowen were beamed to a satellite from Europe but can't tell where exactly. You'll have to check it. Hang on . . .' He swung towards the TV and turned up the volume. 'They're running it again.'

Nick recognised the blonde girl reporter. Remembered her chocolate brown eyes and nice mouth. Wouldn't kick her out of bed. Today she looked flustered, panicky. He forced himself to concentrate on what she was saying, then Bowen's bruised face came on.

'Bloody hell!' He sucked his teeth and listened to the minister's shaky statement. *Kutu*? Have to get the map out.

Then the girl spoke again.

'. . . *a question the government is sure to be asked is how the whereabouts of a Foreign Office minister can be unknown for the best part of a week, without the alarm being raised. This is Charlotte Cavendish for the News Channel.*'

'Couldn't have put it better myself, chuck,' Randall breathed.

'SIS must be shitting themselves,' Mostyn mumbled, glad it wasn't the Yard that was responsible for ministers' security abroad. 'Right . . . Here's the address. Get on over there, collect the tape and find out what they're not telling us. And remember. I've morning prayers at nine thirty. I'll want a report before then.'

49

Harry Maxwell stared at the wall clock, his feet on his desk. Lunch today had been Chinese, collected by his secretary from the Happy Times Food Court in the mall opposite the British embassy.

The representative of the Secret Intelligence Service was wrestling with a complex mental calculation. Had he time to get across town to the Sporting Club for a much-needed hour on the exercise machines before his routine chat with the ambassador at the end of the afternoon? The mick factor was the traffic. With the rains as they were, you could sit for an hour without moving.

He'd just plumped for giving it a try, when the phone rang, the encrypted line from SIS headquarters at Vauxhall Cross.

'Harry, it's Philip Vereker.'

Maxwell swung his feet to the floor. Vereker ran the southeast Asia desk. Ringing at *this* hour meant trouble.

'Good afternoon, Philip,' he answered respectfully.

'Seven thirty in the morning here, in case you've forgotten, and we've just been sucker-punched.'

'Oh?'

'Stephen Bowen's been kidnapped.'

'*What!*' Inside his large frame Maxwell cowered.

'On your patch, Harry, by the look of it. The kidnappers beamed a tape of him to a TV station in London half an hour ago. It's been on the air twice already. They've beaten him up and forced him to spout some stuff about cancelling the arms contract.'

'Mother of Mercy! Do we know who they are?'

'No. But Bowen mentioned Kutu. Said the arms would be used to crush the rebels.'

'That's crap. This contract's for submarines and patrol boats, not rifles and electric shock batons.'

'The point is, Harry, where the hell is he, and why don't you bloody know?'

'Bowen *insisted*, Philip,' Maxwell whined. 'Refused point blank to say where he was going or what he was doing. As soon as the last official engagement was over, that was it. Didn't want to know us any more. Said his official duties were finished and he was taking some leave. Told us to bugger off and leave him alone. Nothing we could do about it.'

'Except keep an eye on him.'

'But there's only me here,' Maxwell protested. 'I couldn't *tail* him.'

'The Indonesians must know where he went.'

'Maybe. I'll ask.'

'Report progress in half an hour. I've been summoned to see the foreign secretary at nine.'

The line clicked off. Half an hour was ridiculous. Could take him days to get information in a country like this. He pushed the intercom button. A click from the speaker as his secretary answered.

'Brigadier General Effendi,' he told her. 'POLRI Intelligence. You've got his number. See if you can get him on the line Vera, there's a dear. Oh, and it's bloody urgent.'

'Right-ho.'

Then the internal phone rang, the ambassador's secretary summoning him. The Sporting Club would have to wait.

London – The News Channel
7.55 hrs

'Downing Street!'

Someone held out a receiver and Ted Sankey grabbed it. Crisp cream shirt, silk tie, very much in charge.

'Yes, Gordon.' The editor recognised the voice of the PM's spokesman. An old friend from Fleet Street days. 'I've no idea why the kidnappers picked the News Channel, chum. Good taste presumably . . . No, we won't stop running the pictures. In fact we're making them available to everyone from eight thirty. BBC, ITN, the lot. Now, when do we get a reaction from the PM?'

He covered the mouthpiece.

'Mandy. Is Angus linked up at Downing Street yet?'

'Five more minutes,' she snapped, taking another call.

He took his hand from the phone. 'Gordon mate, get him out in the street in fifteen minutes, will you? What? Why not? Well what about a quote from *you*? OK, OK. But make sure you come back to us first.'

He listened for a moment then handed the phone to an outstretched hand. He saw Charlotte heading towards him.

'Well done, girl. You're a fucking star, know that?' He stood up and put an arm round her shoulders.

'Can we talk?' she asked.

'Of course. Come into my parlour . . .'

She followed him into his office and Sankey closed the door.

'If you're after a pay rise you'll have to sleep with me first,' he smirked. Sankey's sexist jokes always sounded uncomfortably earnest. 'I tell you, Charl, this story is manna from heaven. *Fucking* manna! Every TV outlet in Britain's going to run those pictures today, and each time there'll be a mench of the News Channel. That's the deal. I tell you, money can't buy that sort of publicity!'

'Ted . . . you're right. We got lucky. A head start. But if we don't move fast we'll be trampled underfoot by the big boys.' She was talking with the excess confidence of someone overdosing on adrenalin. 'And there's only one place to cover this story properly, Ted. Indonesia. I want you to send me . . .'

A patronising smile flitted across Sankey's lips. The girl was talking Chinese. Overseas coverage by the Channel's own staff was strictly prohibited on grounds of cost. Foreign news was bought from agencies, unless it was dirt cheap to cover like a day trip to Calais.

'That's not on, Charlie,' he said gently. 'You know that. We're not in their league. No way we can compete on coverage with the BBC. We only win when we get a lucky break – like this one.'

'We *can* compete, Ted. We're a sleek, lean machine – you're always saying it. We can do things much more cheaply than the big boys.'

Sankey shook his head. Charlie grabbed his arms, the closest to an act of intimacy with him she ever wanted to come.

'At least let me check it out,' she pleaded, eyes burning with ambition. 'I'll do a costing for you.'

Sankey understood. The girl saw the Bowen story as a career breakthrough. He'd been there himself, wanted to help, but he knew that a request for a special budget for the Bowen story stood as much chance of flying as a chocolate aeroplane.

'Look girl, it's the *story* I need you to check out, not some fancy trip to the South Pacific.'

She backed off. Not the right time, obviously. Only one thing on Sankey's mind right now – how to milk their windfall for publicity.

'I'll crack on then.' She made for the door.

'Oh, tell you what,' said Sankey, remembering he was about to get a visit from the police. 'Send one of the techies in, would you? Need a bit of camera work done.' Then with a twinkle in his eye he said, 'Your mate Jeremy would do.'

Her *mate!* Suddenly Charlie wondered if it was Sankey himself who'd sent her the e-mail message branding Jeremy a trainspotter.

Ten minutes later Nick Randall pushed through the glass doors of the News Channel. Days like this gave him a buzz. A new case breaking.

Newsmen must feel the same buzz. But that was *all* he and journalists had in common. To him, this was enemy territory he was entering.

Journalism and his line of policework didn't mix. *His* job was undercover. A nocturnal world of moles. The newsmen's was to flash lights around and turn night into day.

Sankey's secretary led him through the newsroom. The atmosphere was electric. Felt close to flashpoint. A dozen young people on the phone or pounding keyboards. He glanced about, taking it all in, doing a double take when he spotted Charlotte Cavendish. Surprised to see her tucked into a workspace as small as the rest, chewing a fingernail. Less glamorous than on the box.

Then he spotted the camcorder filming him as he walked through, zooming into his face. Anger welled as he was shown into the editor's office.

'*That* is out of order,' he snapped, refusing Sankey's outstretched hand and pointing back to the newsroom. 'No pictures of me, right?' He closed the door to block the cameraman's view.

'What d'you mean, sergeant?' Sankey flushed. It was *his* idea to film the police on the premises and show the viewers the News Channel was in the thick of things.

'I want the tape wiped,' Randall snapped, 'while I watch . . .'

'Now hang on a minute . . .' Sankey bristled. 'This is my newsroom. You can't tell me what to do.'

'And this . . .' Nick jabbed a finger at his own forehead, '*this* is my face. My life depends on people *not* knowing it belongs to a police officer. Understand?'

His grey eyes were pebble hard.

Sankey got the message. His face turned an unhealthy shade of pink. 'Of course. I'm sorry. I'll make sure it's not used, OK?'

'No, not OK, friend,' Nick growled, riled at being thought wet behind the ears. 'I want it *wiped*. In my presence. Here and now.'

Sankey flushed deeper. He felt like a schoolkid caught exam cheating.

'OK, sergeant . . .' He leaned into the newsroom. 'Jeremy! In here please. With the gear.'

Charlotte looked up from her screen and watched her soon-to-be-ex lover lug the camera into the editor's office. Something was up. Sankey gone over the top. Through the Venetian blinds she saw him standing hands on hips and the detective with his arms folded. The visitor was wiry and tough, she noted – like a border terrier – and he looked strangely uncomfortable in a suit.

Back to work. She dialled the Foreign Office in the hope of a statement before her next studio spot.

Inside the editor's office, once the tape was wiped to his satisfaction, Randall accepted a cup of tea as a peace offering.

'You seem to know about cameras,' Sankey remarked, subdued.

'We do use them,' Nick answered tartly.

'Of course, of course . . . OK. Let's get on. I'm busy. First I'll explain how we operate.' Sankey leaned back against the springs of the chair. 'We're a low budget outfit. Most of our output is agency material which we repackage. But in London we shoot our own stuff and do regular reporter live-spots. To link those in, we rent blocks of time on a satellite – Eutelsat, one of the birds over Europe. Half-hour blocks, three times a day when the main bulletins are on. With me so far?'

Nick nodded.

'This morning's booked time was between seven and seven thirty. At five past we had a spot from a reporter at the Wickleigh Hospital. With him was a cameraman and what we call a "flyaway", that's a mobile uplink to the satellite. A dish a metre wide, several boxes of clever stuff and a generator to provide power. All fits into the back of an estate car.'

'Easy to set up?' Nick asked. The kidnappers would be using such equipment.

'A doddle. So I'm told. Never done it myself. Anyway, this morning with the live-spot over they switched off the flyaway, so there was nothing going up to the satellite, right? Anybody tuned to that transponder would just see shush on the screen. Snow. Know what I mean?'

'Go on.'

'And that's what they saw here, in the control room. But only for a few seconds. Then instead of the shush, they got new images. Not from *our* dish, but someone else's. Colour bars and a caption.'

'But they couldn't tell where it was coming from?'

'No. A flyaway doesn't tell the satellite where it is. Whoever broke on to our bird could have been anywhere within its footprint. And that's basically the whole of Europe.'

'I see.'

Useless, Randall realised. Bowen could be anywhere. Here in Europe or still in Indonesia with the satellite uplink feeding taped pictures of him. Good way to preserve the kidnappers' anonymity. But elaborate.

'I'd like to see the tape again,' he said. In case there was something he'd missed.

'Of course.'

Walking back through the newsroom, it reminded him of an incident room at the Yard. Screens, phones, lots of heads down. The big difference here was women. Loads of them in the news business. In Special Branch they were still taboo.

He sat in an edit suite watching the screens.

'This is exactly how the pictures came in,' Jeremy explained.

The terror in the minister's eyes hit him harder than ever in the darkened booth. Randall had seen it before, that look. In a hut in Malaysia many, many years ago. The expression of a man who'd gambled and lost.

'Hold that last frame could you?'

The video froze on the placard resting against the minister's chest, with the word MURDERES.

'Can't spell,' said Sankey. 'Suppose it shows the kidnappers aren't English.'

'Or else they went to the same school as my daughter,' Randall growled. 'Can I have a copy of this?'

'I'll do it now. Beta SP?' asked Jeremy.

'Perfect.'

He slipped a blank into the record machine and dubbed the material across.

As they passed back through the newsroom, Charlotte Cavendish was checking her hair for the studio with a small mirror from her bag.

Once in Sankey's office, Randall turned to him, a new question looming in his head. 'Why'd the kidnappers pick the News Channel?' he asked. 'Why not the BBC? I mean in the news business you're small fry.'

'True. And it's a question I've asked myself. The only thing I can think of is that there's a monthly publication that lists the permanent satellite bookings. If the kidnappers are foreign, maybe they just saw the name News Channel in the book and thought it sounded right.'

'Mmm.' Randall wasn't convinced. 'Any oddballs on your staff?'

Sankey laughed. 'This is TV. They're all fucking oddballs! What d'you mean?'

'Just that the criminals might have chosen you because they have a contact here. Somebody on your staff. If your personnel department can let me have a list, we'll check if there's a name known to us.'

Sankey arched his brows. 'Well . . . fine. We'll bike it over to you later.' The monitor on his desk caught his attention. 'Aha! We're on again.'

He grabbed the remote and wound up the sound.

Charlotte in vision linking into the video of Bowen, the pictures as shocking as ever. Then the scene changed to a drizzly Downing Street and men with umbrellas.

'*A few minutes ago, grim-faced members of the cabinet began converging on Number 10. The foreign secretary was first in, but he refused any comment about the fate of his junior minister.*'

Charlotte again in the studio, her face confident, her voice excited but under control.

'*As of now the mystery of where Stephen Bowen was at the time of the kidnap has not been solved. The Foreign Office says simply he was on leave somewhere in the far east.*

'*It was the News Channel that broke this extraordinary and sensational story to the world this morning. Throughout the next twenty-four hours, and every twenty-four hours, we on this channel will keep you up to date with the latest developments as they occur. This is Charlotte Cavendish for the News Channel.*'

'Bloody good stuff,' growled Sankey, thumping the desk. He turned down the sound. 'The girl's got class. Don't you think?'

'Definitely,' Nick smiled. 'Pity about the looks.'

'Eh?'

Then Sankey chuckled. 'Yeah. You can go a long way in this business with blonde hair and eyes like limpets.'

Randall got up to leave. His gut feeling was that Bowen was a long, long way from London. Solving the crime would be down to the police in whichever country the poor bugger was being held. Another day or two of faffing around covering their arses, then his guvnors at the Yard would appoint a liaison team – men with degrees – to work with the foreign force, and *he*'d be allowed to get back to his Revenue Men. Which would suit him just fine.

'Thanks, Mr Sankey. Thanks for your help.'

Charlotte bounced out of the studio, burning with purpose. She'd asked for printouts of press stories on the Kutu dispute and on British trade with Indonesia. She found them ready for her on her keyboard.

The policeman passed close to her desk as he was being shown out by Sankey's secretary and smiled at her like an old friend. She nodded at him politely, then shuffled through the pages of cuttings. Only a couple of stories about Kutu. The problems there seemed to have been too small, too far away for the British media to worry about – until it got shoved up their noses. She sat and began to read.

FIVE DEAD IN GOLD MINE FIGHT – Daily Telegraph *Monday* 18th *June. Hill tribesmen on the Indonesian island of Kutu fought an hour-long battle last week with crack troops from Indonesia's armed forces (ABRI). Five 'terrorists' armed with rifles and machetes were killed attempting to ambush an army patrol guarding new mine workings, according to official sources.*

Charlie read on, jotting notes.

Kutuan Guerrilla organisation called OKP. Leader – Soleman Kakadi.

Mineral-rich island – copper and gold. 15,000 population – many shipped to other islands by Jakarta government to make way for the huge mine. Torture and abuse common according to Amnesty. Hundreds killed in recent months.

Rights for mine granted to international consortium including British p.l.c. – Metroc Minerals.

Bitter quotes from something called the Kutu Environmental Protection Organization, KEPO, based in Darwin, Australia. Could be useful, she thought, making a mental note to find a number for them.

'God,' she exclaimed, reading on.

Thirteen thousand islands in Indonesia, spread across 3,000 miles of ocean.

'Never knew it was so big.'

The next piece was from the *Guardian*, dated two weeks ago.

ARMS DEAL SET TO SPARK FRESH PROTEST

The British government has learned nothing from recent rows over arms exports, said a spokesperson for Stop The Arms Trade (STArT) yesterday. A deal to sell Indonesia half a billion pounds' worth of submarines, patrol boats and other weapons is expected to be signed in Jakarta when Foreign Office Minister of State Stephen Bowen visits the Indonesian capital next week. STArT supporters plan a twenty-four-hour protest vigil in Whitehall on the day of the signing.

Fewer than fifty people there, Charlotte remembered. Not an impressive turnout. Even the police were ignoring them.

She jotted more notes – STArT chairperson Cindy Holdsworth claiming British-made craft could be used against dissidents fleeing Indonesia by boat – Foreign Office insisting arms only sold when guarantees given they wouldn't be used for internal oppression – past sales included Hawk jet fighters and Alvis armoured cars.

Indonesia ranked top in the corruption league, but near the bottom on human rights – thousands dead in East Timor as a result of Indonesia's invasion in 1975.

Charlie remembered video of the massacre in the cemetery in East Timor a few years back. She stood up, clutching the printouts. Surely Sankey would *have* to see the story was out there, not in London.

'Charlie!'

A shout from the newsdesk. Mandy was jabbing a finger at her TV monitor.

'Line three,' she yelled. 'File footage on Indonesia, Kutu and Timor. Coming in now from Reuters.'

'Thanks!'

Charlie punched the keypad of her own monitor and began to log the pictures. Library shots of Indonesia's ageing president, of Hawk fighters and of the 1991 massacre in East Timor. Then shots of Kutu, volcanic mountains and rainforests. Villages with straw-roofed huts and children with pearly-white teeth.

'Tom wants you to package this for nine o'clock,' Mandy shouted. 'Wants you to wrap it in with the rest.'

'Bugger!' Charlie exclaimed under her breath.

It was going to be like this all bloody day, she realised. Bulletin after bulletin. Update after update. Re-edit after re-edit. Leaving her little time for research. Little time to build her case to be sent to Kutu.

She looked across to Sankey's office and began to scheme. One thing *was* on her side. The man was vain and he was a randy dog. If she could exploit those characteristics mercilessly enough, she *might* yet get her way.

5

Scotland Yard
09.50 hrs

ASSISTANT COMMISSIONER David Stanley was six feet two with heavy shoulders, a shiny bald head and an expression that colleagues described as deceptively avuncular. He stepped out of the lift into Scotland Yard's underground car park where a pale blue Rover Sterling was waiting.

Six months to go before his pension and the longed-for chance to improve his golf handicap, he'd hoped for a quiet end to his thirty-year career in the police, before slipping into a comfortable part-time directorship with a security company. As head of the Yard's Security Group, however, he'd faced crisis after crisis recently. The IRA, the attacks by the Revenue Men, and now this – the unprecedented kidnap of a government minister.

The car climbed the ramp and turned left for Victoria Street. The government's crisis centre, the Cabinet Office Briefing Room (COBR), had gone on-line an hour ago. The PM had summoned everyone at ten.

Assistant Commissioner Stanley balanced his briefcase on his knees and extracted the progress report from DCI Mostyn. What interested him most was personnel – who was on the case. He had the germ of a plan in mind, which – if it worked – might let him leave the Met on the crest of a wave.

DS Randall.

When he read the name his eyes lit up. He knew the man's file almost by heart, as he did with most of those on his team.

Detective Sergeant Nick Randall, pushing forty. Started late in the police, otherwise he'd be a DI by now. Ex-army. Served in the far east – Hong Kong with the Redcaps. Learned Malay so he could liaise with the locals when British soldiers deployed to Malaysia for jungle training.

Something else. Something clever the man had done out there. He closed his eyes to concentrate. In the late eighties . . . It came back. Nick

Randall had been on a team hunting local hoods peddling drugs to British soldiers. Rescued another detective who'd got into difficulties and took out a drug baron at the same time. Won a Military Medal for his trouble.

Assistant Commissioner Stanley stared past the driver at the jam of cars by the Abbey. If the cards fell his way, Randall might be just the man. His lips pulled into a thin line, the closest he ever got to a smile.

The car pulled away from the lights in Parliament Square, its windscreen smearing with drizzle. The sky behind Big Ben was slate grey. Wipers humming, the car turned up Whitehall past tourists peering through the Downing Street gates and stopped outside the Cabinet Office. Bedraggled photographers stood corralled behind police barriers. He checked his cap was straight as the door was opened by the driver. Ten paces across the pavement to the grey stone building.

'Over here, sir!'

Face left then right for the photographers, Stanley ignored shouts for a statement.

Down in the basement, screened against eavesdropping, were the rooms and corridors of COBR, a self-contained living and working space for national emergencies. Usually a Home Office minister presided. Today the prime minister.

Stanley went straight to the main briefing room, which was furnished with a boardroom table in light oak with chairs to match. A dozen officials already there including a couple of women. Home Office, Foreign Office, MI5, and the Secret Intelligence Service MI6. Stanley nodded to the tall, bean-pole thin head of the Asia Desk, Philip Vereker, arrogant eyes behind oval, black steel spectacles, betraying just a hint of embarrassment at his department's failure to keep the minister safe.

Stanley had been at odds with Vereker in recent months. The SIS had run agents tracking drug dealers from Thailand. Done it so successfully they'd proposed taking control of the *British* end of the investigation. *SIS primacy over the police?* The Yard had been scandalised. But today David Stanley saw a chance to get his own back.

Throats were cleared, chairs were pushed back as the prime minister walked in with the foreign secretary. Keith Copeland had a swinging gait because of a leg injury sustained in a car crash years ago. Short of stature, straight-backed and with sandy-grey hair, he'd been the country's leader for less than a year. Forty-eight when he started, he looked ten years older now, and had the shell-shocked eyes of a man promoted beyond his ability.

He sat at the head of the table and flattened the palms of his hands together.

'Good morning, ladies and gentlemen – I would like us to pray a moment. For Stephen's safe return.'

Some eyebrows fluttered, but all bowed their heads. Copeland's reputation for moral rectitude had won him vital party votes in the sudden and unexpected contest for PM. They sat in silence for a full minute. Stanley noticed the MI5 woman doodling on a pad.

'I hardly need say this,' the PM declared eventually, 'but this appalling situation should never have happened. We'll need to look again at ministerial security, even if it means some loss of privacy.'

Beside him the foreign secretary nodded his agreement. The Rt Hon Hugh White MP wore thick-lensed glasses and an expression of permanent anxiety. Whitehall insiders said he had little grasp of geography or history and was firmly under the thumb of his King Charles Street mandarins.

'But inquests are for later. First, the facts. Commissioner Stanley?'

'Early days, prime minister. It's my security group that's leading the investigation of course,' he said pointedly, 'but we'll need substantial help from both the SIS and the Security Service. As yet we don't know whether the crime's been committed in this country or elsewhere. Special Branch at the airports say they're pretty certain Stephen Bowen didn't return to Britain. If he's abroad, it could be the far east, or Europe which is where the TV pictures were beamed from.'

'You've found the transmitter?' Copeland asked.

'No. It puts out a narrow beam, prime minister. Like a laser. Undetectable by normal electronic means.'

'Well you've *got* to find it,' Copeland snapped, 'before these creatures pour more poison into the ears of the media. They're giving Amnesty International a field day, blathering on about Indonesian human rights abuses. It's outrageous the TV people knew about this crime before we did. There's been a serious failure of intelligence.' Copeland glared at the SIS representative. 'Well, Mr Vereker, where the hell is Stephen Bowen?'

The slender Asia-desk head uncoiled like a fern.

'We don't know for sure, prime minister,' he answered crisply, 'but our people in Jakarta have been told he left Indonesia on Wednesday morning. On a flight to Singapore. I got a message to that effect five minutes ago.'

'Oh, really?'

'The Indonesians have produced a video-print of his passport and exit stamp. Mr Bowen's name was on the passenger list for a Premati Air flight to Changi at eight thirty. So now we're talking to the authorities in Singapore.'

'I see. So there is *something* we know that the media don't,' the PM said cuttingly. He pursed his lips. Then a new complication occurred to him. He knew Bowen of old. 'Was he travelling alone?'

'Don't know. They're asking around in Jakarta,' Vereker continued. 'Our people suspect the reason he was being so secretive could well have been a woman.'

Copeland's face was a mask. He knew of other reasons.

'Mmm. Possibly. So, what's being done?' he demanded. 'Commissioner Stanley?'

'Warwickshire police are with Mrs Bowen, in case there should be any attempt to contact her. And in conjunction with the Security Service,' he said, acknowledging the woman from MI5, 'we're checking on the anti-arms trade people in Britain. And any other groups that take an interest in Indonesian human rights. This kidnap does seem remarkably elaborate. Suggests big money behind it.'

'Too well financed for it to be the Kutu resistance?' asked Copeland. The mining project was not unfamiliar to him. 'What do we know about them?'

'Call themselves Organisasi Kutun Pertahanan,' intoned Vereker in an accent he hoped sounded authentic. 'OKP for short. Sworn enemy of KUTUMIN which is an acronym for Kutu Mining – that's the consortium one-third owned by Metroc Minerals. The OKP has a political wing operating semi-openly in the island's capital Piri. Dr Junus Bawi – he's the kingpin. A professor at Kutu University. Placid, reasonable sort of chap. Then there's a small military faction in the mountains run by a wild man called Soleman Kakadi. Used to be a pal of Bawi's until they split over tactics. The mine means depopulating a huge area of the island. Kakadi's guerrillas try to sabotage earth-movers and stuff, and ambush Indonesian soldiers to get their weapons.'

'Yes, but are they up to kidnapping Stephen?' Copeland asked, uncomfortable at being reminded what was being done there.

'Our assessment is no, not on their own. However, with outside help, it's possible. There's a bunch of Australians who've made Kutu a big issue in the Pacific. *They*'ve got money and, I imagine, people who know how to use TV satellites.'

'So what are you doing about them?'

Commissioner Stanley cleared his throat. Time to get his elbow back in.

'At the Yard we have good contacts with ASIO, the Australian security people. It's the middle of the night there now, but we'll be on to them in a few hours. I imagine the SIS will too. Different channels. Belt and braces, prime minister.'

Vereker gave a watery smile.

'And as for Europe,' Stanley continued, 'the French and German liaison officers at the Yard are already kicking arses, so we're confident of a lead soon on tracing that satellite uplink.'

Copeland became agitated. 'Speed is of the essence gentlemen and ladies, if we're going to be able to save Stephen's life *and* the arms contract,' he said. 'I can already feel pressure building to cancel it. Half a billion pounds' worth of jobs up the spout.' He looked round at the assembled faces for support. 'You know, most people in Britain simply don't care who we sell arms to. But when the nastiness of one particular regime gets thrust in their faces by something like this, then they begin to think they have a conscience.'

There was no disagreement. Copeland looked down at the notes he'd made, then frowned.

'So on balance of probabilities, Stephen's still in the far east. Right?'

'Ye-es,' answered Vereker, glancing at Stanley for backup.

'So, what powers do *we* have for pursuing our investigations there?' the PM asked pointedly.

'It's really down to the police in the countries concerned, prime minister,' Vereker explained. 'We can offer assistance and feed them any intelligence we get, but it's up to them what they do with it.'

'I don't much like the sound of that.'

'Probably be wise to put the SAS on standby,' the assistant commissioner suggested, 'for advice if nothing else. And I've a couple of blokes ready to go anywhere at a moment's notice if we get into a hostage negotiation. They've been before, when those students were kidnapped on Irian Jaya a couple of years back. The problem this time of course is we don't even know which country Bowen's in.'

'Isn't there something else we can do?'

'If you're thinking, prime minister, that we should send an undercover team to Kutu to make contact with the OKP, that may not be possible,' Vereker announced. A thin line of sweat glistened on his upper lip.

Assistant Commissioner Stanley felt a buzz of anticipation. He sensed a door opening.

'To be blunt, we're short of resources in the far east,' the SIS man explained, 'what with budget cuts since the end of the Cold War. Our agents in the region are all committed to catching drug smugglers and can't be extracted quickly.'

'God almighty! Another victory to the media!' the PM howled. '*They*'ll be into Kutu like rats up a drainpipe.'

'Wouldn't be too sure, prime minister,' Vereker mumbled. 'The

Indonesians have managed to keep journalists out of there for most of the past year. They can smell a reporter a mile away.'

Assistant Commissioner Stanley cleared his throat. '*We* might be able to help,' he offered quietly. He felt the burn of Vereker's stare. 'It's just occurred to me that one of my officers in the Anti-Terrorist Branch who's already involved in this case happens to speak Malay which I believe is very similar to Indonesian. And he's had experience in hostage situations. I'd be happy to make him available.'

Vereker looked as if he'd been shot. 'Hardly think that's wise,' he protested. 'It'd be extremely embarrassing diplomatically if he cocks up.' He looked to the foreign secretary for support. Hugh White seemed on the point of backing him up, but Copeland cut him off.

'Go on, commissioner.'

'DS Randall could try to get into Kutu and see if he can stand up the OKP involvement in the kidnap, which would leave the SIS to dig up what they can in Jakarta and Singapore where they already have desk men in place.'

'It's a very difficult environment out there,' Vereker whined. 'Not the sort of place for a London bobby.'

Stanley let the sarcasm wash off his back.

'I totally agree. But the man I'm talking about is no London bobby. He's ex-army, served in the far east. Won a medal after negotiating the release of a military hostage, and is one of the best undercover operators we have.'

'Sounds worth exploring,' the PM decided, raising his eyebrows at Vereker. 'Why don't you two come up with a plan in the next couple of hours, then we'll take a decision.' He got to his feet, wincing. For some reason stress always made his leg hurt more.

'Give my office a call when you've worked something out, will you?'

'I most certainly will, sir,' nodded Stanley.

Keith Copeland walked along the tunnel linking the Cabinet Office with 10 Downing Street. Ten thirty. Just over three hours since the nightmare erupted and he'd begun to panic. Time was of the essence he'd told them, but thankfully they'd not understood what he meant. It wasn't just Stephen Bowen's life and the arms contract at risk, but his entire future. The longer this case remained unresolved, the greater the danger of a revelation that would destroy him.

There'd been three hours of speculation this morning by a media short of facts. Time now for him to go on camera and give an impression of being in charge. Couldn't delay it any longer. Yet *in charge* was something he certainly didn't feel.

His boyish-faced press secretary was waiting as he climbed the stairs into Number 10.

'All right, Gordon,' Copeland declared, forestalling the question. 'I know it's feeding time. How many animals out there?'

'A full cage, PM. Shall I tell them five minutes? *If* that gives us long enough to discuss what you're going to say . . .'

'Nothing to discuss. You see I'm not going to *say* anything, Gordon. Words, but no content.'

The press secretary bristled at having his offer of advice rejected. 'Five minutes it is then, PM.'

Copeland slipped into his office and closed the door, desperate for a few moments alone in which to compose his thoughts.

The TV pictures of Stephen had been deeply shocking. Horrible to see such terror in the face of someone he'd known for so long. They'd been at Cambridge together. A friendship, it had to be said, founded more on pragmatism than affection. Thirty years of scratch-my-back that had paid off handsomely just eighteen months ago.

The party had been in crisis. A demand for a leadership contest. Copeland had been pushed into standing. He'd won, but with an infinitesimal margin. Bowen's change of heart had clinched it. His old 'friend' had originally planned to support a competitor.

To Copeland's further amazement, the party had gone on to win the general election by one seat. Which made him prime minister. It had been time to pay his dues, so he'd found Bowen a job in government.

And now he regretted it bitterly. Regretted the deals he'd made to get where he was, and more important, regretted the other little 'arrangements' Bowen had tempted him into.

Outside his front door the media vultures were hovering. But it'd be worse later when they knew more. Best to confront them now.

Gordon was waiting for him in the hall. He checked his watch.

'Two more minutes, prime minister . . .'

'No. I'll do it now. If they're not ready they can lump it.'

The signal was given for the constable to open the door. Copeland strode out towards the microphones on the pavement opposite.

'*We're now live from Downing Street.*' He heard the urgent words of a correspondent alerting viewers.

'It's time I said a few words,' Copeland began, his mind threatening to go blank. 'You er . . . will understand there's little I *can* say at this stage. The situation is still very confused. What is clear is that Stephen Bowen is being held a prisoner somewhere against his will.'

A questioner tried to interrupt, but Copeland held up a hand.

'As you know, last week Stephen was on an official visit to Indonesia.

At its conclusion he decided to spend a few days travelling privately. Perfectly understandable. The far east is a beautiful and fascinating part of the world . . . Anyway, during that time it seems he was taken prisoner. We don't as yet know when or where. As I said, he was not on ministerial duties at the time and therefore didn't need to be in daily contact with officials. Scotland Yard is leading the investigation. They will I'm sure be given the fullest co-operation by the relevant authorities in the countries concerned.'

'Which countries, prime minister? Was he still in Indonesia?' A woman from the BBC.

'I can't answer any questions at this stage. The investigation is very sensitive. I'm sure you'll understand. Now, that's all . . .'

An inbred politeness made it hard to back away. It'd be his downfall one day, his wife always said.

'Will you cancel the arms contract with Indonesia?' He recognised the Glaswegian tones of the terrier from the News Channel.

'I . . .' Dangerous ground. 'The contract was a hard-fought one, involving weapons suitable for Indonesia's national defence and nothing else. There's no question of them being used in any internal repress . . .'

Damn, he thought. Cocked it up.

'*Repression*, prime minister? Why does Britain sell weapons to a country with such a lousy human rights record?'

'The British government has repeatedly made its views on human rights known to the Indonesian government. Repeatedly. Now that's all . . .'

'Is it true, prime minister, that a substantial aid package has been offered to Indonesia as an inducement to buy British arms?'

The prime minister flinched. The man was fishing.

'No. It is not true,' he flannelled. 'We do provide aid to Indonesia, as we do to a great many countries all over the world. But there is no link whatsoever between aid and arms. Thank you.'

He turned on his heels, pulse thundering.

'Any plans to send in the SAS?'

Copeland heard a ripple of laughter amongst the press. As the door closed behind him he paused by the mantelpiece in the hallway to steady himself.

Got away with it that time, he thought. But he knew in his heart that with every hour that passed, his chances of surviving their relentless probing could only reduce.

6

THE WORDS ON the VDU were a blur. Charlotte was flagging. On the go now for nearly nine hours. Her hair felt like it had been rolled in cooking oil. One more bulletin to perform for, then she'd slip out for a sandwich, a Diet Coke and a cigarette.

Her hopes of reaching Kutu were dimming by the minute. Every time she'd cast eyes on Sankey in the last few hours she'd flashed him her sexiest smile, but there was no sign of him softening. And to cap it all a friend at Reuters had warned her the Indonesians were already watching like hawks for foreign journalists. A total waste of time trying to get in, he'd said.

No point in her snuggling up to Sankey for an air ticket, then going all that way only to be turned back on arrival. Suicidal from a career standpoint. However, before she gave up there was one last avenue to explore.

The picture elements for her lunchtime news package were mostly in place. The PM's inadequate statement, police chief arriving at the Cabinet Office, file footage from Indonesia and the kidnappers' video itself. All she needed were new facts to move the story on.

There was a number she'd been trying to ring all morning, but unsurprisingly it had been permanently engaged. This time it rang out.

'*Stop the Arms Trade.*' A mature, female voice.

'Cindy Holdsworth, please.'

'*Not available at the moment. Who's calling?*'

'Charlotte Cavendish at the News Channel. Tell me, do you have a press officer called Melanie?' Some faint memory. Something she'd read. In the *Guardian* probably. A personal connection she might be able to exploit . . .

'*Yes. Melanie Carter.*'

Bull's-eye. They'd been at Oxford together. Hadn't known her well. Not seen her since. But it was an 'in'.

'*She's on another line. It's been very busy this morning.*'

'Not surprised,' Charlie remarked. 'I suppose Cindy's had the police round . . .' she added casually, stabbing in the dark.

'*Oh . . . well I couldn't say.*' Charlie's hook had caught a fish. '*Do you want to hold for Melanie in the press office? You're third in the queue. If you like I can fax you the statement she's given out . . .*'

'Maybe that's best for now. But can you slip her my name before you put the next call through? Charlotte Cavendish at the News Channel. I'm an old friend.'

'*Can't promise. But I'll try.*'

'Thanks. Are the police still there by the way?'

'*I really don't know anything about that, Miss Cavendish,*' she replied testily. '*Now, do you have a fax number?*'

Charlie gave it to the woman then rang off.

Melanie Carter. The only female she'd ever met who didn't seem to mind being overweight.

She tried the Scotland Yard press office number again.

'*Your call is in a queue. Please hold.*'

'Who in the world's got time to hold,' she snapped, ringing off and hurling herself at the fax machine. The first page from STArT began to emerge.

'*The British Government's approval of arms sales to Indonesia is a disgraceful act which gives unwarranted international respectability to a regime that continues to defy the world on human rights. Arrest and torture, imprisonment and murder are the Indonesian government's answers to protests against injustice.*

'*STArT has campaigned for many years against Downing Street's double standards, and will continue to do so with any legal means at its disposal. STArT has never resorted to criminal acts in pursuing its cause and never will. STArT wishes to extend sympathy to Mrs Sally Bowen for the suffering she is undergoing, just as we sympathise with the thousands of victims currently suffering at the hands of the Indonesian regime because of arms sold to them by Britain.*'

Charlie tore off the curling paper. Returning to her desk, she glanced towards the editor's office. The door was closed, but the Venetian blind was open. Sankey sat behind it facing her. Her heart gave a little flutter. Sitting opposite him was Steve Paxton, the blonde, tooth-brush-haired guardian of the Channel's finances. Sankey was pounding his chair arm to emphasise a point.

She felt a tremor in her stomach. Excitement and fear. Sankey loathed

Paxton. Never talked to him unless he absolutely had to. And the only reason she could think of for a dialogue at this particular moment was because Sankey urgently needed money. Money for her to be sent to Kutu.

Help! Her dream could yet become fact.

She returned to her desk, tapped at the keyboard until the PA wires came up, browsed them for anything new, then dialled STArT again. Lucky. It rang out. Twice in a row.

'*Stop the Arms Trade.*'

'Hello. Charlie Cavendish again. Thanks for the fax. Is Melanie free now?'

'*She's on a call. But I gave her your name and she does want to talk to you. Will you hold?*'

'Yes, please.'

She checked her watch. On air again in fifteen minutes. The pictures were edited. Just needed to update her script and record her voice, then tidy up her words for the live-spot in the studio.

'*Press office.*'

'Melanie?'

'*Who's that?*'

'Charlotte Cavendish at the News Channel.'

'*Hello Charlotte! Long time no speak. I've been watching your stuff. Congrats. What can I do for you?*'

'Well, two things, Mel. First, can you confirm the police have been round to see you?' Silence from the other end. 'Come on, I know they've been there.'

'*Then why do you need me to confirm it?*'

'Melanie! Come on. Just a line about what you told them.'

'*We're just not talking about this, Charlotte. Even off the record. The point is we don't have a problem with the police and I don't want the media creating one. You've seen our press release – we think kidnapping's a lousy way to further the cause of human rights.*'

'But do they suspect you?' Charlie pressed. 'Do they think *you*'ve got something to do with Bowen?'

'*You'll have to ask them.*' She lowered her voice. '*Frankly I think they came to see if we had any ideas. But that's utterly unattributable. And you didn't hear it from me.*'

'Fine. Thanks. But do you? Have any ideas, I mean?'

'*Charlotte, you can read, can't you? The press release is quite clear.*'

'Yes. OK, OK. You don't indulge in criminal acts . . .' She remembered now why she'd not kept in touch with Melanie. The woman became supercilious when irritated.

69

'*What was the other thing you were after?*' Melanie prodded. '*No. Let me guess. You're trying to get to Kutu and want some contacts . . . You and the rest of the British media.*'

'More than that, Mel. Advice really. People keep telling me it's impossible to get in.'

She heard Sankey's door open and glanced up. Paxton marched out, glaring at her.

'*Not impossible to get in, Charlotte. Hard, yes. And extremely dangerous. The Indonesians don't like journalists. They've killed a few over the years. But if you really want to try . . .*' She paused as if uncertain how far to go. '*Um, look. There is a woman in Darwin who's made it in a few times. Shot video in Kutu secretly. Quite good stuff. I've seen it. And she knows more about the place than most. I've not mentioned her to anyone else, but if you could come to some arrangement so she does camera for you, you'd have one hell of a headstart. Want me to give her a call? I think you two would get on.*'

'Um . . . well, yes. That'd be great. But don't commit us. If she expects to be paid big money, it won't work. We're cheapskates at the News Channel.'

'*I guessed that. She might do a deal. Want me to try?*'

Uncertainly Charlie flicked a glance at Sankey's office. If only she knew whether his no *had* become a yes. Then she saw Tom Marples frowning at her and pointing at the clock.

'Yes, Mel. Please. See what she says. Got to rush now. Another bulletin coming up. Great to talk. Speak in a while.'

She dropped the receiver back on its rest, then keyed her screen to the script slot. She typed fast and accurately. Her mother had forced her on to a course straight after school.

Mother. *Father*. God! She'd forgotten all about them. Better ring after the programme to see how he was.

'How you doing, Charlie?' Marples yelled, heading out of the newsroom.

'Fine! It'll be there.'

She finished and saved her work, then hit the print key. Five minutes to on-air. Jeremy would be waiting for her to record her track. She ripped her script from the printer and headed for the technical area.

'Charlie?' Sankey's secretary ambushed her by the corridor. 'As soon as you're off air can you see Ted? Quietly. He says it's rather sensitive . . .'

'Oh . . . yes of course.' Her pulse raced. She *had* won! 'Sure. I'll be there.'

But why *quietly*? Why rather sensitive? Suspicion bubbled up in her head. Sankey was a schemer and a ram. Maybe she'd gone too far with her sexy smiles. Wouldn't put it past him to demand some little *personal* favour for sending her to Kutu.

The question was, how would she answer him?

Scotland Yard
13.45 hrs

Nick Randall emerged from Assistant Commissioner Stanley's office, feeling he'd had a collision with a punch-bag. The head of the security group had made it perfectly clear that refusing the mission was not an option.

The world's gone mad, he thought to himself as he stepped into the corridor. Normally if someone were to offer a free ticket to a tropical island in the South Pacific he'd grab it like a shot, but this little outing appealed as much as a month in Wolverhampton.

Stanley had flattered him. Told him he was the only man on the force with the qualifications for the job. That it was a coup for the Met to be able to fill the breach left by MI6. And that the PM himself had given his full backing.

Bollocks. As he walked to the lifts, he knew in his guts that the main reason he was being sent to Kutu was for an over-the-hill guvnor to get his name in lights.

The lift took him to the basement. His mind on autopilot, he opened his locker and sifted through the oddments of clothing he kept there as disguises. His passport was what he was looking for. He found it and returned to the sixteenth floor.

In the assistant commissioner's outer office, Stanley's PA presented him with an application form for an Australian visa.

'Fill it in, then I'll take it with your passport to the High Commission,' she told him briskly.

She was a thirty-something for whom nothing ever seemed to come as a surprise. Nick imagined orgasms wouldn't even quicken her pulse.

'I'll get you some malaria pills too,' she added, 'and here's the chit for your allowance.'

On the rare occasions an officer went somewhere exotic he got a bonus for special clothing. Hadn't happened to Randall before. In eight years with the Met, he'd never gone beyond the M25.

Four floors down to the cashiers' office to collect the money and a wad of travellers' cheques, then to the travel bureau for his ticket.

71

Singapore and Darwin. A 747 leaving at 23.30 from Heathrow tonight. Kutu was best reached from Australia, he'd been advised. He felt as ready for the assignment as for a trip to the moon.

Back on the security group floor he thumbed a coin into a drinks machine and extracted a plastic cup of coffee. In the Ops Room it was quiet. There'd been no more Revenue Men incidents since the Wag's Bar bomb six days ago.

'Having chats with the guvnor, I hear? Our company not good enough for you any more?' cracked a colleague looking up from a VDU.

'Someone wants rid of me, more like,' Nick growled, stopping by the bank of monitors for the surveillance cameras. 'Anything new on the Revenue Men?'

'Sod all. What are you up to?'

'A bit of sightseeing.'

'So you won't be around for the game on Saturday?'

'Shit! Forgotten about that.' Special Branch versus the Flying Squad. Annual match in the Met's soccer league. 'Sorry mate. But Chris can do goal instead of me.'

'He can let 'em in too,' his colleague complained. 'We lost six-two last time he stood between the posts.'

'Well, can't be helped, friend. Tell him to try contact lenses.'

Nick moved to the end of the room and tapped on the SIO's door. DCI Mostyn beckoned him in.

'SIS are on their way over,' he said in his Midlands mumble. 'Fifteen minutes, then they'll brief you. Sounded on the phone like they'd been told to eat shit.'

Mostyn had his collar undone and his tie loosened. One of his big, grubby hands held a small cigar. His was one of the few offices where smoking was permitted.

'Thanks for your report on the News Channel. I agree there has to be a good reason the kidnappers chose that mob. We'll chase their personnel people for the staff list.' He tilted his head and narrowed his eyes. 'How d'you feel about this jaunt?'

'Not happy, sir. Feels like the booby prize,' Nick scowled. 'Working on my tod in a hostile environment with no backup to speak of – not my idea of fun.' He was a team man. Liked mates around him. People he trusted and who trusted him.

'Yeah. Know what you mean. Still, it's better than a panda car and wellies,' Mostyn quipped. 'And you might get lucky. Might find the bugger and get another gong!' He crushed his cheroot into an ashtray.

'Pigs might fly . . .'

'Look, old son, just do what you can. Make Assistant Commissioner Stanley happy, then get back here and sort out these effing Revenue Men.'

Mostyn's phone rang and he grabbed the receiver. Nick ambled to the window, sipping the scalding coffee. Outside, the morning rain-clouds had moved on. Shafts of pale sunlight lit up Horse Guards Parade and Trafalgar Square beyond. He liked London.

He breathed in deeply. Time to stop moaning and get his act together. He would be on his way in a few hours, no matter what he thought. He'd need to pack in some briefings. Work out his kit.

Freelance news photographer would be his legend. He knew the role well. Played it before. And he knew cameras ever since he bought a Canon for baby photos when Sandra was born.

Sandra. Had to remember to ring her. He'd promised to try to see her one evening this week to compensate for Sunday, but now he'd have to cancel again.

'Got your allowance?' Mostyn asked, finishing with the phone and jerking Nick's mind back to the job.

'I have.'

'Don't ever say the Grief doesn't look after you, son. Hey, if you've got any cash left bring me back one of those flowery shirts, OK? Now, here's your bumph. Light reading for the flight.'

He handed over two files of background material, maps and a Lonely Planet guide book on Indonesia.

'You really are going to be on your own out there, old son. We're not declaring you to anybody, not even the Aussies. That's the deal. The SIS resident will be the only friendly face, but he's in Jakarta fifteen hundred miles away. Maxwell's the name. Harry Maxwell. Vereker will fill you on the contact procedure when he gets here.'

Mostyn opened up one of the maps.

'You're familiar with this part of the world, I understand.'

'So it says on my file.'

'Well there's a brief here from the Foreign Office to freshen your memory. And some stuff on Bowen.' He held out a sheaf of photocopies.

One press cutting caught Randall's eye as he flicked through them – Bowen in dinner-jacket surrounded by high-rollers at a roulette table. From the *Sun* in the late 1980s. Snapped at an ill-judged lunch with a casino manager who'd been done for gaming irregularities. THE MP AND HIS DODGY FRIENDS, said the headline.

'One other little nugget for you,' Mostyn growled. 'Before our Stephen became a minister of the crown he was . . . wait for it . . . a non-exec director of Metroc Minerals, the very same British company that's in the consortium digging up Kutu.'

'Interesting!'

'Indeed. But so far that's all it is. No evidence of a link with the kidnap. But at this stage we know sod-all anyway . . .'

'Anything new on the video business? Like where the pics were fed from?'

'Not yet. Every force in Europe's been contacted. Something'll come up . . . We'll be running you as a joint op with Vauxhall Cross by the way, but running it from here, right? I'm your man. There'll be a couple of others manning a twenty-four-hour phone line. Don't know who. Haven't picked them yet. Oh, by the way, we're calling him Bob. The minister, that is. Use that name for him on open phones.'

'OK, sir. Just one question. Supposing by some bloody miracle I do find him in Kutu. How am I supposed to get him out?'

'Up to you, old son. Use your head. You've done it before. Only this time, if you wouldn't mind, try not to kill anyone.'

South London

It took the police Rover an hour to hack through the evening crush to Nick's home in Wimbledon. Balanced on his lap for much of the journey was the briefcase of files he would have to memorise on the flight out.

Vereker of the SIS had been uptight and miserable in the briefing. Harry Maxwell in Jakarta was to be contacted only in emergency he'd said, because the phones would be bugged. What did the geek think he would do, ring up every time he felt lonely?

Vereker had given him just one name in Kutu, Dr Junus Bawi, the university professor who headed the political wing of the OKP. Told him the man phoned Reuters in Jakarta an hour ago to deny any knowledge of the kidnap, but would need checking out.

A deep sense of pointlessness engulfed Randall as the car pulled up outside his house. He was being blasted off into a black void, just because someone up there had a score to settle. He thanked the driver, dumped his briefcase and a professional-looking camera bag on the pavement, then watched the car disappear as he fumbled for his keys.

The house was a two-up, two-down. He'd taken a mortgage on it five years before, when the dust had settled on his divorce from Lindy.

74

Debs had moved in with him three years after that. He'd phoned her at work a couple of hours ago to say he was going away for a few days.

'Hi! That you?' she shouted from the kitchen when he opened the front door. She poked her head into the hall, saw the camera bag and the tension on his face. 'Oh dear . . .'

'Give us a beer, chuck.'

He dropped the bags and followed her into the kitchen. Debbie had changed out of her work clothes into jeans and a pullover. She reached into the fridge and held out a can. He took it, then kissed her on the mouth. She had a pleasant, fleshy face with curly light-brown hair.

'OK. Give me the worst . . .'

'Away for a few days. A week maybe. Can't tell you where, but it's not round the corner.'

She looked anxious. She knew he was on the Bowen case and had seen the video on the evening news.

'Indonesia,' she said.

He pulled a face then ripped the can open and gulped down the lager. He knew she would never repeat anything he told her, but there were rules.

'Got time to eat something?'

'Car's coming for me in a couple of hours.'

She reached into the food cupboard and pulled out a pack of pasta and a jar of sauce. Then she put a saucepan of water on to boil.

Debbie was by no means the most beautiful woman who'd entered his life, but she was certainly the best. She got through to him in a way no other woman ever had. Since she moved in he'd learned to curb his habit of thinking that any woman who smiled at him fancied him. Debbie had told him straight – any playing around and she'd be out of the door.

She had a half-drunk glass of wine beside the stove which she took little sips from as she fried some mince for a Bolognaise sauce. She cast him a glance. Never seen him so uptight before.

'Just tell me one thing,' she said, trying to break through his reserve. 'Is the job do-able?'

He looked her in the eyes. In his guts he sensed that if it *was* do-able, there'd be killing involved.

Couldn't tell *her* that.

'Don't know, Debs. I really don't know.'

7

R AIN HAMMERED AGAINST the warm window glass, smearing the glow from the lights outside. In the huge square facing the British embassy, Jakarta's traffic was dancing its evening quick-slow-slow. Ambassador Robert Bruton slammed down the phone. His collar was undone and his shirt cuffs were held clear of his wrists by sprung metal armbands.

'I want every bloody second accounted for, Cheryl,' he told his unmarried, business-like PA. 'I want to know who Stephen Bowen was with every damned moment he was here.'

Word had just come from Singapore that there was no record of the minister arriving there from Jakarta last Wednesday. Nor of him being in transit. Someone was telling lies. Bruton needed to know who – and why?

'Tell Harry Maxwell he's coming with me to this do. Downstairs in five minutes.'

Ambassador Bruton was a short man with immaculate hair thinned by excessive brushing. He stepped into the small dressing room attached to his office, flicked up his collar and knotted a red and blue tie. His private feelings about Bowen's kidnap were unprintable – served the bastard right for being a secretive, pompous ass.

A touch with the hairbrush, then jacket on and he was ready to go. He closed the security cabinets and spun the combination locks. With a slim, leather attaché case under his arm, he descended the stairs at an undignified speed.

'Harry. Good man.'

The embassy's corpulent resident spy stood by the exit, the jacket of his light-brown suit draped over his arm.

'What d'you make of this denial from Singapore?' Bruton growled.

76

'Difficult to know. Airport records aren't always reliable, but the Changi people were adamant.'

'Buck passing, the lot of them. All terrified of discovering the crime's been carried out on their patch.'

They stepped through the rear entrance of the drab building into the ambassador's racing-green Jaguar.

'You've not been invited to this do, but no matter. Need all the eyes and ears we can muster.'

They sank into the soft, cream leather of the car's rear seat and closed the door, shutting out the clammy heat.

'What's the occasion?' Maxwell checked. 'And where is it?'

'At the Crowne Plaza. It's JAVAIR. The launch of their new turboprop mini-liner. Packed with poker-faced grandees that Bowen would have met.'

JAVAIR was Indonesia's home-grown aircraft manufacturer. Massively subsidised, the diplomatic community nicknamed it a 'bonsai' industry because it never grew however much money was poured into it.

Bruton leaned forward to close the glass panel then turned on the stereo to ensure they couldn't be heard by the locally-employed driver.

'Who's this man *Randall* London's sending to Kutu?' he murmured.

'Special Branch. Not one of ours,' Maxwell answered. 'Scotland Yard seems to think he's James Bond.'

'Make sense to you, sending him?'

'Rather him than me. Kutu's not a place where a white man blends in. My bet is he'll get nowhere. Just hope they don't arrest him as a spy.'

'Soiled underwear for us if they do.'

Bruton pulled a sheet of paper from his briefcase, a list of the people Bowen saw when he was here.

'Can't remember the name of that hostess from the Indonesian protocol department,' he frowned.

'Selina Sakidin.'

'That's the girl. Bowen's eyes were like saucers whenever she came into view.' He scribbled her name then paused, marshalling his thoughts. 'Has to have been a woman – the reason for his secrecy.'

'And you think it could have been Miss Sakidin? Possible. I'll try to speak to her. But we'd better check at the embassy too,' Maxwell added. 'See if anybody in a skirt took leave last week. Bowen was like a dog with two dicks *whenever* a woman hove into view. Took a shine to your Cheryl, I seem to remember.'

The ambassador's secretary was in her late thirties, plain, but not unattractive. Maxwell himself had spent a surprisingly inventive night with her once, after a drunken embassy party.

A fresh cloudburst hammered on the roof. Ahead the road had turned into a small lake. Cars and buses sent up curtains of water as they dodged *bajajs*. Motors flooded, the tricycles were as helpless as drowned beetles.

The Jaguar swung off the main artery of Jalan Sudirman, and climbed the entrance ramp to the covered forecourt of Jakarta's newest hotel. It was in these plush, five-star palaces, glittering with gold and glass, that wealthy Indonesians conducted their social lives.

Inside the suite stood a reception line, with the wizened Sumatran company chairman at its centre. When he saw Bruton, his fixed smile turned to an expression of deep concern.

'Terrible about Mr Bowen,' he declared. He knew the ambassador well – his company relied heavily on British technical advice. 'At least he's not in Indonesia. Very bad for us if such a thing could happen here.'

Maxwell noted his anxiety. There was nothing Indonesians dreaded more than loss of face.

Armed with glasses of fruit juice, they mingled, chatting in the superficial way that Indonesians felt comfortable with. The room held some of the wealthiest and most powerful men in the country, many of them ethnic Chinese. Though a minority in the country, they were the brains of most businesses. Behind the relaxed smiles in the room Maxwell saw fear when they caught sight of Bruton. The Bowen issue was explosively embarrassing for them.

Suddenly Bruton nudged him. Maxwell followed his look. Elbowing his way through the crush towards them was a tall, broad-chested man dressed in the sludge-brown safari suit worn as mufti by all senior Indonesian army officers. Three gold-capped pens glistened in his breast pocket.

'General Sumoto! How nice to see you,' Bruton declared, greeting him edgily. 'You know my *counsellor*, Harry Maxwell . . .'

'Of course.' Sumoto gave a porcelain smile, his small, brown eyes well practised at concealing his thoughts.

The small circle of businessmen around them fell silent. Major General Dino Sumoto was a man of burning ambition and they feared him. A former military commander of the eastern islands that included Timor and Kutu, he was one of many top soldiers seeking to enhance their positions when the elderly president finally gave up his monopoly on power.

'I'm surprised to see you still here, Mr Maxwell,' Sumoto chided, with uncharacteristic directness. 'I thought they'd have recalled you to London to explain how you lost your minister.'

Maxwell swallowed, formulating a retort about the right of an individual to personal privacy. It would *not* be well received. He smiled wordlessly.

'It's a shocking business,' Sumoto went on, shaking his toad-like head. 'Dreadful for Stephen and dangerous for *us*.' He indicated all of them in the circle. 'Ambassador . . . a quiet word if I may.' Towering above Bruton, he took his arm and eased him away from the hearing of others. Maxwell followed closely.

'What's happening? I need to know,' the general demanded, fretfully. 'Your prime minister is saying unfriendly things. On the BBC just one hour ago. He talked about *human rights* in Indonesia.' Sumoto made it sound like AIDS. 'That's our internal affairs, Mr Bruton. Why does he do this? Just because you have protests in London – ignorant people holding banners saying untrue things about us? Is he going to change his mind about the arms contract? We should be told.'

'He was just restating the UN position on human rights . . .' the ambassador soothed awkwardly. 'Nothing new or different. And as far as I'm aware there's no intention whatsoever to renege on the agreements we've signed.'

'I'm relieved to hear you say that,' Sumoto simmered, but he looked nonplussed.

His English had been honed by a year at London's Royal College of Defence Studies. He raised a cigar to his rubbery lips, the finger that gripped it heavy with gold rings.

Sumoto was a major general, in charge of buying new equipment for ABRI, the Indonesian armed forces. Without his backing the deal with Britain would never have happened. Maxwell, however, knew that the backing would have come at a price – something over a million pounds probably, peeled from the commission on the DefenceCo contract and diverted into Sumoto's pocket.

'So what *is* the news of Stephen?' Sumoto pressed. 'He went to Singapore I understand.'

'Well, not according to the immigration officials at Changi, general,' Bruton replied. 'They have no record of him arriving.'

'No? They tell you that?' Sumoto looked momentarily discomfited. 'Maybe they make a mistake.'

Again Maxwell saw fear in the eyes. Fear of the shame and disgrace that would follow if it proved that the kidnap *had* taken place in Indonesia.

'When you talked to him last week, general,' Bruton ventured, 'did Stephen mention staying on for a few days' sightseeing? With a woman friend, perhaps?'

Sumoto pulled himself up straight.

'No. He said nothing of that. We talk business, not social things. But, ambassador, you *must* find him quickly. These people who have him are dangerous. They can easily kill him. Without a second thought. Kutuans – I know them. They're bad people. I was commander there many years.'

'But general, *how* could the OKP have captured Stephen Bowen?' Maxwell pressed. 'Unless he went to Kutu . . . Yet you're insisting he wasn't anywhere in Indonesia.'

'You're right. By themselves Organisasi Kutun Pertahanan cannot do such a thing. But they have friends in other countries. People who interfere in our affairs. People who tell lies about us. It is *they* who have Stephen I think. Maybe Bangkok was where Stephen went,' he added, divertingly. 'Many girls there. That's an easy place for a man to disappear.'

With that thought, he touched hands with them both, then made to move away.

'Stephen's a good friend,' he pleaded finally. 'You *must* save him . . .'

And save the arms contract, thought Bruton as Sumoto drifted off. Unfortunately, for now at least, the two things looked to be mutually exclusive.

'Hypocrite,' he breathed when Sumoto was out of earshot. 'His tears for Bowen are crocodile ones. What he's really scared of is losing his commission.'

'And will he? I mean will London cancel the contract?'

'God knows. We have a weak government led by a weak prime minister. *Anything's* possible. But if we're not cancelling, it's time London made noises that were a little more reassuring.'

Bruton moved off to work the crowd, leaving Maxwell to hover. For a while he kept his eye on Sumoto and wondered. Odd to have voiced his concerns so directly. Javans talked in circles normally.

He looked around the reception room, musing about how much wealth this gathering was accountable for. Musing too about how, one way or another, most of the wealth would have derived from institutionalised corruption.

'Mr Maxwell . . .'

A voice at his side suddenly, which shook him from his thoughts.

'Brigadier! Well met, sir!'

It was Effendi, the police intelligence chief who'd given him the 'evidence' of Bowen's departure to Singapore. Dressed in full uniform, he was short of stature with a round, dark-skinned face and a thin, black moustache.

'Hardly expected to see *you* here.'

An embarrassed laugh. 'My brother,' Effendi explained, teeth gleaming, 'he is a director of JAVAIR.'

Say no more, thought Maxwell. Fingers in pies.

'I see you talk with General Sumoto,' Effendi commented. 'You think he interesting?'

'Well yes. In that he believes it *is* the Kutuans who kidnapped Stephen Bowen – with outside help.' Effendi said nothing. 'You don't agree?'

'No opinion. Because no evidence,' the brigadier answered formally. *And Sumoto doesn't have any either*, Maxwell understood him to mean.

'You like the general?' Maxwell queried, tilting his head to Sumoto who stood less than five metres from them.

'He important man,' Effendi replied, deflecting the question. His eyes gleamed mischievously. 'But he have a special name. Know what we call him?'

'No. A nickname, you mean?'

'*Laba-laba!* You know what that mean? Spider. People call him spider, because he always spinning a web . . .'

They both glanced at Sumoto, who was talking conspiratorially with two others, their heads close together.

'I see what you mean,' Maxwell smiled.

'He like to have people in his power,' Effendi added, embarrassed suddenly by his own openness with a foreigner.

'The succession, you mean? For when the president goes?'

Effendi nodded. 'Of course. Everybody afraid what will happen then. Many people like Sumoto want to fix things so it right for themselves when the time come . . .'

Maxwell arched his eyebrows, surprised at such unaccustomed frankness.

'Why . . . why do you tell me this?' he asked casually.

Effendi smiled enigmatically. 'Because in Java our spiders are dangerous.' He made to move away. 'Best you watch out.'

'I'm grateful for the advice,' Maxwell murmured. 'But there's something else I wanted to ask you about. *Singapore*.'

Effendi's face became a mask again, then he said, 'I know. They say your minister not arrive there, but . . .' He looked genuinely mystified. 'But *our* evidence – it say he definitely leave Jakarta for Singapore. If we find different, then of course I will tell you.'

Maxwell nodded. *If we find different* . . . The enquiry *was* ongoing at least, despite official Indonesian insistence the kidnap was nothing to do with them.

'One final question, brigadier,' Maxwell added. 'We suspect Stephen Bowen might have been travelling with a woman. He was friendly – at an *official* level of course – with Miss Sakidin. From the Ministry of Foreign Affairs . . .'

Effendi's eyes were like glass.

'We already interview every official who look after him when he here,' he admitted softly. 'And *Nona* Sakidin – I speak with her myself this afternoon.'

'Oh, really?'

'Yes. And she confirm what airport police already tell me. Confirm Mr Bowen fly to Singapore on Wednesday morning.'

'Confirm? What d'you mean . . .?'

'Well . . . *Nona* Sakidin – she the person who take him to airport.'

'*What?*'

'Yes. Not official, understand. Just as friend . . .' Effendi gazed at him unblinking.

'A little *personal* touch . . . I understand,' Maxwell nodded. 'But . . . but did she say where Bowen was going? Did she say *why* he was heading for Singapore?'

'On way home to England. That what she say. She think he going home.'

No, thought Maxwell. Didn't add up. The woman was lying. Or *somebody* was.

It was imperative now that he spoke to her himself.

Piri – capital of Kutu
23.40 hrs

The crescent moon shone silver through a mesh of cloud, its long reflection in the ocean blurred by the silhouettes of coconut palms. The Indonesian soldier at the wheel of the truck would have preferred the moon to be full so he could have driven without lights. Safer that way.

Bullets weren't the danger here in town. The OKP kept their meagre stock of guns up in the hills. Rocks were the weapons in the dusty streets of Piri, the island's capital. The helmeted snatch squad he was transporting, crammed behind him in the open back of the truck, was a sitting target.

The convoy followed the curve of the coastal road, skirting the Poteng *kampung* where the troublemakers lived. The military's plan was to leave the town along the coast then curve inland and re-enter Poteng from the west, hoping to catch the ones they were after by surprise.

The thick tyres purred on the tarmac, the first truck followed by three more. The streets of Piri were deserted. Had been since nine o'clock. There was no official curfew in the town, but there didn't need to be. Fear kept people in their homes once night set in.

The soldiers in the truck were not from Kutu. Javans, Sumatrans, Balinese. Conscripts mostly. Night was the environment they'd come to know best. Rested and alert themselves after a day of sleep, they hoped their *victims* would be dulled by exhaustion. They called this Operasi Kalong – Operation of the Bats.

The evening just ended had been more troublesome than most. When word got round that the kidnap of a foreigner had pushed the Kutuan struggle into the headlines around the world, riots had broken out all over town.

Streets barricaded by rocks and burning tyres, bottles smashed under the wheels of army jeeps. Stones and gibes from children who scampered down alleys before they could be caught and beaten. A time of excitement for the Kutuans. A time of tension and fear for the soldiers.

Behind the town rose the steep foothills of the great, rumbling volcano that dominated the island's geographic heart and whose spirit watched over the souls of its people. Black shadows against a near-black sky. It was up there in those foothills that the huge earth-swallowing machines of the Kutu Mining Consortium KUTUMIN were going to rip off the island's vegetation to expose the gold and copper-bearing rock beneath. To the men of Kutu it was a rape of holy land.

Dr Junus Bawi lay motionless on the wood-framed bed, listening to the even breathing beside him of his wife Dana. Beyond her soft panting, his ears were tuned for the more distant sound of diesels and banging tail-boards that would tell him the raids had begun. In the grid of streets that made up the district of Poteng there would be many like him, waiting sleeplessly to be taken for interrogation.

His small, three-room, breeze-block house was nowadays devoid of ornament, the shelves in the day-room bare of books. Too many times he and his family had seen the things they valued smashed and burned by the animals ABRI sent to intimidate them. Better now to possess little and to keep what they treasured in their heads and their hearts.

The door to the bedroom was open to let the air circulate. Humidity was rising. The wet season that had barely begun would peak at the end of the year with cyclones and floods.

83

In the next room lay their child. Junus had told Dana to keep the curly-haired, eleven-year-old boy indoors that evening, fearing the soldiers might shoot rioters like they had in the past.

News about the kidnap had broken in the late afternoon. Bawi had been at the university marking students' work when a colleague burst in with a radio tuned to the BBC. In a breathless silence they'd listened to the report of the kidnap of a man whose name they'd never heard.

Bawi had been gripped by a deep foreboding. An act of violence had been committed against a foreigner in the name of the people he represented – *and he knew nothing about it*. To him it could mean only one thing; the split in the Resistance between himself and Soleman Kakadi had widened to a chasm.

Dr Junus Bawi was professor of languages at Kutu's small university, continuing to teach the island's unique Melanesian dialect despite Jakarta's wish to replace it with *Bahasa Indonesia*. Kutu had been absorbed late into the Indonesian archipelago, after being retained by its European colonisers for twenty years longer than the rest of the old East Indies. Keeping the island's young aware of their culture was the modest, public face of his resistance to Jakarta's rule and exploitation. His involvement with the protest movement was more clandestine.

Suddenly there was a distant clatter of sticks against cooking pots. The sentries had seen the approaching trucks. Bawi's limbs tensed.

His instinct as always was to run, to hide, to avoid the gut-churning terror of arrest. But there was nowhere to go. If he wasn't at home when they came, they would beat his wife to make her say where he was. And if he were found in some other house his hosts would pay the price as well as him. Fleeing to the hills was the last resort, but to him that meant failure. Success was to stay in Piri, keeping the flames of resistance alive in the minds of the young.

He sat up on the bed. Dana heard him, heard the clatter outside, and whimpered like a frightened animal. Bawi swung his feet to the floor. Wearing undershorts, he covered his skinny torso with a white shirt then stepped into thin cotton trousers. Neither spoke.

Dana was shorter than her husband. He watched her remove the flower-patterned night slip, hook a brassiére under her heavy breasts then reach behind to fasten it. Her waist and stomach were ribbed with flesh. She pulled a cotton T-shirt over her head, then looked into Obeth's room.

Tyres squealed at the junction twenty metres away. A tailboard banged down. Rubber soles crunched on the grit of the unmade road. Shouts and hammering at doors opposite. Maybe not him they were after this time. Bawi pushed on his heavy-framed spectacles and ran a comb through his straight, black hair.

Women screamed as their sons were dragged from their beds. He heard the thud of a rifle butt, then silence. A heavy, measured step, outside. Approaching *his* door this time.

A fist crashed on the thin panels. Bawi switched on the lights and opened up. Then his throat dried as he recognised the brute of an arresting officer.

'You must come!' Captain Sugeng's voice was like a whiplash. Dana sobbed wretchedly as she recognised him. 'You and the boy. Come.'

'No!' Bawi protested. 'Not the child.'

'Obeth was seen. Throwing rocks.'

'No. You're wrong. He was here. In the house!'

Sugeng laughed, his thick lips parting to show rows of neat, small teeth. 'You're lying professor. We know your boy. He was recognised.'

The seams of the officer's crisp uniform threatened to burst under the pressure of his muscular body. With a flap of his hand he waved two soldiers into the house.

Bawi followed them to the boy's room. Dana was already there. She threw herself across her son's body but the soldiers slung her on the floor and grabbed the boy.

'My son was here!' Bawi insisted. 'Leave him alone!'

Obeth was dragged out by his hair and frogmarched to the trucks. 'He's a child,' Bawi mouthed helplessly.

'You too, *professor* . . .' Sugeng's voice mocked Bawi's impotence.

'Do you have a warrant?' he asked, suddenly defiant.

The answer was a shove in the back, a hand propelling him towards the lorry. A prod in the buttocks with a gun to encourage him on to the open platform. He looked back at his home. The door was closed again. Sugeng had gone inside.

Bawi swallowed. A taste of sick in his throat. A month ago the same. After his release that time Dana's silence had told him enough of what Sugeng had done to her. Asking for confirmation would have added to her shame. Since then, there'd been no intimacy between them.

Bawi looked round for his son, but the boys were in another truck. About ten of them. He wanted to shout across to be brave, but willed the words instead. They didn't usually harm kids that young, he reasoned. No burns or beatings. Just threats, to terrorise them. And he himself should be all right. Too well known to the outside world to be tortured. Amnesty would make easy capital with it.

The diesels revved. The soldiers clambered on board. As they moved off, Bawi looked back. Just one jeep left. Outside his house. Three nervous soldiers guarding it with their guns. Waiting for their officer to finish with the prisoner's wife.

Bawi swallowed again. Salt tears this time.

The Kadama interrogation centre was at the other end of Piri from Poteng, set back a hundred metres from the coast road to enhance its isolation. Three sides of a courtyard, the outward walls windowless and grey, peppered with ventilation grilles for the cells. Local people seldom hung around to hear the sounds of pain from within.

The truck slowed and turned up the track. Four times in the past two years Bawi had been brought here.

The soldiers ordered the prisoners down. As his legs touched the ground Bawi lost his balance and fell at a soldier's feet. He waited for a kick but instead heard laughter. Some joke about licking boots. And arses.

They stood in a queue before a desk, while a policeman wrote their names in a book. Police and army. No difference. All ABRI. All part of the same regime.

His son was ahead of him in the line, the youngest and smallest of the boys. He knew most of the others. Had watched them grow up. Most were sixteen or seventeen. At eleven Obeth looked out of place and vulnerable. He'd *never* been involved in street trouble. Dana had seen to that.

Dana . . . His stomach clenched at the thought of Sugeng's vile hands on her.

His turn for registration.

'Dr Junus Bawi,' he announced defiantly. 'I want a lawyer with me when I'm questioned.'

The policeman looked up, pained. There was always *one* like this.

'Tomorrow,' he answered, carefully writing the name in capitals. 'Lawyers only work in the day.'

'Then my interrogation must wait until tomorrow . . .'

The policeman shook his head and demanded that Junus hand over his watch.

'Next!'

Bawi was led up a staircase to the first floor. A long corridor stretched the length of one wing of the building. Cracked terracotta floor, rough plaster walls, bare bulbs every ten metres. As he walked where he was pushed, eyes staring fixedly ahead, he passed doors of iron bars, not daring to look in the cells. This wing was for men. The one across the courtyard for women.

A hand on his shoulder. The guard pushed him into a cell then clanged the door shut. On the high ceiling a lamp shone brightly inside a metal grille. Worn tiles covered the floor, white gloss paint on concrete walls, four rattan mats aligned with the corners. On one a middle-aged man slept, knees pulled up to his chin. On the other a younger person sitting cross-legged, stared up at him.

'Professor Bawi!' the youth whispered hoarsely. 'Don't you know me?'

Junus gave him a cursory glance.

'No.'

'I was a student. Three years ago. You remember?'

'No. I have so many students . . .' Junus kept his eyes on the floor. He knew what this was about.

'They keep me here three days, but I tell them nothing,' the youth whispered. 'Bad . . .'

Junus looked away.

'I suppose for you, it is better you co-operate,' the youth went on. 'They know everything about you, so it is better not to lie. Am I right? They know you send supplies to the mountains. Everyone knows. All the students, even.'

'I don't know what you're talking about . . .'

Junus lay down on a mat. No pillow or padding, but the discomfort was preferable to conversation with an oafish stool pigeon.

He heard a whimper from the corridor and a door clanging. Someone returning from interrogation. Then the footsteps of the guards came closer, rubber soles squeaking on the tiles.

The gate opened.

'Bawi! You come.'

Wasting no time, he thought. An urgency he'd not experienced before.

They marched him to the far end of the corridor. A thick wooden door opened into the block that ran between the men's and women's wings. It was here the interrogations were done by the sick men from intel. From somewhere close he heard the dull thud of a beating.

Junus's courage failed him. He sensed suddenly that this time he too would be tortured. For a moment he lost control of his legs. The guards grabbed his arms and propelled him forward, his feet trailing on the ground.

A door opened in front of them and a man was dragged out, the white of his shin bones showing through his bloodied skin.

The soldiers pushed Bawi into a darkened room then closed the door. Pitch black. He felt himself swaying. He held his breath, knowing there'd be others in this room. But how many? And *where*?

87

Suddenly he heard someone clearing his throat. Then a low chuckle.

The light snapped on. A single floodlight on a stand pointed at him. Bawi shielded his eyes. He counted three pairs of legs, one in uniform green behind a table, the others in a darker cloth.

'Dr Bawi . . .'

Junus recognised the voice of Colonel Widodo, head of ABRI Military Intelligence.

'Professor, you're keeping us waiting . . .'

Widodo had interviewed him before. He knew the man's games. He saw the chair, pulled himself straight and moved towards it, his courage returning.

'Why have you arrested me?' he demanded, sitting down.

Widodo brought his fist down on the table with a deafening crash. A flask of water fell to the floor and smashed.

'Because, *kamu*, you are a liar! LIAR!' he screamed.

Kamu was the intimate form of 'you'. Used here it was offensive. Bawi stayed silent. Argument would make things worse.

'But this time you will tell me the truth. You will tell *us* . . .' Widodo swung his left arm wide to indicate his two plain-clothed thugs. Men with stone cold eyes. Bawi glimpsed the hands of one of them. Fingers encrusted with metal rings like knuckle-dusters.

Widodo was squat, with a round, light-brown face and straight, oily hair. Bawi knew his mood could switch from light to dark with mercurial speed.

'What is it you want to know?' he asked, trying to control the tremor of his voice.

Widodo raised a brow and leaned forward, elbows on the table, his chin supported by balled fists.

'Tell me about the kidnap of the English foreign minister Stephen Bowen . . .'

Bawi swallowed to wet his dust-dry throat. He'd guessed this would be it.

'I heard about it on the radio,' he answered. 'The BBC. I can tell you what they said, if you didn't hear it . . .'

Widodo shook his head. He mimed despair. One of the thugs chuckled, the other cracked his finger joints.

'Tell me what *you* know, Dr Bawi. Not what the radio said.'

'That's all I know, colonel. I heard nothing about it before or since.'

'Liar!' The fist on the table again.

'It is the truth . . .' A rough hand slapped his face. Hard enough to twist his neck. He'd not noticed one of the plain clothes men creep round behind him.

'Who planned it? You or Kakadi?'

'I tell you, I know nothing.' Bawi flinched, waiting to be hit again.

'I don't believe you.' Widodo switched his expression to one of pleading. He leaned forward. Bawi smelled garlic on his breath. 'They are Kutu people, the kidnappers. They say it themselves. OKP people. And you say *you* were not involved in planning this?'

'I am a professor of language. I teach students about the culture of their island. Like most people of Kutu I am opposed to the mountains where our ancestors' spirits live being robbed and destroyed by foreigners, but . . .'

'*Foreigners?* You call Indonesians foreigners?' Widodo screamed, his face ablaze. 'Kutu *is* Indonesia!'

Bawi wished he'd chosen better words.

'The English and Australians in KUTUMIN are foreigners. Indonesians of course, are not,' he answered mollifyingly. 'Whatever my views about the mine, I have never advocated violence as a means to oppose it. That is not my way. A kidnap is an act of violence. I could never be involved in such an act, however much violence is used against me and against the people of this island.'

A derisive slow hand clap came from behind him.

'So it is Kakadi?' Widodo's thin, curved eyebrows rose, waiting for confirmation.

'I know nothing about Soleman Kakadi,' Junus answered wearily.

'When did you last see him?'

'You know the answer. You asked me last time. It was one year ago.'

'How often do you communicate?'

'Never.'

'Liar! Why do you still lie to me?' He waved a hand at the thug with the rings. The man stood up and left the room.

Bawi's stomach knotted into a ball.

'Lies, lies, lies!' Widodo muttered, half to himself. He moistened his lips. 'You pretend you don't support violence, yet you send your son out to throw stones at soldiers . . .'

Bawi began to shake uncontrollably. The ring man, he realised, had gone to fetch Obeth.

'I tell you he was not out last night,' he pleaded, pointlessly. 'You've made a mistake.'

No mistake. They knew. But they would use him anyway. Against his own father.

Widodo stood up and stretched. 'Show me,' he said, turning to the side and stifling a yawn.

From the shadows to Junus's right the man who'd hit him emerged with a metre-long cane which he laid on the table. One end was bound with string for a handle, the other frayed and split.

Widodo picked it up, swished it, then thwacked it down, his eyes watching Bawi with cold contempt.

'Children need discipline,' he murmured. 'Don't you agree, professor?'

Bawi's gaze fell to the floor. If there was anything he knew that would stop what was about to happen, he would tell it to them. Even, *Yes, it is Kakadi who is responsible for the kidnap.*

'I don't know anything,' he wept. 'That's the truth, colonel!'

'We'll soon see.' Widodo turned away, pulled a toothpick from his military shirt and worked at his mouth.

Bawi stood up to protest or beg, but a thump on the chest knocked him back on to the chair. He heard the door open and the sniffing of a child. He turned to look. Obeth came in, barefoot in his T-shirt and shorts, his face smeared from crying, one skinny arm gripped like a doll's by the hideous ring man. The thug thrust his thick fingers into the boy's hair and twisted his head round so he would see his father.

The boy cried out and made to go to Junus. Then he saw the tears coursing down his father's face.

'You threw stones at soldiers, little boy . . .' Widodo yelled. 'Very stupid. Very dangerous. You could kill someone.'

'No, no . . .'

A big hand clamped across Obeth's mouth.

'Like your father you don't know the difference between truth and lies. We have to teach you to tell the truth.'

Widodo picked up the bamboo switch and shook it.

'No . . . Please . . .' Obeth blubbed.

Through the shroud of his own tears, Bawi saw the brute holding his son pull the boy's shorts down to his ankles, exposing his small, tight buttocks and hairless genitalia. Then he tugged the grubby T-shirt up over Obeth's head, baring the unblemished brown back.

The man with the rings bunched his fist and ran it down Obeth's flesh, the sharp metal drawing thin, dark rivulets of blood from the smooth skin.

Junus saw his son's legs buckle and water spurt uncontrolled from his penis. He shook with sobs, powerless, knowing that nothing he could say would stop this outrage. They were all victims. Even eleven-year-olds.

Widodo handed the switch to his torturer. Holding Obeth upright by his hair, the brute slashed the sharp strands of cane against the cuts he'd made with the rings. He beat with a practised rhythm until the boy's back and buttocks were cross-hatched with blood.

Then he let him drop to the floor to lie in the puddle he'd made. Bawi blinked the tears from his eyes.

Non-violent resistance – his credo, his mantra, all his life – Kakadi had told Bawi he was wrong. Told him that fire had to be fought with fire.

Yes. Now at last he agreed. They'd left him no choice.

He would join Kakadi, behind the barricades.

8

THE TRAFFIC ON Jalan Sudirman was as slow and dense as a lava flow. The taxi which disgorged the young Chinese woman into the humid heat outside the Australian Embassy had stopped on the wrong side of the dual carriageway.

For several minutes she stared through smudged lenses at the grind of cars and buses, hoping for a gap that would let her cross. Before long she understood what natives of Jakarta already knew – that a gap would never come. Not far down the road was a footbridge.

She was as frightened as at any time in her life by the act of betrayal she was about to commit. More frightened even than during the miserable darkness of the past night, when her pounding heart had made sleep impossible.

She was a dumpy, bespectacled woman in her thirties, with black hair and a round, open face, dressed in a red skirt, tight on her fleshy hips, and a pink silk blouse. She carried the black vinyl briefcase which every member of the delegation had been given before they left Beijing.

This was her second visit here in two years. Relations between Indonesia and China had a history of hostility that had only recently improved. Diplomatic contacts, severed in 1967 after the Chinese communists were accused of involvement in the attempted coup in Indonesia were not restored until 1990. Since then visits by trade delegations had become more commonplace.

Her shoes felt tight. Designed for looks, not walking. They pinched as she climbed the steps of the footbridge. She didn't dare look back, fearful she'd been followed despite the trust she knew the delegation leader placed in her.

Would the embassy let her in? Could she make them understand? The only language she spoke was Mandarin Chinese. In her briefcase was a dictionary. Last night in the bathroom of the hotel room she shared with another woman from the Trade Ministry she'd sat on the toilet, searching for the English words she needed. Then she'd copied the unfamiliar script on to a page of hotel notepaper.

In the middle of the bridge she stopped to ease the discomfort of the shoes. The small obstruction she caused provoked hostility from those brushing past. Javan Indonesians disliked the Chinese in their midst, jealous of their prosperity.

All around towered mirror-polished marble and gold-tinted glass, displays of power and wealth which seemed to mock her. She looked down from the bridge at the oleanders lining the strip between the carriageways. She eyed the swishing conga of vehicles and wondered whether death mightn't be a better solution for her. Then she dismissed the thought. Too much at stake. And it wouldn't just be *her* life she was destroying.

She couldn't call what she was about to do a betrayal of her country. A betrayal of its leaders, yes. But then it was *they* who were the real traitors, killing, imprisoning those who opposed them, and, as she now believed, plotting to extend their iron fist across the South China Sea.

The grey blockhouse of the Australian Embassy looked remote and inhospitable on the far side of the road. Quelling her terror, she tucked the briefcase under her arm and allowed the throng to carry her towards it.

At ground level, the pavement was cracked and uneven. Muddy holes held water from last night's rain. Twice she stumbled, nearly falling to her knees. Suddenly she was there, standing before the thick glass window of the police post at the embassy gate.

'Visa,' she mouthed, the only word in English she had learned to say.

The guard opened the electronic security gate and pointed up the path towards the main entrance. Her mind flipped back three years to the last time she'd approached such a menacing-looking edifice – an abortion clinic in Beijing.

The entrance door swung open as she approached it.

'Good day!' A man in his fifties, smiling politely, held the door for her and tipped his Panama hat in salute. She fumbled with the clasp of her briefcase, thinking to give *him* her note. He gestured with his head that she should go inside.

'They'll help you at reception.'

She guessed his meaning.

The entrance lobby was a sealed chamber, all doors leading from it protected by swipe-card locks. It felt like a prison. She shook with terror.

More armoured glass at the reception desk. Beyond it, a weary-looking official. Communication was by microphone.

'Yes?' The man's voice was de-humanised by the technology that conveyed it.

She pulled out a folded page from a notebook, then held it against the glass. He stared at it, then stared at her. Slowly he raised one eyebrow and his shoulders heaved a sigh.

She'd imagined shouting, people running, bells ringing. Anything but the bored glare she received.

'Passport?'

She let the note drop on the counter and stared down at the words, fearing suddenly that what she'd written was gibberish.

I WANT ASYLUM.

'Can I see your passport?' he repeated. 'Where you from?'

She understood nothing. She'd come as far as she could. She was in their hands now. Her legs buckled. She flopped to the floor and began to cry.

British Embassy – Jakarta
13.15 hrs (05.15 hrs GMT)

Harry Maxwell put the phone down and did a quick calculation. The undercover man being sent from London would be halfway to Singapore by now. Another twenty-four hours at least before he reached Kutu. That's if he got in – the Reuters office had just rung to say there'd been riots in Piri last night, and arrests. When the streets were tense on the island, ABRI tended to close the island to foreigners.

Philip Vereker's signal briefing Maxwell on the Yard man's movements had been full of irony, not least in the codename SIS had awarded Randall – Cuculus. Latin for Cuckoo.

Maxwell sat up straight, the bulge of his stomach just touching the edge of his desk. Vereker had said Randall had been briefed to make contact with Junus Bawi. But according to Reuters the political leader of the OKP was amongst those arrested last night. Bawi was a big fish. Too big for ABRI to arrest just because there'd been trouble on the streets. Why pick him up *now*? Only one reason Maxwell could think of. It confirmed what Brigadier General Effendi had hinted at last night – that they *were* taking the Kutu connection seriously in the kidnap investigation and were putting Organisasi Kutun Pertahanan through the mangle.

It had been an unproductive morning for Maxwell. Several times he'd tried to contact Selina Sakidin. Not at work today, her office had said, but that meant nothing; Jakarta's bureaucrats were well practised at being inaccessible by phone. The woman would be wary of him anyway, not wanting any more light shone on a relationship she'd presumably hoped would stay private.

He pushed back his chair and stared at the wall opposite. Hanging in the middle of it was a carved wooden mask intricately decorated in soft, dark colours. It smiled at him. Like Effendi had smiled. *'Yes, yes, we've checked out Selina Sakidin and it's all above board. Nothing to her relationship with Bowen. She merely took him to the airport to be friendly . . .'*

Nonsense. Maxwell stood up and looked at his watch. He'd thought of hanging around the Ministry of Foreign Affairs to try to ambush her, but knew he'd melt within minutes in this heat. Instead he would make a fuelling stop. He checked his wallet.

'Just going across to the Hyatt for a quick bite,' he announced, striding past his secretary's desk.

'Right-ho.'

Escaping the claustrophobic walls of the embassy was an important part of his daily routine, but when he passed through the security gate into the midday sun he almost turned back. *Breathing* was an effort for him, let alone walking.

Pausing to cross the road, he was distracted for a moment by the pebble-eyed, brown-skinned boys who sprung from the shade to peddle cold drinks when cars halted at the lights. Then, tugging hard on the reins of his mind, he ignored them and walked on.

The Hyatt Hotel rose monolithically on the opposite side of the square. By the time Maxwell reached the sanctuary of its huge, air-conditioned atrium, sweat was pouring from his face. He paused in the lobby to dab his brow with a handkerchief.

Then through the glass he saw a Mercedes with blackened windows draw up outside. A flunkey rushed to do the door.

'Well, well . . .' mumbled Maxwell, instantly recognising the powerful figure emerging from the car. Major General Dino Sumoto pushed through the swing doors, dressed in a dark civilian suit with a slight shine to its weave.

The nickname Effendi had given him was apt. The man had the brooding menace of a tarantula. Maxwell held back so as not to be seen as Sumoto took the escalator up to the reception floor. Then, curious to know whom he was meeting, he followed a few steps behind. The moving staircase bore them to the mezzanine past a marble cascade of crystal water.

In the lobby in front of the reception desk Sumoto was greeted respectfully by a young under-manager who hurried him to a function room at one side. Maxwell watched from behind the fronds of a potted palm. Above the open double doors to the suite he noted its name – Surabaya. Sumoto was greeted with the reverence due a guest of honour.

Maxwell pursed his lips suddenly. The faces in the reception line – they were all Chinese.

He crossed briskly to the bell captain's desk where a board listed the day's functions.

Surabaya Suite – 13.00 hrs. Reception by Trade Delegation of People's Republic of China.

He stepped back in surprise. General Sumoto, a pillar of the right-wing military establishment, attending a reception given by the *communist* Chinese? Indonesia's relations with Beijing might have improved recently, but communists were still bogeymen here. A man in his position had to be careful.

A dark thought came to him. Deeply troubled, Maxwell drifted away towards the coffee-shop before anyone noticed him.

'You want eat lunch, sir?' a waiter asked him.

Maxwell stared through him.

'You want table, sir?' the waiter persisted.

'Yes . . . No. No time. Thank you.'

He turned on his heel and strode briskly towards the escalator. What he'd remembered was that early on in the battle for the arms contract, *China* had entered a bid. It had been rejected quickly on technical as well as political grounds. But had Bowen's kidnap changed things? Was General Sumoto's fear of Britain pulling out of the deal widely shared in the ABRI hierarchy? *Had they decided as a precaution to re-open the bidding?*

Ambassador Bruton would have to find out, and find out fast.

London – Wesley Street, Westminster
Tuesday 09.35 hrs

Sally Bowen had the TV on in the small, chintz-furnished sitting-room, but she wasn't watching. She'd come up to London late last night in a police car. Scotland Yard's idea. They wanted her on hand in case of 'eventualities' and to help them sort through her husband's papers for clues. In the kitchen, drinking coffee, was a detective constable, there to answer the phone. The line was being monitored on the slim chance that Stephen's kidnappers might ring.

She wore a tartan skirt and a red cardigan over her white blouse. She sat on the sofa, a pile of Stephen's personal papers and letters on the low table in front of her. A quick glance through the contents of his desk last night under the heavy gaze of the detective chief inspector from Scotland Yard had revealed nothing useful, but what she had before her now she'd found in a briefcase hidden in a linen cupboard. Her life and Stephen's had been separate for so long by now, what she was doing felt an intrusion into the life of a stranger.

'Can I make you a coffee, madam?'

The detective had stuck his head round the door. Fair hair, round face, hardly looked old enough to shave.

'Oh please not *madam*. Makes me feel ninety.'

'OK Mrs Bowen.'

'But no, I don't want a coffee. Thanks.'

'Manage to get any sleep last night?' he asked. He'd come on shift half an hour ago, replacing the night man. 'Not as quiet as you're used to, I shouldn't think.'

'No. In Warwickshire you can hear the mice breathe at night. Here there's always noise. Cars, boats hooting on the river, and Big Ben of course.'

Sally had hardly slept at all. It was Stephen's smell as much as anything – the leather of his shoes in the wardrobe and the after-shave, scents which had become a turn-off as their marriage died. Last night her emotions had done battle, her lingering dislike of him fighting an upsurge of empathy for his suffering. The video image of him tied to that chair was burned into her brain.

'I'll leave you in peace, then.'

'Thank you.'

When he'd arrived that morning, the policeman had brought a selection of the morning papers. Inside pages carried features about the arms trade, about Indonesia and its army's brutal treatment of rebels in Timor, Kutu and other islands. And about Stephen. Some of it supportive, some cruel. All reported his friendship with the prime minister dating back to university. All had been digging through the Register of MP's Interests and had uncovered his former directorship with Metroc Minerals. Some had even speculated he still had links with the company and that the kidnap was in some way related.

Sally was used to her husband being in the public eye, but what she'd

97

read that morning hurt. They were writing of him in the past. As if he were dead.

Detective Chief Inspector Mostyn had phoned at eight thirty asking her to make another thorough check of the flat. Stephen had never been tidy – another cause of friction. Papers of one sort or another had been scattered around the flat in drawers and cupboards and stacked on shelves in the Georgian break-front bookcase. The young detective had been with her when she found the briefcase, but she'd asked to be alone when examining its contents, fearful of finding something upsetting.

Some of its contents were innocuous enough – bills and receipts. These she scanned and dropped on to the pale green carpet beside her.

Then she picked up a small note written on pink paper.

The handwriting was neat and round. Like a child's, Sally thought. The address was Warwickshire, in the constituency. Effusive thanks for showing the writer round the Commons. Ordinary enough. MPs did that all the time. Then she turned the page.

The advice about working at the Commons was great. When I finish my degree I'll take you at your word. Millions of thanks too for the fabulous dinner – and everything else!!! I'm still tingling!

Sally's stomach clenched into a ball. *When I finish my degree.* God almighty! How old was the silly coot? She peered at the name. Angie. Twenty-one, twenty-two? Stephen was nearly fifty! She stuffed the letter in her handbag, so no one else would read it.

Gingerly she picked through the pile for more handwritten notes, but there were none. Two typed letters from the Georgian Sporting Club, one of his regular gambling haunts. An invitation to a dinner, and another to a cut-price weekend at a casino in Monte Carlo. Never talked to her about his gambling these days. Not since the day she hired a lawyer to end his access to her property. He'd tried to sell some of her family paintings to settle debts.

The next letter had been folded into a small square as if in annoyance at its contents. She opened it gingerly. The Metroc Minerals logo was blazoned across the top. Her heart missed a beat. Maybe the newspapers were right. Maybe there *was* still a link.

As she read the text, she realised it was the same old story all over again. Signed by the Metroc Minerals finance director the letter demanded repayment of a loan the company had granted when he was on the board. A final demand. Dated last month. Threatening legal action.

The loan was for £100,000.

'God Almighty,' she gasped, staring at it in semi-disbelief. She'd had no inkling he'd been that much down.

She sifted the rest of the pile, hoping to find another letter saying the money had been repaid. But there was nothing more from Metroc. Something however from the Sidney Walker Finance Group. A name she'd never heard of. As she read it her hand fluttered up to her mouth.

The letter threatened to send bailiffs round to remove the contents of the flat in lieu of unpaid interest totalling £12,000. Twelve thousand pounds in *interest*? How much was the loan itself, for heaven's sake?

The ball in Sally's stomach turned into a boulder.

A tap at the door and the detective constable put his head round. 'Just checking. Any surprises?'

Sally Bowen looked up startled. For a moment she'd forgotten he was there.

'Umm . . .' she dithered, thinking to hide the letters. The word *loyalty* hovered in her mind. Her loyalty to Stephen, as his wife. Then she thought of the letter she'd just stuffed in her handbag. The pink one. The one from Angie. Loyalty to *what*?

'Surprises, constable?' she said eventually. 'Well yes, I'm afraid there are some. Rather nasty ones.'

9

Singapore – Changi International Airport
Tuesday 19.05 hrs (11.05 hrs GMT)

RANDALL SWUNG THE bag of Nikons on to his shoulder, brushed the food crumbs from his thin cotton trousers and joined the line of bog-eyed passengers leaving the packed 747 at the end of the thirteen-hour flight from London. Burying himself amongst businessmen in suits and young mums with whining children, he filed from the air jetty into the huge, open concourse. The terminal was new since he'd last passed through Singapore eight years ago.

On the flight, he'd slept a little and read a lot, trying to memorise parts of the files given him by Vereker of the SIS. They'd been wide-ranging; a political history of Indonesia and its repressed Democracy Movement, background on the Kutu copper mine and the resistance to it, and an Amnesty report on the torture techniques of the Indonesian security forces. None of it however had helped him decide on a clear plan of action.

Asia was not a part of the world Randall had wished to revisit. Too many reminders. Here at this vast international airport, however, he could have been anywhere, so international were the faces around him.

Out of touch with the Yard for fourteen hours now, a lot could have happened. Bowen might be free, this mission aborted. Wouldn't mind much if it was – relaxing day off in Singapore then back home in plenty of time for the match on Saturday.

Eleven thirty a.m. London time. Mostyn's morning prayers would be over. A good moment to ring him. He spotted a line of booths on the wall to his right.

Over a cream cotton shirt he wore a beige, multi-pocketed vest of the kind used by photographers. He fished in a pocket for a credit card then swiped it through the reader on the phone. He called the DCI's direct line. Mostyn's voice came through loud and clear.

'Evening, guv,' Nick began.

'*Evening*? Who's that?'

'DS Randall, sir.'

'Good man. Where are you?'

'Singapore. Checking in. Anything new?'

'Not a lot, old son. French police have come up with something on the TV side. They say one of those flyaway things was nicked from a car park in Strasbourg last week. Packed inside a Renault Espace. The registration's been flashed all over Europe, so it's a start. How about you? Good flight?'

'Long. Girls were nice, though . . .'

'Yeah, yeah. When do you get to Darwin?'

'In about six hours. Before sun-up tomorrow. Got any contacts for me?'

'Yes, we're looking after you. One of the girls spent last night on the Internet. You know KEPO, the Australian-based Kutu Environmental Protection Organization that has links with the Kutuan resistance? Well it has a home page – whatever that is.'

Mostyn was one of the few senior officers at the Yard who'd failed to become computer literate.

'Using the name of your cover company Newspix, she got through on e-mail to KEPO's main office in Sydney, and they gave her an address in Darwin. Got your pen?'

'Yes, sir. Fire away.'

'Jim Sawyer . . . their man in the Northern Territory.'

Nick wrote down the phone number.

'She's told him you're a snapper trying to get to Kutu as a tourist. He said he'd give you a tip or two. Expecting you to ring Wednesday morning. But look, I've had a long chat with our Aussie security chums. They say they've no knowledge of any subversives in KEPO. They say it's a bunch of environmentalists and human rights wallahs. The closest they've ever come to criminality is blocking the traffic outside the parliament in Canberra.'

Nick groaned inwardly. Another blind alley.

'Great. And there's nothing new on where Bowen *is*, I suppose?'

'No. It's more confused than ever. Looks like Bowen did have a woman, though. She took him to the airport for the Singapore flight on Wednesday morning. The Indonesians have interviewed her. They say she confirms their earlier evidence that he left the country. Trouble is the Singapore police swear blind he never turned up on their manor.'

'That's helpful . . . Anybody from our side trying to talk to the woman?'

'Yeah. Harry Maxwell. Something else you ought to know – the

Indonesians have been rounding up OKP activists in Kutu. Including the man you're supposed to see, Dr Junus Bawi.'

'That's all I need. Covering their backsides, presumably.'

'Presumably. Ring us again from Darwin, OK?'

'OK, guvnor . . .'

He found a luggage trolley and dumped his bag on it. Two hours to wait for the connecting flight. He felt stiff after sitting for so long and began walking to get his circulation going, mingling where he could with other passengers. He paced the length of the building then turned for a second leg, pausing at the flight departure screens to read the gate number of his onward hop.

The concourse was dotted with overpriced shops. He hovered near a boutique where cameras and calculators glittered like treasure. Nice toys, he thought – for those with money to spare. Nice to look at – like the blonde standing at the counter examining a wristwatch, a grey holdall hanging from her shoulder. He ran his eyes down her back. Neat figure, not too tall. Pink shirt, fawn cotton trousers. Nice bum . . .

She sensed him looking and flicked a glance over her shoulder, her black-coffee eyes ringed with lines of sleeplessness. She half smiled – then her jaw dropped.

Randall gulped. He spun the trolley round and propelled it away, aiming for the biggest crowd he could see. Anywhere to put distance and people between himself and the one news reporter in Britain who could recognise him as a policeman.

'Christ!' he breathed.

What the fuck was *she* doing here? Charlotte Cavendish. His cover blown, before he'd even got to Kutu.

'Christ,' he mouthed again, trying to think. 'Now what?'

'You want buy?' The Chinese sales assistant reached for the watch.

'What? Oh, no. No thanks.' She thrust it back and moved quickly away. She was *sure* it was him. All dressed up like a snapper now, pretending not to know her.

Just to see someone she recognised was extraordinarily comforting. Since leaving London she'd felt horribly alone. Fought like a cat for this assignment, now she had it she was scared to death.

What the hell was his name?

She strode out into the middle of the concourse, trying to see where he'd gone. Chest tight with panic, she felt like a prospector who'd found gold and lost it again. That man *knew* things, and as yet *she* knew the bigger part of sod-all. Maybe he even knew where Stephen Bowen was. Prize it out of him and she'd be in for a scoop.

Sankey had told her the detective's name, but she'd forgotten it. He'd told her something else too when he'd signed her up a year ago. Told her that luck didn't fall off trees; people had to make it for themselves. She was about to do just that.

Randall! Nick Randall. Detective Sergeant. She smiled grimly. Things were looking up.

She'd spent the flight from London in a blue funk. Bitten off too much. Travelling to another world, a handful of press cuttings the only information she had on the place she was going to. She, little Charlie Cavendish, taking on the big networks with an amateur Australian camera-person she'd never even spoken to. She, who'd never reported from abroad before. A journalist on the bottom rung, just able to hold her own in a tin-pot, rip-and-read cable channel, making her pitch for the big time, but absurdly ill-equipped for it.

She'd done her best to stifle those fears, stuffing them metaphorically down at the bottom of her bag. Like a child with nightmares whose mother turns the pillow over, so the side with the *good* dreams can get to her.

Luck had teased her. Now she had to find him again . . .

Randall stuck with the crowds, moving where they moved. The woman wasn't visible when he glanced round, so he reckoned he'd managed to lose her for now. He saw a sign for toilets, abandoned his trolley and carted his bag into a cubicle.

Must have arrived on the same plane from London, he guessed, sitting on the lavatory seat and listening to a noisy defecation in the next box. The jumbo had been full. Easy to have missed her. Now, she would probably be on the same flight to Darwin . . . Avoiding her was going to be impossible.

Bloody woman. Woman *and* journalist. Doubly devious.

He began to plan. She knew who he was. No doubt of that. Where they were going there'd be other media around, people she would be bound to talk to. She'd give him away, tell them all that he was a copper, and he couldn't have that. Threats wouldn't stop her. So he would have to try charm.

He checked his watch. Ninety minutes until the connection. Time for some juggling. He flushed the toilet, washed his hands, then made his way to the gate for the Darwin flight. No sign of Charlotte Cavendish amongst the first few passengers already waiting there. An airline rep was checking boarding cards. He presented himself at the counter.

Swamped with dejection at her failure to find him, Charlotte sat in her aisle seat on the jumbo watching the door for the last stragglers to board, hope dwindling. So much for making her own luck.

She'd studied the departure boards and realised there were other flights he could be on instead of this one to Darwin. Probably Jakarta-bound, to liaise with the Indonesian police.

The sense of having missed a scoop drove her back to the fears of inadequacy that had plagued her on the flight from London. For solace she sought refuge in thoughts that were warm and familiar – home, friends and family. But then the worries she'd left behind began to crowd in. Awful ones like the imminent death of her father. And silly ones, like whether asking Jeremy to feed her cat would make the relationship even harder to break. She'd left him her keys.

Yesterday evening there'd been time for only the briefest of phone calls to Devon before racing home to get a bag packed and making for the airport. Her father had sounded all mumbly when she'd told him where she was going, saying he didn't *want* her to go there. Her mother had come on the line and told her not to worry. That Ambrose was easily upset – increasingly frightened of dying – wanted his family around him. Take no notice, dear, she'd said. You just go off and enjoy yourself . . .

Enjoy herself?

Randall. Walking through the door, the last passenger to board, wearing jeans which fitted his terrier look much better than the suit she'd seen him in before. The door clunked shut behind him. Excitement surging through her, she held her breath as he came towards her along the aisle, checking the overhead seat numbers. She felt a schoolgirlish blush spread up her neck as he wedged his bag in the locker above her head.

'Excuse me.' He looked down at her, his smile as warm as a sun lamp. 'I'm in there,' he said, pointing to the window seat.

She let him pass, a smirk spreading across her face.

'What a coincidence,' she breathed.

'Isn't it just . . .' Nick answered, sinking into his seat without looking at her.

'Saw you back at the shops there. We er . . . we weren't actually introduced yesterday,' she said, offering him her hand. 'Charlie Cavendish.'

'Nick Randall.' He gave her the smile again, in no hurry to let go of her hand.

'*Detective Sergeant* . . .?'

'I was hoping you'd keep quiet about that part.'

'Hence your disappearing act,' she replied, confidence surging back. 'Must have been a nasty shock to see me.'

'Yes. But I've got over it now.' He winked at her.

'Good for you,' she breathed, realising the situation had suddenly been turned on its head. Instead of her chasing *him*, *he* had come looking for her. If he fitted her preconception of police officers, he'd be a man who thought with his dick. Fine. Ahead lay a three-and-a-half hour flight. Plenty of time in which to get him to talk.

She fastened her belt as the aircrew began their safety brief. Before boarding she'd had a bit of a wash in the ladies' room and sprayed her neck with Amarige. She leaned towards the window seat slightly, tucking her hair behind her ear and willing the perfume up his nostrils.

'Do I assume we're going to the same place?' she asked coyly.

'Quite possible.'

'Is *he* there – on Kutu – Stephen Bowen?' Too far, too fast. She could tell from his face.

Randall raised his hands in mock surrender.

'Name, rank and number. That's all I can give you, ma'am.'

'Sounds like it'll be a dull flight, then,' she quipped.

He chuckled.

'Take it easy. The wheels aren't even up yet.'

The plane backed from the stand. Nick watched through the window as the terminal lights retreated. His interest in the woman was simple – self-preservation. Nothing else. But Charlie was grinning like she'd won him in a raffle. Have to tell her *something*, but not too much.

As the plane began to taxi he turned and leaned towards her.

'Truth is we still don't know where Bowen is,' he confided, speaking in a voice just above a whisper. 'But that's between you and me.'

'I see. But they've sent you to try to find him?'

Gently, gently. Play it down.

'Big place, the south Pacific. I'm just a little cog in a very big, very complicated machine.'

'But if they're sending someone like you undercover to Kutu, there'll be a good reason for it . . .' she persisted, whispering.

Sure there was a reason. Called Assistant Commissioner Stanley. Whether it was a good one remained to be seen. He didn't answer.

'Look, I realise there are things you can't tell me . . .' she added, oozing understanding. The engines began to roar. 'Oh I h-hate this part,' she stuttered, gripping the armrests.

The 747 careened down the runway and lurched into the air, heavy with fuel and a full passenger load. As it banked for the turn to the southeast, the lights of Singapore's harbour and business district disappeared beneath cloud. When the wings levelled, Charlotte relaxed again.

'Take-offs and landings,' she explained. 'I'm fine with the middle bit.'

'Hold my hand if it helps,' he offered, winking again.

She lifted one eyebrow.

'Been out this way before?' he asked, trying to sound chatty.

'No. I've been nowhere,' she confessed.

'Big break for you then?'

'Yup,' she gulped, her anxiety boomeranging back. 'For me and for the News Channel. We're a bucket-shop news station. Everything done on the cheap. Foreign news, if we ever cover it, is something we buy from agencies. Until today the very idea of sending a reporter to the other side of the world was unheard of. They had to call an emergency board meeting to authorise the money for my air fare.'

She saw his look of disbelief.

'It's true! They've set a daily limit on how much I spend. If I exceed it, the accountants will pull me out.' She laughed. 'Not a problem *you* have, I imagine. Taxpayers' money. No expense spared. By the way, *are* you going to Kutu, or just Darwin?' She answered her own question. 'Kutu, obviously. You'll work with the Indonesian police.'

'That depends,' he mumbled. 'Maybe.'

'But you *are* going to Kutu?'

'That's the idea. What about you? On your own? No camera crew? Don't tell me the News Channel couldn't afford to send one?'

'That's exactly it! Don't laugh. I have to meet someone in Darwin. An Aussie woman who's shot tape there for KEPO – you know the environmental lot?' He nodded. 'Well, the deal is, she'll work for us for free because she wants to go to Kutu again anyway. We just pay her for the footage we use. She keeps the rights to the stuff. I don't know the first thing about her but I'm told she's shot good tape. We have to pose as backpackers, I gather.'

'Don't we all?'

She flashed him a smile. He was giving, slowly.

Her perfume and her mouth were getting to him. He found himself focusing on her lips as she talked. A few years back he'd have pulled her, no problem. But these days he behaved himself. Anyway, sex and the job didn't mix. All he wanted from her was silence about who he was.

'Look, Charlotte . . . or is it *Charlie?*'

'Either. I'm not fussy.' She turned her head sideways, resting an ear against the seat back and half-closing her eyes.

'OK. Charlie it is then . . . Now look, I need your help, chuck.' He saw her eyes glow with anticipation. 'What I'm doing out here – it's sensitive, understand?'

'Sure. But . . . but what exactly *are* you doing?' she asked.

'Never mind for now. The point is that *you* could screw things up for me. I'm asking you not to.'

'Oh . . .' She looked startled. Affronted almost. 'Not sure what you mean.'

'Simply that out here I'm a news photographer, right? But you could identify me to others as a police officer. And I can't allow that.'

'Allow? What d'you mean *allow?*' she smarted, pulling back her head. 'Are you threatening me?'

'No, no. Hang on. I'm asking for your co-operation, that's all. Asking you not to tell a living soul who I am.'

Scotland Yard sending an undercover officer to Kutu was a story in itself, she thought. No one else had it. Her instincts told her she'd be a fool not to use it. On the other hand the trade-off for silence might be worth much, much more.

'There are lives at risk, Charlie,' he went on earnestly. 'Stephen Bowen's. Mine. Yours. This place we're going to isn't Disneyworld.'

Charlie shivered. She'd never travelled south of Nice before and had no clue what to expect on Kutu. Somehow the idea she might be risking her *life* hadn't occurred to her.

'It's OK. Of course I won't tell anyone who you are,' she said meekly. 'We're not *all* irresponsible in the media.'

He touched her hand. 'Thanks.' Question was whether he could trust her. He noticed crow's feet at the side of her eyes and brown roots to her hair. It was the flaws in women that made them truly attractive. Perfection intimidated him.

'Excuse my nosiness,' she continued, 'but what exactly are you going to *do* in Kutu?'

Back on guard.

'I'll find out when I get there. And you?'

'To do a background piece. Explaining why the OKP or KEPO has kidnapped Stephen Bowen.'

'Oh it *is* them, is it?'

'*I* don't know,' she shrugged. 'I'm just assuming that. Do you know different?'

'No, but I don't *assume* things. Maybe that's the difference between a copper and a scribbler,' he goaded.

She ignored the remark. A steward stopped at their row with the bar trolley.

'Diet Coke please,' asked Charlie.

'And a beer for me.'

The steward tossed bags of nuts on to their tables. Dinner would follow in thirty minutes, he told them.

'Always been a *copper* have you?' she asked a few moments later.

'Eight years. I was a soldier before that. Royal Military Police.'

She noticed suddenly that his nose wasn't straight.

'Is that where you got your nose broken?'

Nick put a hand to his face. There'd been speculation from his mates over the years. Punch-ups. Gang fights. Jilted women.

'No. I fell off my bike . . . When I was fifteen.'

She laughed. She liked the answer for its lack of bullshit.

'What time is it?' she asked. 'I haven't reset my watch from London. Still half past one in the afternoon there.'

'9.30 p.m. here, 11 p.m. in Darwin.'

'God, my body clock is never going to adjust. Have you done a lot of this?'

'I was in Hong Kong for a while. With the army.'

'Wife and kids with you?' Charlie checked. 'I assume you're married.' Always best to know.

'Was then. But no, they weren't with me.'

'Must've been hard. You haven't remarried?'

He didn't want these questions. Not when he was working.

'No. And you? Let me guess. Can't be hitched because no husband'd ever let a woman with eyes as seductive as yours run around the world on her own . . .'

She flinched at his chauvinism, then thought better of it. Treat it as an old-fashioned compliment.

'You're right. No husband in my life. Still looking. So I'd watch out if I were you!' she added, nudging him. 'But seriously. Back to business . . .' She leaned towards him so her shoulder touched his. '*You*'re working on your own out here?'

'At the moment, yes.' Couldn't do any harm to tell her that.

She thought about it for a moment. Thought about the pros and cons of making a play for him. In the interests of the story.

'As I said, Nick, you can trust me. I won't let you down.' She rested her hand on his arm. 'But one good turn deserves another, right?' She looked him in the eye. 'You'll keep me up to speed? Tell me what's going on?'

No way. She was asking for the moon on a stick.

'Do my best,' he said.

10

London – The News Channel
Tuesday 13.15 hrs

TED SANKEY SAT at his desk thinking about Charlotte Cavendish. The name had class, like its owner. More class than a downmarket news outlet deserved. The fact that he fancied the woman *had* played some part in his decision to hire her, but it was the confidence she radiated that had got her the job.

Picking staff for a new TV news station was a gamble. Last night he'd taken a bigger one – despatching Charlie to the other side of the world to compete with hacks who had all of her talent, but years of hard-won experience to back it up.

He'd slept badly last night, nagged by fears of it going wrong. If Charlie could only come up with a scoop, or even a handful of respectable, competent reports, then great. The budget men who controlled his life would have to acknowledge he'd shoved the Channel up with the big boys. If she failed, there'd be no sympathy for her, nor for *him* from the board.

On day two of the Bowen story, there'd been little movement, which was good; it would be twenty-four hours before Charlotte was operational. Two new lines had emerged – the discovery that a satellite dish had been stolen from Strasbourg, and the minister's former connection with Metroc Minerals. A whiff of potential corruption to spice the story, but with the man's life at risk, the media had held back on the speculation.

Alone in his office, Sankey sat watching the lunchtime news, which was two-thirds through. His empty stomach churned on the vile, machine-made coffee he'd drunk. His secretary would soon be back from the deli with a sandwich.

Looking to keep his lead on the story, he'd phoned DCI Mostyn earlier, hoping his co-operation with the stroppy DS Randall yesterday might trigger a little inside information, but he'd been abruptly transferred to the press office.

First thing that morning he'd been summoned with the editors of the other TV news companies to a meeting with the home secretary. The government was terrified of what the kidnappers might transmit next on the satellite. The media giving them free access to the airwaves was simply encouraging them, she'd warned. Would they kindly agree not to show it in future?

They'd refused. Wasn't up to the government to say what could or couldn't be shown. But to protect their backs, the TV networks were planning to pool the next satfeed. No more exclusives. If there was to be a fight with the government over broadcasting it, better they stood together.

Sankey had wavered at the idea of a pool. The kidnappers had favoured the News Channel once; they could do it again. And exclusives were like gold at this stage of the Channel's evolution. But he knew he would have to go along with the pool in the end – too risky being a maverick. He was waiting until the lunchtime programme was off the air however before ringing the BBC with his agreement. To keep them sweating.

A tap at his door and his secretary came in with a small carrier bag.

'Ciabatta with Brie and roasted peppers,' she announced. 'You'll love it.'

'What, no corned beef?' Sankey quipped. She was always trying to improve him. Just like his wife had, until she gave up and left him. 'Thanks girl.'

Suddenly there was a shout from the newsroom. Mandy yelling.

Sankey dropped the food bag on his desk and sprinted from his office.

'On six again!' Mandy snapped, pointing at her multi-monitor.

The same colour bars and the message to roll the recording machines.

'Fuck!' Sankey hurled himself towards the control gallery. Four minutes to the end of the live. Ratings dived when this show went off the air.

He banged open the control room door.

'We're rolling on it,' the director assured him.

'Bloody off-air in three minutes, Ted,' Marples panicked. 'What the hell do we do?'

The rest of the afternoon's transmissions were already taped. Extending the lunchtime would mean rejigging everything.

Sankey looked at the station output. A taped item on body make-up was being transmitted. On the studio monitor he saw the presenter, a stylish young black girl, listening on her earpiece to the control room talkback, her face taut with tension.

'Cass, we may cut out of this any second,' Sankey told her. 'You'll have to ad lib an intro.' The presenter nodded. 'Just say we're interrupting for late news on Bowen. Once again the News Channel has exclusive pictures direct by satellite from his kidnappers . . . Something like that. OK?'

Cass grimaced but held up a thumb.

'They're rolling!'

On line six whoever was feeding the pictures had started the clock. Twenty, nineteen, eighteen . . .

Two minutes to off-air. Sankey pounded his head with a fist. What should he do? Record the tape and play it after they'd shared it with the opposition? Never get it on the lunchtime that way. But if they put it out live, he'd be taking a huge risk and be breaking the pooling agreement . . . Except he hadn't told the competition he was accepting it yet . . . They would all cry foul, but he could live with that. One more tasty bite? One more headline-grabbing exclusive for the Channel? The temptation was too strong.

'Cut to Cass! Tell her to do the link. Then take the feed live!'

'I'm not sure that's . . .'

'Do it, Tom! I'm in charge.'

'Seven seconds for the link. Cue Cass . . .'

'*We're interrupting that report because there's some late news on the kidnap of Stephen Bowen. We're just getting these pictures by satellite . . .*'

The director switched to the satellite feed.

Bowen's face filled the screen, hair matted with sweat, mouth sagging. The abrasion on his cheekbone now a deep blue bruise. A plaster across it and another on the end of his nose.

'Fuck!' Sankey breathed.

The minister's grey eyes were screwed up with pain and fear.

'Ted, we *can't* do this live . . . .' Marples insisted. 'We've no *idea* what'll happen.'

'We *are* doing it,' Sankey snapped. 'Just keep your finger on the off button.'

Bowen's face twitched as he began to speak, but his voice was surprisingly forceful.

'*Prime minister – Keith . . . this is for you, this message. Listen. Please. It may be the last you ever hear from me . . . unless you do what they want. I've learned a lot. I know now what vile things are being done to people on Kutu by the Indonesian military. Believe me I know . . . I know exactly . . .*'

His voice cracked, his face convulsed. He shook his head as if he couldn't continue. Then his eyes looked off-camera at an unseen tormentor. Lips trembling he faced forward again.

'They're being tortured, they're being beaten, raped and murdered. We . . . we have to get tough with the Indonesians, Keith. Not just lip service. Not just protests through the UN. We have to put our money where our mouth is. Which means cancelling the arms contract − it's the only way . . .

The OKP are giving you until noon GMT on Friday. Announce it on the BBC World Service. Please. Don't ignore this . . . If you do, they'll kill me. They'll kill me very slowly.

The camera lens zoomed back. Bowen was shirtless, his chest a dark mass of hairs. Sankey watched with horrified fascination, trusting some innate judgement to tell him when to shout 'cut'.

There was something hanging from the minister's nose, attached by the sticking plaster. Looked like a wire . . . Bowen turned his head away and began to whimper and plead.

'No, please . . . FOR GOD'S SAKE!'

Rapidly the picture widened further. Bowen was devoid of *all* clothing. Stark naked, arms out to the side, wrists bound to rings on a wall, a second electrical flex dangling from his penis.

Sankey stopped breathing. Total, horrified silence in the gallery. Suddenly Bowen's body arched like a bow. A scream punched the sound needles into the red.

'Cut!' shrieked Sankey.

Cass back in vision, looking off-camera at the monitor, her serenity shattered.

'Recap,' Sankey croaked, his heart in his boots.

He and the News Channel had just committed professional suicide.

'Tell them latest pictures, Cass. Just in. Dramatic appeal for help. Sum it all up then link out of the show.'

'Twenty to end titles!' the director added with superficial calm.

The presenter turned to camera, her eyes round black dots, her mouth a twisted ribbon of anguish.

'I'm sorry . . .' She pulled out her earpiece and slid out of shot, leaving an empty chair.

'Framestore!' yelled the director. 'Gimme the News Channel caption. Quick!'

Randall listened incredulously, head under the perspex hood of a phone booth in the baggage hall at Darwin. Mostyn's voice seemed half an octave higher than normal.

'I tell you, boy, the clock's ticking now,' he intoned. 'Shaken the bloody government rigid. You should've seen the PM at *Question Time*. Looked like he'd given up the struggle. Total cave-in. Opposition had a stack of Amnesty reports describing torture at the hands of the Indonesian military. East Timor, Irian Jaya, the lot. MPs didn't know who to condemn most, the Indonesian government or the Kutuan kidnappers who demonstrated the Indonesian's techniques on the right honourable member.'

'Definitely OKP, the kidnappers?' Randall queried, deciding Mostyn's pun had been unintentional.

'It's what Bowen said. *OKP deadline of Friday*. I tell you what makes me sick,' Mostyn railed. 'It's when parliament suddenly develops an effing conscience. MPs on all sides claiming they're lifelong champions of human rights and have always opposed selling arms to countries where they torture people. Makes you bloody sick.'

'Know what you mean, sir. But did the video give any clues as to where Bowen actually is,' Randall pressed, cutting through Mostyn's bombast.

'No. Nothing new on that. Except he looked hot and sweaty. He's down your way somewhere, old son. The Indonesians are still playing games – swearing he's not in their country while putting the squeeze on the OKP to find out what they've done with him. What the Brit government needs is direct contact with the kidnappers instead of all this ultimatum by satellite stuff. It's the arms-length business that scares the bollocks off the PM. Terrified the next transmission will show Bowen being cut up into steaks.'

'Even the News Channel wouldn't put *that* out.'

'Don't count on it. Anyway, old son, see what you can glean from the KEPO man, then get yourself over to Kutu quick as you can and find us someone to talk to. When's the flight?'

'Six this evening. That's in . . .' He checked his watch. 'About fifteen hours from now.'

He heard Mostyn curse. 'Nothing sooner? Time's bloody running out.'

'I could try flapping my arms . . .'

'Why not . . .? OK son. Give us another ring before you leave Darwin.'

Thirty passengers had got off the Singapore flight, which was continuing on to Sydney. White- and grey-haired parents and grandparents visiting offspring who'd fled the nest for southern climes, they leaned on trolleys watching out for their baggage.

Charlotte emerged from another phone booth, her face flushed, her eyes gleaming.

'Fucking Sankey!' she exploded. 'Un-bloody-believable!'

'What was it you said on the plane?' Nick goaded. '*We're not all irresponsible in the media?*'

'Don't! Just don't . . .' she warned.

'Your boss allowed pictures of a man being electrocuted to be shown on live TV to an audience of mothers, toddlers and geriatrics!'

'They've just fired him,' she replied flatly.

'Are you surprised?'

Charlotte stomped about, clutching her head in her hands.

'It's a disaster,' she muttered. 'An absolute, unmitigated disaster.' Her face crumpled.

'Carousel's moving,' Randall mumbled.

'Sorry,' Charlie said, wiping her eyes with the back of her hand. 'They've told me to get my bag, then look up the time of the next plane home.'

'*What?*'

'They want me back in London. Immediately. No passing "go".'

'I don't believe it.'

'It was Ted Sankey who pushed to get me out here. Now he's gone, they're reversing all his decisions. They want the lid back on the box and everybody inside it. With a few months' good behaviour they hope they can still keep the licence.' She gave a deep sigh. 'The News Channel is run by eunuchs, Nick. The only manager with balls was Sankey. Trouble was his testosterone level was just *too* bloody high . . .'

She picked up her grey holdall by its thick shoulder strap.

'Shall we share a trolley?' she asked briskly, trying to put on a perky face.

'Sure. I'll get one.'

She watched him walk to the line at the end of the baggage hall, noticing his broad shoulders, straight back and tight butt. He *moved* so well. Pity. She'd begun to believe they'd had something going.

By the time he returned, the first pieces of luggage had emerged.

'What about the woman who was going to do camera for you?' he asked as they watched the carousel.

114

'That's the other problem. She phoned a few hours ago saying she'd gone sick. Cold feet more like. Three journalists got arrested in Kutu yesterday. Including the BBC man.'

'Ouch.' Getting in was going to be even more of a nightmare than he'd feared.

His rucksack came through first. He swung it off the belt with one hand.

'Wouldn't it be the ultimate if they'd lost mine,' Charlotte moaned. 'Look, you go on. Don't wait.' She held out her hand to say goodbye.

'Don't be daft.'

'But I may not even get out of the airport. If there's anything heading north right away, I'm supposed to take it.'

'Are you mad? You'll be dead with all that travelling. Give yourself a break. Tell 'em the first flight was full or something.'

'You reckon?' He was right. Wasn't *her* fault the Channel had fucked up. And she was in no hurry to say goodbye to him.

'Oh *good*,' she said, pointing at the large, maroon backpack being borne down the belt towards them.

Nick leaned forward and lifted it on to the trolley.

The cab driver kept his window open. Eight years since Randall had sniffed the tropics. The light of the street lamps made the wet tarmac gleam. The heat was enough to bring on a sweat, even at night.

'What does it get up to in the day?' Charlotte asked. She'd booked on a flight home the following evening.

'Thirty. Thirty-three. Not bad, but come December when humidity's ninety per cent, you just want to die.' The driver was middle-aged, male and with a dent in his Australian accent that might have been Polish. 'Suicide season – that's what they call the Wet. First time for you in Darwin?'

'Yes,' she answered. 'First time anywhere south of the south of France.'

'Darwin's OK. Growing fast of course. All new since the cyclone in 1974. On holiday?'

'Not exactly, I'm . . .' A prod in her thigh from Nick. 'Well we're sort of on holiday, yes.'

'If you want someone to show you round, you can call me.' He plucked a card from a clip on the dashboard and passed it back.

'Thanks.'

Nick glanced to the right. They were passing an army camp. The chain-link fence, barracks and parked trucks stirred warm feelings in him. Companionship, being part of a team. The good side of serving in the army. Wouldn't mind having that sort of backup to hand right now instead of thousands of miles away.

'That's big,' he remarked.

'Certainly is. The defence forces are taking over the whole flamin' Territory.'

'New, is it?'

'That's right. A few years back the government realised all the military bases were down south but the threat was in the north. So they decided to shift 'em up here. Nobody in Darwin complained. It's all good for business.'

'Threat?'

The driver gave a theatrical shrug.

'We . . . ell,' he drawled, 'nobody ever says, do they? But look at Indonesia – two hundred million people running out of living space. China bursting. And Australia is one huge empty continent. This place could be overrun in no time at all. There's not much to stop boat people getting ashore on this coast, apart from crocodiles.'

'And now soldiers.'

''Sright. They're turning the clock back fifty years. Place was crawling with military in the war. It was the Japs they worried about then, of course.'

Japs and barbed wire. Charlotte thought of her father. Instant guilt that she'd pushed him to the back of her mind. There he was, sitting by the waterside in Devon waiting to die, still tortured by what had been done to him in the camps. Wherever it was he'd been imprisoned, she felt closer suddenly.

They entered downtown Darwin, a grid of streets all but deserted at this hour, the buildings dull, square blocks of concrete.

'Your flight to Kutu's at six tonight, yes?' Charlie checked, pulling her mind back to the present.

'That's right,' said Nick. 'Same time as you leave for London.' He was relieved she'd no longer be around to betray his identity, but he would miss her.

'You've got people to see here first?' she checked.

'Someone from KEPO, yes.'

'Mind if I tag along? I've got a day to waste, and it's either that or visiting a crocodile farm.'

'Which would be like being back in the newsroom . . .'

'Aren't you funny . . .' she scowled.

'Sure. Tag along.' He'd be a more convincing journalist if he was accompanied by a real one.

The Yard's travel office had booked Nick a room at a cheap place next to a bus station. Bleary-eyed backpackers sat slumped against a wall waiting for coaches to transport them across the continent. This part of town looked like it never slept.

Charlotte's hotel was round the corner. She wrote its name down and gave Nick the page from her notebook.

'What time?' she checked.

'Have to call the contact at nine. I'll ring you after that.'

'Thanks.' She shook his hand. 'And thanks for being supportive.'

Her smile was confident again. Grown-up and in charge. Good actress, Nick thought.

"Night. What's left of it,' Nick grunted. He'd get four hours' sleep if he was lucky.

Her eyes gave him a smile that was like being swathed in brown velvet. He closed the car door and watched it drive off.

London, Whitehall – COBR
Tuesday 22.00 hrs

Assistant Commissioner David Stanley ducked when entering the Cabinet Office Briefing Room. Unnecessary, but a habit because of his height. He'd come straight from Scotland Yard where Mostyn had brought him up to speed with developments.

In Parliament Square his car had had to nose through demonstrators several hundred strong. Not the usual leftie do-gooders, but a sober, determined crowd including thirty-somethings in business clothes, sickened by the message hammered home by Stephen Bowen's kidnappers that *their* government, their *nation* was supplying weapons to a regime that silenced its opponents by plugging them into the mains.

The novice protesters had begun assembling early in the evening, after a heavily edited version of the torture video was shown on all TV networks. They'd sought leadership from a core of habitués who'd been there since the day before, pounding out their anti-arms-trade rant which for years had failed to reach a wide public. Suddenly raised to hero status, their well-used placards saying NO ARMS TO TORTURERS became the standards to which the newcomers rallied.

The door to the briefing room opened. Prime Minister Copeland sloped in, his face as haggard and lifeless as in the TV pictures of PMQs. He lowered himself into the large chair at the head of the long table. He looked at Stanley first, then across at Philip Vereker. Just the two of them there.

'What an appalling day,' he announced gravely. His shoulders slumped. Stanley had the odd impression the man's hair had receded since yesterday.

'I feel ill every time I think of what they did to Stephen. What utter bastards . . .' Copeland looked searchingly from face to face. 'You think they *will* kill him if I don't do what they want?'

'Yes, prime minister, I think they will,' said Vereker flatly.

Copeland looked down at his hands. So much on his mind. So much he mustn't show. 'It's hard to think about principles when it's a friend's life at stake. Who is it, Philip? Who's got him?'

'Everything points to an OKP splinter group. Some Kutuan faction that's determined to get the islanders' struggle on to every front page in the world. They're certainly succeeding, but whether they'll pick up sympathy is another matter.'

'Oh, by the way, prime minister,' chipped in Assistant Commissioner Stanley. 'My man Randall's arrived in Australia and is starting to dig. But he won't get to Kutu for another twelve hours. We've told him to try to set up direct communications with the kidnappers.'

Copeland looked confused and cornered, his face drained of all colour.

'Why the penis?' he asked suddenly. He saw the surprise on their faces and flushed slightly. 'Why the nose? Why those two parts of the body connected to wires?'

Assistant Commissioner Stanley shrugged, indicating this was one for Vereker to answer. Torture methods weren't taught at Hendon.

'I believe it's because both organs contain moist conduits into the body . . .' Vereker mumbled awkwardly, 'but I'm no expert.'

Copeland frowned, not understanding.

'Moisture, prime minister. Makes for better conductivity,' Vereker explained. 'For the electric current.'

Copeland swallowed. 'It's so damned clinical,' he breathed.

He opened the folder he'd brought with him and stared at the pages, more to occupy his eyes than because of what they contained. He faced a terrible decision – to back the arms industry and the important principle of never giving in to terrorists, or to go with the flow of the nation's new-found moral conscience, capitalise on it politically – and maybe save Stephen's life.

'The kidnappers have certainly won sympathy here,' Copeland sighed. 'The whips tell me constituency offices are being bombarded with demands that we only sell arms to *friendly democracies*. I blame the media. They've opened their doors to Amnesty and the other lobby groups, swallowing their arguments without question. The fact that the government's trying to run an economy with a flourishing defence industry doesn't seem to get a look in.'

Copeland looked worn down. Stanley had heard it said he'd not *sought* the top job, but had been unable to resist it when it came his way. For a moment the assistant commissioner felt sorry for him. He'd watched him being mauled by the media in the past two days. And he knew what that felt like.

'The trouble is,' Copeland confided, his voice close to breaking, 'I'm far from sure we'll be able to hold the line . . .'

'You'd cancel the arms contract?' Vereker asked, astonished. 'Give in to terrorist blackmail? That'd set a terrible precedent, sir. Think what the Americans would say . . .'

'It wouldn't be put over like *that*, Philip,' Copeland retorted sarcastically. 'No, we would simply be recognising the change in the international climate towards arms sales. Taking the lead in acknowledging the new public morality . . .'

There were some in the party who thought such a tactic might even rescue his government. He couldn't remain in power for long with a majority of one. So there was growing pressure on him to drop the arms deal, to call themselves the party of principle, and to go to the country in the hope of picking up the extra votes they needed.

'To cap it all,' he went on bitterly, 'the halfwits in the European Commission have just proposed a Europe-wide ban on arms sales to countries that don't observe the UN Charter on Human Rights. It's absurd! The French'll laugh their heads off. The reality is that if Europe can't sell arms to autocratic regimes our defence industries would collapse overnight. It'd be economic suicide!'

Copeland clasped his hands and pulled himself together. 'Anyway, that's all political. Where's the investigation got to?'

Stanley sat bolt upright.

'We think the minister's still in the far east, prime minister. We think the videos of him are being airfreighted to Europe to be picked up by whoever stole the satellite transmitter in Strasbourg last week. European police forces are checking all airports that have suitable flights.

'The other main line of enquiry is to do with the News Channel, prime minister. There has to be a reason why the kidnappers picked that station both times. We want to interview Mr Sankey, the sacked editor, but it'll have to wait until the morning. We've found him. But he's in a wine bar, unable to stand or speak.'

'Bloody good thing they sacked him. Outrageous allowing those pictures to be broadcast.'

'Well, he's drowned his sorrows. We're hoicking him out and getting him home. An officer will stay with him until he sobers up enough to make sense.'

'Probably already drunk when he took the decision to show the tape . . .' Copeland ventured.

'That I can't say, prime minister,' said Stanley neutrally. 'But let me tell you what our thinking is. Two possibilities . . .'

Vereker shifted in his seat and sighed. There always were just *two* possibilities with David Stanley, he mused. The man's brain simply couldn't cope with any more.

'One . . .' Stanley continued, 'Mr Sankey may know more about the kidnap than he's saying – i.e. he knows who the kidnappers are and had some deal going with them to get the pictures for his network. On balance, unlikely I'd say.'

Utterly unlikely, Vereker decided. Conspiracy theories gone mad.

'Two . . . one of the people operating the satellite dish may be an ex-employee of the News Channel who knows the times of their satellite bookings and how the company operates. Or maybe he's an ex-employee from one of the channel's rivals with a grudge against his ex-bosses. Giving a boost to the opposition could be his way of getting back at them. We're running checks with ITN, Sky and the BBC, to see if they can come up with names.

'Finally, prime minister, there's the issue of Mr Bowen's debts. Two hundred thousand pounds seems to be the figure owing to the two creditors we've identified so far. There may be more of course, we simply don't know.'

Copeland blinked. He felt a patch of heat spread up the back of his neck.

'Are you suggesting there's a connection between Stephen's gambling debts and the kidnap?' he queried, disguising his terror. 'Surely not.'

'It *is* possible his private activities in Indonesia were for the purpose of raising money illicitly so he could get the bailiffs off his back . . .' Stanley's words drained the remaining colour from Copeland's face.

'I hardly think . . .' Copeland turned to the SIS man. 'Philip? D'you go along with this?'

Vereker removed his round-lensed spectacles and cleaned them with a handkerchief. Without them his eyes looked small and bewildered.

'This wasn't Bowen's first visit to Indonesia by any means,' he answered flatly. 'He first went four years ago when he was a director of

Metroc Minerals. Had some hand in negotiating Metroc's stake in KUTUMIN.'

'We know all about that,' Copeland snapped. He'd spent much of PM's Questions rejecting allegations of ministerial impropriety. 'But the point is there's no evidence Stephen has any on-going connection with Metroc – apart from owing them money. The company's denied it very firmly.'

'Agreed. But David's suspicions are quite natural. Indonesia is the cradle of corruption. Huge sums of money change hands there for services rendered. The minister's insistence on privacy *could* have been because of some dodgy deal.'

'He was with a woman, Philip,' Copeland snorted. '*That's* why he wanted privacy.'

Vereker replaced his spectacles. 'That was part of it, prime minister, certainly.' He held a steady gaze, unmoved from his belief that there was more.

'The woman's a *fact*, gentlemen. And facts are what we should stick with,' Copeland snapped, fearful of where this speculation might lead. 'Now tell me, what are the Indonesians up to? *Do* they think he's in their country or not?'

'I don't think they know, prime minister. But something odd's happened. There are signs that Major General Sumoto, the Indonesian military's procurement chief, believes you'll have to cancel the arms deal.'

'Oh?' Copeland looked up startled.

'General Sumoto has been talking to the Chinese. There's a possibility he's asking them to rebid for the contract. Which is surprising, considering the Indonesian military's traditional hostility to anything communist, but nonetheless a possibility.'

'Bugger,' Copeland hissed. 'So General Sumoto thinks I'm going to cancel . . .' He hated people to prejudge him. Particularly Sumoto who was supposed to be a friend.

'They can see you're under great pressure, sir.'

'Maybe, but the point is I *haven't* made up my mind yet.'

Hadn't, because he couldn't get his brain straight. It wasn't just the conflicting national issues that troubled him, *personal* considerations were affecting his judgement. Cancelling the arms deal would not only lose business for British industry, it would kill off a *private* arrangement he'd made – a deal Stephen had talked him into. At the time it had seemed as harmless a bit of profit-making as the share options given to executives in the privatised utilities, but he knew now that he'd been insane to agree to it. The bait however had been substantial. Losing it would hurt.

Something else was fuzzing his brain, something connected with that – the irrational fear that under torture Stephen might reveal the details of their private deal, tell the world about it on satellite television. The disgrace such an exposure would bring him would not be survivable, politically or personally.

Preventing Stephen from talking had become of overriding importance to him. He kept telling himself he couldn't possibly allow such a consideration to affect his decision, but it was there, needling away like the devil himself.

Terminating the arms contract and getting Stephen safely back to London would be one way of ensuring his silence. But industry would lose big money and so would he.

Reconfirming the contract quickly and resolutely was another way, because Stephen would be killed . . . Big business would be satisfied. His own reputation would be safe and so would his windfall.

But what of his conscience? Could he live with the thought that he'd acted for himself rather than for the country?

Copeland looked up. Stanley and Vereker were staring at him expectantly.

'It's the hardest decision I've ever taken, gentlemen,' he confided softly. 'I don't know what to do for the best.'

I I

Darwin
Wednesday 11.15 hrs

THE TAXI SPED down the highway that cut through the southern outskirts of town, overtaking a coach full of backpackers bound for Ayer's Rock. Under an intense blue sky, commercial estates gave way to bush, an arid flatland of tall palms, stubby cycads and eucalyptus trees. They passed a sign to a crocodile farm.

Randall's head felt fuzzed, his body clock still convinced it was the middle of the night. He'd dozed after checking into the hotel room, but not for long. 'Get in there fast and find us someone to negotiate with,' Mostyn had said. Fine if you're on the sixteenth floor of Scotland Yard. Not so easy from where he was sitting.

Next to him, Charlotte was subdued, depressed, wrapped in her own problems. She'd put on jeans and a white T-shirt. Nick could see that she was bra-less, which was a distraction he could have done without.

'I don't know why I'm doing this,' she announced suddenly. 'Pointless. Embarrassing. What am I going to say to these KEPO people? That I've just popped down from London for the *day*?'

'Say nothing,' Nick counselled. 'Let them assume you're going to Kutu.'

'So humiliating. There's only one thing for me to do when I get back to London . . .'

'Resign.'

The corners of her mouth turned down. 'How did you know I was going to say that?' A patina of perspiration had given her face a sheen.

'Because it's what you *would* do,' he replied dismissively. 'Women think emotionally, not logically.'

'Listen to the little professor! Didn't know you had a degree in behavioural psychology,' she replied snidely.

Randall pursed his lips.

'See that over there?' the silver-haired driver drawled. He pointed into the trees to the right. 'Old air base from World War Two. You can still see the huts.'

Charlotte saw some dilapidated prefabs through the trees.

'The Japs bombed Darwin you know, trying to take out the oil tanks. From bases in the Dutch East Indies. What's now Indonesia.'

Randall guessed all foreigners got treated to a history lesson.

Charlotte imagined her father's prison camp to have been somewhere like this. Heat, dust and a long way from civilisation. She worried his health had deteriorated since she left England, even suspecting in irrational moments that fate was calling her straight home because of it . . .

'What's in the bag?' Randall asked, jolting her from her angst. He rested a hand on the grey holdall wedged between them on the rear seat. 'Camera gear?'

'In a manner of speaking,' she replied coolly, fingering the thick shoulder strap. 'It's a trick bag. The bag's the gear. Hired from a specialist at huge cost. Another reason they want me home.' She held up the webbing and pointed to a rivet. 'See that tiny stud? It's a lens. Next to it, buried in the nylon is a microphone. There's a wafer of electronics in the strap, and a concealed cable running to a hidden compartment for a camcorder. Places to hide cassettes too.'

'Nifty.' Nick had used similar gear on surveillance in Irish pubs. 'Is there a spare pocket I can put this in?' He held up the small Pentax he'd brought with him.

'Sure.' She took it from him.

The driver slowed and swung the car on to a dirt track. A string of poles carried a power cable from the grid lining the highway.

'There's a handful of places up here,' he announced. 'Too darn isolated for my taste. But Jim Sawyer's a botanist so I suppose it's like home to him. Know him, do you?'

'No. Sort of a friend of a friend,' Randall replied quickly.

'Didn't know he had any friends. Except for the women. There's always one here, but different each time I come.'

It was Sawyer who'd given Nick this taxi driver's number. Said it was best to use someone who knew the way.

'Here y'are.' A house of dark green clapboard perched on a rise, almost engulfed by eucalyptus, its corrugated roof patchy with rust. An elderly, dust-caked Land Rover stood outside next to a cleaner, newer-looking Suzuki four-wheel-drive which had the logo of a rental company on the back window. 'Want me to come by and pick you up later?'

'That'd be great,' said Randall. 'In a couple of hours?'

'No worries. If you change your mind, give me a ring on the car phone.' He handed Nick a card. 'That's twenty-two dollars.'

As the car rattled back down the track and the humid heat closed around them the wire mesh door opened and a tanned, bony man aged about forty gave them a searching look. He was bare-chested with baggy shorts and a pair of thongs on his huge feet.

'G'day. I'm Jim Sawyer. Welcome to the outback. Nick and Charlotte, right?'

'That's right.' In the sticky heat Randall was glad he had also dressed in shorts.

Sawyer led them through a musty, parquet-floored living-room and out on to a stone terrace. They smelled charcoal smoke.

'Hope you don't mind eating early. Have to at this time of year if you want a barbie.' Sawyer pointed to the horizon where grey clouds were massing.

A dense, pink frangipani encroached on one side of the paving. Unripe mangoes hung like gonads from trees on a patch of grass beyond.

'Dump your bag down there, Charlie,' Sawyer said, pointing to the left.

A scrawny woman in flower-patterned shorts and bikini top stood by the barbecue, sweat glistening on her bare back.

'Hi,' she said, glancing over her shoulder. She had a sallow face and stringy hair.

'That's Jane,' Sawyer explained. 'And over here there's someone who thinks he knows Kutu as well as just about anybody.'

Easing himself up from a rattan armchair was a ruddy-faced man in his mid-fifties, with hair down to the collar of his faded tartan shirt.

'Brad Dugdale,' he volunteered, holding out a podgy hand. He studied them with a mix of suspicion and curiosity. 'I live on Kutu most of the time,' he added in explanation.

'Now, what *we* oughta know is who *you* two are,' Sawyer asked, eyes hardening. '*Newspix*, your e-mail said? What sort of outfit's that, Nick?'

'It's a picture agency. I'm freelance. And Charlie here works for TV news,' he added, quickly deflecting their attention.

'Oh really? BBC?' asked Dugdale. 'I get over to England from time to time. Might have seen you . . .'

'No. The News Channel. We're on cable. It was us who broke the Bowen kidnap story,' she proclaimed. 'And I'm their senior correspondent.' Bullshit. She felt herself blush.

'Right! Well, we're honoured, then,' Dugdale smiled ingratiatingly. There was the sound of more thongs on the parquet. A man and two women emerged from the house, short in stature, brown-skinned and with flat Melanesian faces.

'This is Thomas and Yuliana,' said Sawyer putting an arm round the man. 'They just escaped from Kutu in a twenty-foot boat. They've both been imprisoned several times by the Indonesian military.'

Thomas wore pale shorts and a patterned shirt, Yuliana a plain pink pinafore dress. The second, older woman went and stood with Dugdale, as if she belonged to him.

'Glad to meet you,' said Charlie extending a hand. The couple smiled blankly.

'They don't speak any English,' Sawyer explained. 'Just the Kutu dialect and a little Indonesian. Teri can translate.' He gestured to the woman with Dugdale. 'Thomas and Yuliana are staying a few days. I've set up interviews for them with the local press. It keeps up the pressure on our government.'

'Pressure to do what exactly?' Charlie asked.

The botanist breathed in as if for a peroration.

'Give these poor folks a beer first, Jim,' Dugdale intervened, slipping an arm round Charlie's shoulders. 'People can die of thirst round here.' He guided her to a chair.

'If you have a Diet Coke . . .' Charlie ventured. 'I . . . I'd prefer that.'

The woman called Jane turned from the barbecue. 'There's some in the fridge, Teri. Can you get them?'

Dugdale's woman padded into the house and returned with a can for Charlotte.

Sawyer pulled a beer from a cool box and thrust it at Nick. His skin was like tanned leather, his cheeks concave as if he'd spent too long in the sun.

'OK. Well as you know I'm the rep of KEPO in the Northern Territory. We've an office in Sydney which circulates all the campaign literature, but I provide most of the data. Darwin's become the main refuge for a lot of Kutuans. Timorese too. Some get out legally on passports, others take to the water. When you've watched members of your family murdered and tortured, you'll take almost any risk to escape. These two . . .' – he indicated Thomas and Yuliana – 'they spent fifteen days in an open boat. Food and water was all finished when our coastguard found them drifting. Another day and they'd have died.'

Nick murmured sympathetically, then asked, 'What's your campaign aimed at, Jim? What're you trying to achieve exactly?'

'To make people aware of what's going on in Kutu. And through that to pressure our government to do something about it.'

'Like what?' asked Charlie.

'Like putting pressure on the Indonesian regime to stop the torture and the killings,' Sawyer added, earnestly. 'And making it illegal for Australian companies to invest in parts of Indonesia where human rights are being blatantly abused.'

Dugdale's eyes looked skywards. 'That's where Jim and I part company,' he growled, shuffling to the cool box for another beer.

'Brad has his own little *investment* in Kutu . . .' Sawyer explained sarcastically.

'Really?' Randall queried.

'Diving. I run a couple of boats for tourists. Take them to the reefs to look at fish. I employ a few local boys, but the customers are mostly from Oz, and when it comes to air bottles and valves they like it better if they see an Oz in charge of things.'

The woman called Jane turned from her labours at the barbecue. 'How d'you like your steak, Charlotte?' she asked in a voice like a strangled cat. 'Well done or burned?'

'As it comes.'

'Good answer,' Dugdale grinned. 'That's what you'll be given anyway.'

Randall took a long draught of the beer, its iciness numbing his throat. He glanced from one man to the other. Sawyer was simple to categorise; a well-meaning do-gooder, probably somewhat naïve. Dugdale was less easy.

'What's your role in KEPO then, Brad?' he asked casually.

'Don't have one, Nick. I'm just a hanger-on. I support all the human rights stuff of course, but er . . . I mean who *wouldn't* when you know what the Indonesian army does to these people.' He nodded towards the couple who'd fled by boat.

'But you're not in favour of stopping Australian investment in places like Kutu . . .?'

'I'm a realist, chum. Our politicians won't take a stand like that. They're petrified of doing *anything* to upset the Indonesians. There's two hundred million of the buggers just north of here. If they decide they need our empty spaces and start flooding across in boats, we wouldn't stand a chance. All the smarmy boys in Canberra want is to be allowed to lick the Indonesians' bums and hope they leave our continent alone. Now . . . I admire Jim here for his principles – trying to get our government to act tough – but it won't achieve anything.'

'But kidnapping a politician might?'

'Eh?' Dugdale spluttered into his beer. 'Now you're putting words in my mouth.' He looked momentarily uncomfortable.

'What's the kidnap done for KEPO, Jim?' chipped in Charlie,

deciding as the only real journalist present that it was time to assert herself. 'Good publicity for you or bad?'

'We're all keeping well out of it,' Sawyer snarled. 'Already had the police round asking whether I've got your bloody minister banged up in the house. Let's get this straight. KEPO is about preserving Kutu. The land and the people. It's about *protecting human rights*, OK? Now you don't do that by depriving some other poor bugger of his human rights and sticking electrodes up his dick.'

Jane turned from the barbecue again. 'Food's ready folks.'

Dugdale grabbed a plate, draped it with salad and a hunk of bread, then added a charred piece of meat.

'Come on,' he urged, remembering guests were supposed to go first. 'Get stuck in.'

'Is that why you Poms are here?' Sawyer whined disparagingly. 'To pin this kidnap on the poor bloody Kutuans?'

'Just trying to find out what it's about, that's all,' Charlie soothed.

'It's the kidnappers themselves who keep linking it with Kutu,' Nick reminded him.

'Yeah, but that's impossible,' Sawyer insisted. 'It can't be the OKP.'

Dugdale caught Nick's eye. *Don't be too sure*, his expression said.

'Look at those two.' Sawyer gestured at Thomas and Yuliana. 'The Kutuans are simple folks, not international terrorists.'

Charlotte crossed to the table and picked up a plate. A blackened steak wasn't what her stomach wanted, but there was no choice.

'Talk to *them*,' Sawyer insisted. 'After you've eaten something, do an interview with them. Why not?'

'Fine,' said Charlie. 'I'd like to.'

Nick perched with his plate next to Sawyer.

'Tell me about the Kutuan resistance, Jim. How does your outfit tie in with them?'

'We don't. Separate organisations. We communicate that's all. There are people on the political side of the OKP at the university in Piri. They're on the Internet. So we get info from them which we use in our campaigns in Australia, the States and at the UN. But we only give moral support. Nothing financial.'

'You don't supply weapons? Explosives to blow up earth movers,' Nick prodded.

'No. We do *not*,' Sawyer glared. 'I wonder if you folks realise what the OKP's *massive* guerrilla force amounts to. There's about eighty blokes up in the mountains, that's all. Maybe a hundred. They live off berries in the forest, armed with machetes and the odd stolen rifle. Just get *that* image into your heads, rather than some fantasy of jet-setting revolutionaries equipped with cheque books and satellite dishes.'

'But they're not without powerful friends,' Randall persisted. 'Sympathisers who could have staged the kidnap on their behalf.'

'Look, I *know* all their friends. And it's not on.'

Randall glanced up to find Dugdale watching him with intense interest. 'What's your view, Brad?'

'Don't ask him – he knows fuck-all,' snapped Sawyer, ripping the ring-pull off a fresh can of beer and putting it to his lips.

'That's right,' Dugdale winked. 'I only *live* there . . .' He finished a mouthful of meat, then put his plate to one side. 'Look folks, my position's a little difficult to say the least. I have to make compromises all the time, and that's what sticks in Jim's throat. He doesn't believe in them.

'Now . . . in spirit I fully sympathise with what the Kutuans are after – of course I do. Who wouldn't? I mean they want to keep their land, don't they? It's natural. But I don't get *involved* with their cause like Jim does. I can't. The Indonesians'll tolerate us foreigners only so long as we're useful and don't interfere. Now, I've got a house there, I've got my business, and . . . and I've got Teri. So I put a little money in the right pockets to make sure I don't get hassled, and I button my lips when it comes to politics. If I didn't, they'd soon kick me out. And I've no desire to have to leave the place.'

Sawyer snorted. 'Course he doesn't! There's a few thousand rich mining executives about to descend on Kutu, and they'll all be looking for someone to take them scuba diving . . .'

Charlotte noticed the refugee couple looking uncomfortable and out of it. 'Maybe I'd better have that chat with Thomas and Yuliana,' she suggested.

'Teri'll translate,' Sawyer replied quickly. 'That's why she's here.'

Charlotte grouped some chairs together at the far end of the stone terrace.

Randall retrieved his Pentax from Charlie's camera bag. First he took pictures of her with the refugee couple, then quick shots of Sawyer and Dugdale while they weren't looking.

He put the camera away and drifted back over to them.

'So what are your plans, Nick?' Dugdale asked, putting a matey arm on Randall's shoulder then flopping down next to him.

'Going to Kutu on the six o'clock flight this evening. As a tourist,' Randall told him.

'Are you? Well I'd advise you to behave like one, chum. They'll be watching you. And the first time you do anything that doesn't fit, they'll have you in for questioning. You heard about the BBC bloke, did you?'

'Not any details.'

'Went in Monday night. Also posing as a tourist. Arrested Tuesday morning trying to get to see Junus Bawi at the university. Him and about three other journalists. All being expelled today. You'll probably see them coming off the plane that you're getting on tonight. There's only one flight a day.'

'I realise it's not going to be easy,' Nick replied, dispirited.

'Are you errm . . . together?' Dugdale asked, out of the side of his mouth. He pointed to Charlotte. 'I mean *together*, you know.'

'No.'

'Pity. Might have helped. People on their own stand out in Indonesia.'

Randall glanced across at Charlie, engrossed in her interview. Not only were they not a couple, Charlotte wasn't even *going* to Kutu. He turned back to Dugdale for more details.

'What's the procedure when you land at Piri?'

'They look at you. On the tarmac, in the terminal, there'll be people watching. Men staring at you. At passport control they'll give you a sixty-day tourist visa, so long as you can give the name of a hotel you're staying at and have a ticket out. They want to be sure you'll leave again.'

'And after passport control? They do a body search?'

'If they think you're media they might, but normally, no. They always search your baggage. Don't carry anything political – books and the like. And nothing pornographic. They'll pinch that for themselves.'

'Right. Then after customs, you're on your own?'

'On Kutu you're never on your own. They'll be watching all the time. The guy who gets you a taxi will be working for the police. In the street they'll come up and ask you where you're going. Always with a big smile like they're just friendly. Shaking intel off is going to be your biggest problem.'

Nick felt the gnawing of despair. On his own he'd be a sitting target.

Charlie came over and touched his arm. 'Can I have a quiet word?'

'Sure.' He stood up and followed her across the terrace.

'Wouldn't mind filming an interview with this couple. They're good,' she whispered. 'Just one problem. I need help with the camera.'

'I'll have a go.'

She dug into her grey 'trick' bag and pulled the Handycam from its concealed pocket.

'The thing's perfectly normal I think, apart from the connections on the back for the sneaky stuff.'

Nick turned it over in his hands, conscious of Dugdale watching him. 'Got a tripod?'

'Yup. And a pair of clip mikes.'

He worked out the gear, then set it up. The couple from Kutu looked curiously detached.

'They've done this before,' Charlie confided. 'About a hundred times by the sound of it. Every TV station in Australia!'

'Keep Teri's face out of it, OK?' Dugdale called anxiously from the other side of the patio. 'Don't want anyone knowing it's her doing the translating.'

Nick clipped microphones to the man's shirt and the woman's pinafore top. He checked the camera alignment and pressed the start button.

'Camera's running.'

'Thomas,' Charlotte began, 'tell me what happened to you when you protested about the destruction of your village.'

She nodded to Teri to translate her question.

Solemnly the man began to talk, crinkly black hair shiny with oil, skin the colour of roasted coffee beans and small black eyes that gave short, sharp clues to the distress he'd suffered. Then he paused. In a voice that betrayed her nervousness Teri began to translate.

'Thomas say KUTUMIN want make road through his village. But he and Yuliana they no want. Some people they leave the village when the soldiers come. But Thomas he refuse. So they take him from his house to the middle of the village so other people see, then they beat him.'

'What with?' Charlie asked.

'With their guns,' Teri explained. Thomas used his hands to demonstrate how they'd clubbed his head and body with their rifle butts.

Charlie grimaced. 'When did this happen?'

'About six months ago.'

'Then what happened?'

Thomas began talking again. At one point he turned to his wife and she lowered her eyes in shame. Then he reached over his own shoulder to touch the top of his back.

'The soldiers, they take away Thomas and Yuliana and some more people. Then they burn the village. Next day the machines come to build the road to the mine. The village is finish. No more village. Thomas and Yuliana they are take to prison. Soldiers they ask them many questions. About OKP. About the men who hide in the mountains with guns. They say Thomas give food to OKP. Yuliana also they do very bad things to her.'

131

'Was she raped?' Charlie pressed.

'I think yes,' Teri whispered, embarrassed. 'But Kutu women not like say such things.'

'And Thomas?'

'They burn him to make him confess. You wan' see?'

'Well, yes . . .' She swallowed, dreading the next part.

Thomas had been waiting for the cue and began to remove his shirt.

'Hang on a second,' Nick interrupted, switching off the camera. 'Let's get that microphone out of the way.' He unclipped it from Thomas's clothing and gave it to Charlie to hold. 'Right. Now Teri, tell him to start again. I'll go in close. Fingers on shirt buttons.'

Charlotte looked up, impressed by the sudden creativity of her stand-in cameraman.

Thomas removed his shirt and turned his muscular back to the lens. Half a dozen small round scars visible, two of them livid red, not yet healed. They spread over the hard ridge of his spine from right shoulder to lower left ribs, like stepping stones across a river.

'How did they do that?' Charlotte asked, wincing.

'Cigarettes.'

Charlotte paused to let the camera linger on the burn marks.

'What happened then?'

More questions and answers in Kutun.

'They send them to camp near airport at Piri. They want take them another island. Many thousand Kutuans already gone. But Thomas and Yuliana, they no want. One day they run from the camp. Priest he help them find boat. With some others. Fifteen days on the sea. No food and water. Then here in Australia.'

Charlotte imagined the hell of crossing five hundred miles of sea in this heat. She gave them a tight smile, then turned to Nick.

'That's great,' she whispered. 'Let's have a few cutaways. You know, a shot of Yuliana listening to him, then one of me.'

Dugdale came over, still anxious about Teri being seen on camera. 'Got enough now?' he queried.

'Nearly.'

'Three of the others died on that boat, y'know,' he confided. 'Coastguards found them ten miles off shore. Out of fuel and drifting. With their food finished and less than a litre of water between them, they were *all* waiting to die basically.'

Nick finished the shots, rewound a few seconds of tape to check it, then packed everything away, making it look as if video equipment was something he handled every day. A quarter to two. The taxi would be back soon, and time was short.

'When are you going back to Kutu, Brad?' Nick checked.

'Tonight. Same flight as you . . .' His face was a blank, but his eyes were oddly calculating.

'Good,' said Nick. Dugdale would be useful. And away from Sawyer he might open up more.

'But I warn you, I won't know you from Adam on the plane. So don't try and talk to me. They're watching remember and I've got my own back to protect.'

'Well, fine. But maybe we can have a drink together in Piri?'

'Sure thing . . . if they let you in,' he added sceptically. He dug into his pocket and pulled out a wallet. 'You'll find me at Captain's Bar. Teri's family runs it for me.' He handed them a card.

'You'll be trying to see Junus Bawi I expect,' Sawyer chipped in. 'Every journalist does.'

'His name's on my list,' Nick replied.

'Well, be careful. They arrested him Monday night. I heard he's been freed, but he won't want to see *you*. Too bloody dangerous. You could do better trying the priests. None of *them* has been arrested in the last few days. I'll write a couple of names down.' He went briefly into the house to get a pad.

'There's many religions in Kutu,' Dugdale explained. 'Allah's spreading fast but the Pope's still strongest. Up in the mountains they're catholic/animist, worshipping trees, rivers and the spirit that lives in the volcano as well as the Heavenly Father.'

A car hooted. The taxi had arrived. Sawyer handed Nick the note and fixed him with an eye like a vulture.

'Just remember ABRI doesn't like journalists,' he warned. 'If they can, they'll think of a way to put a bullet in your head and make it look an accident.'

Nick reached out his hand. 'Thanks for the warning. And for the lunch.'

It was Dugdale who led them back through the house. Nick sensed he wanted a word with them away from the others. It was a question, and it came as he held open the fly-screen.

'Tell me folks, just suppose you two *did* find out something about your kidnapped minister when you're in Kutu. Something nobody else knows . . . what would you do about it?'

Randall stared at him. Odd question, he thought.

'What d'you mean?'

'I mean would you put it straight on the TV, or ring up your prime minister for a quiet word?' Dugdale's watery eyes were studiedly neutral.

'Depends, I suppose,' Nick replied carefully, trying to divine what was behind this query. 'If it was important enough I guess we'd make sure it got to the right place.'

Dugdale nodded as if it was the answer he was hoping for.

'Why d'you ask?' checked Randall.

'Oh, just curious to know how you guys work.' He smiled dismissively, then shook each of them by the hand. 'Captain's Bar, remember. Welcome's warm and the beer's cold. Oh, what were your surnames again?'

'Randall and Cavendish,' Nick replied.

'Yeah! That's it. See you later!'

The taxi rattled away from the house, with Dugdale watching them thoughtfully.

'What was he on about?' Charlotte breathed.

'No idea.'

Randall was sure the question had not been innocent. Sure Dugdale knew more about the kidnap than he'd said. And sure that when the time was right, he'd want *them* to know it too.

He glanced behind. Through the dust being kicked up by the taxi he saw Dugdale open the door of the Suzuki and lean inside.

'*God!*' Charlie exclaimed, thinking through the interview she'd just done. 'Did you see those scars on Thomas's back? How can anyone *do* that to another human being?'

'Mmm.'

Randall's mind was on fast forward. He *had* to get in to Kutu. And for that to happen, he *had* to have Charlie with him as cover. But there were just minutes left in which to persuade her.

A flock of brightly coloured rainbow lorikeets swooped across the road in front of the car before alighting in eucalyptus trees. The first drops of the afternoon rain splattered on the windscreen.

'Just in time,' the driver mused. 'You'd have drowned back there.'

The clouds burst, water drummed on the roof cutting visibility to a few metres. The driver turned up the radio so he could hear it above the noise of the rain.

Randall looked at Charlie. Her blonde bob hung forward, half-obscuring her face. He felt sorry for her. Sorry he was about to manipulate her.

'Kutu is a big story. Pity you're going to miss it,' he remarked, leaning towards her sympathetically.

The rain became a curtain of silver threads, parted by the bonnet of the car. Spray hammered the wheel arches.

'Yes. Damn everybody!' Charlie exploded. 'Can you imagine what it feels like, knowing I'm sitting on the edge of this *huge* story and being told to catch the first plane home?'

'Well, why take it?' His words fell out with deceptive indifference.

'What?'

'I mean, do you *always* do as you're told? Nice for your boyfriends if you do . . .'

'What d'you mean?'

Randall gave her a disparaging look.

'I thought journalists were supposed to live by their wits,' he remarked softly, so the driver wouldn't hear. 'Not by what some goon says in an office eight thousand miles away.'

'You mean refuse to go back?' she croaked, astounded the thought hadn't occurred to her. 'Defy orders and go to Kutu?'

'Why not? If all you're going to do when you get back is resign. Why not do it *now* if you have to? Resign here. Turn freelance. If you get a good story in Kutu and the News Channel doesn't want it, someone else will. The BBC maybe. Their own man's been thrown out. This could be your big chance.'

Staring straight ahead, she tucked the loose hair behind her ears. Nick noticed her cheeks had turned pink. The driver was chuckling at some wacky nonsense from a caller to a phone-in programme.

'It's a thought . . .' she breathed. 'But, but the trouble is not just London . . . it's that camerawoman. She's let me down too . . .'

'If that's your only problem, I suppose *I* could help you out . . .' He'd closed the trap.

She faced him, mouth gaping melodramatically.

'*You* act as my cameraman?'

'Why not? Did all right back there, didn't I? I know video cameras. I've used sneaky gear like this.' He patted her grey holdall.

She shook her head. 'It's too risky . . . I need a pro with me.'

'The whole trip's risky. You knew that in London before you came out here. The only difference is you'd have a bloke you know little about holding the camera, instead of a woman you know little about.'

He *had* to persuade her. He *needed* her.

'We could pretend to be on honeymoon . . .' he suggested glibly. More than once he'd adopted that cover with a WPC.

'Oh of course!' she snapped, flushing a deeper red. 'What else . . .? Is *that* what this is all about?'

'*Pretend* to be on honeymoon,' he whispered, remembering she'd never done this sort of thing before. Go gently, he told himself.

'Didn't take the Indonesians long to rumble the BBC guy,' he went on. 'The trick is to *convince* the buggers we're tourists. Now if we went in as a *couple* – particularly a honeymoon couple – well everybody knows there's only one thing *they*'re interested in, so the police wouldn't bother with them. Look, it's not a come on, Charlie. I don't even fancy you.' The last bit was a lie. The heat had made the thin cotton of her T-shirt cling to her breasts like a second skin.

'Look, I don't *know* you . . .' she whispered, crossing her arms. She was wavering.

'Share a room with me for a few days and you'll know me quite well,' he joked. 'Seriously, it's no big deal, chuck. In public we'd be luvvy-duvvy, but in the bedroom I'd sleep on the floor, whatever you like.' He meant it. This was work. 'It's *acting*, that's all. You must do a bit of that every time you go on camera.'

'Rubbish,' she snapped, angry at the way he was railroading her. 'When I'm on camera that's *me* you're seeing.'

'OK Charlotte. Have it your way.' He folded his arms. Have to shame her into it. 'Beats me why you came out here in the first place . . .'

Charlotte's stomach tightened. The chance of a mega-scoop drew her like a grail. But those cigarette burns on Thomas's back had given her an unnerving insight into what it might take to get it. And there was the other problem. Could she trust Randall?

'Stop playing games with me,' she hissed, jabbing him on the shoulder. 'Why should *you* care whether I go to Kutu or not? What's going on in that scheming mind of yours?'

The taxi nosed into the outskirts of the town, the road's grassy banks luminous with bougainvillaea and magnolia. The rain had eased for the moment. The driver hunched forward, his mind on the radio.

Time, Nick realised, was now desperately short.

'OK, it's self-interest, I'll admit it. Working on my own I'm going to fail. With a woman as cover I've got a chance. Not a great one, but better than nothing. *You* happen to be a woman. And at this moment in time you're the only one available. Simple as that.'

She chewed her lip, tortured by indecision.

'For God's sake, girl, I'm giving *you* a chance too. You'll get your story. You'll be a winner.'

Charlie looked away. With him she would have unique access to what was going on. Not often that a reporter found herself teamed with an undercover cop. But now she'd smelled the danger of the place, her self-confidence had vapourised. She was scared, desperately scared.

The driver tilted his head to one side. 'Where do I drop you folks?'

Nick looked at Charlie. Decision time.

'Um . . .' she dithered, biting her lip. Oh what the hell . . .

136

She nodded.

Randall smiled.

'Downtown,' he told the driver. 'We've some shopping to do.'

12

British Embassy, Jakarta
Wednesday 12.05 hrs (05.05 hrs GMT)

IF HE'D HAD any hair worth tearing, Harry Maxwell would have
ripped it out. The Indonesians were being exceptionally opaque. No
collateral whatsoever from his contacts or Bruton's that the arms
contract was to be re-opened. He'd begun to think his judgement had
been blown off the rails by paranoia.

And Brigadier General Effendi had gone deaf. Maxwell's first call to
him at POLRI HQ had been just after eight a.m. *Busy in a meeting.* A
promise to call back, then nothing. He'd tried again an hour later. Then
an hour after that.

Selina Sakidin. *She* was the reason for Effendi's reticence. Guessed he
was going to request an interview with her. *Drove Bowen to the airport*
. . . Yes, but why, why? Did she sleep with Bowen the night he waved
goodbye to the ambassador and moved hotels? Must have done. And she
must've known his plans.

The phone rang and he grabbed it. At last. Maybe.

'Mr Maxwell?'

'Yes?' English accent. Didn't recognise the voice.

'This is Mr Cuculus speaking . . .'

Who the . . .? Ah.

'Oh, yes.'

'Trying to trace a British friend of mine called Bob. I'm told you're
the man at the embassy who can help. I expect it's a busy time just now.
Maybe you'd like to ring me back?'

'Yes. Yes I would. In about fifteen minutes.'

'Fine. Want to take down the number?'

'Go ahead.'

Randall read it to him. Maxwell recognised the code for Darwin.

'Thanks.' Randall hung up.

Damn! Why *now* of all times? To be safe for the call back Maxwell would need to use a public phone. There were several booths in the shopping plaza, but it would mean being gone a good half-hour. Sod's Law said that's when the brigadier would finally return his call.

And the ambassador wanted a progress report in a couple of hours so he would have something for London when they woke up.

The phone rang *again*. Damn, damn!

'Maxwell,' he snapped.

'Harry!'

Antipodean accent this time. Hunniford, his ASIO counterpart at the Australian Embassy.

'Mike, hi! Bit of a bad time. Can I call you later?'

'I've got something you'll want to see right away. A little curio I picked up at an antique stall.'

Maxwell perked up. Antiques? Hunniford despised the stuff. The word was a code.

'I see. Bit frantic, to tell you the truth . . .'

'I'll meet you somewhere.' The Australian's voice was cool but insistent.

'Right, well I was planning to eat sushi at that Jap place on the sixth floor of the plaza opposite.'

'Know the one. See you there in half an hour?'

'Right. Fine.'

He dropped the phone back, alarmed. Hunniford was a back-slapping Bondi beachboy. Never heard him so earnest before.

Maxwell opened his wallet. Over a hundred units left on his phone card. He'd need all of them, ringing Darwin.

'I'll be gone an hour,' he told his secretary, hurrying through the outer office into the corridor. 'If the brigadier rings tell him I'm *desperate* to speak to him and will he give me a time.'

'Will do.'

Outside, the traffic was flowing unusually smoothly. He crossed the wide avenue at the lights, ignoring a shout from the street boys selling drinks, and mingled with the office-workers on their lunch break. Perspiration trickled down the inside of his arms. He envied the locals. Whatever the heat they never seemed to sweat.

Inside the shopping mall with its excessively cold air-conditioning, he made for the phones in the basement. He tapped in the Darwin number and it answered immediately.

'Hello?'

'Cuculus?'

'That's right.'

'Sorry about the stupid name they gave you.'

'Don't worry. Expected nothing else from your lot . . .' said Randall sarcastically.

'Oh . . . Well, fine. Now what can I do for you?'

'Just touching base,' Randall told him. 'Flying to the island this evening. Wanted to know what the local *boys in blue* are up to.'

'They're still adamant *Bob* isn't anywhere in the country, including the *island*,' Maxwell told him, using Bowen's code name and avoiding words that might alert a sleepy eavesdropper. 'So, officially, they're giving us the big shrug, saying it's not their problem. *Un*officially they're dead worried. You heard about the arrests on the island last night?'

'Yes. Is the university man still being held? Someone told me he'd been released.'

'Haven't heard. Don't know. Wish I could tell you more.'

'And the woman who took Bob to the airport? You've spoken with her?'

'Not yet. I think the police have her under wraps, but I'll keep London posted.'

'Thanks. Look, one other thing. There's a bloke I've met here who's dropped a couple of hints he may know something. Name of Dugdale. Brad Dugdale. Australian, but lives on the island with a local woman. Runs a bar and sub-aqua for tourists.'

'How did you meet him?'

'Through the environmental lot. Brad's on the fringe. Said nothing specific about Bob. Just a nudge and a wink. If I get in, I'll try and catch up with him tonight. Name mean anything?'

'Nope. But I'll ask a friend. Care to tell me how you're operating?'

There was a pause. He could almost hear the Yard man pondering how much to reveal.

'In Australia I'm a photographer. *There* I'll be a tourist,' Randall said eventually.

'Working alone?'

Another pause.

'Not entirely. Look I'll be ringing London on and off, so if you get anything, leave a message at the er . . . at the *cuckoo's nest*. OK?'

Maxwell smiled. A policeman with a sense of humour. He'd need it in the days ahead.

'One other thing,' said Maxwell. 'There's a theory that our friend still had links with Metroc Minerals. You know he was a director of the company but had to break the link when he got office?'

'Indeed.'

'Speculation is he still had a finger in the pie and went to the island for some financial reason, travelling via Singapore to cover his tracks,' said Maxwell dismissively.

'You don't sound convinced?'

'Open mind. One thing though – the Metroc reps in the KUTUMIN office in Jakarta have had their lips taped since this thing broke. Won't even socialise with us. Nor with anyone from the Brit community.'

'I'll bear that in mind. Anything else?'

'No. But time's running out. So, good luck. And watch your back. You'll be a long way from friends out there.'

'Thanks a million.'

The line clicked and purred. Maxwell extracted his Telkom card. Five points left. Rather you than me, Mr Randall, he thought.

Five minutes to go before meeting Hunniford at the sushi bar. Maxwell took the escalator to the third floor then walked through the female clothing department towards the main stairwell in the central core of the mall.

The plaza was one of Jakarta's glitziest, its galleries dotted with women and girls picking through racks of designer jeans and sweatshirts. To mingle briefly with their trim, gentle bodies gave Maxwell the sort of lift others took cocaine for. But how did they manage to look so elegant on wages of a few pounds a week? *Biznis*, he guessed, the brown-envelope economy that kept Indonesia afloat.

When he reached the main escalators, the stairwell resonated with heavy rock music. In the basement they were demonstrating megabass sound systems. Indonesians, he'd quickly discovered, loved noise.

Stepping off the moving tread Maxwell walked into the sixth floor food hall and joined the line at the sushi bar. In the centre of the space was a wide seating area, encircled by take-outs from half-a-dozen cuisines.

He paid for his selection, collected a cold drink from a machine and made his way to an empty table for two. Hunniford had appeared at the back of the queue and pretended to ignore him.

Four minutes later the Australian joined him.

'G'day. How goes it?'

'Don't ask.' Maxwell pulled wooden chopsticks from their paper sheath and separated them.

Hunniford's chunky-chinned face was impassive as he sat down. Maxwell found the man overbearing. Too much of an all-rounder for his taste.

'So what have you got for me?' he asked.

'Don't rightly know, sport,' Hunniford answered, his face perplexed. 'Could be something . . . or nothing.'

'Try me . . .'

'Well, yesterday morning we had a visitor at the embassy. Chinese woman seeking asylum.'

'A Chinese from China?'

'Yes. Here with the trade delegation which you doubtless know about.'

'I certainly do.' The meeting room at the Hyatt yesterday. His interest ratcheted up a notch.

'Her name's Liu Jiefang. Means *clean and fragrant*, according to our Mandarin speaker. Anyway, she passed out in our foyer at about eleven o'clock yesterday. Scared to death and four months pregnant.'

'Uhuh,' Maxwell grunted, wondering if this had anything to do with Stephen Bowen.

'We think having the baby is her main motive for wanting asylum. Claims the child's father was executed last month. Some figure in the democracy movement we'd never heard of. She says she'll be forced to have an abortion if she returns to China. She's had one termination already apparently and says she'll kill herself rather than go through it again.'

'Careless girl,' Maxwell murmured, wishing Hunniford would get on with it.

'Quite. And under normal circumstances not grounds for asylum. But there's something else . . .'

'Ah. I assumed there would be.'

'She's come up with an extraordinary story. Liu's thirty-five, employed by the Ministry of Foreign Trade, so presumably a trusted party member. Says she worked for the State Council a year ago, handling position papers. Stuff that was highly classified.'

He paused to take a bite of raw fish.

'Go on,' said Maxwell tensely. Time was pressing.

'As one might expect, a big wadge of files concerned the South China Sea – Beijing's claims to the oil round the Spratleys, and more. Liu Jiefang maintains the council is obsessed by the fact that Indonesia, the largest country at the southern end of the sea is potentially hostile.'

'This place is hardly a military threat,' Maxwell chided.

'No, but an economic and political one. The Chinese want to dominate trade in the whole region, right? And Indonesia's big enough to block them at this end of the South China Sea. Well, the State Council in Beijing knows perfectly well nothing much'll change here while the old president remains in power, so,' he continued, watching for Maxwell's reaction, 'they're making plans for the day when he's not around anymore.'

'Hoping whoever takes over will be more China-friendly? Not surprised.'

'Not *hoping*, Harry. *Ensuring*.'

Maxwell put down his chopsticks and stared.

'Meaning what?' he growled.

'Meaning they intend to make sure the job goes to the contender who's the *least anti*-Chinese.'

Maxwell blinked.

'Make *sure*? What's *that* supposed to mean? Some sort of coup here? Backed by *China*? Liu whatsername's having you on,' Maxwell mocked.

'Not a coup. Last thing they want is a rerun of 1965. No. According to Liu Jiefang they want to persuade the Indonesian military to manipulate the succession in a way that'll be favourable to them. Persuade them with money – and with equipment.'

Maxwell shook his head. This didn't make sense.

'She's up in the clouds, Mike. You know what the Indonesians think of the Chinese. There's no way any faction hoping to take power here would align itself with Beijing. ABRI – the military – they simply wouldn't stand for it.'

'My sentiment exactly, sport – until I gave it some more thought. Listen, the Javans may hate the Chinese, but they're happy to use them when they've got something they need. After all, Chinese businessmen *run* this place.'

'Yes, but they're not mad enough in Beijing to think that wads of their money can buy influence with the Indonesian armed forces? Need more than that, chum.'

'That's why I said money and *equipment*.'

Maxwell felt a shiver run down his spine.

Hunniford paused, as if checking it through in his mind one last time before hitting Maxwell with the clincher.

'You know what the girl said, Harry? Four of the blokes in her trade delegation are in the *arms* business. Two are *naval* specialists, here specifically to pitch for your submarine contract.'

'Ouch,' Maxwell spluttered, his nightmare suddenly confirmed. 'Had a horrible feeling about that. Chatted with Sumoto on Monday night. He seemed to have it fixed in his head that London's going to renege on the arms deal to appease the kidnappers. And yesterday I spotted him talking to the Chinese delegation.'

'*Sumoto*? Christ!' Hunniford's eyebrows arched like croquet hoops. 'You do realise the significance of this.'

'Well, naked opportunism by the Chinese, I suppose.'

'You're missing the point, Harry. When did the Chinese get here?'

'Don't know . . . Sunday?'

Hunniford nodded. 'And when did you first know your minister was a hostage?

'*Monday!*' Maxwell felt the blood drain from his face.

'Exactly.'

So *before* the news broke about Bowen, *before* there was the remotest possibility of the submarine deal being re-opened, the Chinese were preparing to pitch for it!

'That's bloody odd,' Maxwell whispered, sensing a chasm opening in front of him.

There were only two explanations. Either the Chinese had been tipped off before they arrived that the British contract was likely to fail – tipped off by someone connected with Bowen's captors. *Or* it was the Chinese themselves who'd kidnapped Bowen. Nabbed him in the hope of getting the arms contract and through it the chance of an improved relationship with ABRI . . .

'My God!' he mouthed. 'This is extraordinary. You think *Beijing* . . .?'

'No,' said Hunniford. 'I simply don't believe the Chinese would risk taking a foreign politico hostage. *Whatever* the stakes. But there's the other option . . .'

'Somebody here . . .' Maxwell stammered. 'Somebody here who *wants* China to have the contract, so they kidnapped Bowen to pressure Britain into cancelling . . . The Kutu thing's just a blind, a smokescreen . . . But who?'

'Sumoto?' Hunniford shrugged.

'Never!' Maxwell scoffed. 'The man's on *our* payroll.'

The two men stared at one another. Maxwell held out his hands as if using them to wrestle.

'This is madness. Let's recap. You're saying . . .'

'Liu Jiefang's saying . . .' Hunniford corrected.

'OK. The woman's telling you that Bowen's kidnap has something to do with a Chinese push for arms sales to ABRI?'

'*She* didn't know anything about Bowen. That's *my* deduction.'

'But she did say that China hopes to buy influence with ABRI by providing them with the arms they want?'

'Buy influence with *some* part of ABRI, yes.'

'Doesn't add up,' Maxwell concluded. 'Why should switching the supply of a few patrol boats and submarines from Britain to China influence any part of ABRI?'

'It wouldn't, on it's own. But suppose your government *does* pull out of the arms deal because of the hullabaloo over human rights, and suppose other western countries follow suit, China's chances of grabbing the arms business will rocket. So, maybe that submarine contract is just for starters,' Hunniford pressed. 'To set a precedent, to open the way to other deals. Think of what China could offer? All sorts of stuff the West simply *wouldn't* sell here. Chemical, *biological* weapons. Who knows what . . .'

'Now you're fantasising,' Maxwell exploded. 'Forget Bowen for now, what's Beijing's strategic objective – according to your defector?'

'To extend their influence down here. Eventually to have a military presence on the southern rim of the South China Sea – even if it's just visiting rights. Which frightens the pants off *us* of course. Particularly after the recent missile tests around Taiwan and the Chinese press talking about the need for *living space*. Last thing in the world Australia wants is a Chinese military force a few hundred miles north of Darwin.'

Maxwell folded his arms. Was this what was driving Hunniford's imagination? The old Aussie paranoia about invasions by little yellow men? Hunniford's eyes were as unrevealing as black holes.

'Are you giving her a visa?' Maxwell asked suddenly.

'Liu Jiefang? Yes. She's on a flight to Sydney tonight.'

Maxwell pondered for a moment. One fact was central. The Chinese appeared to have foreknowledge of Stephen Bowen's kidnap or its anticipated outcome. And General Dino Sumoto was behaving in a way that broke all the normal parameters.

'Food for thought, Mike,' Maxwell muttered. 'In fact a bloody great banquet.'

'Thought I should tell you . . .'

Sumoto. *Laba-laba* – the spider. Watch so he doesn't bite, Effendi had said.

Suddenly Maxwell felt a pressing need to get away. To dig. To cross-check. Time was desperately short. He looked at his watch.

'Thanks Mike,' he said, standing up. 'Let's stay in close touch.'

'Of course.'

'Oh, one other thing. Nearly forgot.' The phone call with Randall. Maxwell sat down again. 'There's an Australian who lives on Kutu. With a local woman.'

'There's loads of 'em down there. Deadbeats mostly,' Hunniford replied.

'Yes. But there's one in particular. Dugdale? Brad Dugdale. Just wondered if you knew the name . . .'

Hunniford frowned. 'Where's this come from?'

'Can't tell you that.'

The eyebrows arched again. 'Well, if it's the bloke I think it is, he's got an interest in junk from World War Two. Shipwrecks, that sort of stuff.'

'Could be. He runs diving for tourists. Know anything else about him?'

'Yeah. Let me think. Heard something a few months ago. He came to our attention a year or two back when some wartime papers got declassified under the fifty year rule. A load of reports about special ops against the Japs on Timor and Kutu. He was picking through them with such thoroughness the Records Office thought it suspicious and passed his name to us.'

'Nothing on him, though.'

'No. An OK bloke so far as we could tell. Marine archaeology turned out to be a hobby he hoped to make money out of. TV documentaries. Last I heard he was looking to hire a floating crane to salvage some rusty hulk or other.'

'Interesting.'

Hunniford blinked suspiciously.

'I must push,' Maxwell announced. 'Thanks again, Mike. Speak soon.'

Maxwell took the escalators to the basement, pausing at a bookshop to buy a new phone card.

The number he called was in a run-down quarter in eastern Jakarta, a small office with a handful of computers and a modem through which the Association of Free Journalists kept a line open to the outside world. The voice that answered belonged to the young man he'd sat next to in court two days ago.

'Zis is Hans,' Maxwell growled in a laboured German accent. 'Can you meet wiz me in one hour?'

'Just now?' Abdul stalled. He sounded stressed. 'Very busy just now.'

'It is wery important . . .'

'Yes? Oh . . .'

Maxwell heard a sigh and a keyboard clicking.

'OK, then I try. One hour. Usual place.'

'*Ja. Gut.*'

There *was* no usual place. Each time they met, Maxwell set a rendezvous for the next time. Effendi's phone tappers would have the AFJ on their list.

He took the escalator to the ground floor and hurried from the building. The sky was still clear outside. He pictured the young journalist fighting through the traffic on his motorbike, the sun turning his crash helmet into a sweat box. Perspiration was streaming from his own brow by the time he slipped through the security gate into the embassy.

'Not a dicky bird,' his secretary announced as he passed through her office into his own. 'No word from the Brigadier General.'

'Damn. And I have to go out again as soon as I've done a note for the ambassador.'

'You look as if you're melting,' she told him, her nose wrinkling with disgust.

'Thanks.'

Inside his office he closed the door and scribbled a quick, ground-holding memo. The ambassador would complain at its brevity, but that couldn't be helped.

His next destination was less than a mile away, but the drive cut north through the tangled heart of Jakarta and took forty minutes. The taxi's air-conditioning was on the blink. By the time they reached the old Dutch colonial district of Batavia, Maxwell was in serious need of a drink.

He paid off the driver outside the schooner harbour of Sunda Kelapa, jammed on a wide-brimmed hat, then turned and walked over an iron bridge. Below its girders lay the stinking, grey sludge of a canal, its banks lined with evil-looking slums made from plywood and rusting corrugated iron.

At the end of the bridge was a maritime museum. He turned into its courtyard, relieved to see a thin, bare-chested youth selling drinks from a stall. He bought a can of Fanta, gulped down the contents, then bought another.

Across the cobbles at the door to a nineteenth-century wooden watchtower, he paid the few hundred rupiahs entrance fee, removed his hat, then climbed the winding stairs inside. There was a viewing platform off the top floor which was small and seldom visited.

Abdul was already there. So, unfortunately, was a party of young schoolgirls who giggled at Maxwell's paunchiness and dripping red face. Abdul showed signs of alarm.

'Hello mister!' An urchin-faced girl in maroon skirt and white blouse grinned, then overcome by embarrassment buried herself amongst her fellows for safety.

'Mister you speak English?' dared another.

'*Pergi! Pergi!*' Abdul shooed them away. Their teacher rounded them up, smiling her apologies and led the troupe down the perilous open staircase.

'Unusual to find anyone else here,' Maxwell panted, after the children had gone.

Abdul's slight frame was clad in black trousers and a white shirt. He nervously jingled the keys to his motorbike.

'This not good time for me,' he complained. 'Very much work.'

'Well, I'm very grateful to you for coming.' Maxwell knew the signs and handed over an envelope of money. Abdul's anxious brown eyes brightened momentarily and he smiled his thanks.

They stepped on to the little shaded wooden platform that overlooked the mast-lined harbour. It was so narrow their shoulders touched. Maxwell tried not to be distracted by this bodily contact with someone he found disconcertingly attractive.

'You have contacts in ABRI, Abdul,' Maxwell began, speaking softly and checking behind to confirm they were alone. 'Good contacts I think.'

'Some young officers they talk to me private,' Abdul confirmed, running a hand over his shiny, black hair. 'There are some who have the same ideas as us.'

'Such as . . .?'

'An Indonesia with a government that is fair and not corrupt,' he frowned, surprised Maxwell needed to ask.

'They talk about such things in the army?' Maxwell asked, deciding an oblique approach was the only way to get the information he needed.

'Privately, yes. Loyalty – it's a big discussion for them. Whether ABRI should serve the president and his cronies, or serve the Indonesian people . . .' Abdul glanced behind, nervous at Maxwell's line of questioning.

'And this loyalty question. It divides the armed forces?'

'Divide?' Abdul looked suspicious. 'Not divide. They don't fight over this. They have strong discipline in ABRI and the president's men are in charge.'

'Of course. But your friends are able to be open about the way they feel? Sometimes?'

The journalist looked down at the courtyard, then chuckled impulsively. 'You hear about the wrist watches?'

'No.' Abdul's upper lip was downy like on a pubescent boy. Maxwell's mind began to wander. 'Tell me about the wrist watches?'

'If you wear watch on right hand instead of left, it supposed to show you are *ABRI Marah Putih*. That mean loyal to Indonesian people first, loyal to *president* second! Like a sort of badge.' He laughed again, exposing neat white teeth. 'Or maybe it just show you're left-handed . . .' he joked.

148

Maxwell smiled. He knew of another issue preoccupying the army. *Dwi Fungsi* – dual function – the long-established policy of military units running businesses and local government as well as soldiering. Many officers thought the army *too* focused on internal affairs instead of training and equipping itself to face threats from *outside* the country.

'And those officers loyal to the *people* first,' Maxwell checked, 'are they the ones who want a change to *Dwi Fungsi?*'

'Most, yes.'

'So on *Dwi Fungsi*, ABRI *is* split?'

'Split, you cannot say. Just a difference of opinion.'

Any suggestion of division within ABRI made Abdul bristle, Maxwell noticed. Indonesians had pride in their armed forces, even if they feared them.

'But suppose the president died tomorrow and ABRI had to choose a new leader, this difference of opinion might become something more?'

Abdul glanced at his watch. 'It's possible.'

'Like it could split the army?'

Abdul turned and went back inside the watchtower. Maxwell saw him stop by the top rail of the staircase, listening. Then he came back out on to the balcony.

'You're very nervous today,' said Maxwell.

'I don't like talk about these things.'

'Why not? What are you afraid of?'

For a moment Abdul wouldn't answer. Then he whispered, 'My brother – you see he is a soldier.'

'Ah . . . I understand. Just one more question though. On which wrist does Major General Dino Sumoto wear his watch?'

Abdul flinched at mention of the name, but he recovered quickly.

'Maybe on both wrists,' he replied eventually. 'For General Sumoto, most important thing is power. He support whichever side can help him get it. He dangerous. Many people afraid of him.'

Abdul included, Maxwell guessed. But dangerous enough and desperate enough to involve himself in the kidnap of a foreigner?

'Why? Why are many people afraid?'

For a good fifteen seconds Abdul didn't reply.

'Because they remember 1965,' he whispered eventually. 'The coup, the massacres. Nobody want that again. And Sumoto – he is a man who could make it happen one more time.'

'How? Does Sumoto have a power base in the army?' Maxwell pressed.

'Yes,' Abdul replied, half covering his mouth with his hand. 'KODAM Twelve.'

'That's the military district that includes *Kutu*,' Maxwell checked, his pulse quickening.

'Yes. Sumoto was commander KODAM Twelve for many year. Most officers there wear watches on right hand. They think it stupid for soldiers to build roads and trade coffee beans. They want to be in an army that can fight anybody in the world. Want more training. More equipment. And even if Sumoto no longer their commander, they think he give them what they want if he get more power.'

'Sumoto is rich?'

'Oh yeah. He made good business in Kutu. Found out where KUTUMIN want to build processing plant and harbour for the mine, then he bought the land before they got the licence. Sold it to them at big, big profit.'

'Ah . . . And what has he done with the money?'

'Invest it. His business partner has fingers everywhere. Premati Airline, for example. Sumoto has big share now.'

Premati. The airline which claimed to have flown Stephen Bowen to Singapore.

Maxwell stared at the horizon, not seeing it. The nightmare was taking shape, putting on flesh.

'How?' he pressed. 'How would Sumoto give KODAM Twelve what they want?'

Abdul shook his head. It was a road down which he could go no further.

'I don't know,' he shrugged.

'But you said they want new weapons? What exactly?'

'I don't know,' he hissed.

'Can you find out?'

The journalist turned on him. 'Why you ask this? Your country must know what ABRI want. You been selling them weapons many years.'

He saw Maxwell's hesitation, then his eyes widened.

'You think maybe there are *two* ABRIs? The one *you* know, and the one General Sumoto want to make?'

Maxwell nodded.

'And you think people you deal with now won't be in charge in the future? You worry some other country get the business?'

Maxwell nodded again. Let him think that.

Abdul grunted. He looked relieved. If the motive for the questions was money, it was one he understood.

'So, Abdul, it would also be helpful to me if you could find out which country your friends in KODAM Twelve imagine their new weapons would come from,' Maxwell added.

Abdul sucked his teeth. 'Not easy to find this out . . .' he prevaricated. 'So busy just now.'

Maxwell knew what he meant. The material Abdul wrote didn't earn him much. 'I'd pay double.'

'Well . . . maybe tonight I can talk with someone.'

'Ring my home. You have the number. Just give a time, I'll understand. Then we'll meet at the Hot Rock Café, Jalan Thamrin. It stays open late. You know it?'

'Of course.' It was where gold-digging Jakarta girls went to pick up wealthy foreigners.

They heard voices and feet on the stairs. More visitors.

They shook hands. Abdul would leave first.

'Tell me,' Maxwell asked on impulse, as the journalist gripped the top of the stair rail. 'I've often wondered . . . are you married?'

Abdul smiled. 'Not yet, *tuan*. Not yet.'

Maxwell returned to the viewing platform. He stayed looking out towards the elegant lines of the cargo-carrying sailing craft until he heard the rip of a motorcycle engine starting up.

British Embassy, Jakarta
15.25 hrs (08.25 hrs GMT)

Maxwell asked the ambassador to meet him in the 'box'. Off the second floor corridor and shielded from eavesdropping, this steel-lined, windowless cell was the embassy's safe room for confidential conversations.

Ambassador Bruton listened with stony concentration, his hair as immaculate as a sculpture, his face growing steadily grimmer. As Maxwell wound up, he pushed the metal shirt bands up his arms.

'It's an extraordinary theory, Harry, but you've no actual proof that Sumoto's the villain,' he commented eventually.

'Not yet. All I'm certain of is that the Chinese *are* after our naval contract.'

'Then we must make absolutely sure they don't get it,' Bruton snapped, eyes burning. 'The PM has bloody well got to stick to his guns.'

'How's it looking in London?'

'Better. The arms industry is launching a counter-offensive in

Whitehall against the human rights people. With luck, the memo I'm about to send should clinch it.'

Then Bruton began to look uncomfortable.

'Bowen . . .' Maxwell murmured, reading his thoughts.

'Yes . . . The buggers'll kill him, I'm afraid.' Bruton stared at the ceiling and put a hand to his mouth. 'But he'll get a good write-up. Better than he deserves. *Gave his life for his country* . . . Tell me I'm not being callous, Harry.'

Maxwell looked at his hands. In war there were always casualties.

'Realistic, ambassador,' he assured him. 'You're being realistic.'

'Feel sorry for his family. Two teenage children,' Bruton sighed, thinking of his own son and daughter. 'When does the Scotland Yard man get to Kutu?'

'Tonight. Odd thing is *he* thinks he's getting signs that Bowen *is* being held by the OKP.'

The ambassador frowned. 'Well one of you has to be wrong. Tell you what,' he decided suddenly, 'I think it's time our friends in DefenceCo dropped a little hint to their *agent* here about what the Chinese may be up to . . .'

Nice one, thought Maxwell. DefenceCo's agent was a member of the president's family. A rumour fed to him would spread through the anti-communist old guard like a brush fire.

'I'll dig out my tin hat.'

His secretary leapt up as Maxwell walked through her office into his own.

'Just missed him. Brigadier General Effendi.'

'Damn.'

'But he left a message. Sounded worried.'

'Oh?'

'He said he'd be more than happy for you to talk to Selina Sakidin. Just one problem . . . She's disappeared.'

13

THE INSIDE OF Ted Sankey's head rumbled like a cement mixer. From the familiar pattern of light leaking round the thick curtains, he knew it was his own flat he was lying in. What he couldn't understand was why he was wearing a tie.

His bladder threatened to explode. He rolled off the bed and using a chest of drawers as a hand hold, groped his way to the en-suite bathroom to relieve himself. Tie, shirt, trousers, socks, all still in place from the night before. Then he remembered.

'Jesus,' he croaked, aiming in the rough direction of the toilet bowl.

When he'd finished, he wrestled with the child-proof cap of the paracetamol bottle, cursing its designers, then downed some tablets with a tooth mug of water.

He pulled back one curtain in the bedroom, shielded his eyes from the daylight and decided to leave the other as it was. Then he perched on the end of the bed trying to decide whether to throw up.

The memory of yesterday when he blew it in the control room came back like the wallop of a sandbag. The biggest mistake in his life, and there had been a few. The most disastrous misjudgement of his career.

He remembered the half-angry, half-apologetic phone call from the chief executive saying the proprietors had granted him fifteen minutes to clear his desk and leave the building. He remembered the shock on the faces of the newsroom journalists, and the smirk from that bean-counter Paxton. He remembered taking refuge in the wine bar down the road and the stream of supporters who'd come to commiserate. What he didn't remember was leaving the place.

His flat in Fitzrovia was a ten minute walk from the News Channel building in Wendover Street. He'd bought it when he took the job, because it was close. Handy, he'd thought, for sex in the lunch-break if opportunity knocked. It had from time to time.

'I can fuck any woman I want,' he muttered to himself. The words had become his mantra since his wife left him. Believing them was what kept his pride intact. Beryl had run off with a double-glazing salesman in a Ford Mondeo estate. It was the cliché that had hurt, almost as much as the loss of her. There'd been no children and the divorce had been clean and mechanical.

How had he got home last night? The question nagged. Couldn't have walked. There was a vague memory of being carried and people he didn't know trying to talk to him.

He turned to check the time on the red display of the bedside clock. A quarter to seven. A drink was what he needed. Tea. Maybe with a shot of whisky. Hair of the dog.

He opened the bedroom door and made for the kitchen.

'Morning Mr Sankey.' A voice. From the living room. Through the open door he saw a young, shirt-sleeved male rise up from his sofa, pushing the aerial into a mobile phone. 'Thought I heard you moving about.'

'Who the fuck . . .?'

'Last night. We had a little chat. Helped you home. Remember?'

Vaguely. Strangers asking him questions. Bundling him into a car.

'Detective Constable Harding.'

'Oh, shit. Who did I hit?'

'No one, sir,' the constable grinned. A strapping lad with dark hair that needed a comb running through it.

Sankey clutched his forehead and massaged his temples. He needed some tea urgently. He continued his drift towards the tiny kitchen. He shook the kettle, found it full and switched it on.

'Want some tea, sergeant?'

'Detective constable, sir. Joe, if it's easier. And yes, I'd love a cup.'

Sankey perched on a stool and rested his elbows on the worktop.

'D'you mind telling me what this is about?'

'You had a chat with us last night, sir. Me and my boss, Detective Chief Inspector Mostyn. Only, you weren't too coherent. Thought we'd try again this morning. So we brought you home and I slept on your sofa. DCI Mostyn's just on his way back over. I rang him a few minutes ago.'

Mostyn. The boss man at the Yard.

'I talked to one of your blokes on Monday,' Sankey frowned. 'Detective Sergeant Randall. Awkward bugger.'

The young policeman smiled.

'That was after the first satellite transmission. Now there's been another we thought you might have remembered something else.'

'Must be joking. Can't even remember who I am this morning . . .'

'You were certainly well pissed last night,' the DC confirmed, grinning. 'Pissed as anyone I've ever seen.'

The kettle clicked. Sankey groped in a cupboard for two mugs, then in another for the PG Tips.

'Milk and sugar?' he enquired, without turning round.

'Two sugars please.'

As he was pouring, he heard the letter box go and the morning papers thump on to the doormat.

'I'll get them,' said Harding.

'Thanks.'

Sankey sat back on the stool and sipped the scalding liquid.

'You've made the front page in the *Sun*!' The policeman sounded impressed. He dumped the papers down on the kitchen table.

'Christ!'

For several minutes Sankey flicked through the pages, cringing at what they'd written about him and about the irresponsibility of the News Channel in putting the pictures out live.

'Oh, God!' he moaned repeatedly.

The doorbell rang.

'That'll be DCI Mostyn, sir. All right if I let him in?'

Sankey waved his approval. He peered anxiously at the man who entered – late forties and looking strangely grubby.

'Morning Mr Sankey. How's your head?'

Sankey shook it and winced. 'Don't ask. Have a cup of tea and tell me what you want.'

When Sankey reached for another mug, Mostyn enquired with his eyes if the DC had got any more out of him. Harding shook his head.

They sat around the small Formica table.

'We need your help, Mr Sankey,' Mostyn insisted, coming straight to the point. 'The kidnappers chose you twice for their transmissions. Has to be a reason. Perhaps they know you. Know people in the company maybe. Conceivably you may know *them* if you think hard enough about it.'

Sankey blew out through pursed lips, his breath carrying enough proof spirit to make Mostyn quail.

'I'm sure I don't . . .'

'Think about it. Why pick you?'

'Haven't a clue . . .'

'And why the second time? Chose their moment, didn't they? Just before your lunchtime news went off the air. If you wanted a scoop they'd left you no time to record the feed and check it first. Must be someone with inside knowledge, Mr Sankey.'

Sankey frowned, his brain like a car engine on a damp morning. Suddenly he realised they probably suspected *him*.

'Now wait a minute . . .' He looked at one face then the other. Both expressionless. 'Are you accusing me of something?'

'No, sir,' Mostyn answered smartly. 'Just very curious.'

The *why* question had plagued him too. There had to be a reason for choosing the low-audience, lowly-rated News Channel in preference to one of the main outlets.

'Maybe they realised the only chance of getting their horror movie on the air was by giving it to a daft chancer like me . . .' Sankey said forlornly.

'Maybe.'

'I meant that as a joke,' he added, hurt. 'It's called self-deprecatory humour.' He felt pleased he'd been able to pronounce the word.

'But perhaps it isn't a joke,' Mostyn pressed. 'Perhaps the kidnappers *do* know you. Knew you'd take a chance if it meant boosting your ratings. Think, Mr Sankey, think.'

Sankey gulped at the tea, desperate for the fluid and the stimulant even if it meant burning his throat.

'Wait a minute, gents. What are we talking about here? The people who kidnapped Stephen Bowen, or the people who beamed pictures of him up to a satellite?'

Mostyn smiled fleetingly. He could see Sankey's mind was beginning to work.

'I think we're talking about the latter. About somebody who knows how to operate a stolen flyaway. Maybe even someone who knows how to steal one.'

Suddenly Sankey breathed in sharply. He'd remembered someone.

'Tell me, sir,' urged Mostyn.

'Hang on.'

Think it through, Sankey told himself. Don't say anything stupid. He remembered the day, about two weeks ago. A talented technician looking for work. Just resigned from the BBC, so he'd said. Learned later he'd been sacked on suspicion of stealing camera equipment.

'Ricky Smith.'

'Go on, sir,' Mostyn said, turning to the constable. The name was familiar.

'Came to see me a fortnight ago, looking for work. Just gone freelance, so he said. Good professional reputation. Handsome bloke. Impressive to meet. Said I'd give him a try. After we'd talked he hung around the newsroom chatting up the girls and playing with the computer system.'

Dead smooth, the bugger was. Acted like he owned the place.

'Shit!' he exploded. Another blast of alcohol vapour. 'Ricky Smith. Beeb sacked him for theft. Could well be your man. He'd know how to operate a flyaway. And have the bollocks to pinch one.'

'And with a grudge against the BBC?' Mostyn checked.

'Could be.' The tea had got his mind going. 'He could've found out about our satellite feeds off the computer.' Then he had second thoughts. Thin evidence on which to accuse someone. 'I don't know. Jumping to conclusions. Can't see how he would have got involved.'

Mostyn turned to the DC and nodded. Harding extracted a photocopy from a briefcase.

'Could have been set up like this,' the DC asserted. 'Advert in the classifieds of a trade magazine a month ago.' He pushed it across the table for Sankey to read. A struggle to focus but he managed.

Adventurous, multi-skilled TV News technician wanted. Experience of flyaways essential. Needs to be used to taking risks. Box XW273.

'Oh yes,' Sankey murmured. 'Ricky would have gone for something like that.'

'Not seen it before?' Mostyn asked.

'No. Never. Who placed it?'

'Somebody who went in personally to the magazine office, paid cash and left a false address. Came in a week later to pick up the replies, three of them. The girl in classifieds said he was middle-aged with long hair in need of a wash. Thinks he had an accent. South African, Australian, she wasn't sure.'

Mostyn watched for some sign of recognition from Sankey, but there was none.

'Tell me, Mr Sankey . . . what are your plans? Out of a job, I gather. My condolences.'

'Yeah. So I am. Dunno. Start thinking about it when I get rid of this hangover.'

Had to see a lawyer and try to squeeze some compensation from the bastards at the News Channel.

'Would you do me a favour?' Mostyn asked, handing Sankey his card. 'Don't go far without talking to me first. Just in case we want another word. And by the way. Everything we've talked about in this room is confidential. You'll understand that, even as a journalist. Don't want to see any of this appear in print, right? There's someone's life at stake, remember.'

'I'll remember.'

'Right then. Thanks for your time. Sorry to jump on you so early.'

Mostyn stood up and held out his hand. 'Think of anything else, give me a call, right?'

'Right.'

The DC nipped into the living room to collect his jacket. Then followed Mostyn outside.

'Thanks for the use of your sofa,' he said, closing the front door behind them.

Sankey loped back into his bedroom and wrestled the tie from his neck. His clothes stank. He stank. He'd take a shower.

He felt lower than he could ever remember. Much lower than when the wife left him. There'd been an inevitability about that; they'd both played around. But this time it felt like he'd lost everything. His job, his reputation and above all his pride. Some jerk of a technician had taken a quick look at him and decided he was the one man in the TV news business he could con into doing a live transmission of the untransmittable.

He kicked off his trousers, then picked them up carefully from the floor. He inspected the silver-grey fabric for stains from drink or bodily fluids, then folded them along the remains of their creases and slipped them into an electric clothes press.

He removed his pants and socks and stood naked, staring down at the bulge of his stomach. His liver hurt when he pressed it. He decided never to drink alcohol again.

He felt acutely insecure suddenly. He had little recollection of what had happened in the bar and wanted reassurance. The clock said nearly seven thirty. He bumbled into the living room, cluttered with yesterday's half-read newspapers, and picked up the TV remote. The News Channel was into its commercial break. A good time to ring.

He returned to the bedroom, perched on the mattress and dialled the direct line to the newsdesk, finger poised over the rest, ready to ring off if it wasn't Mandy on duty.

'Newsdesk.'

It was.

'Mandy, it's Ted.'

'Hey! What happened? Last I heard you got carted off by the police!'

'Don't bloody tell everyone, girl . . .'

'Don't have to. Most of the newsroom was *there*!'

'Shit! Did I make a complete cunt of myself?'

'No. You were just brain-dead and legless. How's your head?'

'Still attached to my shoulders. Just. Look . . . what's going on? What are people saying?'

'Well . . . not a lot yet. It's heads down and get on with it. Tom Marples running the meetings and guess who's taken over your office for now?'

'Oh, no,' Sankey moaned. 'Not . . .'

'Steve Paxton. Yes. Taken complete charge of the housekeeping. Budget cuts all round.'

'Hell! So what's happened to Charlie? Is she there yet?'

'Funny you should ask. Just been speaking to her. Paxton ordered her home again to save money . . .'

'*What?* The berk! What a waste . . .'

'But, Ted, *but* . . . Would you believe it, she's refusing to do it. She rang up from Darwin airport a few minutes ago to say she's found someone who'll do camera for free and she's going to Kutu tonight. And if the company fires her, so be it, she said.'

'Plucky little girlie. I knew she had *balls* when I picked her . . .'

'*Eh-h?*' giggled Mandy. 'Muddling up the sexes this morning, are we, Ted?'

Whitehall
10.45 hrs

The line of motor coaches wound its way through Trafalgar Square into Whitehall. One from every DefenceCo factory in the country, they'd formed into a convoy at a service station on the M25. Banners naming the plants hung from the side windows.

TV cameramen filmed their progress past the Cenotaph. Two coaches from the Clyde had travelled overnight to get here. Others from Lancashire had set off in the small hours. The men in those from the Home Counties however had breakfasted at home. Most of Britain's 100,000 workers dependent for their livelihoods on arms exports had sent delegates.

The demonstration had been organised at astonishing speed, triggered by the galling sight yesterday of the prime minister caving in at Commons Question Time. Managements and unions galvanised by a common belief that unless they rammed a steel rod up the government's backbone, the anti-arms-trade lobby would have a sudden and unwarranted triumph.

The convoy turned left at Parliament Square, then left again on to the Embankment, to park in a line outside the Ministry of Defence. Doors hissed and drivers stepped down to unlock baggage spaces. Then the passengers disgorged, stretching stiff limbs and turning up noses at the unfamiliar noise and smell of the capital. Some wore raincoats and suits, others overalls and anoraks, all with the common aim of ensuring the arms contract with Indonesia went ahead, whatever some fuzzy-haired lunatics did to a not very popular cabinet minister.

From the lockers they pulled out their placards, then formed up in the roadway for the march into Whitehall.

10 Downing Street
11.30 hrs

Prime Minister Keith Copeland replaced the receiver with a twinge of relief. The most difficult aspect of his decision was now behind him – telling Sally Bowen that he simply couldn't yield to the terrorist demands that would save her husband's life.

In the end the decision had been easier to take than he'd feared. It was the Cabinet that had forced his hand. In the minds of his ministers, the principle of never being seen to give in to terrorists became paramount. Tragic though it was, better that one roguish minister should lose his life than that the whole government should lose its credibility. The colleagues had concluded too that the tide of public opinion was turning. After initial gains by the human rights lobby, money was winning over morality again – as in the end it always did.

The decision was the right one, taken for the right reasons, of that he was satisfied. The fact that it was also the best way of protecting his own back and the nest-egg he'd been banking on for his retirement was incidental.

Copeland got up from his desk and stepped into the entrance hall, just seconds before the big black door opened to let in the Indonesian ambassador. Tall, wearing a dark suit and with slicked hair, the diplomat's mouth was clamped into a smile that was shaped by protocol. Copeland reached out his hand.

'Good morning, Your Excellency. Thank you for coming.'

'Good morning, prime minister.'

The Indonesian looked overawed; he'd not been in Number 10

before. Unsettled too by the battery of cameras that had recorded his arrival, and by the pair of microphone stands waiting in the road outside.

The PM led his guest into a reception room. They sat and said nothing while coffee was poured. Then they were left alone.

Copeland spoke first. He talked of the moral debate that had raged in the Commons and in the country, and of the deep concern about human rights that the kidnap had brought to the surface.

The ambassador's square, bespectacled face looked grim, ready to reply that such matters were his country's internal affairs, not the concern of foreigners.

'You'll understand, Your Excellency,' Copeland continued solemnly, 'that as the elected leader of the British people it is my duty to give voice to their very real concerns and to pass them on to you. However . . . it is also my duty to ensure that the decisions I take as head of the government are in Britain's national interest. In the past couple of days I have listened to wise counsel from all sides. After much careful consideration I have decided to *resist* the pressure in Britain and elsewhere to cancel the arms contract with your country. I propose to announce this to the media shortly and would be very pleased if you would do me the honour of standing beside me when I do so.'

'You want to reconfirm the contract?' the ambassador checked, muddled by the verbiage. He looked absurdly relieved. 'Shake hands for the cameras?'

'Umm, yes.'

'Sure. Why not.'

They talked for a little longer, Copeland asking whether the Indonesian police had any new leads on the kidnap. The ambassador's response was pre-scripted. An echo of what had been said before. No evidence whatsoever that Stephen Bowen was still in his country. No evidence that any Indonesian was involved in his kidnap.

Did he *know* about Sumoto, the PM wondered? Ambassador Bruton had rung two hours ago hinting at the general's chicanery.

Copeland led the way on to the pavement, his confidence returning. Half an hour ago he'd received a boost to his spirits, a call from Assistant Commissioner Stanley at Scotland Yard. A photo of a rogue TV technician called Ricky Smith, wired to the Paris police, had been recognised by a cargo clerk at Charles de Gaulle airport. The man had collected two packages airfreighted from the Indonesian island of Bali, one on Sunday evening, the other on Tuesday morning. The timing was right for these to have been the tapes of Stephen Bowen.

The net was closing. Soon the kidnappers would lose their power to manipulate the minds of millions.

Sally Bowen hunched on the sofa hugging her knees, never more miserable and alone. She'd wanted the children with her, but their house-tutors had urged her to leave them at school where they could be kept busy. Best for them, if not for her.

The television was on. Good of Keith to give her notice of his decision. Now, there he was in Downing Street, saying it to the world. Announcing in effect that his forty-nine-year-old minister of state at the Foreign Office would never see fifty.

It seemed so callous. War widows must have felt the same, she reasoned, although dying for some great principle must be more honourable than dying for money.

It numbed her to see Keith Copeland shake hands with the Indonesian ambassador. Their smiles, the togetherness . . .

In the back of her mind she'd always harboured the naïve concept that life was sacred and beyond price. Wrong. Every man had a value – and Stephen's was not high enough. Friendship meant nothing either. Stephen and Keith, buddies since Cambridge – irrelevant when the chips were down.

There was another numbness inside her that came from not being sure of her own feelings. She herself had wished Stephen dead in recent years – and meant it. What the kidnappers had done to him however was worse than death and she feared there'd be more to come before the end.

She rested her chin on her knees. Then she strained forward, peering at the screen. How *could* he smile at a time like this? Suddenly she was angry.

Why? Why so satisfied? Why not more regret at what he was having to do?

She reached a hand to the sofa table and picked up the small piece of oblong card she'd found tucked at the back of Stephen's desk drawer that morning. Was *this* why? This airline boarding pass? She'd been clutching it for hours, staring at the words written on it, debating whether to hand it to the police.

Impossible! A man who'd risen so high could never be so low . . . But she couldn't but wonder what he would have said if she'd mentioned it when he rang . . . *Might* it have changed his mind?

'Oh God!' she gasped. Perhaps the evidence she held in her hand could have saved Stephen's life . . .

The flight had been to Zurich, two months ago.

The words written on the boarding pass were perfectly legible and in Stephen's hand.

Keith's account: N465329.

Over the Kutu Sea
18.45 hrs (10.45 hrs GMT)

A PATTERN WAS emerging at last. For the first time Randall felt on the track of something more concrete than a mirage. The breakthrough that mattered was the discovery by the French 6ième Division that the Bowen video-tapes had been airfreighted to Paris from *Bali*. Just five hundred miles from Kutu, Bali was the nearest point with flights to Europe. If the tapes were sent from there, the kidnapped minister could not be far away.

In his phone call from Darwin airport to the unlisted number at Scotland Yard they'd also told him about Ricky Smith and the possibility that he might have been recruited by a middle-aged Australian. Randall had shipped the cassette of photos he'd taken at Sawyer's house on the evening flight to London, so the Dugdale and Sawyer shots could be shown to witnesses.

The setting sun streaked fire across the horizon and bathed the wings of the Premati Air 737 in pink light. To their right, looking east, the distant rim of Kutu's solitary volcano thrust up through the low cloud, its crater smudged with smoke. Then the view was gone as the airliner dipped through the grey into the dusk below.

Although encouraged that his mission had some purpose, Randall felt deeply uneasy. Charlie sat beside him with her head resting against the window, her face grey with terror. Mad to have involved her in this mission. Working with a woman *always* made him jumpy. And a woman *journalist* . . . But there'd been no alternative. Not if he wanted to avoid being kicked out of Kutu as soon as he arrived. Kept telling himself that Charlotte Cavendish was a grown-up – big enough to know what she was doing. Here at her own risk. If things went wrong she could take care of herself.

Three rows in front sat Brad Dugdale and Teri. No contact on the flight, just like he'd told them when they'd met at Sawyer's place. The

Australian had the aisle seat, his tanned, bald crown showing above the seat back. Randall was sorely tempted to go and ask what he'd meant by his odd question earlier – *if you learn something in Kutu about Bowen, will you pass it on to your PM?* Innocent curiosity? Or a probe to gauge whether beneath their guise as journalists, they'd been sent by HM government to make contact with Bowen's kidnappers?

Dugdale *knew* something. Randall felt it in his bones. But now was not the time to press him. They were being watched.

Time. That was the trouble with this job. Running out fast, yet everything he did took loads of it. Thirty-six hours to get here. Forty-eight hours since the kidnappers wired Bowen up with electrodes. For all he knew, the man might be dead by now.

A ping from the overhead loudspeaker made Charlie look up. The seat-belt sign had come on. She wished to God she'd taken the other plane. *Any* plane, so long as it was bound for a country where they *didn't* burn men with cigarettes and rape their wives for disobeying orders. Her heart was jumping about like a demented butterfly.

'What happens when we land, Nick? Tell me again,' she flapped.

'We go with the flow. We're tourists,' Randall said, giving her hand a reassuring little squeeze. She'd be OK, he told himself, so long as he kept her calm.

Their cover story was sketchy. Known each other three months – married in London just two days ago – he in the travel business, she a teacher.

'I'm sure we've forgotten something,' Charlie fretted, fiddling with the plain gold ring they'd bought in Darwin. They'd had to begin their newlyweds impersonation straight after take-off when they noticed one of the cabin crew kept looking at them and dropping things as if serving coffee wasn't his normal job. They'd kissed and cuddled a bit. Not a problem. Acting. Like Nick had said.

'There is one thing,' he remembered. 'I don't even bloody know how old you are.'

'Twenty-nine. You?'

'Thirty-seven. Any brothers and sisters? Parents alive?'

'Only child. And yes. But my father's dying from a brain tumour. They live in Devon.'

She'd phoned them from Darwin airport a couple of hours ago. Her mother had cried. Told her Ambrose had lost his will to live. Just sitting there waiting to fade away. Wouldn't even speak to her.

'I'm sorry.'

'It happens,' she replied, needing not to think about it just now. 'Yours?'

'Fit as a fiddle. They live in the Dordogne now. Not real parents. I was adopted at birth. They had two natural kids as well. Two brothers.'

'Oh. Anything else I should know about? Fatal diseases, scars – unpleasant personal habits?'

'No to the first two. Have to make your own mind up on the last.'

She managed a smile. That's better, he thought.

'Look. You can see the ground.'

In the purple evening light the soil was red-brown, dotted with small, rusty-roofed houses amongst sparse palm trees. Beyond, a darker, denser vegetation clung to the land, here it rose steeply away from the coast. The sight of it sent a new stab of terror through Charlie's innards.

When she'd phoned the newsroom to say she was defying orders and staying, she'd experienced a few seconds of power-crazed exhilaration before panic had set in. Her decision to go to Kutu with Randall had been spur of the moment, not thought through. The more she *did* think about it, the more she realised the perils. Her worries about Randall weren't professional. Not scared he'd hold the camera the wrong way up or anything like that. The trouble was quite simply that he was a bloke and he had a different agenda. No loyalty to her or to news. When the chips were down, he'd revert to being a cop and forget her needs as a journalist.

She glanced sideways, head pressed back into the seat so he wouldn't see her looking. He was staring in front, preoccupied, keeping his thoughts to himself. He'd made a long call to London from the airport but wouldn't talk about it, a silence that irked her and did not bode well for her hopes of getting an inside track from him. He was clearly a man used to taking care of number one. But then, what man wasn't? Thoughtfully she put her fingers to her lips. If she *was* to get him on her side, she would have to work at it.

Through the window she saw the ground approaching fast. Her heart leaped again.

'God, here comes the part I really hate,' she whispered, tensing for the landing.

The wheels touched smoothly and the engines roared into reverse. Randall leaned over. She realised he was nervous too.

'Just play girly from now on, OK?' he murmured into her ear. 'Leave the talking to me.'

As the machine taxied to the terminal, Randall saw military jets on the far side of the field and two sludge-green army helicopters.

No more than thirty passengers on the flight, mostly Indonesian businessmen and ex-pats like Dugdale. Tourism was down as a result of Kutu's unrest. As they stood up to retrieve bags from the lockers,

Randall caught Dugdale's eye for an instant. A nervous, knowing look from the Australian before he turned quickly away.

On the tarmac the hot, damp evening air glued the shirts to their backs. Hibiscus and bougainvillaea bushes flanked a small, brightly-lit terminal, but any impression of island paradise was dispelled by the sight of soldiers on the half-dark tarmac ringing them and the plane in a loose cordon. At ease but alert, the men held automatic weapons across their midriffs, watching that none of the new arrivals should escape the scrutiny of the immigration process. The knot in Charlie's stomach grew to the size of a brick.

Nick slung an arm round her shoulders. His other hand clasped the grey holdall with the stud lens in the strap. The camcorder itself he'd removed from the bag and slung round his neck like a tourist. His own camera bag had been left in a locker at Darwin coach station after stuffing it with Vereker's files, the Yard's Nikons, and Charlie's interview with the Kutuan couple at Sawyer's place.

In front of the terminal a policeman checked faces, feet apart, hands behind his back, bull neck bursting from an immaculate uniform. Charlie avoided his eyes.

Just married, just married, she told herself, guessing at how it would feel.

Inside, ceiling fans stirred air that was heavy with clove-scented cigarette smoke. They joined the passport queue, conscious there were people in it with hard, piercing eyes who had not come off the plane.

Uniforms everywhere. Charlie's knowledge that the men wearing them belonged to a force which regularly practised torture made her shudder. At the head of the queue pebble-eyed officials questioned the new arrivals.

A voice screamed in Charlie's head. *They'll never let us through!*

'Hold the bag a tick,' Nick whispered, standing back from the line and raising the Handycam. He sensed eyes turning his way, which was what he wanted.

From nowhere a uniformed arm grabbed his shoulder.

'Mister! No picture!'

A round, brown face, black, suspicious eyes and a finger waving.

'Yeah, but we're just married,' Randall protested, loudly establishing their cover. 'Just wanted a shot of the wife. Can't do any harm.'

'Is forbidden. No picture in airport.'

'Oh really? OK, chum. Sorry 'bout that. Fair enough.' He stepped back in line next to Charlie. Understanding his purpose, but unnerved by the attention they'd attracted, she lit a cigarette.

The Dugdales had their papers stamped and walked through. Familiar faces, Randall guessed, judging by the way the officials beamed. He watched them disappear amongst the throng of prune-faced porters beyond the immigration desk. Dugdale must have the poise of a tightrope walker he decided, one minute supporting the Kutu rebels, the next glad-handing it with the military.

Soon it was their turn. Charlie clamped her jaws to stop her teeth chattering. The round-faced official who'd stopped them filming hovered behind the desk, listening and watching as the other man went through his checklist of questions.

'Why you come to Indonesia?'

'Tourists,' Nick replied.

'Show me return tickets.' Routine – to make sure they intended to leave again. 'How much money you have?'

'Enough,' said Nick, showing his travellers' cheques.

The seated officer held their passports under a lamp. He had eyes like drills.

'What work you do?'

'Not work. We're tourists,' Nick stressed.

'Yes work. When you home, what work?'

'Travel business.'

'And I'm a teacher,' Charlie added.

'We only got married two days ago, so her passport's in her old name,' Nick explained.

Round-face was unimpressed. He stepped forward, hand outstretched. 'Show me video camera. You take picture outside?'

'No. Nothing.'

He switched the camera to playback, rewound a few seconds of tape, then watched in the viewfinder – touristy shots Randall had taken back in Darwin of Charlie pulling faces outside the airport.

'You be careful,' he warned, handing back the camera. 'No picture police or soldier. Where you stay?'

'Cendana Hotel.' The Cendana was a wind-surfers' place down by the beach. Dugdale had recommended it. Almost empty at this time of year, he'd said. No need to book.

'Cendana full, Mister. You stay at Touristik.'

Randall's heart missed a beat.

'Is that on the beach?' he asked edgily, guessing the Touristik was where they put foreigners they were suspicious of.

'Not far.' The passports were returned with visa stamps. Round-face drifted away as they walked through the barrier.

'They're so bloody suspicious,' Charlie whispered, trying to smile. 'Wherever I turn there's some little sod watching.'

One of the wizened porters touched Nick on the arm. '*Tiket*,' he demanded. '*Tiket, tiket!*' He pointed to where the cases were emerging. Nick gave him their luggage tags.

'Keep an eye on the bugger while I change money,' he murmured to Charlie.

Waiting at the exchange window for the clerk to complete her work, he noticed round-face slip through the exit doors.

By the time Randall was done, a customs official was already searching their rucksacks. When he finished, he pointed to the grey shoulder-bag. Nick slung it on the counter. Involuntarily Charlie put a hand to her mouth.

The official pulled back the zip and a handful of condoms spilled out.

'On honeymoon,' Nick grinned sheepishly. Charlie looked away. Randall, she'd decided, had all the subtlety of a carthorse.

Mildly amused, the official put the contraceptives to one side, then pulled out the flippers, snorkels and beach towels they'd bought in Darwin. He probed the lining that concealed the camera cables. Charlie held her breath, but he found nothing and pushed the bag back towards them.

Randall refilled it and pulled shut the zip. A cursory scan with a hand-held metal detector and they were through the exit doors into the open air.

'Where you go, Mister?' A Melanesian gestured towards his battered blue taxi.

'Cendana Hotel,' Nick replied, optimistically.

'*Cendana*? No. Cendana full. I take you Touristik.'

Round-face had done his work. The porter loaded their bags in the boot then held out a hand for payment.

The road into Piri was potholed and pitted, the sky now purple and black. Where the scrub ended and the town began, night food stalls sold fried rice and chicken legs under the glow of oil lamps. Ancient buses rattled past, horns blaring, their fronts ablaze with coloured lights. Along the banks of a drainage ditch, lines of tin shacks jostled for space. Through the open window came the aroma of food, tainted by sewage and the pungent smoke of rubbish fires.

The smells stirred memories he'd tried to forget, like a postcard from the past that he'd hoped would never come. The twang of the voices, the lurching trucks draped with Christmas lights – and the smoke. His mind jerked back.

1988 in Malaysia. He'd been hunting drug pushers trying to sell smack to squaddies on R&R after jungle training. Up to his neck in a nightmare operation run jointly by the SIB and the Malaysians. They'd had some success, closing in on the top man. Nearly close enough to nail him, but then Randall's buddy on the SIB team had gone missing while posing as a buyer.

He'd volunteered to go find him, but had been told no. Fears it would wreck the investigation. Squaddies were getting hooked – too much was at stake. He'd been ordered to leave his mate to take his chances. The man had known the risks, they'd said.

Balls to that. Randall had gone secretly and alone to the village where his partner had disappeared. The smell the same as here. Fires of wood and rubbish. Inside a house of bamboo and thatch he'd found four thugs trying to club his mate to death.

He'd got him out. Saved his life. But used the Browning to do it. Had to shoot one of the dealers.

He shuddered at the technicolour memory.

'You all right?' Charlotte whispered.

'Yeah.' He puffed out his cheeks.

He'd saved his mate, but got hauled across the carpet for compromising the investigation. Then lady luck had stepped in; the man he'd killed was the kingpin they'd been after. The peddling ring fell apart, so the grown-ups back home gave him a medal.

He shook his head like a wet dog, booting the memories back to the mists.

Charlie saw his jaw clench with tension and didn't like it. She wanted him strong, confident, one hundred per cent, because everything she saw through the taxi window scared the pants off her. In one short plane hop they'd moved from a world she understood to one she didn't.

'Where you from?' the driver asked, turning his head.

'England,' said Nick.

'Ah! *Inggris*. You speak Indonesian?'

'No.' No mention of his rusty Malay. The driver was bound to work for intel.

'What your name, mister?'

'Nick. And this is Charlie.'

'My name Toni. You want, I your guide.'

'We'll see . . .'

They were into the town proper by now. Wider streets, official-looking buildings. A square dominated by a fine Dutch colonial mansion.

'Governor palace,' the driver announced. '*Vehry* old.'

Nick spotted two jeeps parked at the side of it, stuffed with troops.

'Much trouble here at night?' he asked. 'We've read something in the papers.'

'Ya, ya. Just some troublemakers here, they no want the copper mine.'

'But you do, yes?'

'Ya, ya. Good business,' he cackled. 'But I think in the night time it better you stay in hotel. Is safer.'

Randall threw Charlie a glance. She grimaced, trying to look brave, but a bruised look in her eyes said, *you got me here, you bloody look after me.*

'There's a curfew?'

'No. No curfew. But bar, restaurant all shut.'

'Really? Well it won't worry us. We go to bed early.' Nick leaned over and gave Charlie a kiss on the mouth.

She shoved him away. 'Don't overdo it,' she whispered.

The driver was watching in the mirror and cackled again.

'Just married,' Nick explained, putting on his sheepish look.

'Ohhh . . . then you vahry happy people. Tomorrow I take you beach, coffee plantation, typical Kutu village. Maybe you interest war cementery. Japanese they kill many prisoner here. Australia, India, and *Inggris.*'

'There was a Jap prisoner of war camp *here?*' Charlie piped up, startled.

'Ya, ya. They use prisoners to make airfield.' The driver pointed back over his shoulder to where they'd come from.

'My father was a POW,' she murmured to Nick out of the side of her mouth so the driver wouldn't hear. 'Tortured by the Japs,' she went on, her voice dry with tension. 'Never got over it. He can't talk about it. Never even said where it happened.'

'Malaya probably,' Randall mumbled. 'It's where most of them were.'

Charlie pictured her father sitting on the terrace in Devon, staring out at the mud and sand of the estuary, listening to the curlew cries, waiting to die. Her eyes began to water. She tried to banish the image. This wasn't the time to be maudlin.

The taxi turned up a narrow hill, past dusty hardware shops closing up for the night. Soon the Hotel Touristik loomed, a shabby, low building, with a once-white facia and an entrance of darkened glass. As they got out, two-stroke motorbikes buzzed past like wheeled chain-saws.

Inside, the lobby echoed to the noise of an over-loud television. The duty manager was expecting them. Round-face must have phoned. Next to the reception desk sat two men in tight shirts and trousers.

Nick returned their dead-eyed look. There were two ways of

watching people. His way, which meant the target never knew about it, and the way they did it here, openly, brazenly with a technique designed to intimidate. Charlotte's drawn face told him their method was working.

'We give best room for you,' the manager grinned. 'Bridal seat . . .'

'Suite,' Charlotte corrected him, her mind on automatic.

Randall paid off the taxi driver and pocketed the business card he thrust at him. They signed in, then a porter slung a rucksack over each shoulder and led them through the hotel to an open, lantern-lit courtyard and swimming pool around which the bedrooms were situated. Two middle-aged Dutch couples were eating their evening meal there. In the far corner a small, three-man gamelan orchestra of percussion and strings twanged and clunked their way through a Javan melody. The porter stopped outside room twelve.

Randall put a hand on Charlie's arm. 'Watch what you say in here,' he warned under his breath. 'The room may be bugged.'

Charlie gulped. Microphones? In the *bedroom*? Checking they were the honeymooners they claimed to be?

'Jesus!' she breathed.

Menteng, Jakarta
Mid evening

A grey Merc cruised along a dimly-lit street of two-storey houses, past the heavy metal gates which shielded the well-off residents from intruders. Major General Dino Sumoto sat in the rear, glaring vacantly through the tinted windows, his wide, thick lips set in a tense line. His hands were flat on the seat to each side of him as if to steady himself. In front his regular driver sat stiff-backed and drove with an immaculate serenity.

General Sumoto was in a state of shock. The unthinkable had happened. A British prime minister renowned world-wide for weakness had refused to bow to pressure. The arms contract Sumoto had banked on being cancelled had instead been reconfirmed.

Sumoto was used to winning; for two decades almost everything he'd done had worked the way he'd intended. His easy rise to a position of power in the armed forces, his almost effortless accumulation of money and supporters, all this had encouraged him to believe the time had come for the biggest gamble of his life. Above all there'd been the advice of his *dukun*. The general was a Muslim, but like many powerful Javans, including the president himself, when big decisions were due he relied on a soothsayer who listened to the spirits of trees, rivers and mountains.

But the signs had been wrong. The *dukun* had misread the spirits. He was about to lose, a contingency he'd not planned for.

The car slowed and swung on to the narrow concrete ramp that bridged the deep storm drain running along the roadside. The driver stopped and flashed his lights. At the familiar signal, the dark green, steel gate rolled back. As the car drove through, the house-guardian stood to attention and saluted.

The centrally located district of Menteng was where Jakarta's old money lived. A few blocks away from Sumoto's home the president himself had his house. For an ABRI *apparatchik* this was the only suitable place to live, even if *Sumoto's* wealth still had the smell of the mint about it.

His driver jumped out to open the rear door.

'I'll need you again soon,' Sumoto snapped as he walked into the house. 'To collect someone for me. So don't go to sleep.'

Sumoto had lived alone here since the separation from his wife a year ago. A young Sundanese couple ran his home for him, sharing the housekeeping and cooking. Hearing him enter, the manservant emerged from the kitchen.

'Tea,' said Sumoto. The servant bowed his head and retreated.

The living room had a well-polished parquet floor and furniture of dark wood, the seating upholstered in deep reds and greens. The general sank into an armchair and switched on the TV with the remote. A news bulletin in five minutes. Not that it would tell him anything he didn't know.

The general was of a culture where open displays of anger were unacceptable. However fierce the fires inside him, his face must remain a mask of self-control. But fury tore through him now, burning his stomach. He had a need for the soothing tea.

That the misjudgement which had brought disaster was *his* and his alone had not occurred to him. In his mind the failure of his plan was the fault of others – treachery, maybe even by the spirits. He'd been misled. Those responsible must pay the price.

Above all he'd been misled by Stephen Bowen. *He* who'd spoken so bitingly about his prime minister's feebleness under pressure. *He* who'd innocently cautioned that if the fickle spotlight of the world's media happened to focus on Indonesia's harsh suppression of unrest in Kutu or East Timor it might force Britain to withdraw from the arms deal.

Sumoto pulled one of the gold pens from the breast pocket of his dark safari suit, tapped it against the chair arm and reassured himself he could still be safe. In his head he went through a checklist of vulnerability. First – his dealings with the Chinese. Meetings with the trade delegation had been more social than business. The real contacts, the ones that had dealt in specifics, had been secret – his involvement blurred by go-betweens. Nothing there to draw him to the attention of his commander-in-chief. Nothing to link him with the kidnap of Stephen Bowen.

He *was* in danger, however, from those he'd had to trust. The bit-part players who'd done his dirty work. Some would stay loyal through thick and thin. But there were others whose loyalty he'd had to buy. And people who could be bought once, could be bought again – by somebody else. *They* were the ones whose silence he now had to ensure.

He looked around the room. His father would have been proud to see him in this house, a boy from simple peasant stock. Prouder still if he'd succeeded with his plans.

Blood had been shed to get him where he was. His father had done it in the 1940s – to give the nation its freedom. Dutch blood. And *he* had done it when the nation faced internal strife in the 1960s. Communist blood.

The sacrifice of lives – little had been achieved without it in his nation's history.

Major General Dino Sumoto was still destined for greatness, of that he was sure. He had lost a battle today, but not the war. He would still win. But to do so *he* had to survive.

The news bulletin was on. Pictures of the president visiting Sumatra where there'd been an earthquake. Scenes in the hospital. Victims being comforted by the nation's leader. Nothing about the arms contract with Britain. Nothing about Bowen; thanks to the efforts of the information minister the kidnap had been all but ignored by the Indonesian media.

He switched off just as the tea was set down on a small, inlaid table at his elbow. He poured some into the thin porcelain cup and sipped.

Of all the decisions he now had to take, there was one that would be desperately hard. A decision he was not ready for, but for which he had to prepare.

The jasmine-scented liquid warmed and calmed his insides. He rose from the chair and crossed to an alcove lined with books where the telephone sat on his leather-topped desk.

Hand hovering over the phone, he looked down at the silver-framed photographs that ringed it. Distracted for a moment, he picked up one from 1965 – his class at the military academy.

He remembered the bloodshed that had followed. Ironic he should have been bent on eradicating communism all those years ago, yet now be seeking communist help. The world had changed in thirty years and so had he.

He replaced the photo and dialled quickly before he could change his mind about what he had to do. The bird-like voice answered after a couple of rings.

'I want you here,' he told her gruffly. 'I'm sending the car.'

'Yes,' she replied flatly, as if she'd been expecting it.

He replaced the receiver then walked through the house to the side door where the driver was waiting. He gave him the address, making him write it down, then told the oaf how to find the correct apartment and sent him on his way.

On his way back in, Sumoto called into the kitchen.

'I have a guest for dinner. We can eat in one hour.'

She had never been to this house before. More discreet for them to meet away from the wagging tongues of Menteng. It was why he'd rented the small apartment close by – so he could make use of her when he wanted. But the situation had changed. Away from him she was a danger now. He needed her here, under his control. So he could take his time in deciding what to do with her.

One more phone call. To Kutu this time – the headquarters of KODAM Twelve. On the island there was some cleaning up to be done.

Hotel Touristik, Kutu
20.05 hrs (12.05 hrs GMT)

They'd spoken little in the bedroom for fear of being overheard. Heart in her mouth, Charlie had changed into a clean bush shirt.

As they passed through the courtyard on their way towards reception the Dutch couple smiled at them again, but it did nothing to reassure her. Charlie carried a Lonely Planet guidebook to look like a tourist. Her trick camera bag hung from Randall's shoulder. In the foyer the manager glanced up in surprise.

'Hello, mister! Where you go?'

'For a walk . . .' Randall snapped, looking round for the intel men. One of them was watching TV. His fat face twisted towards them.

'Everything closed in Piri . . .' the manager warned. 'Not safe. Better you stay in hotel.'

'Shan't be long . . .' Nick shoved open the door to the street. He heard the scrape of the chair behind him as the policeman scrambled to his feet.

Outside, the road was eerily empty now, as if the town had been hit by the plague. They marched over broken paving stones, heading downhill towards the town centre.

'You sure about this?' Charlie whispered, hoarse with nerves. 'You don't think they'll shoot us?'

'No, chuck. I don't,' he answered, walking faster.

'But, I mean, d'you even know how to find Captain's Bar?' Charlie felt her courage about to fail totally. The place was horrendously spooky. 'Maybe we should wait until morning.'

'It's near the harbour,' he said, grabbing her arm to hurry her along. Looking round in the vain hope of a taxi he spotted the policeman slip from the hotel. 'Shit!' They wouldn't get far at this rate. Then suddenly from up the hill came the heavy thump of rock music. A minibus approached, its front aglow with coloured lights.

'This'll do,' Randall murmured.

'We can't go in *that*,' Charlie hissed, appalled.

'We're *going* to. And it's called a *bemo* according to the book you're holding.'

When the minibus was almost on them, he stepped out into the road. It braked sharply and a skinny teenager swung from the door to let them board, his fist full of grubby banknotes.

They crammed in beside a dozen, small, neat-bodied locals. Dark faces, white teeth, bright shirts and dresses. As the vehicle took off again Nick saw the intel man curse and run back to the hotel. He turned to the boy with the money.

'*Pelabuhan, Berapa?* How much to the harbour?'

'Six hun'red,' he answered tensely.

A loudspeaker wedged beneath the benches pounded a bass beat that shook their innards. Oblivious to the sound level, the other passengers gaped like children at their white faces. Charlie forced a smile.

At the bottom of the hill a coin was tapped on the overhead rail and the *bemo* stopped to let two passengers off. The faces of those remaining were tense and watchful. Two unlit army trucks passed in the opposite direction. The passengers looked away, avoiding each other's eyes. More stops, more passengers out, all in a hurry to get off the streets.

'D'you get the feeling this is the last bus?' Charlie whispered timorously.

'Yes.'

'So how the hell do we get back to the hotel?'

'Leave it to Allah, love.'

Charlie was not amused.

The driver killed the music. He slowed down, window open, listening. At each bend in the road he stopped to look before pressing on. By the time they reached the harbour, they were the only passengers left. The money collector swung into the road to let them off, eager to see the back of them.

As the *bemo* sped away silence closed in. They stood in an empty square that smelled of rotten fruit. Earlier in the day there'd been a market here. At one end street lamps above a closed Telkom office cast an insipid light. At the other the patchily floodlit port was framed by the dark shapes of dockside cranes. Nearby they heard unseen waves caressing a shingle beach.

'Christ, it's *so* eerie,' Charlotte breathed.

Randall's skin crawled as if they were being watched. He looked round, but saw no one. He heard Charlie's teeth chatter again. Odd how they did that when she was scared. Like a character from a Disney cartoon. He slung an arm round her shoulders.

'Don't worry. We'll be OK.' Then he pointed. 'Down there, look.'

A glow of red neon from a side street that could be the bar. They hurried past the iron harbour gates, glimpsing a sandbagged sentry post behind it.

'They're everywhere,' Charlie hissed, 'watching, listening. It's Orwellian.'

They reached the corner of the side street, then Randall jerked her sharply back into the shadows.

'A jeep,' he growled. 'Outside the bar. With its lights off.'

'Oh Christ!' she whimpered. 'Now we're for it. They guessed where we were going. Told you we should've left this until morning.'

Then they heard the engine start, the gears crunch and the vehicle drive off into the night.

'See?' Randall said. 'The jeep's nothing to do with us. Now just cool it. We're tourists, remember?' She would balls things up for them if she didn't pull herself together. 'OK. Let's go for it.'

The first door they came to was a restaurant, closed and in darkness. The second was Captain's Bar, but locked. Randall knocked on the bottle-glass panel. No response. From inside came the sound of a television. He knocked harder.

Through the glass they saw shadows move, then heard the lock being turned. Teri's face peered out, alarmed.

'Hello. Remember us?'

Recognising him, she unhitched the chain and let them in. 'This late not safe,' she muttered as they slipped past her into the half-lit bar.

A small, empty drinking den, with a ship's wheel on the back wall draped with fishing nets. Behind the counter an elderly man with the same broad, Melanesian face as Teri – her father, they guessed – hunched on a stool, staring at the TV. Teri whispered to him, explaining who they were. He listened without taking his eyes from the screen.

'Is Brad here?' Randall asked.

'Yes. I get him. You want a drink?'

'A beer. You too?' he asked Charlie. She nodded, biting her lip.

Teri disappeared through a bead curtain into the back, while the old man flipped the caps off two bottles and gave them glasses. The curtain parted again and Brad Dugdale poked his face through, startled and flustered. He pointed at his watch.

'Not too clever being out this late,' he warned. 'Didn't they tell you at the Touristik?'

Randall blinked. So the man knew they weren't at the Cendana . . . Somebody must've told him. The soldiers in the jeep? But why?

'Yeah, well we're not the clever sort, friend,' Randall mumbled distractedly.

Dugdale knocked the top off a bottle and put it to his lips, eyeing them like a car salesman finding punters on his forecourt.

'Suit yourselves,' he shrugged. 'So, now that you're here, what can I do for you folks?'

'Just thought we'd have another word. See what else you know.'

'About what, chum?'

'About the kidnapping of Stephen Bowen . . .'

Dugdale's eyes flickered. 'Like Jim Sawyer said, we're all steering clear of that one. Don't really know anything about it.'

Dugdale swigged from the bottle again, watery eyes watching from beneath heavy brows.

'OK, but there must be loads of gossip, Brad,' Randall pressed, sensing the man was playing with them. 'Who do people think's got him? The Kutuan resistance?'

'Maybe,' Dugdale hedged. Then his eyes narrowed. 'They certainly *could* have done it despite what that fart Sawyer told you. The OKP's got plenty of friends in the media, too. People who'd help with the TV side of things.'

'Do *you* think he's here? On the island?'

'I . . . I don't know.' He glanced uncomfortably towards Teri and her father, who were both listening. 'Tell you what, why don't we go and sit at a table. More comfortable.'

They crossed to the far side of the small bar. Teri slipped away through the bead curtain. The old man concentrated on the TV again.

'Tell you something,' Dugdale confided, leaning across the table so their heads were close. 'I *have* just heard a rumour that'll interest you . . . They say some European who was a dead ringer for Bowen was seen arriving at Piri airport in the middle of last week on a private jet!'

Randall perked up. This matched the speculation Maxwell had come up with.

'You think it's true?' Charlie asked eagerly. The cosiness of the bar had made her feel safer again.

'Search me. As I said it's just a rumour.'

'Where'd you hear this?' Randall asked, suspicion growing that it was all too pat.

'Immigration feller at the airport.'

'But those blokes would *know* if it were true. A plane coming in – there'd be records kept.'

'Records? Not in this country, chum. Not if you don't want there to be and have the right connections. The rumour is, you see, your man Bowen had some private little swizz going with KUTUMIN and came here incognito.'

Same line as Maxwell again. Plausible. But then the best rumours always were.

'Could be why ABRI's so darned jumpy at the moment,' Dugdale continued, reinforcing his message. 'After telling the world so many times that Bowen's not in Indonesia, it'd be dead awkward if they've found out he *is* here after all. Loss of face could be terminal. For someone . . .'

Randall drank from his glass. It still didn't add up.

'OK. Suppose Bowen *did* fly here,' he pressed, 'how could the OKP have nabbed him?'

Dugdale gave a huge shrug.

'Now there you've got me, sport. I've no idea. Maybe he was at one of the KUTUMIN sites when the OKP attacked. They're doing it all the time. Perhaps old Soleman Kakadi – the bloke who leads the wild fellers up in the hills – maybe he just took a look at Bowen and said *hey, he looks important. Let's have him.*'

'So it would be Kakadi,' Nick checked, 'if it *was* the OKP.'

'Oh yeah. The other bloke, Junus Bawi, he's a softie. Believes in passive resistance. He's already gone on record saying he's not involved. And Bawi doesn't lie.'

'So how do we find Soleman Kakadi?' Charlie asked earnestly.

'Haven't a clue, my dear. And I don't want to know. Because if I did, some uniformed gentleman from ABRI might come along and squeeze my nuts until I told him. But you could try the priests. Sawyer gave you the names.'

'Yes. But tell me, what's the military doing about Soleman Kakadi?' Nick probed. 'Trying to catch him presumably.'

'Between you and me there's not too much they can do,' Dugdale confided. Sensing Randall's scepticism he was concentrating his answers on Charlie, who hung on his every word. 'They haven't the manpower. Kakadi has millions of trees to hide in and most of ABRI's men are busy in places like East Timor. They haven't used KOPASSUS here for example – the counter-terrorist boys. They're the *real* hard bastards – famous for not taking prisoners. But they're too busy elsewhere. All ABRI does on Kutu is guard the places where the work's going on for the mine. Here, I'll show you.'

He got up from the table. Close to the door was a pinboard with tourist information on it and messages for backpackers. He switched on the light above it.

'Look.' A small map showed Kutu shaped like a leg of lamb. 'In the middle is the volcano they call Jiwa – Spirit Mountain, OK? Piri's down here on the coast. It's between Piri and the volcano where the mine'll be.'

'They're not digging yet?' Charlie checked.

'No way. Got to finish building the road to the coast first.' He drew a finger across the map, from the centre to a point west of Piri. 'That's to bring the ore to the new deep-water harbour, also being built. And there's a valley to be dammed for a reservoir.'

'And Soleman Kakadi is up in those hills?' Randall asked.

'I imagine. Twenty, thirty k's away. The whole island's less than sixty across.'

'And with him is Stephen Bowen . . .' Charlotte mused. 'Maybe.'

'Well . . . for all I know, yes . . .' Dugdale hovered like a salesman close to a deal. Then he switched off the wall light and sidled back to the table.

Randall followed. Speculation, all of it.

'Great story that airport rumour. Pity there's no evidence to back it up,' he said dismissively, sitting down again.

'Evidence?' A smile flickered on Dugdale's face then died again. 'Who knows, maybe you'll get lucky.'

Suddenly there was a rap at the door. Charlie jumped in her seat.

'This could be for *you*,' Dugdale warned, tensely. 'Sit tight. Pretend you don't know me.'

He crossed to the bar. Randall saw fear in his eyes, the fear of a man who was only tolerated here if he kept his nose clean.

'Teri!' Dugdale barked, tapping on the counter. The woman emerged through the beads and he shoved her towards the door.

Three uniformed soldiers burst in, an officer with a pistol holster, his men with rifles. Charlie grabbed Randall's arm.

'*Selamat malam*,' said Dugdale, greeting them with a rictus of a smile.

The military ignored him, one soldier pushing through the beads into the kitchen, the other guarding the door. The officer stared at Randall and Charlie. Then a look of relief came over his face. He turned back to Dugdale.

'*Selamat malam*,' he responded finally.

'Christ!' Charlie breathed, her heart thumping wildly. 'I thought they were going to open fire.'

The officer was a lieutenant, smart and fit-looking with a tough face the colour of Thai curry. He talked to Dugdale in Bahasa.

Randall strained to listen. 'He's asking about us,' he whispered. 'Asking how long we've been here.'

'Oh help.'

'We came for a drink, remember,' said Randall, resting a hand on her arm. 'We're tourists.'

He downed the remains of his beer.

They watched in silence for a couple of minutes, then Dugdale leaned across the counter towards them.

'Hey, Mr Englishman, whatever your name is! I've fixed you a lift back to your hotel. The lieutenant says he'll take you in his jeep. Right away. You won't get a taxi at this time of night.'

They stood up.

'And in future, remember they don't like you going out in the evenings.' Dugdale's face glistened with sweat. 'Safer to do as they want here . . .'

The lieutenant ordered his soldiers out, then stood by the door, slapping his thigh with impatience.

'Hey, if you want to do some scuba diving I'm your man,' Dugdale added as an afterthought. 'Take a brochure.' He grabbed a pamphlet from the bar counter and thrust it at them. 'Tells you about the boats. Only, ignore the stuff about the *Morning Glory*. She's er . . . she's out of commission at the moment.'

'Thanks. Nice idea.'

'Watch yourselves, now.'

Outside, the jeep's engine was already running, the two riflemen perched on the mudguards to make room in the back. The officer swung in beside the driver. The soldiers smelled of sweat and thick cotton, oil and webbing. A smell of violence, Charlie thought.

'Good of you to give us a lift,' Nick shouted above the engine roar as they sped up the hill from the harbour. The jeep's lights were out.

The lieutenant ignored him. No English. The streets were empty and silent, the soldiers uptight and watchful. Reminded Randall of the Falls Road when he'd first joined up. Next to him Charlotte sat straight backed, her side pressed against his.

Shadowy vehicles passed the other way, trucks full of civilians under arrest. Men and women. Charlie's mind clicked back to the job. She needed *pictures* of stuff like this. But with spies watching everything they did, filming anything significant here was going to be a nightmare.

London – Waterloo Station
12.45 hrs

The Eurostar from Brussels due in at twelve thirty arrived two minutes early. Detective Constable Joe Harding stood in the little darkened room behind the immigration barrier, watching through the one-way glass. He felt a little frayed after his night on Ted Sankey's couch. With him was a short, plain-clothes officer from the Transport Police.

The French had excelled themselves. A motorcycle patrolman in the northern city of Lille had spotted an Espace in the railway station car park with its lights on as if dumped in a hurry. The car was left-hand drive, but had British plates that had proved to be false. The Espace was the one stolen last week from Strasbourg's Palais des Nations. The television 'flyaway' it had originally contained was missing, however.

Lille was on the Eurostar route from Brussels to London.

The photo in Harding's hand showed a young man with a wide grin and long hair. Ricky Smith. He guessed he would look different today.

The passengers were mostly businessmen in suits. Their passports were given a cursory glance by the immigration officer. A young man with hair cropped to within a centimetre of his scalp presented his maroon document. Upon reading the name the immigration man scratched his cheek. At the signal Harding hurried out into the customs hall.

Ricky Smith had a face bronzed by a sun-lamp, a denim shirt open to his navel, and a gold medallion glittering against his sternum. His face wore an expression of unjustified self-confidence.

'Excuse me sir, could I see your passport?' The transport policeman blocked the TV technician's path.

'Eh? Just done that, mate,' Smith protested.

'Don't fuck us about, Ricky,' Harding snapped, gripping his arm.

Wesley Street, Westminster
12.59 hrs

Since watching Keith Copeland condemn her husband to death on television just over an hour ago, Sally Bowen had paced around the little flat, clutching the boarding pass on which the unexplained account number was written. From time to time she stopped to stare from the window.

She'd decided she couldn't let it go. She was still Stephen's wife, whatever she thought of him. Still the one person he would be counting on to save him if she could. In her hands she held *something*. Didn't know what. Didn't understand the relevance of the words: *Keith's account: N465329.*

It might be nothing. But knowing how gambling had stripped Stephen of all financial morality, knowing how close he and Keith Copeland had become in the past year, she realised that what she held in her hand could just turn out to be a lever as strong as a crowbar.

The television was on with the volume low. She heard the jingle for the lunchtime news, crossed to the set, turned up the sound and sat on the edge of the sofa.

'*PM gives final "no" to Stephen Bowen's kidnappers,*' the newscaster intoned. '*Police say the minister's whereabouts are still unknown.*'

She watched as they reran the shot of Copeland with the Indonesian ambassador. That smirk on his face. That dreadful smugness. That appalling look of satisfaction just after condemning Stephen to death. It decided her.

She stood up, paced to the rosewood table with the phone on it and dialled the number for 10 Downing Street.

'Hello? This is Mrs Sally Bowen speaking. I'd like to speak to the prime minister.'

'*I'll put you through to the secretary, Mrs Bowen.*'

A moment later a man's voice came on.

'Mrs Bowen? The prime minister's in a meeting just now. Can I help?'

'Yes. I want to see Keith. He said I could. Whenever I liked. I want to fix a time. As soon as possible. It's really quite urgent.'

Kutu – Hotel Touristik
21.25 hrs (13.25 hrs GMT)

Inside the lobby of the Touristik Hotel the intel man who'd let them slip through his fingers an hour and twenty minutes ago gave them a look that could have flayed the skin off their backs.

'Evening,' said Randall.

They walked past him into the empty, central courtyard.

'That's one very unhappy bunny,' Randall muttered. 'Now, I don't know about you, but I've got to eat something. You hungry?'

'Yes. If we're not too late.' The dining terrace was deserted, the gamelan orchestra gone, the tables draped with white cloths but no cutlery. Charlie put a hand on his arm. 'They wouldn't bug this bit of the hotel would they? Put things under the tables?'

Unlikely, thought Randall. Beside the lit-up swimming pool however the furniture was plastic and portable. Safer to sit there.

'Over there,' he pointed, leading the way.

They sat, looking round for some sign of serving staff. Charlie lit a cigarette and drew on it tensely, relieved to be back in the hotel.

'So, what d'you make of all that?' she prodded, desperate for Randall to open up. 'Our Australian friend and his rumours . . .' She'd watched Nick's face while Dugdale was talking and was convinced something had clicked with him.

'Not sure,' he shrugged. 'But I think he's up to something.'

'Knows more than he's saying, you mean?'

'Maybe. Had a feeling at one point he knew where Bowen was . . .'

'Wow! Why d'you say that?' She hunched forward, drawing in a mouthful of smoke.

Randall puffed out his cheeks. 'Just a feeling . . .'

'. . . born of years of policemanly experience, I suppose,' she needled, hoping to goad him into giving away more.

'If you like.'

'Or . . . because of something you *know*. Something about Brad that's come up elsewhere? Something dug up by MI6 perhaps?' she gushed, desperate for Randall to give. 'Something they told you on the phone when you spoke to London from Darwin airport, perhaps?'

'Hey, hang on chuck. Hang on. You're way off beam. And anyway, don't push your luck. When there's something I can tell you, I will. OK?' His voice was firm but gentle. *He*'d try it on if *he* were her. 'But the answer's no. None of that stuff. It's just a gut feeling.'

Charlie sat back and flicked ash on to the soil of a pot plant. 'Well, do your guts also tell you whether we can get anything to eat around here?' She peered into the shadows that ringed the dining area, then looked at her watch. It felt like midnight. 'Only half past nine. Must be *someone* around still.'

Nick tapped his metal watch-bracelet on the table, hoping the noise would attract attention. He felt desperately tired suddenly. The lack of sleep was catching up.

A waitress appeared, dressed in knee-length skirt and white blouse. Silently and from nowhere.

'Kitchen close . . .' said the woman. She had a pretty face but sad eyes.

'You can find us something,' Nick replied, slipping a banknote into her hand.

'*Terima kasih!*' she smiled, bowing. 'You like *nasi goreng?*'

'She says there's fried rice with chicken and veg,' Nick translated.

'Fine. Anything.'

'Beer to drink?' he checked.

'No. Diet Coke.'

'And a beer for me,' he told the girl.

'The power of money,' Charlie breathed as the waitress disappeared.

They sat staring into the clear blue depths of the pool. For a full minute neither spoke. Then Charlie broke the silence, reading his thoughts.

'Soleman Kakadi.'

'Yes. All the signs seem to point. Tomorrow we have to find a way of getting to him.'

Charlie felt warmed by the way he'd said *we*. He gave her a smile that was a little sheepish. Looks like a kid at times, she thought. He'd be cuddly if he let go a bit. She stubbed out her cigarette.

'Got any kids?' she asked suddenly.

'Eh?'

'On the plane from Singapore you told me you were married once.'

'Yes. One daughter,' he frowned, not wanting the distraction of thinking about Sandra.

'How old?'

'Fifteen.'

'And trouble, I imagine,' she smiled. 'What happened?'

'What d'you mean?'

'Between you and your wife. You broke up . . .'

Randall puffed his cheeks. 'Look, I really don't want to talk about it . . .'

'Sorry.' She blushed. 'That was rude. Typical journalist. Never know when to stop.' She smiled meekly. 'It's just that when I share a bed with a bloke I like to know a bit about him.'

He sat up with a jolt, sensing her remark had been more than an idle one – that she was telling him something. A gentle come-on perhaps? Too bad. He'd decided right at the start that, however tempted, sex with Charlie was a complication he could do without.

He was about to remind her of his promise to sleep on the floor, when the waitress returned, beaming. She set a tray down, off-loaded bottles and glasses, then the two plates of food.

'That was quick,' Charlie breathed. 'How much did you tip her?'

'Too much by the look of it.'

'*Selamat makan*,' she purred, slinking away.

'What did she say?'

'Nothing much. Just *enjoy your meal*. But it'll probably be cold.' He took a forkful of rice. 'It is.'

Charlie didn't care, so long as it stopped her stomach rumbling.

'How much of this language can you understand?' she checked.

'About half. It's not hard to learn, but I'm rusty.'

Charlie watched his mouth as he ate, her fear of the place sufficiently diminished to wonder, just for a moment, what he would be like as a lover.

'Look, as far as the bedroom arrangements are concerned . . .' Randall began, deciding he'd better clarify matters. He stopped mid sentence. Footsteps were crossing the terrace to their left. They both looked. It was the intel man sneaking past hoping not to be noticed. He disappeared through a door.

'That . . . that's the room next to ours,' Charlie gulped.

'Yes.'

Their eyes locked.

'Umm . . . so there'll be somebody actually in the room next door to us, listening?' she whispered huskily.

'Looks like it. Listening and maybe watching, I suppose . . .'

Her jaw dropped. Then she frowned. 'This is actually quite serious, isn't it?'

'How d'you mean?'

He saw a blur of embarrassment in her eye.

'Well, we're . . . we're supposed to be on honeymoon, right? And, as you so perceptively said in Darwin this afternoon, there's only one thing honeymooners do when they get into bed . . .'

She half smiled. She was floundering. Wanting him to tell her what to do.

Randall knew that look. Knew what it meant. Knew for certain that if he wanted to make love to her, he could. Visions of having sex with her deluged his mind suddenly, flushing out all thoughts of Bowen, of Dugdale and the job. Everything that mattered bleached out by a testosterone surge . . .

That was the trouble with sex. It took over. Took over completely. And he mustn't let it.

'Turns you on, does it, chuck . . .' he growled, in an instinctive and clumsy put-down to cover his confusion, '. . . the thought of being videoed shagging?'

She put a hand to her mouth. That aspect of it hadn't occurred to her.

'But then I suppose being videoed is what you get paid for . . .' he went on, labouring the joke until it hurt. He bit his tongue.

'Thanks.' She looked bruised, and turned her eyes away.

'Sorry. Didn't mean . . .'

'Forget it.'

But she couldn't. There was nothing funny about this situation. It scared her to death.

'Look, I'm serious,' she continued, looking down at her plate. 'What . . . what are we going to do about that bloke?' She shivered at the thought of him behind the wall, watching their every move, listening to their every breath.

'OK . . .' Randall reined in his imagination. Back to the job. Back to what mattered. 'Let's *be* serious then. They *will* be listening. But what they'll be listening for is some bit of careless talk. Some clue that we're journalists or Amnesty workers instead of who we say we are. That's what it's all about. So, we just have to stick to our legend like glue.'

'It was your idea.'

'What was?'

'The *legend*. Being honeymooners.'

'Well . . . sure.' She was making a point again, he realised. Making the point that they would have to do *something*. 'Well yes, I suppose the guy listening to the bugs might find it odd if . . .'

Charlie reached down suddenly and slapped her leg. 'Talking of bugs . . .'

Mosquitoes flitted round the light above their heads. Nick dug in the grey holdall and found a stick of repellent, glad of the distraction. Charlie smeared it on her legs and arms.

'You *are* taking malaria pills?' he asked, then wished he hadn't. He was *not* responsible for her. Couldn't afford to be. The woman had *chosen* to come here.

Charlie nodded. 'Of course I am.' She looked at him expectantly. She wanted a decision. 'They might find it odd, you said, if . . .'

'I was only thinking,' he muttered uncomfortably, moving the food round his plate, 'that maybe we should give them *something* for their bugs to bite on.'

'Yes,' she replied, lowering her eyes again.

'I mean just something for their tape. Sound effects.' He paused, waiting for a reaction, but there wasn't one. 'Tell you what, we could just turn the telly up loud and then provide a backing track of screwing noises.' He shrugged at the nonsense of it. 'How about that?'

Charlie lifted one eyebrow. This was becoming a black farce. She was scared stiff. Not of sleeping with a relative stranger – she'd done that a few times in her life – but scared of this place, of the spooky, sinister men who lurked in every shadow. Scared too of the dangers she would face tomorrow if she was to get the story she'd come for.

What she needed above all was for Nick to be on her side. To help her get at the story, and to keep her safe. In short she needed him to *care* about her. If achieving that meant being videoed shagging as he so poetically put it, then so be it.

'Look . . . I think maybe you're making more of a problem out of this than you need . . .' she said softly, reaching out and touching his hand. 'This honeymoon thing – it's acting, Nick. Like you said back in Darwin. *Whatever* we do it's acting . . .' She held his look until she knew he'd understood. 'So just give me the script, will you? Or we can ad lib it. Whatever . . . it's fine by me. You lead, Nick – I'll follow.'

She withdrew her hand.

'You're the boss, Nick.'

Yes, thought Randall. That was just the bloody trouble.

15

London – 10 Downing Street
19.00 hrs

PRIME MINISTER COPELAND stood in the middle of the room, eyes
glued to the TV set in the corner. There'd been a murder and the
Channel 4 News was leading on it. The chief executive of Capital
Electricity p.l.c. had been shot dead an hour ago. Bullets fired through
the window of his 7-series BMW while being driven home from his
office in Battersea. He'd demanded an urgent report from the Met.
Assistant Commissioner Stanley was on his way over.

Three days ago the press had written about the executive's £125,000
pay increase. On top of an annual salary of £575,000. A *productivity
payment*, Capital had called it. For raising shareholders' profits by sacking
2,000 workers and freezing the pay of the remaining staff.

The Revenue Men had struck again.

'Bastards!' Copeland hissed. He meant *all* of them. The terrorists for
mounting such an atrocious attack – and the City men whose greed
tempted other men into sin . . .

He switched the set off. It sent shivers up his spine watching it. Every
outrage by the terrorists felt like a move up the path towards his own
front door.

Envy was the sin Copeland was most prone to. Nearly thirty years of
public service in the House and in government, and now managing
director of UK Ltd., and what did he get out of it? A spurious sense of
power and a wage that was a fraction of what the top businessmen
earned. Which was why Stephen Bowen's suggestion of a little sleight of
hand as a way to feather his nest had been so cruelly tempting . . .

With the panache of a poker player Stephen had slipped him the
proposition at a time when he was riddled with doubts about his
suitability for the job. For the first time in his life a chance to acquire
capital, a lump sum as a cushion for early retirement. Not a huge

amount. About the same as a year's pay for an electricity company chief
. . .

And no one could ever know. No names. Nothing in writing. A secret between him and Stephen which neither would ever reveal because each had as much to lose. A secret that had been as safe as houses, until Bowen fell into the hands of monsters who could make a man reveal anything.

The buzzer went.

'The assistant commissioner's here, prime minister.' His personal secretary's voice. 'But I'd like a quick word myself first if I may.'

'Of course. Come on in.'

The secretary was late thirties, five feet ten, curly hair and contact lenses. A grammar school boy.

'It's Mrs Bowen,' he explained. 'She's rung twice. Wants to see you. You've been so busy today . . .'

'Yes quite. But yes, I *must* see her. Poor Sally. What's it about, d'you know?'

'She wouldn't say. Book her in first thing tomorrow, possibly?'

'You've got my diary . . .'

'Nine o'clock then. I'll ring her. And one more thing. The foreign secretary's coming over in ten minutes . . .'

'Oh.'

What was *that* about, he wondered?

'Thank you. I'd better see David Stanley quickly.'

'I'll bring him in.'

The assistant commissioner was dressed in a dark grey suit. Normally he wore uniform for a meeting with the PM but there'd been no time to change.

'Come and sit down, David,' Copeland said, pointing to a floral print armchair. 'Good of you to come over. I'm sure you're as pressed as I am.'

'Indeed, prime minister,' he replied sharply. His place was back at the Yard, not here.

'Yes, well I had to know about this murder. For heaven's sake – high-powered rifles being loosed off in a London street – this is one hell of an escalation.'

'It is sir. And makes us increasingly certain there's an Irish connection with the Revenue Men. First it was Semtex. Now an Armalite.'

'But you're no nearer finding them.'

'Well, I wouldn't say that,' he replied testily. 'But arrests aren't imminent. However,' he continued quickly, 'in the Bowen case we do have a man in custody . . . Ricky Smith, the TV technician who beamed the pictures to the News Channel. Picked him up at Waterloo station at midday.'

'Excellent. Has he talked?'

'No. Not a word. But we found a piece of paper in his pocket with some figures on it. Turned out to be a reference number for a package on a flight from Bali that landed at Heathrow this afternoon.'

Copeland's eyebrows rose expectantly. Stanley took in a deep breath. The news he'd brought was not pleasant.

'The package contained a human ear, prime minister. We believe it belongs to Stephen Bowen.'

'Oh, my God!'

'And there was a note with it. This is a photocopy.' He reached into an inside pocket and extracted a single sheet of A4 folded down the middle.

As Copeland read it a wave of nausea engulfed him.

You want Mr Bowen back? We send him to you, one piece each day. Signed OKP.

'My God! They're monsters!' He wrung his hands. 'Where is he, David? Where have they got him?'

Stanley scratched the side of his face. 'We're waiting to hear from DS Randall. If Mr Bowen's on Kutu, Randall will find him, I have every confidence of that.'

The secretary buzzed again. The foreign secretary had arrived. Relieved, Stanley got up to go. The two visitors nodded to one another as they passed in the doorway. Copeland waited until the door was closed.

'What's up then, Hugh?'

He despised Foreign Secretary White. He'd appointed him because of his reputation for gravitas rather than for his ability, which was slight. The man was a cipher, but, he feared suddenly, potentially dangerous.

Tall and skinny, White savoured what he was about to say.

'Tomorrow my department will be issuing a statement on overseas aid, Keith. Featured prominently in it is the loan to Indonesia for the construction of the power station on Kutu. You'll remember the project. *My* department opposed it as being too controversial, but *you* pushed it through Cabinet. Well, tomorrow, I think the press are going to be asking you why you did.'

16

Hotel Touristik, Kutu
Thursday 05.45 hrs

CHARLIE AWOKE WITH a start. For several seconds she didn't know where she was. Then Nick's light snoring reminded her. She turned towards the sound. A trace of dawn light filtered through the fanlight above the door to the room, just enough to show the mountain of his bare back. She wanted to snuggle up to him again, to draw comfort from that mound of bone and muscle – but she didn't, knowing that to do so was taboo.

The bridal suite was spacious but windowless, kept cool and fresh by an air-conditioning unit. In the middle was the king-size bed on which they lay, with a headboard of padded white plastic.

She began to wonder what the man in the next room had made of it last night – their ludicrous faked orgasms struggling to be heard against the babble of a TV soap in Bahasa.

After their glutinous meal they'd taken turns in the bathroom, making the most of the half-blocked shower and scratchy towels. Then, dressed in clean briefs and a T-shirt, with a dab of Amarige on her neck, she'd joined her notional husband under the thin top-sheet, more unnerved than ever by the thought of the monster listening next door.

The room had been in darkness apart from the TV glow in the corner. Too dark Randall had said for a camera to see them. *Sound would be enough.*

As soon as he'd said it, she'd realised there wasn't going to be any intimacy between them. For a moment she'd felt hurt. Embarrassed even at having made her readiness to perform so obvious. Then she'd told herself quickly that it really didn't matter a row of beans if he wasn't attracted to her. This was work. Nothing else.

During their desultory theatricals, they'd lain side by side not touching. Then Nick had switched off the TV, and they'd listened to the rattle of the air-conditioning, hovering on the brink of sleep.

In the darkness Charlie's fears had begun to multiply again. The terrors that had come and gone through the day – eyes that stared, uniforms and guns, imagined torture chambers. From the sound of Nick's breathing she'd known he was still awake too. A hug was what she needed. For comfort and security, nothing else.

She'd risked a whisper. 'How about a little cuddle?' He'd hesitated, as if even that might be unprofessional, but had then rolled towards her, holding her briefly, a hand on her shoulder, letting her cheek rest against his chest, but keeping their nether regions chastely apart. Then he'd quickly turned away again, mumbling 'g-night'.

She'd got the message. For him, everything they did together was to be strictly business.

Eventually the rattle of the air-conditioning had become hypnotic and she'd dozed off.

Then a couple of hours later she'd been woken by his laboured breath against the back of her neck, the weight of his arm round her waist and his fingers loosely cupping her breast. She'd kept very still, knowing he was asleep, knowing that while he stayed that way she could draw the comfort from his body that he'd denied her earlier. Very slowly so as not to wake him, she'd eased the ridge of her spine back into the curve of his stomach. He was erect.

They'd lain like that for a while, their breathing synchronised. Feeling the pressure of his body rise and fall, Charlotte had imagined a bond growing osmotically between them that might yet ensure his protection when the crunch came.

He'd rolled away from her eventually, mumbling nonsense words. She'd lain awake a little longer, keeping as close as she dared without waking him, dogged by the self-mocking thought that going to bed with a man as a security blanket seemed to be becoming something of a habit. That thought triggered a string of others – Jeremy, the newsroom, her cat, her father – everything peeling like damp wallpaper from the back of her mind.

Then she'd slept again. Until now.

Nick was woken by the clatter of a bucket in the courtyard outside. In his dream he'd been with Debbie, driving through Wimbledon searching for a Chinese takeaway that had moved.

For a few woozy seconds he assumed it was Debbie in the bed beside him and slung his arm round her. His hand closed on a breast that was small and quite firm. Debbie's were like soft cushions.

He pulled back his hand, abruptly remembering where he was and who he was with. Charlie gave him a knowing look that made him spin fast through his memory. But it was OK. He *had* behaved.

'Hi,' he croaked, groggily. 'Forgot where I was for a minute. Sleep OK?'

'On and off.'

Randall had wanted her very badly last night. He'd yearned for the pleasure she would give him, like an alcoholic did for whisky. Lying there after the TV was off, listening to the lightness of her breathing, her fresh-washed smell enhanced by some scent or other, his mind had kept saying – *can't do any harm, she wants it too, so why not, for God's sake?* The *job* was why. And Debbie was why.

He sat up and blinked towards the daylight coming in above the door. Then he looked down at the floor beneath it. He rubbed his eyes to clear them. Something had been pushed under the gap like a morning paper.

He extracted his legs from beneath the sheet, swung them from the bed and crossed the room. A plain brown envelope. No writing on it. Flap sealed.

Concealing it from Charlotte, he took it into the bathroom, closed the door and switched on the light. Gingerly, out of habit, he felt the envelope to see if it was thick enough to hold the components of a bomb. Too thin. He slit the flap with the nail file Charlie had left on the shelf above the basin.

He frowned. Nothing inside the envelope except a small plastic folder which looked strangely familiar.

'Christ,' he growled, realising suddenly what it was.

He tilted the envelope so the folder slid into his hand. Holding it by its edges to avoid smudging prints, he opened out an English driving licence. The name printed on it – *Stephen John Bowen*.

He goggled.

Brad Dugdale's words came flooding back. '*What'll you do if you find something. Tell the PM?*' Then the fleeting smile in the bar last night. '*Evidence? Maybe you'll get lucky . . .*' No wonder Dugdale knew where they were staying. He'd made it his business to find out.

Randall stared down at the licence. Evidence yes. But of what? That Bowen was here, or simply that someone wanted them to think he was? And *had* Dugdale stuck the envelope under their door himself? Too bloody dangerous, surely . . . If the police had caught him with it, he'd be done for.

There could be another explanation of course. That it wasn't Dugdale at all. That word had got to Soleman Kakadi that there were Brits in town and the OKP chieftain had decided to make contact. A supporter amongst the hotel staff, perhaps. The waitress in the restaurant, even. Picked their room simply because she knew they were British. But odd to leave no message. No way of communicating, of opening a dialogue. Without that, what was the point?

He slipped the licence back into the envelope.

Urgent that he phone London, but not from the hotel. Overseas calls from Kutu might all be monitored, but a public phone would be safer than here. There was the Telkom office down by the harbour.

Then what? Break cover and take the licence to the local police? No way. He'd be shoved on to the next plane out. Deciding what to tell the Indonesians was for London to handle.

Should he sit around the hotel then, hoping that whoever had slipped him the licence would make themselves known? Not with intel sniffing about.

No. There was only one thing to do. Find Dugdale again. Beard him with the licence and tell him to come clean.

Randall heard a smoker's cough from the bedroom. Charlie mustn't know about this yet. Couldn't risk her feeding news of it to the News Channel. He folded the envelope as small as he could then stuffed it into his washbag.

He filled the basin to shave. He could sniff her perfume from somewhere. After a moment or two he realised the smell was coming from him.

Piri town centre
08.05 hrs (00.05 hrs GMT)

In daylight the harbour square had been transformed into the bustling market place they'd got the whiff of last night. *Bemos* cruised through the crowd, their money-collectors leaning out for business.

They'd come here because he needed to phone, he'd told her. He'd not said why. Bowen's driving licence was hidden in his money belt.

The sun burned the tops of their heads as they walked through the throng – men in dark trousers, women in bright cotton skirts. Most of the chatter was in Kutun, a language unconnected with the Malay that Randall understood. Faces turned to stare. The white man was clearly still a stranger here. Nick began to see differences in the islanders. The native Kutuans had boxy, aboriginal looks, the neater Malay faces belonged to Javan *transmigrasi*, here to work on the mine.

At the Touristik Hotel they'd been served breakfast by their waitress from last night, her face this morning brightened by a smile like a melon slice. Randall reckoned he'd seriously misread the noughts on the banknote he'd given her. But the girl had been *too* smiley, too easygoing. Couldn't have been she who'd slipped the envelope under their door. If there was an OKP activist in the hotel it wasn't her.

Charlie had been quiet at breakfast. Worrying about her father, she'd said.

They reached the Telkom office with its banks of direct-dial phones. Randall didn't want Charlie hovering when he made his call.

'Hey, why not take some shots of the market while I'm on the blower,' he suggested. 'Tourists do it all the time. Could be good background stuff.'

'Won't fit in,' she countered. 'Anyway I don't want to get more noticed than's inevitable.'

'Well what about getting us a couple of drinks?' There was a stall outside selling sodas.

'I'll stick with you if you don't mind,' she insisted.

He'd overdone it. Made her suspicious. They stepped into the air-conditioned cool of the telephone office.

'Well, hold the camera-bag, then,' he said brusquely, giving it to her.

'Aren't you worried the phone'll be bugged?' she whispered, slipping the strap over her shoulder.

'Yes chuck, but I've no choice.'

Randall queued to buy a phonecard then took it to a booth and dialled. The number answered at the third ring. Just after midnight in London.

'*Hello?*' Mostyn's voice. Working late.

'Hello! This is Nick.'

'*Oh, hi! Havin' a good holiday?*'

'Yeh! It's great. Beautiful place.' Sticking to the legend. Chatty – like a bloke on honeymoon. 'Hot as hell, mate. Hot as hell. But you know what? I got given something this morning. Something belonging to Bob. His D.L.'

'*Oh really? How's this line, by the way?*'

'Not too good.'

'*Right . . .*' Care needed. '*So, you reckon Bob's there?*'

'Looks that way. I'm trying to find out. Be nice to meet up with him. Bugger owes me a beer! Any messages?'

'*Yes. One from the Vauxhall bloke you rang yesterday . . .*' Vauxhall. Vauxhall Cross – SIS HQ – Harry Maxwell. '*Said things could be more complicated than we thought. Said it may involve big wheels.*'

'Any names?' Have to risk it.

'*Yes. Got a pen?*'

'Shoot.'

'*I'll spell it. S-U-M-O-T-O. Said you'd know the name. It was in the brochure you took away with you.*'

'I do,' Randall frowned, surprised. 'Any explanation?'

'*No. May be a connection, that's all. Said to listen out for the name. And watch your health. Lots of nasties about, he said. Oh, and you asked him about another feller.*'

'Yes.'

Brad Dugdale.

'*They have heard of him. Specialises in underwater archaeology. Seems to have something big on 'cos he's been trying to hire heavy lifting gear in Australia. Wants to make a TV documentary about it.*'

'Does he now!' So Dugdale had a TV connection. 'That it?'

'*No. There's more. The boss here has reconfirmed the export order, so Bob may not have much of a future. And related to that, we've found the bloke who was the er . . . distributor in Europe . . . Know who I mean?*'

'Yes.' Ricky Smith.

'*He's told us bugger all, but he had something on him that used to be Bob's. A hearing device.*'

'Oh, fuck!'

'*Nice people. So keep in touch.*'

'I will. Any of this public yet?'

'*The fact that we've got hold of the European distributor, yes. But no names and nothing about the body part.*'

He rang off. So, Bowen had been as good as condemned to death and the terrorists had begun cutting him up. Animals!

Concentrate. Sumoto. He racked his brains to remember the biog from the SIS file. A major general. Former military commander at this end of the archipelago, now head of procurement at the Defence Ministry in Jakarta. A key figure in swinging the arms deal to Britain instead of France. Sumoto was on *our* side – that was the main point, so how on earth could he be involved in the kidnap?

Baffled, he decided he'd better move.

He swung round – and collided with Charlie. She blocked him, her face flushed. She'd heard what he'd said.

'Who's Bob?' she demanded. 'It's Bowen, right? And what's D.L. stand for?' In her pouch-pocketed, fawn bush shirt and fawn slacks she looked like a little girl who'd dressed up in battledress to look tough.

'Not here,' he whispered, jerking his head towards the door.

'Yes. Here. Tell me. Then it's *my* turn to phone,' she said petulantly.

'No way, love.' He took her arm and hustled her outside. The heat hit them again like an open oven.

'Know what you are, Nick?' she seethed, wrenching her arm free. 'A cheating bastard.'

'Hang on a minute . . .'

'No. *You* hang on. We had a deal, remember? I keep quiet about who you are, you keep me up to speed with the story!'

They were being stared at. Couples didn't do their squabbling in public in this part of the world.

'Cool it,' Nick breathed, moving her away from the Telkom office. 'I was going to tell you . . .'

'Oh yes? When?'

'Now. After I'd made that call.'

'Right. Well here's your big chance.'

He guided her away from the staring crowd, towards the side-street where Captain's Bar was.

'Look, you're right. Bob is Bowen. Somebody stuffed his driving licence under our door this morning,' he muttered. 'Could've been an OKP sympathiser in the hotel, could have been Dugdale. I'm about to try to find out. But you can't use any of this. You know that.'

She did. But it wasn't the point. His grey eyes and firm-set chin had that stony look again. The one that shut her out. So much for nocturnal osmosis.

A dark green truck full of shiny-helmeted soldiers entered the square, the crowd parting respectfully to let them through. Randall shrank back, fearing it was them the soldiers had come for. Then the lorry drove into the port. A guard change.

Suddenly he began to look around as if taking in the sights. Intel would be here somewhere. He spotted them quickly. Not hard to see. No attempt at concealment. Two men sitting on the steps of a bank. Javan faces, eyes accustomed to instilling fear. One of them got up and ambled towards the Telkom office. To check what number he'd rung, Randall guessed.

Big wheels. General Sumoto. What on earth had Maxwell meant? He'd have to ring him direct. But first he had to pin Dugdale down.

At Captain's Bar the door was locked. Nick hammered on the blue-painted wood, then tapped more gently on the bottle-glass above it. Eventually he heard the lock turn.

A man opened it. In his twenties, chest like a gorilla, but the same flat face as Teri. Could be a brother.

'Bar closed,' he scowled. He made to shut the door again, but found a foot in the way.

'I want to see Brad,' Randall insisted, holding up the scuba-diving brochure Dugdale had given him last night.

'Brad no here.'

There was a movement in the half-darkness inside the bar. A woman cleaning the tables.

'Teri!'

She looked up, then came to the door muttering in Kutun. Standing beside one another it was obvious they were siblings.

'Brad not here,' she repeated.

Charlie leaned close to Nick's ear. 'We've got company,' she whispered.

He glanced round and saw the intel men strolling towards them.

'Look, last night I fixed with Brad to see him this morning. To book some diving.'

Teri looked past him, saw the policemen, said a few words to her brother and he stood back. Inside, the bar smelled of the bleach she'd been using as a cleaner.

'Where is Brad?' Nick demanded when the door was relocked behind them.

'Not here.' Teri positioned herself behind the counter. 'Back tomorrow maybe. When you want to dive? This my brother Dedi. He can take you.'

Dedi's muscle-packed frame was squeezed into blue shorts faded by the sun and a striped T-shirt.

'We want to talk to Brad, Teri. Can you get him?'

She laughed nervously. 'I tell you he not here.'

'Why don't you go and have a look? Maybe he's upstairs . . .' Randall snapped.

Teri frowned, puzzled he should disbelieve her. She spoke in Kutun to her brother, a twangy, complaining sound. Then Dedi rounded on Nick, hands on hips, chin thrust forward.

'Brad back tomorrow, maybe. What you wan', Mister?'

They were telling the truth. He realised that now. Brad must have deliberately taken himself off for the day to keep out of their way. His suspicions grew.

'OK. No Brad,' he conceded.

Back to plan A. To contact the priests in the hope of finding a way through to Soleman Kakadi. Maybe these two could help.

'Teri. Yesterday in Darwin Brad and Jim Sawyer gave us the name of some priests. We want to get in touch. Can you tell us where to find them?'

Teri looked distinctly uneasy. 'I just work in this bar, Mister,' she protested. 'Kutu very dangerous place. Best thing keep away from trouble. Men outside – they watching you.'

'Teri . . . we have to contact Soleman Kakadi,' Randall insisted. 'Through the priests is the only way we know of doing it.'

Teri rocked her head for a long while. Then she seemed to have an idea. She whispered to her brother, suggesting something which he strongly resisted. Eventually she seemed to half convince him.

'We not know how you find Soleman Kakadi,' she said formally. 'But maybe best you talk with Father Pius Naplo.'

'Church of Santa Josef?' Randall checked.

'Twenty kilometres from Piri,' she told them, keeping her voice low. 'You have to pass where they build new harbour. Many soldiers there, because OKP make damage. ABRI block road. But tourists can pass if they with guide, to go to beaches at Santa Josef. For diving . . .'

Nick understood at last. He turned to her brother. '*You* can take us there?'

Dedi looked distinctly uninterested.

Nick dipped into the pocket of his thin slacks and extracted a folded wad of money. He peeled off 100,000 rupiah, the equivalent of thirty pounds. Dedi was still unmoved. Nick doubled it.

'OK,' the Kutuan sighed, eyes flickering at what to him was a huge sum. 'I take you to beach at Santa Josef. For *diving*.'

'Sure. But the church is nearby? We could walk to it?'

'Next to beach,' Teri explained. 'Next to home for orphan children.'

'Orphans . . .? Because of the fighting?' Charlotte checked, seeing an opportunity for some meaningful pictures.

Teri looked uncomfortable. 'Some there because of fighting. Yes.'

'We go now?' Randall pressed. Time was whirling by.

'Maybe ten minutes,' said Dedi. 'I must get equipment ready.'

Air bottles rattled in the back of Dedi's blue minibus as the wheels hit potholes on the coast road out of Piri's centre. A smelly outboard hung from a rack. On the roof was an upturned inflatable. In the bay to their left the sea bobbed with fishing boats at anchor. On the driftwood-littered beach, outrigger canoes soaked up sun between coconut palms.

Randall felt he was floundering. Too much about this case that he didn't understand. Bowen's licence – Dugdale – General Dino Sumoto – Soleman Kakadi. Was there some link between them or not? He was running out of time to find out. The chances must be high by now that Bowen was already dead. He looked out to sea.

'Are Brad's boats out there?' he asked, sitting in the front next to Dedi.

'Ya. See two boats?' Dedi took a hand from the wheel to point. Moored away from the fishing fleet, a fast-looking power boat with a high bridge was tied alongside a larger schooner with a roomy superstructure at the stern.

'Which one's the *Morning Glory*?'

'Big one.' A light swell had set its mast rocking.

'What's it used for? Brad said it was out of commission?'

'Brad have big plan,' Dedi told him. 'Year ago he find small submarine used by Aussies when Japs here. Very deep. Need special gear. He going to put it on *Morning Glory*. Use her as salvage ship. He make movie 'bout it. For TV. He say I can be star,' he concluded with a modest smile.

Wartime minisub – Special Ops. No wonder Dugdale had got on to the files of the intelligence services.

'Does he have permission?'

'Soon. Permission come soon, he think.'

In the meantime, out there at anchor was a big, roomy boat. A perfect place to stash a hostage. Randall stroked his chin.

No. *That* brainwave made no sense whatsoever. Involving himself that deeply would be *far* too big a risk for Dugdale to take. He remembered the man's fear when the soldiers stormed into the bar last night.

Charlie sat behind him on the middle bench. She leaned forward, resting her arm on the back of his seat so her mouth was close to his ear. He smelled a little of sweat, but not unpleasantly.

'What was the news from London,' she asked, trying to sound casual.

Randall quickly selected something to tell her. 'Bad news for Bowen. The government's reconfirmed the arms deal.'

'Oh God! So . . . so he's a dead man. Or will be soon,' she whispered.

'I fear so. One other thing – and this isn't public yet – we've picked up a bloke called Ricky Smith. He's the satellite freak who beamed the videos to your lot at the News Channel.'

'Wow. That's something.' The name was vaguely familiar, but she couldn't place it. 'Who is he? What's he said?'

'Nothing yet. And I suspect he's just a gofer.'

'For whom? I mean . . . Jesus! I'm lost, Nick,' she confessed. 'Have to admit I simply do not understand what's going on.'

'Makes two of us.'

She didn't for one moment believe him. 'That driving licence of Bowen's,' she pressed, 'what's your hunch about where it came from?'

'I just don't know, Charlie. And that's the plain truth.'

Was it? Or was he just stringing her along? She sat back, arms folded.

She felt desperately isolated with no other hacks around. Either it meant she was on her way to the scoop of a lifetime, *or* there was a damn good reason she was here on her own. Like the others were covering the *real* story somewhere else . . . Fear gripped her that she'd got it *wrong*. Then she stuffed it to the back of her mind. At least they were on the move now, following leads. *And* she was with her personal detective. However secretive he might be, they were together, going to the same places, covering the same ground. Not even Kate Adie could have bettered that.

Anyway, instinct told her they *were* on the right track. They *would* get to Kakadi. It *would* be an exclusive. This *was* going to make her career.

Still had nothing on tape though. Couldn't be happy until she'd got some shots down. She checked over the camera bag, making sure the leads from the stud lens were connected to the hidden camcorder.

'Heyup!' growled Randall suddenly.

She followed his look. They were on the edge of town. Burning tyres blocked access to side turnings. A grid of streets, tin-roofed shacks, and not a soul in sight. Charlie jabbed on the recorder and swung the strap to the window.

'This Poteng,' Dedi intoned, jabbing his foot on the accelerator. 'Last night ABRI they shoot two boys here. Arrests. Many arrests.'

No troops now and in a few seconds they'd passed the area. Charlie replayed her brief shots through the viewfinder, then frowned with disappointment. Too fast. A blur. Nothing usable.

'Why so many arrests?' Randall asked. 'Why now, Dedi?'

The Kutuan answered without hesitation. 'Because of Englishman.'

Randall stroked his chin. If ABRI were rounding so many people up to grill them about the kidnap it could mean they were as baffled by it as he was. He looked at Dedi, trying to guess where his sympathies lay. He decided to test him with a name.

'Sumoto,' he asked out of the blue. 'You know him, Dedi? General Dino Sumoto?'

Charlie perked up her ears. Something *else* Randall hadn't told her about.

The Kutuan's reaction was instant. He flexed his hands and blew through pursed lips. 'Bad man, bad man,' he muttered. 'When he boss KODAM Twelve, that when we begin have troubles. Anybody who against KUTUMIN, Sumoto send soldiers to take him and beat him. *Mayjen* Sumoto, he want the mine very much, because it make him very rich. He buy land cheap, then sell to KUTUMIN for big profit.'

'I see. But he's not here now. Has a new job. In Jakarta.'

'Ya . . .'

There was a *yes, but* in the way Dedi said it. Then he tensed up, hunching his gorilla shoulders and stepping on the brake.

A roadblock. They'd reached the site for the new harbour. Soldiers in the road with automatics, levelled at their windscreen. Beyond, they could see heavy trucks manoeuvring. Somewhere nearby a pile driver thumped rhythmically.

When they stopped, a policeman in dark glasses and knife-edge creases came to the window. He stared in to see what they had with them, checked Dedi's papers, then shoved open the rear door.

'*Paspor*,' he asked. 'Where you go?'

'To the beach. Diving.' Randall pointed to the gear in the back. The policeman nodded. He flicked quickly through their passports like a man just going through the motions.

He knew all about them. Been told they were coming. The realisation made Randall uncomfortable. Shouldn't have surprised him. Intel had repeatedly proved their thoroughness.

They were waved through. The road traversed the construction site. Giant earth movers levelled the shore and rust-red, steel piles reached into the sea for a new jetty. The site was dotted by sandbagged sentry posts, with roofs of palm fronds. To their right a new road of red earth cut a swathe through the lush foothills which rose sharply to a ridge of dense forest.

Good bandit country.

Beyond the harbour, a large area set back from the shore had been cleared of trees.

'For power generator,' Dedi explained. 'They say it to make electricity for *all* people of Kutu, but we don't believe. It only for the mine, for places where mine workers live. They all Javans. No work at mine for people of Kutu, because they say we lazy,' he added bitterly. 'But not true. They afraid we sabotage mine because we no want it here.'

Afraid with justification, Randall guessed. Dedi's bitterness revealed precisely where his sympathies lay.

A second checkpoint as they left the site, then the tarmac ended and the road turned to dirt. The trees thinned and a broad beach of fine sand curved away to the left. The minibus bumped on to a long wooden bridge that crossed a dry river bed.

'KUTUMIN going to use this river to wash poison from the mine into the sea,' Dedi announced acidly. 'Diving finished here then.'

'Hey, can we stop a minute?' Charlie asked. 'I'd like a shot of this.'

Dedi hummed uncertainly. He looked behind to see if they'd been followed.

'Quickly, quickly,' he told her.

Charlie got out with the camcorder and took some shots to illustrate the environmental impact of the mine. Something on tape, even if she never used the shots. Made her feel better.

They continued, the track cutting inland through dense vegetation and hamlets of thatched, wood-framed houses. In the bare earth yards, small pigs dug for roots under flame-flowered trees. Then the road dipped again. They'd crossed an isthmus and the wide blue sweep of the coast was back in view. Islands of black rock lay a kilometre or two off the coast.

Charlie was brooding about the name that Randall had come out with, her suspicions growing like algae.

'Who's General Sumoto, Nick?' she asked sharply.

'Bloke who used to run this place, chuck,' he replied curtly.

'That much I gathered, *ducky*. But why were you asking about him?'

Nick turned to her. 'Nothing special love, honest.'

Like hell, she thought. Later. She'd try him again later. Ahead lay Santa Josef.

According to the guidebook, the village had been settled two hundred years ago by Portuguese missionaries as a fever treatment centre. Today it was a decrepit huddle of semi-derelict houses, with the church and sanatorium set back from the road at the far end.

They passed through it, then Dedi swung the minibus on to the beach and stopped by a giant fig tree.

'I make boat ready,' he said stiffly, opening the rear doors. 'Maybe you like take walk now?' He nodded towards the church. Behind it, through a dip in the distant ridge they saw the far-off, smoking crater of Mount Jiwa.

They approached the long, low, stone-built sanatorium. From inside came the sound of children chanting. The central doors had been hooked open to let air circulate. Inside, the once-white walls were flaking and stained. A bespectacled nun in mid-blue habit bustling along the corridor jumped at the sight of them.

'*Selamat pagi*,' Nick smiled.

'*Selamat pagi*,' she replied, pushing the glasses up her broad, flat nose. '*Saya mencari bapak Pius Naplo.*'

Randall hoped his Malay made sense. He'd asked for the priest. She beckoned with a downward motion of the hand. They followed her.

The dark terracotta floor tiles needed sweeping. On the left were dormitories. Some had iron-framed beds, others just soiled mattresses side by side on the floor. There was a smell of urine.

Then out into the sun's glare again, across a paved yard to a small modern house. The sister opened the fly screen and tapped on the door frame. The Kutuan who opened it had short, curly hair and gold-framed glasses. Mid-thirties, he wore a plain shirt and dark trousers.

The nun spoke a few words in Kutun then left them.

'You want speak me? I am Father Pius Naplo,' he asked, agitated. His English was heavily accented. He beckoned them into a small office, equipped with fax machine and a PC.

Randall explained they were journalists.

'They allow you in?' Naplo looked surprised.

'We're here as tourists,' Charlie added.

'Ah. Of course. Then take much care. Why you come to me?' he asked, his knowing eyes belying the innocence of his query.

'The British government minister who's been kidnapped . . .' Randall explained.

'Mr Bowen.' He waved a hand towards his hardware. 'I keep in touch. Internet.'

'So we heard. From Jim Sawyer.'

Naplo gave a nod of recognition.

'Father, we want your help. Something mysterious happened last night. A document belonging to Stephen Bowen was put under the door of our hotel room.'

Naplo's face gave nothing away.

'A driving licence. It seemed like a message from his kidnappers. As if they were giving us proof that he's here on Kutu.'

Suspicion crossed the priest's face like a squall.

'Why you come tell *me* this?' he demanded. ABRI intelligence was not beyond using foreigners as spies.

'Because we think whoever did it must work for Soleman Kakadi . . .' Charlotte explained carefully. 'And we thought you could help us find him.'

Naplo raised his hands in a feeble protest. 'Me? Why? I am priest. We care for orphan children here.'

'. . . orphans of the OKP,' Nick pointed out. 'You must be in touch with them.'

Naplo stared down at his empty desk.

'When you see Jim Sawyer?' he checked.

'Yesterday. He said to contact you rather than Junus Bawi because you hadn't been arrested recently.'

A thin smile crossed Naplo's face then vanished again.

'You think it is Soleman Kakadi who take prisoner Mr Bowen . . .' He sounded as if they'd confirmed his own fears. He glanced at his wristwatch and then through the window as if looking out for someone.

'It looks that way. Won't know for sure until we ask him.'

Naplo seemed undecided. He tapped his finger nails on the desk, then stood up abruptly.

'The man who bring you here, the guide, what his name?'

'Dedi. He works . . .'

'I know him . . .' He made up his mind. 'Wait here please.' He pushed open the door and crossed the yard to the orphanage.

'What's going on?' Charlie whispered.

Randall shook his head. He looked round the room. Against the back wall a low bookcase contained UN Human Rights Commission reports and a handbook from the International Committee of the Red Cross. Above it hung a print of a madonna.

Three minutes later the priest strode back across the courtyard, dressed now in a white cassock and clerical collar. He wasn't alone.

The Kutuan who followed him wore dark-framed spectacles and was exceptionally thin. The white shirt he wore hung from him as if it had been put on a frame to dry.

'Hello,' he said in a soft, nervous voice, offering his hand. 'My name is Dr Junus Bawi.'

The dilapidated green minibus clattered up a rutted track into a banana plantation, then cut through gum trees towards the hills. Age and the elements had turned the machine's once shiny paint a dull matt.

At the back sat a terrified woman and a boy still below the age of puberty. The woman dabbed her eyes with a handkerchief.

'My wife and my son,' Junus Bawi murmured, turning his head towards them. Randall and Charlie were wedged beside him on the middle seat.

Father Naplo was driving. 'Hospital about one hour from here,' he told them, over his shoulder. 'Malaria, leprosy . . . You will see our work – and the valley that KUTUMIN want to fill with water.'

'Soleman Kakadi – he's at the hospital?' Randall checked.

'No. But not far away from the village,' Bawi confirmed. 'He will send someone to take us to him.'

Bawi had revealed he was on the same mission as they were. To find Kakadi. When Randall had told him of the sudden unexplained appearance of the driving licence, he'd looked sad. It seemed to confirm his fears about the depths to which his former partner had sunk. Yes, the licence could have come from Kakadi, he'd said. OKP sympathisers were everywhere, even in hotels watched by intel. Easy for someone to have got the licence to them.

'*You* think he's got Stephen Bowen?' Randall checked.

'I fear it . . . I fear it is true, because, you see, *ABRI* thinks it. When they interrogate me . . .' He looked away and bit his lip. '. . . not just me but everyone they arrest, they ask them where is Kakadi, where the Englishman? It is the reason I am here now. Because if Kakadi has done this, then it is urgent that I see him again. To tell him it is an evil thing. A thing *against* our people. ABRI is using it as a reason to beat us. To torture us. They will use it as a reason to turn their most terrible weapons against us.'

With his straight black hair, his heavy, earnest spectacles and his naïvely determined chin, the professor had the look of a missionary.

'Did they torture *you* when they arrested you on Monday?' Charlie asked softly.

The question was too abrupt. It pushed Bawi to the verge of tears. 'My son,' he choked, inclining his head towards the rear seat. 'They . . . they beat Obeth to try to make me talk.'

Charlie stole a glance behind. The boy was hunched forward, clinging to a handrail, his mouth set in a grimace of pain. *Had* to have some of this on tape, she told herself, but couldn't bring herself to ask.

The minibus reached the crest of a ridge, overlooking a wide sweep of coast behind them. Then it turned a corner. Straw-roofed houses straddled the road in a straggly village where barefoot women in long skirts carried firewood on their heads.

'Your wife and son,' Charlie asked suddenly. 'Why did you bring them with you?'

'Not safe for them to stay,' Bawi explained. 'You see, ABRI does not permit me to leave Piri. But I had to – to talk with Soleman. The only way to get out without being stopped was by fishing boat, last night. If Dana and Obeth had stayed, ABRI would have beaten them to make me come back. So it is better they are with me, even if now we are all exiles.'

'You're not going back to Piri?' Charlie asked.

Bawi stared through the window, seeing nothing, his mind in the back of that army truck on Monday night, looking back at his house, picturing with vile accuracy what Captain Sugeng was doing to his wife.

'No,' he murmured. 'We shall stay in the valley that is to be filled with water. With the people who live there, and if it is the will of the spirits we will die there.'

Charlie's jaw dropped. 'That's awful,' she breathed.

Bawi turned away so she wouldn't see his eyes.

The track became rougher. The forest began to envelop them, intensifying the sense of gloom and despair which Bawi's brooding presence cast upon them.

'Soleman Kakadi,' Randall asked gently. 'You and he were close friends once?'

Bawi stared ahead. For a moment Randall thought he hadn't heard him.

'It was four years ago that geologists discovered Kutu is rich with gold and copper. When the news spread, village headmen came to Piri to see the island's leaders,' he began, as if it was a well-rehearsed speech. 'They knew there would be a problem. The Kutuans in authority on the island had been put there by the Indonesian governor as puppets. Men who were told what to say and were paid for it. Those so-called leaders of ours said Kutu people wanted the mine, despite knowing that most islanders were against it.

'So the villagers who feared they would lose their land decided they must find another way to oppose the mine. They came to see us at the university – I and some colleagues, we were well known for defending the Kutuan culture and language against the Indonesian president's wish to make us like Javans.

'One of those village headmen who came to see us was Soleman Kakadi. He was a little older than me and he was strong. When he spoke, people stopped what they were doing and listened. He and I had many long talks. Out of them was born the idea of Organisasi Kutun Pertahanan with the two of us as leaders, he representing the farming people and me – well, representing the intellectuals, I suppose. The OKP was a *cultural* organisation. It had to be. Real political activity is banned in Indonesia, as you know. We gave ourselves the task of trying to make environmentalists around the world understand how much of Kutu would be destroyed by the mine. We had some success. But the pressure was not enough to change anything. A year ago KUTUMIN was given the rights to develop the mine.

'Something else happened at that time. Soleman Kakadi was having much trouble from ABRI. The soldiers used to search his village for weapons – he had none then. But they would break things and search the women by making them undress in front of all the men.

'Then Kakadi was told that his village which was close to the sea must be evacuated, because KUTUMIN needed the land for the workers coming to build the mine. Soleman refused to allow this. He was arrested and beaten. While he was in prison, ABRI burned down the village. Kakadi's people were given some money as compensation and taken to another island. Some, it is true, were happy to go – in every community there are people who can be bought – but many were not.

'When Soleman was released from prison and learned what had happened, he came to see me. He was on fire with anger. His lands

208

were gone and his family too. The money given for his crops was an insult. He came to me and said, Junus we must now fight. Talking is no good. We are losing. The only way to stop the mine is with guns and with explosives.'

Bawi sighed. It had been a policy of madness and desperation that Kakadi had embraced. But he now understood the passions that had driven him to it.

'He asked me to get help from my contacts in other countries. Asked me to arrange for weapons and uniforms to be smuggled into Kutu so that he could create a guerrilla army. I told him this was impossible. That nobody would help us that way. And that it was not right. Fighting, killing was never right. He was angry. He said I was like the rest. That I had been bought by the Indonesians. Then he left. That was the last time I saw him.

'One month later an ABRI supply convoy was ambushed. Crossing a bridge in the open country – Kakadi and his men had weakened it. The trucks fell into a river. That's how the OKP guerrillas got their first guns.'

He fell silent. There was no more to be said.

But there *was* more. Randall sensed it. Some other clue in this.

'You said it was ABRI that took away Kakadi's land,' he asked softly. 'What did they do with it? They *gave* it to KUTUMIN?'

For the first time, Bawi allowed a smile to cross his lips.

'No,' he muttered. 'They don't give anything. They sell. The commander of KODAM Twelve – *he* sold Kakadi's land to KUTU-MIN. People say he made millions of dollars for himself.'

'General Sumoto . . .' Randall breathed.

'Oh. You know of him?' Bawi asked, surprised.

'Beginning to . . .'

Charlie put a hand on his arm. 'Please tell me, Nick . . .' she begged. 'Just who is this guy Sumoto?'

Suddenly they were hurled forward as the priest braked sharply. Through the windscreen they saw the trail in front was blocked by logs.

'Christ, it's an ambush!' Randall growled, ducking instinctively.

Father Naplo looked unperturbed however. He killed the engine, then held up a hand for silence. Forest sounds replaced the grind of the motor; leathery leaves rattled, birds shrieked high in the canopy. Beyond the barrier, Randall spotted the conical muzzle of a machine gun poking through the scrub, and behind it, a pair of eyes.

Naplo listened through the open window, his ear turned the way they'd come, listening for some noise that would say if they'd been followed. Nothing. After more than a minute, four men in combat fatigues rose from the foliage clutching rifles.

The priest turned to his passengers in triumph. 'These are Soleman's men,' he beamed.

One came forward to shake the priest's hand, his wild black eyes firing darts of suspicion at the two white passengers. His face was thin and aboriginal, his features half hidden by hair and beard.

Naplo explained in Kutun who the strangers were, then the patrol leader grinned, exposing teeth stained red with betel juice. He reached in through the windows with rough, earthy hands.

'We can get out now,' Naplo announced, opening the driver's door.

Dr Junus Bawi was welcomed by the guerrillas with an embrace he seemed reluctant to accept. For a year he'd opposed what these men were doing. Now he was as much an outlaw as they were, but the fact of it would take some getting used to.

Suddenly a shout cut short the reunion. The guerrillas' smiles vanished, replaced by fear. The machine-gunner jabbed a finger at the sky, then with his fellows fled the open ground for the protection of the trees.

'Back in!' the priest shouted. 'Quick.' He scrambled into the driving seat.

Then the sound that had alerted the more sensitive ears reached the rest of them. The roar of a jet.

One foot on the step of the minibus, Randall held back and caught a glimpse of the small, grey dart flashing overhead. A British-built Hawk fighter.

He swung himself on to the seat next to Charlie. 'What's happening?' she hissed. 'Why are they so scared?'

'Frightened of being bloody bombed, that's why,' he growled.

Within seconds of the jet's passing, two of Kakadi's men rolled aside the logs blocking the road. The priest wound up the engine, then gunned through the gap and accelerated away in a cloud of dust.

Naplo half-turned his head. 'Maybe plane come back to attack,' he panted in explanation. 'OKP men they very scared.'

'Photo-reconnaissance more like,' Randall whispered to Charlie.

'Don't care what it's doing, if it comes over again, I need it on tape,' she whispered, lifting the grey holdall on to her knees. She unfastened the hidden pocket and pulled out the Handycam.

Naplo was driving like a madman, the suspension crashing and banging. Hot air and dust blasted in through the open windows.

'First time I see fighter plane here,' he told them nervously, half-turning his head.

As the track climbed, it narrowed so that branches scraped both sides of the vehicle. The path ran parallel to a boulder-strewn river, the water a trickle now, but it would be a torrent in the rains.

Ten more minutes and they emerged on to a plateau no wider than a football field. Maize grew in strips between banana plants, and pigs lay in the shade of acacia trees. Straight ahead where the road ended, was a handful of low buildings clustered round a tin-roofed church. The tiny, isolated settlement lay in a gap in the hills. Beyond they could see a wider valley and on the far horizon the simmering bulk of Mount Jiwa.

Relieved to have arrived unscathed, Naplo stopped the bus in front of a long, wood-framed building encircled by verandas, its roof daubed with a large red cross. At the side, fenced off from animals and children, Randall noticed two satellite dishes, a large one for TV reception, a smaller version for a satellite phone. Communications. Could prove extremely useful.

From the buildings and the planted areas, faces began to appear, alerted by the sound of the motor. Most were adults, some moving with difficulty, their limbs misshapen by leprosy.

'They will be curious,' Naplo stated. 'Not many visitors here.'

They got out and drank from their water bottles. 'Where do all the patients come from?' Charlie asked. A small crowd gathered at a respectful distance. Three children put hands to their mouths, awed by Charlie's blonde hair.

The priest swept an arm towards the volcano. 'Between here and Jiwa are many villages. And much disease. But soon no more. KUTUMIN will make this a lake. They build barrage here between the hills where it is narrow.'

Charlie decided she'd need some shots of this place. She switched on the Handycam and videoed the people who were to be driven from their homes.

Father Naplo led Bawi into the mission hospital. 'We'll find out if there has been word from Soleman,' he called over his shoulder. Bawi's son walked with him, wincing with pain. Charlie panned the camera over to them. The back of Obeth's shirt was criss-crossed with blood.

She switched off, sickened. 'That's horrific,' she murmured, sweating profusely. Randall nodded. 'My God! It's so unbelievably hot,' she went on a few moments later. She was beginning to wilt.

'Get in the shade and keep an eye on Bawi,' Randall told her. 'See what the news is of Kakadi. Give me the camera. I'll do some shots for you.' It was about time he gave her a hand.

'Well thanks. You know what I want?'

'Wideshots, close-ups and faces of villagers. Right?'

'That's about it.' She drifted away, glancing behind a couple of times to check that he knew what he was doing.

Randall took pictures of the valley, the hills and the church. Then he crossed to a grass-roofed hut where giggling children were helping their mother grind maize.

Suddenly, from behind him he heard a low rumble that built quickly to a roar. The Hawk was back.

Ducking for cover under the roof-overhang, he swung the camera towards the sky, the lens on wide. A black dot appearing above the trees, the fighter hurtled towards him, low this time, not more than five hundred feet up.

Eye to the viewfinder. The plane's dart entered the frame as if aiming for it. He zoomed in, following the Hawk across the sky, then pulled wide as it banked over the wooded peaks and climbed like a toy into the sun.

He ran back to the hospital. Around him the village stirred with nervousness.

'Get it?' Charlie came running out towards him.

'Yes.'

'Great.'

'Kakadi's blokes are already here,' she told him. 'And they're in a hurry.'

'Good. So am I.'

He packed the camera into the holdall. An ominous feeling gnawed his guts.

That was twice the Hawk had buzzed them. Twice. Dead overhead.

As if it were following them.

17

IT WAS THE minibus the fighter had tracked, Randall decided.
Followed the priest's dull green vehicle up from the coast like a
beacon.

Why? That was what worried him. Because of *them?* Or because of
Dr Junus Bawi?

They were on foot now, a small crocodile with Kakadi's men at front
and back heading for the dense forest where ABRI's foot-soldiers had
never ventured. Under the thick tree canopy they should soon be safe
from the watcher in the sky.

In single file, they climbed the side of the fertile valley that was to
become a lake – towards the distant hills that were to be blasted into
fragments for the ore they contained. From the position of the sun,
Randall knew they were moving east. He slung the camera bag round
so that it nestled in the small of his back.

The narrow, winding track skirted terraces of rice, bananas and
cabbages. Coconut palms rustled in disorderly clumps, and huge green
fruit hung from *nangka* trees. In the paddies men and women bent over
their work, their brown legs caked with mud, their heads shielded from
the sun by hats of straw.

Heavy clouds massed round the distant peak of Jiwa, but the sky
above remained scorchingly clear. The rainy season which was in full
spate elsewhere in the archipelago was still more of a threat here than a
reality.

Kakadi's men were nervous. Just two of them, boys almost, with wild
eyes and heads of stringy black hair, their bodies had been reduced to
skin, bone and sinew by the deprivation of life on the run. One carried
an assault rifle, the other a machete. Dressed in stained dark green, their
rolled-up trousers exposed wiry, muscular calves. The man at the rear
kept turning round to scan the ground behind with binoculars.

Before they'd begun their march, Randall had stuffed a hiker's
compass into his shirt pocket. He took it out now to check their
direction.

Charlie was glad of the walking boots she'd put on that morning. A twisted ankle would be no joke. Glad too of the long-sleeves that protected her arms from the sun and the sharp-edged scrub they were walking through. She slowed her pace until Nick drew level.

'Could do with some shots of me hiking with these guys,' she whispered. 'To cover my commentary links.'

'They won't like being filmed,' Randall replied.

'They won't know, if you do it with the bag.'

He swung the holdall forward, reached into the end pocket and touched the buttons. Charlie strode ahead again, trying to look intrepid without overdoing it. Nick videoed her for half a minute then switched off.

'No way of checking this without them knowing what we're up to,' he whispered.

'Can't be helped. Anyway, I trust you.'

Her soft brown eyes held his for longer than necessary. Randall smiled. He knew how desperate she was to penetrate his defences in the hope he would share his knowledge with her. He watched her walk ahead again, her compact body weaving lithely through the foliage. She'd smelled delicious in the bed last night. Resisting temptation had its down side.

The track petered out amongst tall ferns. In front loomed the dark wall of the woods. Guided by some feature in the foliage which only the young jungle fighters could recognise they slipped into its gloom, weaving between trunks and creepers.

For fifteen minutes they followed their escorts up the steepening slope, the sky almost invisible under the dense canopy of branches. Then they stopped abruptly, the lead guide muttering in Kutun and waving them to wait while he probed the trees for some marker left there earlier.

'They have put mines here,' Junus Bawi translated. 'In case we are followed. We must go round them. Stay very close.'

The guide found his tell-tales and led them thirty paces to one side through thick undergrowth, parting branches and fronds gently, the man at the rear ensuring the foliage swung back to leave no trace of their passing.

Soon they were climbing again. Then after ten minutes they paused to regain their breath in the sweltering heat and to drink from their water bottles.

Suddenly they froze, flasks to their lips, heads cocked to one side. Through the mesmeric chirping of the tree crickets there burned another sound, the whooping roar they'd come to dread. The Hawk was back.

Galvanised by terror, Kakadi's men shoved their three charges against the trunks of trees, where the overhead branches were at their densest.

'Fuck!' growled Randall as the jet crackled overhead, its thunder reverberating through the forest. The bugger was still on their tail, despite the protection of the trees.

Scared now, Charlie pressed herself against him. Without thinking, Randall put his arms round her.

Right on top, he thought. The plane was right on bloody top again.

'Is that damned thing following us?' Charlie whispered as the noise subsided.

'Yes. I've a nasty feeling it is.' He let go of her.

How, though? Could the pilot *see* them through the branches? Randall's knowledge of thermal imaging was minimal. No idea if the technology was up to it.

Kakadi's escorts huddled together, arguing. One kept pointing to the valley, wanting to turn back, but the man with the rifle didn't. And since he had the gun, he had the final say.

The reverberations faded. Bird screeches filled their ears again. The guides resolved their differences and relaxed a little, relieved the plane had passed without dropping bombs. Then they hurried the party onwards, driven by the desire to be somewhere else in case the Hawk returned.

They climbed for a further fifteen minutes. Then the ground levelled and the trees thinned. They'd reached a small clearing of long, dry grasses, a natural rendezvous in an anonymous forest.

'We wait here,' Bawi croaked. With his white shirt and library spectacles he appeared out of place in this wilderness. 'We stay under the trees. Soleman will come soon.'

He sat on a tree stump, hands clasped, cracking the joints of his fingers. For him, the moment of truth was near. For twelve months he'd argued against Kakadi's methods, so vociferously that at one point Soleman had threatened to have him killed. He'd changed his view now, but was far from sure of the welcome he would get. Particularly when he demanded that Stephen Bowen be freed.

Charlie found a square of ground free of ants and squatted, glad of the rest. It was an eerie place. The forest hummed and rustled, the air pierced by screeches. She felt eyes watching her, eyes of creatures she couldn't see. She glugged down more water and told herself to grow up.

She took stock. If all went well here, she would have the most amazing story, providing she could get her tapes out of the country. She stole a glance at Nick. He sat on a boulder deep in thoughts he was keeping to himself.

Always a mistake to think you can change a man, she reminded herself. Their jobs were chalk and cheese. His to *keep* secrets, hers to prise them out. So far he was winning hands down. A worrying thought struck her. What if she got something on tape which he didn't want her to broadcast? Would he try to stop her?

The tapes. Have to make sure they stayed in *her* possession, not his.

Randall stood up. In his head the name Sumoto reverberated like the gongs of the gamelan orchestra in the Touristik Hotel.

General Sumoto. The man who'd driven Soleman Kakadi to take to the jungle. '*Could be involved with the kidnap*,' Maxwell had said. *How? With* Kakadi or *against* him? A heavy feeling in his chest told him the situation was about to go pear-shaped.

He moved from his rock and crouched down by the professor. Fearful of being cut out again, Charlie slid over to join them.

'Dr Bawi, tell me . . . tell me about General Sumoto,' he stumbled, not sure exactly what it was he wanted to ask. 'He still has connections with Kutu?'

Bawi was taken aback. 'Why you ask about Sumoto?'

'Just curious.'

'Well . . . it is right you should be.'

Suddenly a strong gust of wind rattled the fronds of a tall palm on the other side of the clearing. Bawi looked at the sky, suspecting the approach of rain. Then he pointed at the shaking tree top.

'You know what Kutuan people say about that? Those rattling leaves? They say it is *Gundrowo*. The soul of a man who died in torment and can find no rest. He cannot reach the land of the spirits, so he shakes the palm trees in his rage.' Bawi furrowed his brow. 'Whether it is true or not I don't know, but I tell you, when General Sumoto was commander of KODAM Twelve, the noise in the palm trees used to keep me awake at night . . .'

'Gosh,' breathed Charlie, wishing she'd videoed him saying that.

Randall's chest tightened further. He wanted facts not fantasies. 'But now he's gone, does he still have influence here?'

Junus Bawi looked down at his hands. 'When a man's fingers have been so deeply steeped in the blood of this island, he remains a part of it until he dies,' he pronounced. Then he straightened up. 'Kutu, as you know, is in the ABRI military district of KODAM Twelve. When he was in command of it, General Sumoto used to call KODAM Twelve *his* army. There are many officers here who are still loyal to him.'

'Senior officers?' Randall checked.

'The ones who have the greatest power,' Bawi replied. 'Colonel Widodo. Chief of military intelligence . . .' In his mind he saw again the colonel's emotionless, wooden eyes watching his son's back being shredded by the cane.

'The chief of intel?' Randall croaked. 'He's Sumoto's man?' Suddenly the pieces began to fit. 'The arrests, the interrogations, they were all ordered by Colonel Widodo?'

'Yes, I think.'

'And it was *he* who convinced you that Soleman Kakadi kidnapped Stephen Bowen?'

'Well, yes, I suppose so,' Bawi confirmed, baffled by Randall's drift.

Sumoto. Just listen out for the name, Maxwell had said. Not enough. The clue should have been bigger. And now it was too bloody late. Whatever sort of circus Sumoto was running, they were all in the middle of it. All of them were his puppets.

'One other question. There's an Australian living in Piri. At one time I thought he had connections with the OKP. He's called Brad Dugdale? Does the name mean anything to you?'

Bawi looked further confused.

'I know the woman he lives with. But Mr Dugdale is a businessman. He must be friends with ABRI, not with us.'

Randall's mind flashed back to the jeep waiting in the alley when they'd arrived at the bar last night.

'Why do you say that?' he croaked, guessing the answer.

'Because to have a business in Kutu, you must pay ABRI money. The military controls everything, including business permits. And to get one, you must pay twice. An official fee, and a commission to the man who arranges it. It is how the officers live. ABRI wages are bad. The junior officers need the bribes to feed their families. But if you are a KODAM *commander* then the bribes can make you rich.'

From the woods they heard noises. Twigs snapping. Low voices.

'Nick!' Charlie hissed. 'They're coming. Camera!'

Randall ignored her. The links in the chain – they were nearly in place. He leaned forward.

'Brad Dugdale. Would *he* have known Sumoto? Paid him money?'

'Most certainly,' Bawi confirmed.

'Nick, for God's sake!' Charlie snapped. 'Film it or gimme the camera!'

Battledressed figures moving towards them through the trees. Nick rummaged for the Handycam, switched on and zoomed in.

Soleman Kakadi towered above his men, a striding black giant. He was dressed like them in grubby green battledress, a pistol holster on his webbing belt, a short-barrelled assault rifle slung across his chest. A handful of hungry-faced fighters hovered around him like pilot fish with a shark.

Through the lens Randall saw Kakadi's eyes lock on to the camera. Not the self-satisfaction of a man expecting a date with the media, but fear – and then anger.

Half a dozen men with him. No sign of Stephen Bowen. But then there wouldn't be, would there?

'Please,' Bawi said, flustered, 'let me speak with him first, alone.'

The professor rose unsteadily and moved towards his former partner, arms outstretched in greeting. Kakadi's face was a mask of suspicion. Then a stream of invective exploded from his mouth. Bawi recoiled. Kakadi pointed at the camera.

Randall swung it away. Kakadi's soldiers were fanning into firing positions to guard the rendezvous, their ageless, war-hardened faces nervous and watchful. Their weapons were modern FNCs, captured from ambushed ABRI patrols.

Randall was bowstring tense. He knew now they'd walked into a trap. What he didn't know was how it was to be sprung. Everything that had brought them up here, the hints, the suspicions – all of it could be sourced now to people connected with General Sumoto.

'I need to do a quick standupper,' Charlie whispered, touching Nick's arm and nudging him towards the brighter light of the clearing. Kakadi's fury she saw had subsided. He and Bawi were conversing less heatedly. 'Frame me to one side with the two of them in the background. OK?'

'Fine. Hang on. Warning light. Need to change the battery.'

He fumbled in the bag for the spare power-pack, brushing aside a loose AA battery from a walkman. Odd. Hadn't packed any. Must be Charlie's. He found the fresh nickel-cadmium cell and clicked it on to the camera.

'Ready?' he asked, anxious to get this over with.

'Ready,' she replied. The sun struck like a blow-torch as they stepped from the shade. She ran a hand through her hair, checked her clothing for undone buttons, struck an authoritative pose, then began.

'I'm standing in the very heart of the mountains controlled by Kutu's OKP guerrillas. The kidnapping of Stephen Bowen has split the Kutu resistance down the middle. Today the pacifist leader of the OKP's political wing has defied the house-arrest imposed on him by Indonesia's military rulers and has come up here to plead with his guerrilla counterpart for Stephen Bowen's release.'

She held her look, then he switched off.

'Just a scene-setter,' she said awkwardly. 'To show I'm here.'

Suddenly there was an angry shout, a frantic waving for them to get back under the trees. A black finger jabbed towards the sky.

Half a second later Nick heard the whistle-crack of the jet. The Hawk. Dead overhead like a homing pigeon. Followed them like an arrow, straight to the man ABRI most wanted dead – Soleman Kakadi.

'Film it! Film it!' Charlie shrieked, as they ran for cover.

'No way,' Randall panted. He wanted them out, now. Away from there before it was too late. But a flustered Junus Bawi beckoned them over. Kakadi wanted to leave in a hurry but would speak with them if they were quick.

'Straight in,' Charlie insisted. 'Interview. Still running?'

'Yep.'

'Hello, Mr Kakadi,' Charlie began, crouching in front of him. 'Charlotte Cavendish from the News Channel. Can you tell us, are you going to release Stephen Bowen?'

Kakadi's ebony face was blank, his chiselled expression haughty, his eyes withdrawn.

'He speaks no English,' Bawi explained, softly. 'But he has already told me . . . that he knows nothing about Mr Bowen.'

Charlie gaped.

'He . . . he doesn't *have* Stephen Bowen?' she stammered.

'No,' said Bawi, confused and embarrassed. 'The first that Soleman heard of the kidnap was from me when I sent the message yesterday that I wanted to meet him. You see, the batteries in their radios are dead. They have not heard any news for two weeks . . .'

Battery. Randall gulped. The loose one in the bag. The one that belonged to Charlie's Walkman. She hadn't *got* a bloody Walkman!

'Fucking hell!' Nick switched off and stood up. 'Everybody get out of here. Quick!'

Charlie turned, startled by his outburst. 'What's up?'

'They're coming! For him! For Kakadi. Tell him, Junus. It's a trap. The soldiers are coming!'

The whites of the guerrilla chief's eyes were streaked with malarial yellow. Bawi jabbered in Kutun, translating.

Then they heard it. All of them together. A sound from hell that turned their guts to water. The heavy thump-thump of twin-blade rotors. Randall switched the camera back on. Evidence. That's what he needed. Evidence on camera of a conspiracy still well beyond his comprehension.

Kakadi's head whipped towards the noise. On his face, the pain of betrayal, then hatred. He stood up, a murderous look in his eyes, his big

219

hands clamped round the stock of his FNC. He swung the barrel up to the firing position.

'Chri-ist!' Charlie cried as the muzzle levelled with her mouth.

Then, as suddenly as he'd stood, Kakadi spun away, hammering like a boar through the long, dry grass, yelling to his men.

Randall pointed the camera at his fleeing back. 'Get away from the clearing!' he snapped to Charlie. 'Into the trees.'

Just the three of them left. Him, the girl and Bawi. Kakadi and his men evaporating like tree spirits. Abandoning them to their fate.

The rotor clatter grew to a roar. He swung the camera towards it, then the mud-green machine filled his viewfinder, sweeping over the rim of the trees, chain gun poking out like the beak of a pterodactyl. Randall's stomach clenched. He knew what those guns could do.

'Fucking run!' he yelled.

Camera off, feet flying over roots and rocks, they fled into the dark of the forest hacking with their arms at the creepers. Thick foliage closed around them.

Then, behind, came a sound like an earthquake as the chain gun ripped the air.

'Down!'

Flat on the earth, Charlie's quivering breath beside him, the thunder of the gun made the ground shake. But the shells, Nick realised, weren't coming their way. Cautiously he rose to a crouch, found a gap through the leaves and aimed the camera. Framed by the lens, he saw flames spurt from the helicopter cannon, the spent cartridges cascading to the ground.

Just fifty metres away the shells smacked through the trees, splintering trunks. The gunner was firing blind, putting down a sweep of fire that would shred anything in its path. Including Kakadi and his men if they were there.

Then the UH-1 jinked away, its pilot running for cover, the chain gun falling silent. As the echoes died they heard the sharp crack of assault rifles, the OKP firing back.

Camera off. He thrust it at Charlie. 'Hold this a minute.'

'Oh my God,' she trembled. 'What are we going to do?'

There was one thing *he* had to do. His fingers dived into the grey bag, scrabbling round until they closed on the short, thin tube that he'd thought was a battery. He pulled it out. Even *looked* like a bloody battery . . . apart from the little wire trailing from it.

What a mug! Check, check. Standard Operating Procedure. And he bloody hadn't. Walked into this wasps' nest of a country like it was an

English village. SIS would piss themselves if they knew. He held out the device in the palm of his hand.

'What is it?' Charlie croaked.

'Tracer beacon. We left the camera bag in our room when we had breakfast this morning. We've been fucking bugged, Charlie. Followed every bloody inch of the way.'

He rose to a crouch again, wrenched his arm back and hurled the device towards the clearing.

The thunderclap of grenades way off in the trees threw him down again. They heard a shout, then a scream, then a long burst of automatic fire. Bawi clutched his head in his hands, certain he was about to die.

Through the foliage Randall saw two more helos skim the trees, heading to cut off Kakadi's retreat, their doors open, commandos poised to abseil through gaps in the canopy.

'Who, for Christ's sake?' Charlie gaped. 'Who put that bug in our bag?'

'Same person who put Bowen's passport under our door . . . Somebody with a bunch of airborne infantry at his disposal . . .'

'I don't understand . . .' she cried. 'You mean Sumoto? Who *is* he?'

Junus Bawi had lost his spectacles in the scramble through the trees. He blinked about like a mole, feeling for them on the ground.

'KOPASSUS,' he breathed. 'These men are KOPASSUS.'

The hard boys who don't take prisoners. That's what Dugdale had called them.

'It's what I told you,' Bawi wailed, 'the Javans are using Mr Bowen as the reason to destroy us.'

'But Soleman Kakadi hasn't fucking got Bowen,' Charlie screamed, despairing of ever understanding.

'No . . .' Bawi was boiling with hate now for the intel man who'd tricked him. 'That *is* the truth and you must report it on the news. Quickly. Tell the world before they kill us all.'

The only report on the news would be of their own deaths if they didn't get the hell out of there, Randall decided. First thing was to move further from the clearing before ABRI brought the helos in to lift out casualties.

'*Nick!* Tell me about Sumoto, for God's sake!' Charlie yelled.

No time. He was calculating how many soldiers there could be. Eight to ten in each aircraft. Maybe eight machines, a dozen at the most. So, sixty men. A hundred. Snatch squads, that's all. In quick. Kill or capture, then out quick before the guerrillas hit back. *Their* best chance was to find good cover and lie low.

Charlie, he saw, was now trembling like a leaf, hit suddenly by the desperateness of their plight.

'It's not *us* they're after, is it?' she whispered, hoping Bawi wouldn't hear. 'You and me, Nick. I mean *we*'ll be all right, won't we? What if we were to walk into the open waving something white and say we're British journalists? You speak the language, Nick.'

'The Geneva Convention doesn't work here, love,' Randall warned her gently. 'If we tell 'em we're journalists they'll put a bullet in our heads and pretend it's an accident.'

And in Darwin Jim Sawyer would say that he'd told them so.

'No. We move deeper into the trees and lie low,' he declared, taking charge. 'Can you see without your glasses?' he whispered to the professor.

'Enough,' Bawi answered, crawling closer. 'Enough to be able to follow you.'

Randall tugged the compass from his pocket. Rotor clatter to the north and east. Kakadi must be trying to escape towards the volcano. The KOPASSUS commandos would hope to turn him, to drive him and his men back towards the valley where more soldiers would be waiting. Like a pheasant shoot, beating the guerrillas towards a line of guns.

They had to go the other way. South and west, along the ridge, then try to find another way down to the valley.

The chain gun hammered again, a sound like a tree trunk being torn apart by giants. Further away this time.

'We'd better move,' he told them. 'Follow me and keep low. Use the trees for cover. Stay about five metres apart, and if I hiss, get down.'

He headed south, trying to avoid the thorny creepers that could slash an arm, hoping the noise of the fire-fight had frightened off the snakes. He stopped at the first tree, listened, then moved on, glancing back to check the others were following. The helicopters he guessed were holding off beyond small arms range.

On again. Then a fresh burst of shooting. Nearer. Much nearer. Less than fifty metres to their left. The helos must have dropped a patrol right close to them.

He fell to his knees, crawled forward then slithered into a dip in the ground littered with moss-covered rocks. Good cover. To find them a patrol would have to be right on top.

Charlie slid after him, then Bawi a few seconds later.

'We'll stay put for a while,' he breathed. 'Stay silent too.'

Close by, a fierce fire-fight broke out. When it ended the echoes were pierced by the terrible screams of a wounded man. Charlie covered her ears. Then came a single shot and silence.

No prisoners.

They heard a turbine whine and glimpsed the fat, dragonfly shape of a helicopter pass swiftly overhead. Then a different sound, short and sharp like a door slamming. Randall recognised it instantly. A second later the machine that had passed them detonated in a sheet of flame.

'A missile,' Nick breathed. 'Kakadi's got bloody missiles.' As the thunder of the explosion died away, metal fragments clattered through the trees.

Randall crawled up the slope. Less than a hundred metres away the forest was ablaze. If they weren't shot, they could be burned to death. He slithered back into the hollow.

'Time to move again.'

West now, he decided. Towards the valley. He led them away at a crouch. Then the trees thinned. Open ground to be crossed and no way round it.

'One at a time,' he whispered. 'Wait till I reach cover, then follow. Keep low.'

From the direction of the blazing helicopter came shouts of panic, of men distracted. He stood up and ran.

Crack! A high-velocity round inches over his head.

Fuck! His guts did somersaults. Blown it.

Crack! Crack! Two more shots. Bark flicked off a branch as he reached the tree.

'Nick!' A scream from Charlie, well behind.

A half-turn. A split second's hesitation. Go back for her? Suicide.

'Keep down!' he yelled.

In front of him the ground fell away towards the valley and safety. Behind, there were men trying to kill him. No choice. Heart pounding, feet dancing, he ran downwards, weaving through the trees.

Another shot, muffled this time, then the clunk of heavy metal in the branches above and a thud as a rifle grenade hit the soil behind him. He flung himself flat, fingers in his ears.

The explosion hammered the earth. Grenade fragments spattered the leaves above his head, but none touched him. He lay in dense ferns. As birds screamed at the disturbance, huge red ants scurried past his face.

He lay still, straining to hear above the thunder of blood in his temples if the others had tried to follow.

Nothing. No feet pushing through undergrowth. No sound of a chase. Maybe it had been a lone sentry they'd stumbled across, too concerned for his own safety to come after them.

Nick crawled forward beneath a screen of ferns, the camera bag nestling in the small of his back. Had to find cover. Then locate Charlie and Junus Bawi. *His* team. Had to see them all right.

Two more shots suddenly. Single rounds. Aimed with deliberation, but not at him.

Then a woman screaming hysterically.

'Christ!' he gasped.

They'd got Charlie.

Charlie cowered on her haunches, back against a tree, her hands smothering her unstoppable yells, staring at Dr Junus Bawi sprawled face down in front of her. Blood gushed from the mess that had been his head. A red stain spread from the middle of his white shirt. The two soldiers who'd killed him were short, squat men, but they towered over her, their young, dirt-smeared monkey faces taut with the elation that came from killing one of the enemy.

Charlie shook uncontrollably. 'I . . . I'm British,' she babbled between screams, terrified she was next. The soldiers levelled their guns at her head, but seemed uncertain what to do.

She gaped at Bawi. Seconds ago a human being, now a doll with a head of crimson sponge and a pool of dark-red treacle under his chest. Suddenly her stomach spasmed. She turned to the side and threw up.

Randall hid behind the thick roots of a huge tree, his mind in bits. Images of Charlie badly wounded flashed through his head. She'd be lost. Panicking like hell. And this was *his* fault. Should never have arm-twisted her into coming with him.

'God what a mess . . .' he muttered.

He listened, praying for another shout, something to show she was OK after all. He felt powerless. No weapon. No backup. Crawling up the slope to try to help her was madness. He'd be picked off like a duck at a fairground.

Backup. He thought of the Ops Room on the sixteenth floor of the Yard. A long, long way away. A big friendly machine full of blokes who got you out of trouble. Run by rules. Rule number one: working with women led to trouble.

He listened again. Nothing. He moved his face along to a dip in the root until he could look back through the ferns. He flinched and ducked down. Crouching on the ridge above half-hidden by a rock, a helmeted soldier was searching for him with binoculars.

He frowned. Why hadn't they come after him? Too few of them. Scared of Kakadi's men now they'd seen what they could do to a helicopter. But they knew he was down here – the other half of the bait in their trap. They'd want to scoop him up. Need to, to prevent word of the raid getting out. But they wouldn't hang around for ever, so at least he had time on his side.

Suddenly from the direction of the valley below came the deep bass boom of a mine explosion, followed quickly by another.

Maybe *that* was why the soldiers on the ridge hadn't followed. Leaving him to be caught by a patrol coming up the hill – a patrol that had just walked into the trap set by Kakadi's men.

From the ridge above he heard the muted crackle of a tactical radio. The commandos were getting new orders.

Charlie. Her scent haunted him. Smelled it in his head.

'Oh, fuck!' he breathed. Don't let her be dead.

The soldier guarding Charlie stood an arm's length away, but she caught his odour. Same as in the jeep last night. The sour stench of unwashed battledress. From his contemptuous stare she knew that her life was as insignificant to him as piss.

She trembled like a jelly, no longer daring to look at the mess of Junus Bawi. The flies were at his head already.

She took deep breaths to steady herself. Think, think. She at least was alive. They could've killed her, but hadn't. Because she was white, perhaps. A foreigner. Hard to explain to the big wide world if they murdered a Brit up here.

But who would know?

She felt desperately alone. Like a severed limb. She wanted to cry out for Nick and get a shout back to show he was OK. But they'd fired bullets and a grenade for Christ's sake! How could he be OK? Dead like Bawi, maybe. Or worse, wounded and in pain.

She wanted the soldiers to find him – to save his life, and so they could be together again. But the bangs from down the hill had made the commandos jittery. The one with the binoculars had rolled away from the ridge, shouting into his radio. Now he was kicking through the scrub looking for a fallen branch. When he found one he unhooked the machete from his belt and hacked the wood to length.

Body pressed to the forest floor, Randall heard rotors heading for the clearing. Medevac, he guessed. Or maybe KOPASSUS were pulling out . . . He eased himself back to the gap in the roots to risk another look.

'My God!' he gasped.

Evidence. Get it on tape. He reached into the bag for the video camera, touched the record switch and aimed the lens at the ridge.

Junus Bawi strung on a pole like a slaughtered pig. Two soldiers carrying it, with Charlie towed along behind, her hands bound with rope.

He breathed again. At least she was alive.

18

In THE CLEARING the first machine was down, its rotor swishing perilously close to the trees. A swirl of dust and grass stung Charlie's eyes. Numbed now by what had happened, she bowed her head, wishing her hands were free to shield her face. The plastic tie cut into her wrists.

The soldiers restrained her at the edge of the perimeter. The helicopter wasn't ready for them. Laid out on the ground in front of her were the men KOPASSUS had killed. She looked at them dumbly. Six bodies, including one of the stringy-haired youths who'd led the way up from the mission hospital – the boy with the machete. But Soleman Kakadi was *not* there. At that she felt a quiet sense of relief. KOPASSUS had missed the big prize. Bawi's corpse lay at the end of the row, his smeared white shirt out of place amongst the dirty green uniforms of the fighters.

Two soldiers ran from the helicopter with green plastic sacks. They spread them out, pulled back zips, then heaved the corpses into them one by one. Charlie gagged and turned away.

As the grinding whine of the jet tunnelled into her brain, she became conscious of twenty or thirty soldiers ringing the clearing, gawping at her. She felt raped by their eyes.

Above the rim of trees a second helicopter hovered, waiting its turn. To her right four men tramped out of the forest. One was bare-chested, a large, blood-stained field dressing taped to his brown shoulder, his face contorted with pain.

With the body bags aboard, the loadmaster beckoned to the injured soldier. He limped towards the open door, a second dressing on his leg. Once he was seated securely, it was Charlie's turn. Shoved forward, she ducked under the rotor, its down-draft tugging at her clothes. She was lifted into the machine and strapped into a canvas seat.

The helicopter shook wildly. An alien box of grey alloy, bare pipes, stained webbing and scratched Perspex. Charlie looked through the window that overlooked the far side of the clearing. More bodies there. A second neat row in the grass. Her heart leapt to her mouth. Nick? No.

All in ABRI uniform. She began to count, then a rough hand twisted her face from the window. OK for foreigners to know about ABRI's gains, but not its losses.

The engine note rose, the machine lifted, shaking more wildly still. A stench of jet exhaust blew in through the door. Outside, grass and twigs whirled in a frenzy. As they rose above the trees, the nose dipped and the helicopter accelerated low over the forest canopy jinking left and right, before climbing and settling on to an even course.

Opposite her, his knees touching hers, the injured commando sat slumped in his straps, eyes closed as if he'd passed out. Crouched by the door, the loadmaster watched the dark carpet of foliage zipping beneath them, his face hard, exhausted but relieved. At the rear of the cabin were the body bags. Up ahead, the two pilots in green bone-domes slouched in their seats smoking cigarettes like Vietnam-jocks.

Heading for Piri, and the interrogation centre where they tortured people . . .

She bit her lip, swallowing the tears that were welling up. Delayed shock spread through her like a nicotine surge after a month of abstinence. She was losing it. Any second she'd be screaming, howling, thrashing about in total, blind panic. She ground her teeth and told herself to get a grip.

It was no good wishing. Wishing that she'd never come to Kutu, or that she'd stayed in Piri, or at the mission hospital, or that Nick was here to hold her hand. He was gone. The person she'd been depending on to keep her out of trouble could even be *dead*. She was on her own now, so she'd have to be grown-up. To be cool. To think.

Torture was what terrified her most. The visible scars on Thomas's back, the unseen ones in his mind. No. They wouldn't do that to *her*. Not to a foreigner who had the power to tell the world about it and get listened to.

She opened her eyes again, stuck forward her chin and began to plan. No looking back. No agonising over what *might* have been. A strategy for the here and now.

Questions. What would they ask her? What should she tell them?

By now they would know full well she was a journalist. Must have known all along. Which was why they'd planted the bugging device on them.

She tried to concentrate, to remember precisely what had happened, what Bawi had said. The name of General Sumoto came back to her like a spectre at the feast. The man was big and he was bad, but that was all she knew. The kidnapping, the helicopter raid – Sumoto was behind all of it? Was *that* what she'd understood Randall to be driving at with his questions? What about Dugdale? Where did he fit in, if at all? God knew. Wary. That's what she'd need to be.

What would they do with her? Put her on the first plane out? Fine. Great. The sooner the better. But what if they didn't? There'd be questions. They'd demand her tapes.

Tapes! She sat up with a jolt. They were with Nick. Christ! No chance of a story now. No material for the scoop that would carve out a new future. Then she felt ashamed – thinking about her career when he was down there in the forest in God knows what sort of shape.

Then she realised something else. If he *was* dead, there'd be no one to tell London that she'd been taken prisoner. ABRI could do what they liked with her, torture her, murder her and nobody would ever be the wiser. She shrunk back into her seat. He *couldn't* be dead, she told herself. At this very moment he'd be hacking his way back to civilisation to set diplomatic wheels turning. *Nick* would ensure she was treated well . . . *And* he'd make sure her tapes were safe . . .

And pigs flew.

Ten minutes later the helicopter dipped towards Piri. She saw the town sprawled below, and beyond it the translucent blue of the sea. As it neared the ground the machine juddered, then sank on to its skids. Dust swirled in through the open door.

Paramedics scrambled aboard to help out the wounded soldier. She watched him being stretchered to an ambulance a few metres away. Then it was her turn. The loadmaster unclipped her belt and helped her roughly to the ground, her hands still bound behind her back. Beyond the perimeter of the whizzing rotor she was passed into the custody of an officer with a fat, square face and rubbery lips. His well-pressed uniform contained his flesh like a sausage skin. A name-flash on the breast pocket said Sugeng.

'Come!'

Like with the soldiers in the forest clearing, she felt his eyes defiling her. He propelled her away towards a bleak barrack-like building which enclosed three sides of a wide yard. She looked up, gulping at the bars on the windows.

At a counter inside she was asked for her passport. She froze. Hadn't got it. With Nick in his money belt. She felt cowed suddenly.

'I . . . I'm afraid I don't have it with me,' she stammered.

'*Nama dia Charlotte Cavendish*,' the officer told the clerk, who wrote her name in a ledger. 'Take off your watch, Miss Cavendish. What you have there?' His hand reached towards the breast pockets of her shirt as if about to search them himself.

'Cigarettes. And a notebook and pen,' she said, pulling them out. The pen and cigarettes went into a plastic bag with her watch.

Holding her notebook as if it were the evidence that would hang her, he pushed her up two flights of stairs on to a long landing that smelled of fear. At intervals iron bars from floor to ceiling marked the entrances to cells. They stopped by the third. Sugeng took a knife from his pocket and cut the plastic that bound her hands. Then he opened the door, pushed her inside, and locked it again.

The cell was bare and it stank of vomit. Blotchy white walls, a tiled floor. Two other women there, staring at her.

One of them was Teri.

London – Fitzrovia
Thursday 06.50 hrs

Ted Sankey was woken by the phone, his head a little clearer on the second morning of his involuntary unemployment.

'Hell,' he wheezed, noting from the digital clock that it was not yet seven. 'Hello?' he grunted, stretching the receiver coils across the pillow.

'Ted?'

'Ye-es. Who's this?'

'No names. But you know my voice, mate?'

Sankey rolled onto an elbow, wide awake suddenly.

'Yes, mate.' It was Gordon Wiggins, the PM's press secretary. 'What can I do for you?'

'The footbridge over the lake in St James's Park – you know it?' Wiggins's voice was clipped and strained.

'Of course.'

'Meet me in half an hour. OK?'

'Er . . . yep. All right.' Had to be important.

Click.

Adrenalin propelled him from the bed to the bathroom. Was it a *scoop* his old chum was offering him? A helping hand up off the floor? Five minutes, then he'd need to be outside looking for a taxi. Lightning fast shower and shave.

Gordon Wiggins. Good bloke. Ten years ago they'd been reporters on the *Mail* together. Gordon had become chief political correspondent.

Then when Copeland became PM he'd turned spin doctor at Downing Street. But he'd never done a 'deep throat' before.

Ten past seven when he finally found a taxi in Charlotte Street. Still in good time.

'The Mall,' he told the driver. 'Halfway down.'

A grey, chilly morning, the air soiled and grubby with the approach of winter. Leaves from the plane trees in the park had created a carpet of yellow-green, shiny wet from the drizzle.

Sankey turned up the collar of his white trench coat. No umbrella with him, the soft rain felt cold against his face. Along the path to the lake he saw a pair of joggers. Fit-looking men in tracksuits with short hair and serious faces. Officers doing staff jobs at the Defence Ministry he guessed, keeping up their training for the day they were allowed to be soldiers again.

Standing alone in the middle of the bridge, Gordon Wiggins looked like a caricature of a 1950's spy. Maroon anorak with the hood up, dark glasses and leaning over the rail. He was throwing bread to the ducks.

'Watcha mate,' Sankey breathed, positioning himself beside him but with his back to the rail so he could watch for anyone coming. 'What's with this Len Deighton stuff?'

'It's big, Ted. Very big. Can I trust you?'

'Course you bloody can, mate!'

'They could gaol me for this . . .'

'They'll never know, Gord. Not from me. That's a promise.'

Wiggins threw the last crust at a Canada goose honking down the lake. He glanced about him to check they were alone.

'There's a cover-up, Ted,' he murmured. 'Don't know all the ins and outs, but there was a statement due on aid to Indonesia from the Overseas Development Administration. Should have been out this afternoon – only it won't appear.'

Sankey leaned in closer. 'Why not, Gord?' he whispered.

'Because the PM's ordered the Foreign Office and the ODA to delay it for a month.'

'Why's he done that?'

'Because eighty million pounds of that aid is a soft loan to build a power station on the island of *Kutu* . . .'

'O-hh . . .' Sankey realised it was significant but wasn't sure why exactly.

'It's a project the foreign secretary himself didn't want anything to do with,' Wiggins continued *sotto voce*. 'He thought it dodgy – because all his officials did and he always goes along with what they say. *However*, a few months ago a certain junior minister by the name of Stephen Bowen went to the PM behind his boss's back and lobbied hard *for* the power station. And after a while by some miracle of Bowen's persuasive powers, Copeland decided that the Kutu power plant was, upon further reflection, the best bloody thing since sliced bread. And he managed to bulldoze the proposal through Cabinet committee.'

'I see.' The plot was thickening, but Sankey was still unclear. '*Why* didn't the F.O. want to fund it, Gord?'

'Because, Ted, with overseas aid it's nice to be able to show that it's helping *poor* people in the country it's given to. But the Kutu power station is designed purely for the new copper mine, not to make life better for the downtrodden Kutuans.'

'I see . . . but does that make the aid illegal or something?'

'Not exactly, but listen,' he whispered, easing closer. 'You haven't heard the half of it. This mining consortium KUTUMIN – it's owned one third by a British company, Metroc Minerals, one third by an Australian outfit and one third by a bunch of Indonesians.'

'Yeah, I know that.'

'OK. But KUTUMIN has a real problem. Until the power station's up and running they can't dig up the mountain and start raking in the profits. However, they're insisting the Indonesian government funds the power plant, not the company. Because, they say, it'll end up as part of the national infrastructure, so shouldn't be a *company* asset.'

'Sounds reasonable,' Sankey muttered. He was worrying about Charlie suddenly. Wondered if there'd been any word from her.

'Sure. But listen, Ted. This is complicated. It's all to do with who's got a finger in the pie . . . who stands to gain from the spending of British taxpayers' money. Now, have you ever heard of a man called General Sumoto?'

'Nope.'

'You have now. Listen. General Sumoto has a big personal financial stake in KUTUMIN. He also happens to be high up in the Indonesian armed forces. So high that, without his support, Britain would never have got that nice, juicy arms contract. Get me?'

'A-hh . . .' Sankey smelled the story at last. 'Let me get this straight. British taxpayers fund a soft loan to Indonesia so the power station for the mine can be built. That makes KUTUMIN happy, which makes General whatsisname happy, yes? So, in return he makes *us* happy by giving us the arms contract, right?'

'Looks that way.'

'Bit like the Pergau Dam in Malaysia?'

'Sort of.'

Sankey frowned, trying to remember the arguments used back in 1994.

'Tell me, would this power station be built by British companies?' he checked.

'Yes.'

'And by helping get the Kutu mine started, it would be doing *something* for the local economy?'

'You could argue that.'

Sankey scratched his head. This didn't make sense. The government had all the excuses it needed. So why was Gordon taking a huge risk in leaking all this to him?

'So why *doesn't* the PM argue it, Gordon? Why not let the aid figures be published and then bluff it out like they did over Pergau?'

Wiggins did a slow, full-circle turn to check they were still alone. He watched a jogger go past, then faced Sankey again.

'That's the point, Ted, I don't know . . .'

Sankey pursed his lips.

'*That* is the whole point,' Wiggins repeated, earnestly. 'The only reason Copeland can have for delaying the aid figures is to cover something up. Something *else*. Some other scam which *he* knows about, but nobody else does, not even the Foreign Office. I've talked to them, Ted, and they're as baffled as you and me.'

'Scam? What sort of scam?'

Wiggins removed the dark glasses. With his young face beneath the anorak hood he looked like a truanting schoolboy.

'Something involving Bowen and involving money,' he warned softly. 'Loads of it. Look, Stephen was on the board of Metroc until a year ago, right? No further connection with the company, *so they say*. Personally I have my doubts. Anyway, what we *do* know is this; Bowen was in bad need of cash. Hundreds of grand down on his gambling. Threatened with public exposure, facing the end of his political career. We also know he got *deeply* involved in the dealings with Indonesia, which, remember, is a country where making money from influence peddling is as easy as wiping your bum.

'Now, when Bowen did his lobbying for the power station loan – against the advice of his officials and behind the back of his boss – he was taking one hell of a big political risk. Must've had one hell of a good reason to do that. And for a man in his position what could that reason be other than money?

'And, Ted, Copeland took a huge political risk when *he* backed the power station aid bid. Why? To help out his old chum Bowen? Hardly. Charity is not in our dear PM's nature, despite his sanctimonious image.

233

'No, Ted. I can smell it. Copeland's in there too. Hands in the trough along with Bowen. Can't prove it. But the man's scared, Ted. Scared witless.'

'*With* you, Gord. With you all the way,' Sankey breathed, his mind racing ahead. 'Only problem is how do we use it . . . But use it we will, mate. Use it we will.'

Then another question came to him.

'Why are you telling me all this?'

Wiggins looked depressed suddenly.

'Sinking ship,' he mumbled. 'And between you and me I'm fed up with the half-truths of politics. Prefer the lies at *our* end of the briefing room.' His smile was like that of a dog used to being kicked. 'And anyway, whoever pays me I'm a hack at heart. And when you get a sniff that the PM's got his hand in the till, it's not the sort of thing you *can* keep to yourself.'

Kutu
16.20 hrs (08.20 hrs GMT)

Randall stopped to listen, like he had a hundred times in the last three hours. Bird shrieks and the buzz of insects. Nothing human. He sat on a fallen tree and thought of Charlie. She *was* OK, he told himself. To be certain, he took out the Handycam and replayed the shots he'd taken of her being marched off. No sign of injury on her. No blood. They could've killed her if they'd wanted; the fact that they hadn't must mean they intended her no harm. The soldiers had been pros and would treat a foreigner with care, he reassured himself. Anyway, there was nothing he could do to help her now. Had to concentrate on saving himself, then find Stephen Bowen.

He stared up at the sky. Small patches visible amongst the branches. Must be what a prisoner felt, glimpsing light through the bars of his cell. Grey clouds were sweeping in, threatening rain. He sniffed at the air. Then he furrowed his brow and sniffed again. Wood smoke. Always the bloody same for him in the tropics. Got himself into trouble and smelled bonfires . . .

Smoke!

'Christ!'

He stood up again, sniffing deeper to check he'd not imagined it. His drinking water was long gone and dehydration did funny things.

Definitely smoke.

He smiled fleetingly with relief. Must be near the valley at last. At times he'd thought he would die in the forest. He pushed on rapidly, soon seeing daylight ahead. On the tree line he stopped, crouching to scan the paddies below him. No soldiers. No sign of *any* living creature for that matter.

He crept forward, taking advantage of cover until he could see the village. Then he stopped dead.

'Fu-uck . . .' he gasped. 'The world's gone mad.'

The smoke. He understood it at last. Understood the deserted fields. The houses where he'd videoed children a few hours ago had been put to the torch. All gone, reduced now to blackened timbers and smouldering thatch. A blue haze hugged the valley bottom. Out of it rose the white bulk of the mission hospital, miraculously untouched. Spared the rage of the soldiers. If the villagers were alive, that's where they'd be.

The phone – the satellite dish he'd seen when they arrived from the coast. Please God, let it have survived. The thought of being able to communicate again with friends, with people on his side, had sustained him for the past three hours.

Back into his head came the image of Junus Bawi, strung on the pig pole. Down there somewhere were Bawi's wife and son, waiting for news. Or not. Dead too, maybe. Or taken by the troops. Hell.

Evidence. Needed it for himself – and for Charlie if she ever got to make a report. He dug out the Handycam again and videoed the view.

A path led him down to the village. He began to picture what must have happened here – soldiers dropped into the valley to ambush the fleeing OKP guerrillas – walked into a minefield – lost some men – then took it out on the villagers. To his right a patch of trampled cabbages would have been where the machines had landed.

There was still no one to be seen. But no bodies either. No sign of killing. All taken away? Transported from the valley? Was he now alone up there? Unnerved, he left the path and crouched amidst banana plants to watch and listen. The silence was eerie. Just the crickets. Then, faintly, from afar, he heard music. A single female voice at first, high and tremulous, then the drone of untutored throats singing 'The Lord is my Shepherd'.

Not until he reached the edge of the hospital verandah did he see the people jampacked inside, squatting on the ground, spilling through the doors. The entire population of the village sheltering there with the lepers and the malaria victims.

Heads turned. Eyes turned. At the sight of him, a ripple of movement carried word of his arrival to the headmen inside. Seconds later Father Pius Naplo picked his way through the carpet of legs and stood on the verandah looking down at him. His cassock was streaked with blood. He was shocked at Randall's own bedraggled state, shocked to see him alone.

'Father, I don't have good news for you. Junus Bawi . . .'

'You are alone . . .'. Naplo interrupted.

'Yes.' He could see the priest expected the worst. 'Dr Bawi – I'm afraid they shot him.'

'Ohhh . . .' Naplo emptied his lungs and bowed his head. He squeezed shut his eyelids as if unable to witness more tragedy.

'They came in helicopters,' Randall explained. 'To try to catch Soleman Kakadi.'

Naplo crossed himself.

'I don't know, Father. Don't know whether they found him or not,' Randall went on, forestalling the question. 'I didn't see.'

'And the woman who was with you?' Naplo asked eventually.

'They took her prisoner.'

He looked forlorn. 'That is bad. Very bad.' Then he tilted his head on one side, seeing a grain of hope. 'But maybe they don't hurt a foreigner.'

'Father, you have a satellite telephone here?' Randall pressed, desperate for contact with a world and a culture he understood.

From Naplo a blank stare, then a turn of the head. Nick followed his look. Under a large fig tree, twenty metres away, four dead bodies had been laid out, one of them a nurse.

'I'm sorry,' Nick murmured, embarrassed that he'd not asked what had happened here.

'Come.' The priest walked down the steps and took his arm. He led him to the end of the building where the satellite dishes were. The chain link fence surrounding them had been flattened, the antenna for the satphone smashed to pieces.

'You see . . .' Naplo gestured. 'We cannot even tell anyone what has happened here.'

Randall's heart sank.

Naplo took his arm and led him towards the smouldering shells of the houses.

'Come. You journalist. You see. Soldiers burn everything. Anybody try to stop, they shoot them. Four people killed here, ten more wounded.' The priest's voice teetered on the edge of hysteria. 'ABRI say KUTUMIN start building dam across the valley tomorrow, so all people must leave.'

Randall grimaced. 'And will they?'

The priest spread his arms. 'ABRI send trucks tomorrow. The people cannot fight this. Not even if Soleman still lives . . .'

Randall looked at his watch. The day was slipping away.

'Father, I need your help. I have to get to a telephone. It's desperately urgent that I tell people what happened here today.'

'Yes. You must. I will bring you to Santa Josef soon. But first there is Doctor Bawi's wife and son. I must tell them what happen. I think they already fear it when they see the helicopters fly towards the mountain. After, I will take a wounded man to Santa Josef. He very bad. Need hospital in Piri. The nurses make him ready now. Maybe in ten, fifteen minutes I go, and you can come with me.'

He waved an arm at the devastation around them.

'Take pictures. Show people in England what kind of army they sell guns to.'

London – Downing Street
09.00 hrs

Sally Bowen felt queasy. Nerves. The taxi dropped her by the heavy steel gates at the end of Downing Street. She gave her name to the policeman and was allowed into the road. She'd never set foot here before. Such a narrow, insignificant street for a nation's leader to live in. More imposing on TV.

She'd slept very little last night, and had then spent a good hour trying to decide what to wear. The well-cut suit of the loyal political wife, or something simpler in which to appeal to Keith's better nature. In the end she'd settled for the dark-grey Jaeger skirt and a cherry-coloured turtle-neck pullover that went well with her blonde hair. The more she'd thought about it, however, the more she'd despaired of being able to change his mind and persuade him to negotiate with Stephen's kidnappers.

'Morning, Mrs Bowen.' The policeman guarding the broad, black door nodded respectfully. He tapped and it opened. Inside, she was shown into a little drawing room where a fire crackled in the grate. Keith Copeland emerged through a door at the other end.

'Good morning, Sally,' he said, accentuating his limp as he crossed the floor. He gripped both her hands. 'Let me say once again how terrible I feel about this whole business. You've been an absolute tower of strength. How are the children?'

She detached her hands from his. She fancied there was something reptilian about his look this morning, but she could have been imagining it.

'They're being kept busy at their schools,' she replied insipidly. 'I don't think it's sunk in yet that their father's about to die.'

'No,' Copeland gulped. 'I . . . I suppose that must be a good thing.' They sat in a pair of regency stripe armchairs. Between them was a small Georgian table set with a coffee pot and two cups.

'May I?' he asked, offering to pour.

'Thank you . . . Keith, I've come to make a plea,' she announced bluntly, determined not to be soft-soaped.

Copeland winced. This wasn't going to be as easy as he'd hoped.

'To ask whether there isn't *something* more that can be done to save Stephen's life.'

'Sally, everything possible *has* been done. *Is* being done. Let me assure you of that.'

'Except negotiations,' she insisted. 'You're not even trying to negotiate his release!'

'But there's no one to negotiate *with*, Sally,' Copeland protested. 'We don't know who these people are. We're trying extremely hard to find out.' Should he tell her about the Yard man in Kutu and the fact that Stephen's driving licence had turned up? No. Too sensitive at this stage. 'But there's one thing you have to understand, Sally. No government can afford to give into threats from terrorists.'

'That's rubbish,' she murmured, unimpressed. 'Governments do it all the time.'

'Not British governments. But I say again, if we can only contact the kidnappers then maybe some sort of deal can be struck. But on the issue of the arms contract, no. We can't budge. You understand that, surely?'

She felt he was lecturing her. Treating her to a TV performance rather than conversing with her.

'You were good friends, once,' she said, trying to shame him.

'Still are, Sally. Still are,' he insisted. 'Believe me I feel this whole business as personally as you do.'

'You helped each other out politically, didn't you?'

Copeland recoiled. What did she mean? What did she know?

'Well, yes. In a manner of speaking,' he admitted, warily.

'Financially too,' she continued, looking him straight in the eye. She fancied she saw the blood drain from his face.

'I'm not quite sure what you . . .'

238

'The bank account in Switzerland. The one Stephen set up for you . . .'

Copeland gaped. His jaw moved wordlessly. Panic choked him. It was as if the sea were closing over him. Stephen must have told her. Betrayed him.

He swallowed, pulling himself together. He looked at Sally. County clothes. Farmyard brain. A silly woman, that's how Stephen had always described her. She *couldn't* know. Had to be guessing.

'I don't know what you mean by that, Sally,' he mouthed, playing for time. 'In fact I have no *clue* what you're talking about.'

Sally sensed she'd got him. She opened her large black handbag and pulled out the boarding pass.

'*Keith's account: N465329,*' she read. When she looked up, she knew it was true. Copeland's face had imploded.

Then suddenly it managed to re-inflate.

'I don't understand,' he said softly. 'What is it you have there?'

'An airline boarding pass,' she said defiantly. 'From when Stephen went to Zurich a couple of months ago. To set up the bank accounts for you and him. For some reason he wrote the number of yours on it.'

She let her accusation hang in the air.

It *was* a guess, Copeland realised. A number on a card could mean anything. He breathed again.

'No, my dear. You've added two and two and made five, I'm afraid – or rather I'm *glad* to say. I don't have a Swiss bank account. If I *had*, there'd be nothing to put in it,' he assured her. 'May I see?'

He held out his hand.

Sally felt her resolve crumble. Politicians always managed to make her feel out of her depth. Stephen had done it too.

'May I?' he repeated.

She gave him the boarding pass.

'Well, well . . .' he said, shaking his head. 'I have simply no idea what this is, Sally. I suppose there must be hundreds of thousands of Keiths in England. But I can assure you *this* one isn't me.'

He was about to hand it back to her, then had second thoughts. He levered himself to his feet.

'Tell you what,' he said, walking over to the fireplace. 'I think we'd better dispose of this, don't you?'

He threw the ticket into the flames. Sally gasped, reaching out a pointless hand to stop him.

'There,' he murmured, watching it burn. 'Wouldn't want anyone else jumping to the wrong conclusion.'

He limped back towards her.

'It's been very hard for you, Sally. I'm so sorry.'

Kutu

On the nightmare drive to Santa Josef, every rock, every pothole jolted a moan of pain from the youth laid out on the rear seat of the battered green minibus. A nurse dabbed at his forehead with a wet cloth and tightened his bloodstained dressings. Randall tried to shut out his cries and to think. To put what he knew into some sort of order.

Fact number one. The Kutuan resistance movement, the OKP, was *not* involved in the kidnap of Stephen Bowen. Of that he was now certain.

Fact two. General Dino Sumoto probably *was* involved. Backed by supporters in KODAM Twelve. Why? Hadn't a clue. Maxwell might know by now, if only he could contact him. All he'd come up with by himself was that Sumoto wanted to destroy the OKP. But to do so by kidnapping an official of a foreign government and blame the OKP was to play with stakes that were extraordinarily high.

Fact three. Sumoto had made big money from KUTUMIN and probably stood to make much more. So, it was rumoured, did Stephen Bowen. Could they have cooked up the kidnap between them? To provide an excuse to smash the Kutuan resistance, so the mine and their money flow could proceed unhindered? Could the kidnap be a *hoax* even – Bowen faking his terror, faking his injuries and the torture, and now sipping gin with Sumoto waiting for the pay-off?

Not credible. Fantasy. But where *was* Bowen? The sixty-four-thousand-dollar question. Somewhere on this benighted island – of that Randall now felt almost certain.

And where in this equation did Brad Dugdale fit – if at all? He *was* linked with Sumoto, if only through the payment of bribes to him.

It was Dugdale who'd fed them the rumour of Bowen being seen at Piri airport. Dugdale who'd hinted heavily that Kakadi was the kidnapper . . . So, had he been used by Sumoto to set Charlie and him up as the bait to trap Kakadi? Had he fed them the driving licence? What else could he have done? Used his TV connections to set up the European end of the kidnap? *Maybe even have provided the boat on which Bowen was now hidden . . . ?*

Suddenly Naplo stamped on the brakes. They'd reached the village on the hill overlooking Santa Josef, the bamboo houses turned pink by the glow of dusk. In the middle of the track stood a woman in nun's habit, flagging them down. It was the sister from the orphanage.

She came to the window and yammered breathlessly. Naplo buried his head in his hands. Eventually he looked up again and turned to Randall.

'Sister Angelica say ABRI cut telephone from Santa Josef,' he declared. 'Soldiers waiting now at the orphanage. Waiting for *you*.'

Randall gulped. Waiting to trap him. To shut him away with Charlie so there'd be no witnesses to what KOPASSUS had done. Nobody to blow the gaff on Sumoto . . . His stomach somersaulted. Charlie. She could be in greater danger than he'd imagined. If even half his suppositions were right, she might not be in the hands of professional soldiers anymore, but in the clutches of General Sumoto's men.

God, he needed that phone. Needed to get the whole British government machine working on getting the girl free again.

'Damn, damn, damn!' he hissed.

'For a telephone you must now go to Piri,' Naplo said forlornly. 'There is no other place. But I cannot take you there. Not even to Santa Josef now. They will arrest me as well as you. But Sister Angelica – she has a plan. She will take you to the man who brought you from Piri this morning. She has spoken with him.'

Dedi. But was he part of the conspiracy? He and his sister? Or had Dugdale used them too? Whatever – he had no alternative. Randall thanked the priest and got out. The minibus rattled onwards immediately in a cloud of dust and exhaust. Solemn-faced, Sister Angelica pointed towards a small motorbike with a pillion, which she pushed off its stand and kickstarted into life.

The track she took was no more than a path, weaving through patches of maize, banana and cabbage down to the coast. They bounced along without lights, the ride increasingly hazardous as the sunset glimmered its last. Finally the machine purred on to the flat of a beach, weaving through coconut palms. The moon shone through thin clouds, turning the heads of the trees into black paper cutouts.

The nun stopped and killed the engine. Randall slid off the pillion and looked around. Close by, the burly Kutuan rose up from the sand where he'd been squatting.

As soon as she saw him, Sister Angelica restarted the bike and rode off without a word.

'You alone, mister?' Dedi asked.

'Yes,' Nick confirmed. 'The soldiers have taken Charlie prisoner.'

Dedi made a clicking noise with his tongue.

Randall stepped round until his back was to the moon and he could see Dedi's expression in the light.

'And they killed Junus Bawi,' he added.

'Ahh . . .' The Kutuan's shoulders slumped as if he'd been punched. 'Ohhh . . . Bad, bad, bad thing . . . Oh . . . people very angry now. Big, big trouble now. You see.'

He began rolling his head, muttering in Kutun. Then his eyes looked up and locked. He stared fixedly at a point beyond Randall's shoulder, terror on his face.

'Aieeaieeaiee,' he wailed softly. Distraught, his hands hovered as a shield as he gazed towards the moon. Then he fell to his knees.

'What is it, for Christ's sake?' Randall hissed, turning to look.

The crown of a palm tree stood out stark against the moonlight. Its fronds were shaking, yet he could feel no wind.

Randall crouched on the sand beside the Kutuan. 'Dedi,' he whispered. 'What is it?'

The man looked to be in a trance.

'*Gundrowo!*' he whispered, pointing.

Randall gripped him by the shoulders and shook him. Dedi was all he had in this god-forsaken place. Couldn't have him collapsing into a bundle of gibbering superstition.

The Kutuan's face began to relax once more. Randall looked behind and saw that the fronds of the tree were still again.

'Dedi, you have to help me,' Randall insisted. 'I have to find a telephone.'

Like asking for a drink in a desert.

'OK, mister. OK, mister. I take you Piri in the boat,' Dedi answered, recovering quickly. Randall could see he wanted to be rid of him. 'I put you on town beach. No one see. Plenty telephone in Piri. Then I come back here. Tomorrow morning I drive back Piri in minibus and tell soldiers you not come back from mountain. OK, mister? Then they think you also dead up there.'

Late at night in Piri, on his own, he'd be picked up within minutes. And if he found a phone to use, one call to the Scotland Yard number he'd rung earlier and intel would nail him. But what else could he do?

'OK, mister?' the Kutuan repeated.

'OK. But you've got to help me more than that,' he replied gently. 'I need to know about Brad. Where was he this morning?'

'He gone to the boat, mister.'

'The *Morning Glory*?'

'Yes, mister.'

242

Another piece of the jigsaw clicking into place. Could Dugdale have been taking food there? For the hostage and his guards?

'Dedi . . . who else is on that boat?' Randall pressed.

'Nobody, mister.' There was surprise in his voice. 'Boat empty. Waiting for salvage equipment from Australia.'

'You sure? When did you last go on board?'

'I don't know. Not for many weeks.'

'Well, I want to go there,' Randall declared. 'Right now.'

London – the News Channel
10.55 hrs

Mandy was finding it hard to concentrate this morning. A numbing lack of direction had pervaded the newsroom since Sankey's sacking. She'd just put the phone down and had already forgotten what the caller said.

There was a lull in the newsroom. There'd been an early morning recap on the killing of the electricity boss yesterday, but little movement on the story. And on Bowen there were rumours of a man in custody about to be charged with some minor involvement, but no confirmation from the Yard. And nothing yet from Charlotte Cavendish. Now that the PM had refused to back off on the arms deal, the next break on the story was expected to be Bowen's corpse turning up.

She had a need for more coffee. She pushed her chair back, stood up and stretched. She wore a loose-fitting black skirt that concealed her bulges, a black silk blouse and a cardigan. Halfway across the newsroom she stopped in her tracks.

Sankey walking in through the door. White coat over his arm, grey suit immaculately pressed, hair freshly trimmed.

'Ted,' she mouthed.

'Find Angus for me, girl,' he snapped, as if he'd never been away.

'Angus Addy? Sure, but why? What's going on?'

'I'm back, Mand,' he whispered. 'I've just told the proprietors about an exclusive I've got. Back on the payroll. Calling me a consultant for now, but just you watch; I'll have my office back by the end of the day.' He winked hugely. 'Now, I need somewhere with a phone to park my bum. Steve Paxton's room's empty, isn't it?'

Mandy's face widened into a grin. 'It certainly is,' she said.

They turned to look at the glass-walled editor's office. The even pattern of the Venetian blind was broken by a hand parting the slats. Through the gap the bristle-headed accountant watched aghast.

Kutu – Kadama interrogation centre
19.05 hrs (11.05 hrs GMT)

A single bulb hung from the ceiling, dazzlingly bright.

Charlie kept her eyes on the floor in a yoga-like attempt to control pulse and terror. She'd been over five hours in the cell, petrified of the questioning that was certain to come, yet desperate to get it over with. She'd left the cell just once, to be taken to the toilet – a stinking pit overflowing with excreta. Afterwards, she'd resolved not to eat or drink again until they released her.

When Charlie had arrived there Teri had pulled faces to indicate that the third woman in the cell might be an informer, a thin sobbing Kutuan who made out she spoke no English. Then in stilted whispers, taking care not to be overheard, Teri had explained how two intel men had come for her at Captain's that afternoon. Men she'd recognised. Men who'd been in the bar from time to time, drinking with Brad . . .

Three hours after Charlie's arrival, Teri had been taken for questioning, her face bleached by fear and by the uneasy realisation that in some incomprehensible way she'd been betrayed by the man she lived with.

After Teri had gone, Charlie had sought to control her own panic by constructing in her head the story she would write once she was free. A massive, angry story about the rape of an island, the crushing of a community by an industrial monolith, the cold-blooded murder of a peace-loving man, and – in the midst of it somewhere – the kidnapping of Stephen Bowen, but almost dwarfed by the wider abuse of human rights that she was witnessing.

That was the story she would *like* to write, but it wasn't the one the Channel would take. They'd want Bowen, Bowen and Bowen. The Channel's audience were assumed to care infinitely more about the fate of a single famous Brit than about atrocities on a faraway Pacific island.

The problem with the kidnap story was that she no longer knew what it was, now her assumption that Bowen had been taken by the OKP had been blown out of the water. And the Sumoto link was one she simply didn't understand. Connected *somehow* – that was the implication of what Randall had said. But the kidnap and the helicopter raid on the

OKP – all done by the same people? *Couldn't* be. That meant the *people* were the Indonesian army, or a part of it. Surely not.

She kept thinking of Nick. Thinking of that warm, unconscious mound of muscle and bone she'd snuggled up to in bed last night. Yet all she could see now was a vision of him lying on the ground with his skull blown apart like Junus Bawi.

And she thought of Sumoto. Just a name – yet central to everything apparently. There was another name too – one belonging to Sumoto's key man in Kutu – but she'd forgotten it.

Noises from the corridor. A woman whimpering. The barred door clanged open and Teri fell inside, pushed by a sweating guard. He shouted in Kutun as she sank to the floor, her blouse held together with two buttons done up in the wrong holes. The shirt tails hung loose over her skirt. She put a hand under the fabric and began massaging a breast. She seemed in shock, too shocked to cry, but quivering as she breathed.

'Are you all right?' Charlie asked lamely.

Teri looked down, panting. She stopped the massage of her breast but kept a hand over it for comfort. Then, slowly with the other hand she began to rebutton her blouse. 'They make me undress . . .' she gulped. 'They bastard!'

Charlie's stomach clenched. She'd rather die than have them do that to *her* . . .

She kneeled beside Teri and gave her a sisterly hug. 'What . . . what did they ask you?' she whispered close to her ear, hoping the other woman wouldn't hear.

'Ask if I know where is the kidnap Englishman,' Teri muttered, not caring if the informer did hear. 'Is stupid. Why they think I know . . .?'

Why indeed, Charlie wondered, increasingly confused. Unless she'd misunderstood him, Randall's theory was that these people *knew* where Bowen was, because *they*'d got him . . .

Teri's face crumpled. She covered it with her hands, then lay on the floor.

Ten minutes passed. It felt like an hour. Then the door clanged open again.

'Cavendish!'

The guard grabbed Charlie's arm and jerked her into the corridor. Heart hammering, limbs limp as putty, she was hustled to an interrogation room. Not as she'd expected. A small office with filing cabinets and a desk, behind which sat a stocky man in uniform. A round, light-brown face, oily hair and gold half-moon glasses over which he peered as she sat. The guard left them. They were alone.

Charlie quivered with fear but sat up straight and took in a deep breath. The officer looked reassuringly senior and sophisticated.

'I want to speak with the British Ambassador in Jakarta,' she announced, a flash of courage returning.

Suddenly his benign expression turned to outrage. He crashed his fist on the table.

'You think this is a Telkom office?' he screamed.

Charlie flinched. 'It . . . it's my right, that's all . . .' she stammered, all courage evaporating.

'Rights? *Spies* don't have rights!' He smacked the table with the flat of his hand.

Charlie gulped. 'I'm not a spy.'

The officer looked sceptically at the folder on his desk. From it he took the immigration card she'd completed on arrival at the airport.

'Charlotte Cavendish,' he read. 'Born in year 1967, profession teacher.' He looked up quizzically. 'True or untrue?'

Charlie didn't answer.

'They employ teachers at the News Channel?' he goaded, holding up her notebook.

Her heart sank. She pulled herself up straight again. No point in bluffing. 'No . . . I'm a journalist. I put teacher on the form because I knew if I wrote journalist I wouldn't be let in. But that doesn't make me a spy.'

'And Mr Randall – he is also a journalist?'

She hesitated, wondering if they knew the real truth about Nick. Wondering if it would *help* saying he was a policeman. Couldn't risk it.

'He's a photographer,' she answered simply.

The colonel looked down at the file again.

'You tell a lie to come into Indonesia. You travel to part of this island that is forbidden to foreign visitors. And you meet with murderers in order to help them . . .' His voice had a twang like a taut elastic band. 'That makes you a spy. And dangerous.'

'No,' she answered defiantly. 'It makes me a journalist trying to find the kidnappers of Stephen Bowen.'

'And you did find them . . . Tell me, what did they say to you, Dr Junus Bawi and Mr Soleman Kakadi . . .?'

Charlie frowned. Did he believe this, or was it a game?

'They are not the kidnappers,' she answered flatly.

The intelligence officer laughed. 'They tell you that? You make interview with them on your video camera?'

Charlie glared defiantly. 'Yes,' she replied. 'It's all on tape.'

'You have the tape? No.' He answered his own question. She'd been searched. 'Mr Randall – he has the tape, yes?'

'Maybe. I don't know . . .' Her heart flipped, suspecting they'd caught him too. And that now there was no one to alert London as to what was happening to her. She bit her lip.

'Well, I tell you – they trick you,' the officer oiled. 'Bawi, Kakadi – they think you foolish, ignorant foreigner who believe anything they say. But I *know* they have Mr Bowen. Very close to where we catch you today. *Very* close. I tell you little secret, Charlotte Cavendish, we nearly rescue Mr Bowen today. Those soldiers . . . that why they there.'

Charlie gaped. The gunship scytheing everything in its path, the cold-blooded execution of unarmed Junus Bawi, all that was part of a *rescue* mission? Disbelief was written on her face.

Seeing it, the officer's eyes hardened again.

'Under law of the Republic of Indonesia you can go to gaol for long time,' he warned suddenly. 'You understand me?'

Charlie didn't doubt it. She nodded.

'But maybe I can avoid that. You answer my questions?'

'I'll try,' she replied meekly.

'Where is your friend? Your *husband*?'

His eyes mocked her. She felt herself blushing, guessing he must've listened to the idiotic tape recorded in the hotel last night.

'I don't know.'

So they hadn't found him. She didn't know whether to feel relief or despair.

'Where you arrange to meet if you get separate?'

'Nowhere. You see we weren't expecting . . .'

'I think maybe he get killed by OKP,' the colonel added as if it were a matter of supreme unimportance. 'They do a lot of shooting. Kill one of our soldiers,' he added, feigning outrage.

Killed many more than one, Charlie remembered.

'So what they tell you about Mr Bowen?' he continued. 'Bawi – Kakadi – they tell you some story about who kidnap him?'

'No. They seemed to have no idea who did it,' she answered firmly, trying to keep her mind focused. 'Dr Bawi thought Soleman was responsible until he found out Kakadi didn't even know who Stephen Bowen was.'

The colonel pulled his face into a broad grin. 'They very good actors. Should be in *Ramayana!*' Then the grin vanished. 'Why you go out from hotel last night? Why you want to talk with Mr Dugdale?'

Jumping about to confuse her.

'For a drink. Captain's Bar is listed in my guide book . . .'

Suddenly he slammed the table again. 'You lie!' he screamed.

Charlie quailed. 'It's not a lie. We . . . we went there for a drink.'

'Ohhh . . . you very stupid woman, Cavendish! Teri tell me many things 'bout you . . . How they meet you in Darwin, how you come to Kutu on same plane . . .'

Charlie blanched. So *this* smooth, sophisticated man was the one who'd stripped Teri naked and done unspeakable things to her.

'I ask you again,' he snapped, standing up and walking round behind her chair. 'Why you want to talk with Brad Dugdale?'

Charlie's throat was as dry as hay. She swallowed, desperately trying to understand the drift of his questions.

'For a chat. That's all,' she croaked.

The intelligence officer stood close behind her. She could smell garlic on his breath. She flinched as his hands touched her shoulders.

'We . . . we wanted to ask him what he'd heard about the OKP, about the kidnap . . .' she stammered, a shiver running up her spine. 'That sort of thing. Just gossip.'

His fingers closed on her neck, as if to caress. Or to throttle.

'You think Brad Dugdale know something about the kidnap?' The voice was gentle. Politely curious.

'Well . . .' she trembled, 'Nick thought so. Thought he might be involved in some way . . .'

'Oh?' Gentle again. Ever so gentle. His fingers slipped forward, feeling the ridges of her collar bones and the ribs above her breasts. 'Your friend, he think Brad Dugdale is one of the kidnappers?'

Mind racing. Trying to fathom the significance of this. Suspecting she'd said something she shouldn't have.

'Just a suspicion. No more than that. Probably totally wrong . . .'

Then it clicked. Clicked who this was. Clicked what these questions were about and why they'd asked Teri what *she* knew of Bowen's whereabouts.

The hands lifted. Then a single finger pushed up under her hair and caressed the nape of her neck. She shivered. Slowly the colonel walked back to his seat. When he sat and looked at her his eyes were as cold as an executioner's.

This was *Sumoto's* man, she realised. *He* knew all about Bowen. What he *didn't* know was how much *they* knew – her, Nick, Teri and Brad. That's what the questioning had been about. To find out how much *they* knew. So he could decide who would have to be silenced . . .

'Could I, I wonder . . . could I know who you are?' she stammered hoarsely, dreading but needing the confirmation. She'd remembered it – the other name Bawi had mentioned.

'I am Colonel Widodo,' he said, unblinking.

Charlie closed her eyes. Inside her head she began to scream. *Nick!* For God's sake get me out of here – *before they kill me.*

19

Hot Rock Café, Jakarta
19.15 hrs (12.15 hrs GMT)

THE HEAVY RHYTHM from three hundred watts of music power throbbed through the throng like a communal heartbeat. The dimly-lit bar was already crowded despite the earliness of the hour. From the ceiling hung strobe lights, flashing to the beat.

Maxwell stood close to the bar holding a tall, cold glass of lager, its sides wet with the humidity generated by the lissom bodies around him. He was tense with anticipation; London had been calling for news but there'd been little to give. Then Abdul had rung an hour ago. Finally.

Maxwell checked his watch. His source was late.

The Hot Rock Café was a Jakarta pick-up joint used by Caucasian ex-pats looking for sex with smooth-skinned locals, a place where Maxwell easily passed unnoticed amongst the dozens of sweaty white males. The feral atmosphere of the bar appealed – tense, jaw-flexing foreigners and watchful, smiling Javans who would make money from them.

Maxwell himself had scored here. Twice. Once with a woman, once with a young man. Both very clean, very anonymous, and very accommodating.

'Hello, Harry.'

Abdul. Mouth close to his ear so he'd be heard above the beat, hand lightly touching his arm. Maxwell jumped.

'Oh, there you are,' he shouted above the din. 'What d'you want to drink? Beer?'

'No. Orange Fanta.'

Maxwell nudged his way to the bar then returned with a can. They pushed through the crowd until they found a corner where the music was less loud. Abdul upended the can as if he had no intention of staying long.

'You hear about *Mayjen* Sumoto?' he asked excitedly, mouth to Maxwell's ear again.

There'd been a rumour the general had been summoned to the president's palace that morning.

'Nothing specific . . .' Maxwell replied, cautiously.

Abdul turned to face him, watching for the impact he knew he was about to make.

'The president,' he announced, 'he give Sumoto the sack! General been told to take his pension . . .'

'Mother of Mercy!' This was more than Maxwell had expected. Much more. 'You sure about this?'

Abdul cast a nervous glance towards the door. The bar was still filling up, people queuing for hamburgers and steaks.

'In Indonesia we never *sure* about anything,' Abdul replied, his voice heavy with irony. 'But yes. About Sumoto, my friends in ABRI say this is true. They *very* unhappy.'

'Your friends in KODAM Twelve?' Maxwell checked.

'Yes, but also in other KODAMs. All officers loyal to people before president are angry. Because they think Sumoto was for them.'

Abdul checked again that no one was in earshot. His face came so close to Maxwell's they almost touched.

'You ask me 'bout weapons, Harry.' Another quick glance behind. 'Well, Sumoto promise them *rockets*,' he whispered hoarsely. 'Sumoto tell them he get ballistic missiles from China. Range two thousand kilometres. Such weapons make ABRI very strong. But, before China sell missiles to Indonesia, Indonesia have to change . . .'

'Let me guess . . .'

'Must have new president, China say. President who want to make good friends with Beijing . . .'

'And how would such a man be chosen?'

'By ABRI generals who want the same as Sumoto. There are some.'

'He was planning a *coup?*'

'No. But a change in the army leaders. Using KODAM Twelve to force out any generals who not want to go . . .'

A coup by another name. Maxwell sensed that Abdul was relieved that Sumoto had been stopped.

'You're glad he's been sacked?'

'Ya . . . maybe,' he wavered. 'You see most people want change in Indonesia, but not change that way. No more blood. Enough people killed already. And Sumoto he want to move too fast. Too dangerous, you understand?'

'I understand. He took a big risk, didn't he?'

'Ya . . . He want power very much. So much it make him blind. He want to be commander-in-chief of ABRI. That first, then who knows . . .'

An ABRI complete with an arsenal of ballistic missiles that could hit Australia. Flesh on the bones of the Aussie nightmare.

But he'd blown it. Sumoto, the Java spider, had built a web too weak to hold what he'd hoped to catch with it. With a wave of his feather duster, the president had simply swept it all away.

'I think maybe they charge him with treason,' Abdul went on. 'Because he have secret contact with China. And because he plot against the president.'

'Where is he now?'

'Nobody know that. But he not under arrest.'

Quickly Maxwell correlated his thoughts. There was a vital piece missing from the puzzle – proof that it *was* Sumoto who'd kidnapped Stephen Bowen to abort the arms deal with Britain and prime the pumps for his push for power. All the evidence pointed, but was circumstantial. What he needed was proof that would stand up in court.

'Tell me something else, Abdul,' Maxwell asked, trying to make it sound like a disconnected issue, 'what are people saying about the kidnap?'

'Oh . . . nobody know anything 'bout that,' the journalist replied dismissively. 'But I think the Englishman's in Kutu. The resistance – OKP – maybe they have him. They are like children. Stamp their foot because they don't want the mine.'

For all his liberalism Abdul was still a Javan, Maxwell reminded himself. Little sympathy for far-off Melanesians resisting Javan rule. The young man began to tap the table in frenetic accompaniment to the music beat.

'I go now,' he shouted. His eyes looked at his fingers, reminding Maxwell there was unfinished business.

Maxwell nodded, put a hand in his trouser pocket and pulled out the brown envelope, twice as fat as usual.

'Thank you, my friend.' He touched him on the forearm.

Abdul was on his feet in an instant. A peremptory nod and he was away through the crowd.

Damn, Maxwell thought, losing sight of him. He'd forgotten to fix a location for their next meeting.

Harry Maxwell got the taxi-driver to drop him short of the embassy. An automatic precaution in a city where nobody was quite what they seemed.

It might well have been the action of the British ambassador that had prompted General Sumoto's dismissal by the president, Maxwell realised. Bruton had had a quiet word with DefenceCo about Sumoto's contacts with China. Then DefenceCo had spoken about it to their Indonesian agent. Then *he* must have raised it with his supremely important relative . . .

The meeting with Abdul had left him deflated. The kidnappers had given a deadline of noon GMT Friday. Bowen would die then unless there'd been a favourable response from Britain. Twenty-four hours left – assuming they bothered to wait now that Keith Copeland had reconfirmed the arms contract.

If only he had *proof* of Sumoto's guilt he could slap it on the desk of Brigadier General Effendi and demand that POLRI take action. But he hadn't – unless the elusive Cuculus had unearthed something in Kutu.

The evening rain had stopped but there were puddles to be avoided as he walked the last thirty metres to the embassy compound. As he neared the security gates he became conscious of a car coming slowly up behind him. Out of the corner of his eye he saw the bumper draw level with his legs. It was a Toyota, new and shiny in the pink light of the street lamps. When the car slowed further, he felt an irrational stab of fear.

'Mr Maxwell!' A little girl voice. Strained. From inside the car.

He turned to look. Heart-shaped face, very pretty. At first he thought she was a prostitute kerb-crawling, but it was stretching things that she should know his name.

Then with a jolt he realised he was looking at Selina Sakidin.

She drove him without speaking to a part of the city he was not familiar with, just a short distance away. Then she swung the car down a narrow, dimly-lit street of modest houses and stopped. She killed the engine, but kept her eyes on the road in front, with frequent glances in the mirror. She was flustered and panicky, not knowing where to begin.

'The police told me yesterday you'd disappeared,' Maxwell murmured, accusingly.

'I was at the house of General Dino Sumoto,' she admitted softly.

Maxwell stared at her open-mouthed, her whispered words the tumblers of a combination lock clicking into place. The proof he'd been looking for was sitting in front of him.

'Ahh . . .' he sighed. 'Were you indeed!'

Dressed in salmon pink skirt and jacket – her work clothes – she *looked* like someone's mistress, now he thought about it. The face of a woman satisfied with what she'd got from life, but not with the way she'd got it.

'I so very sorry, Mr Maxwell,' she blurted out, her voice cracking. Her shoulders began to shake. 'I done a terrible thing. Now he going to kill me. You got to help me, otherwise I going to die . . .' Her voice spiralled upwards. She spread her hands over her face and wiped the tears downwards.

'I done such a terrible thing. Help me,' she begged. 'You must help me!'

'Now, calm down, my dear . . .' He offered the neatly folded handkerchief he'd put in his pocket that evening. 'Of *course* I'll try to help. But you've got to help *me* first. Understand?'

'Yes,' she whimpered.

'Right.' He took in a deep breath and crossed his fingers. 'Do you know where Stephen Bowen is now?'

'Yes.'

Maxwell's heart galloped.

'He on a boat. He been there since Wednesday last week when I go with him to Bali. General Sumoto – he do this. He make prisoner of Stephen – I don't know why. He not tell me. But now he very angry your prime minister not cancel contract. He send a message to the boat last night. He tell them to take Stephen to Kutu. He tell them to kill him and put him on the beach to make it look like Kutu people do it.' She began to sob again.

'My God!' Maxwell gulped. No time to lose. 'Pull yourself together, Selina. Where's the boat now?'

'I don't know. On its way to Kutu, I suppose.'

Maxwell visualised the map of the archipelago. Kutu was about an hour's flying time from Bali. Which made it around four hundred and fifty miles.

'What sort of boat?'

'Like a *pinisi* . . .'

The high-prowed ketches that brought timber from Kalimantan to the old harbour at Batavia. How fast would they go? Twelve knots at the most, he guessed. Three hundred miles a day top wack. Thirty-six hours for the voyage.

'When did the boat leave Bali?'

'I don't know if boat was still at Bali last night. But General Sumoto call it at ten.'

Arriving Kutu around ten tomorrow morning at the earliest. That's if his figures were right and the *pinisi* was coming from Bali waters. He needed to return to his office and check the maps.

'You have a name for the boat?'

'*Berkat Amanat*. It mean Blessed Messenger.'

'And how many men on board?'

'I think two. And Stephen.'

Maxwell jotted notes on the small pad he carried in his shirt pocket. By rights, he should turn her in. Hand her straight to Brigadier General Effendi and let POLRI sort things out, but in this country life wasn't that simple.

'Why haven't you told this to the police?'

She looked aghast.

'You not understand, Mr Maxwell? General Sumoto he have a lot of friends. He very powerful man. If I go to the police, I never seen again. I finished. I dead.'

'But the president's just sacked Sumoto,' Maxwell protested.

'Make no difference. You don't understand. Dino he still very powerful. If you big man in Indonesia – maybe in ABRI, or businessman or minister – then only one question matter: who take power when the president goes ... And Dino got many friends. He still very important to whoever become new president.'

What role did Effendi have in the power play, Maxwell wondered? Surely *he* couldn't be a Sumoto man? Not after coming out with all that spider stuff.

Selina fiddled with the bangles on her left wrist which glittered dimly in the light of a distant street lamp. Maxwell let his eyes linger on her face. Fetching, terribly fetching, with the sort of facial perfection that made European men go weak at the knees. Poor Bowen. Must have felt he'd won the jackpot when she gave herself to him.

Questions.

'Tell me the full story, Selina,' he murmured. 'Tell me everything that happened. Why you?'

'Because I girlfriend of Dino Sumoto,' she whispered, head down in embarrassment. 'Dino, he live away from his wife one year, now. He good to me. Give me money. Car. Nice clothes. Then, last week he tell me I must do something very special for him. He know it my job to look after Mr Bowen when he here on official visit. He say Mr Bowen like me *very* much ... Then he tell me let Stephen make love with me. I say *no*, *no*, but he tell me it *very* important to him. For his business.'

Her mouth turned down again.

'I had no idea 'bout what they going to do to Stephen. Believe me,' she pleaded. 'Dino just say to make sure I pick up Stephen from hotel and take him to Bali. He tell me to let Stephen do whatever he want with me ...'

She wiped her nose with the back of her hand, ashamed.

'How did you get to Bali? Via Singapore?'

'No. He fix it so it look that way. But we fly by executive jet. It belong Dino's business partner.'

Her expression clouded as she remembered Bowen's greedy selfishness when he'd made love to her on the plane's soft, cream, leather upholstery.

'Dino,' she went on, 'he meet us in Bali where his partner have a boat. We go on board, and leave the marina. Then we have lunch and plenty drink. But in Stephen's glass they put some drug. He fall asleep. Then we meet with the *pinisi* and some intel men carry Stephen across . . .'

'Intel?' Maxwell exclaimed. 'How d'you know they were intel?'

'I know because of their way.'

And in her line of business she *would* know, he realised.

'I see.'

It raised a huge question. How much of ABRI military intelligence was caught up in the conspiracy? How many involved in the plot to manipulate the succession?

'What happened next?'

'Dino tell me stay in Bali, while he return to Jakarta. Then on Friday a man I never seen before bring me a cassette and tell me take it to airport and send to Paris airfreight, for collection by . . . oh, I don't remember the name.'

'Ricky Smith,' Maxwell offered.

'Ya, I think. I have to call a phone in France and tell him the number of the freight papers. Please, Mr Maxwell, I didn't know what's on that tape. Believe me, they tell me nothing . . .'

'Yes, yes. I believe you. Go on.'

'On Sunday they bring me another tape. I send that off too. Same place. Same phone call to France. Then Dino he tell me to come back to Jakarta. Next day, Monday, I hear on the news what they done to Stephen. Dino say he kill me if I tell anyone what I know.'

'But you did speak to the police on Monday?' Effendi had told him that same night.

'Ya. I tell them a lie. Tell them that I take Stephen to Soekarno-Hatta for Primati flight to Singapore. Dino tell me to say that . . .'

Maxwell began to smell a rat. Everything she did was on Sumoto's orders. This too?

'And why are you telling me this now? Did Sumoto send you?'

'No, no!' Selina began to cry again. 'I . . . I escape from his house . . .'

she gasped between sobs. 'He . . . he tell his guard to keep me there, but . . . but I give the guard money and he leave the door open.'

'And where was Sumoto when this happened?' Maxwell asked, his voice tinged with cynicism.

'General Sumoto gone away. This afternoon, after he meet with president he come back to his house. He very afraid. I never seen him like that. Then I hear him call someone on the telephone. Someone in Kutu. He give him order, like the man at other end was a soldier. Tell him the boat will come tomorrow. Say to him, *"You know what to do."* Then he say – *everybody who know 'bout Stephen, you make them disappear* – that what he say to him.'

'Who? Who knows about it? Did he give any names?'

'Give one name. Dugdell, I think.'

Dug*dale*. So . . . Randall *was* on the right track. And by now could be in extreme danger. Somehow he had to get a warning to him.

'Selina, you said Dino Sumoto had gone away . . . Where to?'

'Kutu, Mr Maxwell. He gone to Kutu. To make sure nobody left alive who know what he done.'

Kutu
21.20 hrs (13.20 hrs GMT)

The inflatable nudged round the headland. At the far end of the bay the lights of Piri sparkled on the water. In the midst of its spatter of brightness the skeletal schooner rig of the *Morning Glory* stood out. The fishing boats they'd seen moored around her earlier were now at sea, their catch lights strung out across the horizon.

The *Morning Glory* was in darkness. It had the appearance of a dead ship. As they approached slowly, Randall waited for some twitch of his guts to tell him this was indeed the place where Stephen Bowen was being kept prisoner. But his guts were silent.

With the outboard at low revs to limit noise, it had taken two hours from Santa Josef, with just the weak light of the moon and the Kutuan's knowledge of the coastline to keep them off the rocks. They'd given a wide detour to the construction site for the new harbour. Arc lights burned through the night there to deter attacks, the ABRI guards alert for an OKP assault from any direction, including the sea.

Dedi cut the engine and dipped a paddle into the water. His breathing was laboured. Any moment he feared they'd be picked out by the searchlight on the old harbour watchtower. Every few seconds he rested his paddle to listen. The silence was total. Beyond the shore lights Piri had bolted its doors for the night.

Fifty metres from the schooner now. No glimmer of light, no sound. They lay on the boards, letting the inflatable drift closer. Twenty metres. A soft lapping of water against the schooner's hull. Too dark to see if there was a lookout. The neoprene bow nudged the planking. They listened again. Nothing. Not a breath. No feet scuffing across the deck to ward them off. Dedi pressed his ear against the side, listening for movement within the hull. Hearing none, he eased the rubber boat towards the boarding ladder near the stern, then gripped the steel side rails, looping the painter round one of them. He placed his foot on a rung and eased his weight onto it gently so as not to make the boat rock.

Bare-footed and silent, Dedi stepped on to the deck of the *Morning Glory*. Heart thumping, Randall followed. From the distant shore came the sudden growl of tyres on the coast road. A riot-squad heading for Poteng. A relentless military that showed no mercy.

And Charlie was their prisoner.

He heard a lock click as Dedi opened a hatch and went below. Torchlight glowed softly from the square aperture of the companion-way.

Seconds later a head reappeared.

'Come. No one here.'

Below deck, Dedi swung his torch round a lounge the width of the hull, created from part of the cargo hold. Off it was a galley. The Kutuan retrieved two plastic bottles from a store cupboard and a packet of biscuits. Gratefully Randall gulped the water and took a handful of the digestives.

'Nobody here, see?' Dedi repeated. He sounded relieved, but in the low torch light looked as if he knew something was seriously wrong.

Randall's suspicions remained. He could trust nobody.

'What about the rest of the boat?' he growled. 'Show me round.'

Dedi took him down a wood-panelled gangway, pushing doors open to show two, four-berth cabins. A companion-way at the end led below. To the engine space, he said. Then on the right, directly beneath the large wheelhouse, was the captain's cabin. With a bunk and lockers on one side, Brad clearly used the rest as an office. The torch picked out a table spread with charts, an old roll-top desk with a swivel chair secured to the deck by a hook, and a filing cabinet.

Randall pulled a small Maglite flashlight from his pocket and twisted it on. As he shone the beam on to the chart table he had the impression of looking at a display case in a museum. Everything laid out to be seen.

'Always like this, Dedi? Everything spread out all over the place?'
'No.' The Kutuan frowned. 'Maybe Brad leave in a hurry.'

In the centre of the table, in a cover of clear plastic was a chart of the waters around Kutu, a large, red cross chinagraphed at a point off the northwest coast.

'What's this show, Dedi?'

'That mark where Brad find World War submarine. I tell you this morning . . .'

'I remember.' He leaned forward to look more closely.

Suddenly some extra-sensory twitch that he'd never been able to define told him he was on to something. Somewhere in this mess he knew he would find the key to the maze.

He widened the torch beam, picking out a thin pile of photocopied pages. On the uppermost sheet was a blurred photograph of a miniature submarine. From out of its tiny hatch poked a bony face under a misshapen cap. Below the photo, a name. *The Witch*. And a date – August 1945.

The pages looked to have been copied from Australian government archives chronicling a Special Forces mission to Kutu – still under the control of the Japanese then, but just days before the surrender.

Randall skim read. It talked of Japanese atrocities inflicted on Allied prisoners extending the airfield in Kutu and reported that documents recording the maltreatment had been moved to the villa of the Japanese commandant for destruction in the event of defeat.

Two officers from Aussie Special Forces were tasked to raid the island by miniature submarine and seize the papers for use as evidence in war crimes trials. The raid itself was a success apparently, but ultimately a failure when the sub sank making its escape. The two crew were never found.

Randall turned the pages. Technical spec on *The Witch* . . . Biogs of the men involved . . . Interesting tale. Dugdale was right. It'd make a great TV documentary.

But he'd still not found the clue which he was convinced was there.

He came to the last three sheets. Different. Handwritten. Barely legible. A photocopy of a diary, the writing a faded, looping scrawl. It took a moment to get the hang of the script, but as he read further his pulse began to quicken.

The diary had been written by one of the men on the raid the day before they'd set off – a confession to his family in case he didn't return. It revealed another, sensational reason for the mission to Kutu. One that made Brad Dugdale's obsession with the wreck only too clear.

The diary stated that the Jap commandant on the island had used the war years to feather his nest, looting homes wherever he'd served. Paintings from the houses of Dutch settlers – artifacts of gold and silver – and a collection of diamonds and other gems that weighed several kilos.

This was what had really drawn the two Special Forces adventurers to the Kutu mission. At the end of a war that had been long and harrowing, mentions in despatches were not enough for them. The jewels were the reward they wanted.

The diary was unsigned. He flipped back to the men's biographies and read the names again.

Lieutenant Martin *Dugdale*.

'Ahh . . . Bingo.'

A father? An uncle? The age would be right. So, it wasn't just a piece of *history* Brad planned to salvage, but a fortune in stolen gems.

Nick put down the photostats. The trouble was none of this seemed to have any link with the kidnap. He glanced up, wondering if Dedi knew something that would cast more light. Then he gaped. The Kutuan was holding a mobile phone.

'Christ! Where'd *that* come from?'

Dedi pointed to a bracket on the wall.

'It belong Brad. He leave it here by mistake.'

'Does it work?'

'Can use in Piri and up to three kilometre offshore,' he explained calmly.

'Can you dial abroad on it?'

'I think.'

Randall breathed out. The Gods were smiling on him.

'First I call Captain's Bar,' Dedi said, switching on and dialling. He dropped into the swivel chair.

'Don't say anything to them about me,' Randall warned.

The number answered almost immediately. Dedi spoke softly in Kutun, then he gave a little gasp. As he listened, his eyes widened with horror. A few more words, then he cut the call.

He stared straight at Randall.

'Soldiers come to bar this afternoon. They take Teri. And Brad he gone too!'

'Brad's been *arrested*?'

'I think. My father just say Brad never come back from boat. He tell me keep away from Captain's Bar or they take me too.' His face sagged with bewilderment.

Dugdale arrested? Why, why, why? Randall was desperate to phone Maxwell. But first he *had* to find the missing clue. He leaned across the chart table, supporting himself on his hands. The link with the kidnap *was* here. He could smell it.

The filing cabinet. He looked up and stepped over to it. The drawers were locked.

'D'you have a key to this?' he asked Dedi.

'No. Only Brad.'

On top of the cabinet was a black box file. He looked at the label on the spine. One word written on it. *Permit.*

He opened the lid. Inside was a pile of letters Dugdale had written to the headquarters of KODAM Twelve. Requests for a permit from the Indonesian navy to dive on the wreck of the *Witch* and to salvage her. Letters addressed to the then commander – *Major General Dino Sumoto.*

Randall read fast. The last reply – sent just over a month ago – had talked of unresolved problems, of the need for fees to be paid. It gave a date and the name of a hotel in Bali, saying that Dugdale should meet Sumoto there privately to settle the outstanding difficulties.

'Yes!' hissed Randall. He had it. He'd closed the circle.

He could see it now. Dugdale desperate for the permit that would make him rich. Sumoto's price – help with an international crime that only a Caucasian with contacts in the TV business could provide.

'Now I need that phone,' Randall whispered, holding out his hand. Dedi reached it across to him.

A standard Japanese-made analogue cellphone. Easy to be monitored, simple to locate when switched on. About the most insecure form of telecommunications there was. But beggars couldn't choose. Had to gamble that ABRI's phone-monitoring abilities were as under-resourced as the rest of their garrison.

A call to the Yard number he'd rung that morning would be suicide. He knew the intel watchers had noted it. Any automatic intercept system would pick it up immediately. So, it would have to be Jakarta. Have to take his chance on someone being there.

The number rang.

'*Hello?*'

'This is Cuculus,' Randall announced.

'*Thank God!*' replied Maxwell.

20

South Devon
Early afternoon

RAIN SWEPT UP the wide estuary in a slow-moving wave, uniting the sky, the sand and the gold-flecked woods in a skein of grey.

Colonel Ambrose Cavendish stared from the dormer window that overlooked the river, a silver-haired stick of a man in green tweed and cavalry twill. The climb to the little-used, bare-floored boxroom at the top of the house had taken it out of him. His hands clutched the sill as he panted for breath.

It had rained like this fifty-odd years ago, he remembered.

In Kutu.

Solid sheets of water that had surged in from the direction of the ocean to turn the foot-hardened earth of the Japanese prison camp into a lake. Water that had flooded latrines and spread the ordure of a thousand sickly men, so that when the sun dried the ground, it was laid out for all to see and to smell, like a past they couldn't escape.

And now it was happening again. Of all the islands in all the oceans of the world, fate had taken his own daughter to Kutu, the source of the guilt that had gnawed at his soul for half a century and, he believed, created the cancer that was consuming his brain. It was inconceivable to him that she would *not* discover his secret. Instead of dying with a *private* shame, it would be exposed like that excrement in the prison yard.

He turned away from the window, but left it open so he could feel the cool dampness of the air – and to let out the smoke.

The attic had been a child's bedroom in the distant past, the walls still covered with a faded paper of cavorting rabbits. When he and Verity had moved in twelve years ago, they'd stacked the bare boards with old suitcases and boxes of junk.

Verity would be away for two hours at least. She'd gone food shopping at Tesco's in Ivybridge. Time enough.

He knew precisely where to find the small leather-bound suitcase

262

with the brass locks that hadn't been opened for fifty years. Since the day they'd moved in, it had remained hidden by a tea chest full of the books he'd accumulated during twenty years of army life, tucked into the corner furthest from the door. A small time-capsule, buried in the top of the house like a tumour, benign only for as long as people remained ignorant of the significance of its contents.

To reach the corner he pulled aside a pine blanket box that had belonged to Verity's mother, then reached down behind the tea chest.

The tan bag was little larger than a briefcase. On the lid were his initials A.C.C. Ambrose Carmichael Cavendish. A relic from boarding school. He laid it on the floor beside the galvanised bucket he'd brought up from the scullery, knelt down, then felt in his jacket pocket for the key which he'd kept with his cufflinks in an old tobacco tin for fifty years.

The locks turned stiffly. He pushed aside the catches and the tongues sprang open. Before lifting the lid, he hesitated, bracing himself. His eyes had not seen the contents since his return to England in 1946. He brushed the dust off the lustreless hide, then opened it.

The photograph was on the top, as he knew it would be. A picture of himself and his brother standing proudly in their uniforms, side by side on the day of their commissioning. For a moment he couldn't remember which was him and which George. Twins. Identical piercing eyes, almost white in the faded sepia of the print.

Then he saw the difference. The slight bow of the head, the turn of the mouth that was the outward sign of the inadequacy that had always dogged him. Ambrose had found himself.

The picture had been taken in 1941. Second lieutenants in the Service Corps. After six months in Britain, both had been posted to Wavell's High Command in Java. Then in March 1942 with the Japs about to invade, they'd escaped the island by ship. The vessel had been torpedoed. Dutch, British, Sikhs and Hindus, all who survived the sinking became prisoners of the Japanese.

He laid down the picture on the open lid. Three years they'd spent in prison camps together, he and his brother. Never apart. Then finally at the labour camp in Kutu, death *had* separated them. Beneath the photo in the box was the letter his father had written him after his own liberation – the first word from home in over three years. He picked it up. It told of his father's heartbreak at George's execution in the camp. George – the favourite son. Told too of his mother's demise a year earlier. More junk in the box. Uniform pips, medal ribbons. He let them run through his fingers like sand.

He'd remained in Java on military service after his release from detention. A year had passed before returning to England. The homecoming came back to him as vividly as yesterday. Mentally scarred by the hell of the camps – needing to talk about it but unable to – he'd met a wall of non-interest in England. *'Don't tell us what you've been through, chum – we've had it just as bad here.'* But they hadn't. Nobody had it as bad as that.

He stared at the wall, monstrous memories spooling through his head. The oven-like punishment cages. Spread-eagled on benches being beaten with sticks. George's death in the blazing sun.

He pulled out the rest of the papers. Army stuff certifying his release from POW status. Spidery notes he'd scribbled during captivity. And the official report on George's demise . . .

That was the paper he burnt first. He held it over the metal bucket, touching its corner with the match flame, watching the fire blacken and curl the paper, the ink still legible. Then he tamped the ash to dust.

Next he burned the photograph, then everything else in the case, until it was empty – except for the .38 service revolver in its cracked, leather holster.

Ambrose slipped the gun from its cover and held it by its grip. It felt strange to touch after so many years. He turned the chamber, checking the bullets were in place. Always known that one day he would need it again.

Then, from below him in the house he heard the phone ring. Verity probably. Ringing from Tesco's to see he was all right. It threw him into confusion. By rights he should ignore it. In a few minutes time whatever conversation he had with her would be irrelevant. Yet, like life itself, the insistent ringing was hard to turn his back on.

With the pistol dangling in his hand, he descended the narrow staircase and entered their bedroom.

'Hello?' he croaked into the mouthpiece.

'Colonel Cavendish?'

'Um . . . yes.'

'This is the Foreign Office here. I'm ringing about your daughter Charlotte. I understand she's a journalist. And she's in Kutu.'

'Yes. Oh, dear.' Heart in mouth. Concern about her suddenly, instead of himself. 'What's happened?'

'Now you're not to worry, colonel. But we've had a report she was caught up in a bit of a skirmish. She's not hurt, but we believe she's been arrested by the Indonesian armed forces. Our embassy out there is trying to get some information, but it's nine o'clock at night in Jakarta, so it could be another twelve hours before we hear anything.'

'Twelve hours?' he mumbled.

An eternity. Another one. The revolver was still dangling from his right hand. He held it out in front of him. Couldn't do it. Not now. Not until he knew she was safe.

'Well ... well we'll be waiting for your call then ...'

London – COBR
14.15 hrs

Philip Vereker stepped from his car on to the Whitehall pavement to see David Stanley's uniformed back disappearing through the varnished entrance to the Cabinet Office. He caught up with him in the lift down to the briefing room.

'David. I want a quiet word before we go in,' he whispered. There were others in the lift.

Once through the security barrier into the COBR area and alone, they stopped.

'This journalist woman who's been arrested, Charlotte Cavendish – what's her relationship with your man Randall?'

'*Relationship?* What d'you mean?' Stanley protested.

'Maxwell told me Randall wasn't just filing a missing persons report when he talked about her. He sounded *concerned*. As if it was personal.'

'Meaning?'

'Meaning was this pretty young journalist who's now in the hands of ABRI intelligence an *intimate* of Randall's?' he growled. 'Does she know he's a British agent? Has he told her everything? And is *she* going to tell the whole bloody world when she gets out of there? He's your boy, David. It's *you* the shit'll stick to if he's screwed up.'

Stanley drew himself up straight. The men were of similar height, but he had the advantage of age.

'DS Randall's proved his worth a hundred per cent in the last hour, Philip. And he's a professional. I have every confidence in him.'

'He's also a man with a long-standing reputation for making a play for any woman who comes within reach,' Vereker scowled, moving on swiftly into the meeting room.

Stanley began to sweat. Vereker had found some dirt that was news to him.

Prime Minister Copeland looked tense but determined. The leak on the News Channel lunchtime bulletin about his withholding the aid statement had driven him into a corner. He wanted to curl up and hide, but knew he couldn't. He would have to fight. Until the bitter end.

The source of the leak, he suspected, was sitting right beside him. Hugh White, the foreign secretary, wore an indignant, surprised expression, like a man who's rear had been penetrated by a poker. The large, thick lenses of his spectacles needed a clean. The men stared away from each other as if communication between them might never be possible again.

'Ah, there you are,' Copeland snapped, wearily. 'Let's get on. I've got PMQs in an hour.' The latest developments from Indonesia had been phoned through to him a few minutes ago.

Vereker stood his briefcase on the floor beneath the light oak table and sat down.

'Prime minister, as you know, we think we have a handle on where Stephen Bowen is,' he began.

'But . . . but is he still alive?' Copeland stammered, unsure whether he wanted the answer to be yes or no.

'We don't know that,' said Vereker. 'General Sumoto's ordered his men to kill him, but it may not have happened yet. Detective Sergeant Randall's been despatched to try to intercept the boat that Bowen's on and to save him if he can. I don't hold out a lot of hope, however.'

'Randall's a resourceful man, prime minister,' the assistant commissioner interjected.

Copeland nodded like a robot.

'General Sumoto has embarked on what one might call a cull,' Vereker continued bluntly. 'Killing anybody who could reveal his involvement in the kidnap. If Randall falls into his hands I don't give much for his chances.'

His words had a chilling timbre.

'Well then General Sumoto's got to be stopped,' Copeland insisted, lamely.

'*We* can't stop him, prime minister,' Vereker went on. 'The Indonesians could of course. But *will* they? Depends on how much of their police and armed forces organisation is allied with Sumoto. The general's played his cards extraordinarily close to his chest. The CIA don't know any more than we do. Which puts us in a real dilemma over how to proceed.

'We have one trump card. Selina Sakidin. Sumoto's mistress. She's told us the whole story and is currently hiding at the apartment of our man Harry Maxwell. She thinks some of the police are on Sumoto's side and if we hand her over to them they'll kill her to silence her and to protect the general. Maxwell thinks she's wrong. Thinks *his* contact in POLRI is straight.

'Now, here's the question. Do we ensure the survival of this key witness by getting her out of the country to safety, and hope Randall works a miracle on his own? Or do we hand Miss Sakidin over to the Indonesian police with everything we know about Sumoto and demand that they deal with him?'

Copeland frowned in disbelief. 'Are you telling me the Indonesian police genuinely still don't know what Sumoto's been up to?'

'It really does look that way, prime minister. Astonishing as it sounds. For the kidnap he's made use of a very small, very loyal group of supporters. And any whose loyalty he's not sure of he's had killed. Or is in the process of killing.'

Copeland supported his chin in his hands and pondered. Saving Stephen was almost certainly a lost cause, but he wanted no more deaths on his conscience.

'If we leave it to the Indonesians to sort out,' Copeland asked thoughtfully, 'could Randall be recalled? For his own safety.'

Vereker pursed his lips. 'Possibly. I'd have to check with Maxwell.'

'I'm very concerned for him,' said Copeland. 'To risk Randall's life trying to save a man who's probably already dead – it can't be justified. Miss Sakidin should be handed to the Indonesian police immediately.'

'They won't thank us,' interjected the foreign secretary.

Copeland looked through him, irritated by his intervention.

'Us telling them what's going on in their own country,' White went on. 'It'll be a huge embarrassment to them. And if you embarrass the Indonesians they won't want to know you afterwards. We could lose trade.'

'Lose even more if Randall gets caught and they put him on trial as a spy,' Copeland retorted cuttingly. 'But you're right,' he added, mellowing. 'It *may* need some finessing.'

There was a sharp tap at the door. One of the officials manning the phones put his head round.

'Beg pardon, prime minister, but Ambassador Bruton's on the line.'

'Put him on the conference phone,' Copeland ordered, reaching forward to press the key on the box in the centre of the light oak table.

'*Hello?*' Bruton's voice, echoing, from Jakarta.

'Good afternoon ambassador. Keith Copeland here.'

'*Good evening, sir. I've just had a rather disturbing call from our friends in ABRI. Thought I'd better let you know right away. They've been on to their HQ in Kutu about Miss Cavendish. They say they've never heard of her, and certainly haven't got her under arrest. They say no Europeans whatsoever were involved when their commandos struck at the Kutuan guerrillas this afternoon.'*

The News Channel
15.25 hrs

Ted Sankey picked up the waste basket that held the last of the detritus left on his desk by the accountant Paxton and placed it outside his door. He'd got his office back. For a moment he stood in the doorway surveying his newsroom kingdom.

Since the lunchtime scoop about the aid cover-up, Sankey's phone had rung constantly. Ironically, the first call had been from Gordon Wiggins demanding to know the News Channel's source. Sankey had pictured the tape recorder spinning on Wiggins' desk. Then the broadsheets had been on, frustrated by the stonewalling response they'd got from the Overseas Development Administration and the Foreign Office. They'd asked if he had more details, but he hadn't. Now they were all waiting for PMQs. Copeland's chance to explain himself.

Three minutes to go. Sankey switched his monitor to the parliament feed.

The triumph of his return to the helm of the News Channel had been dampened by the alarming call from the Foreign Office reporting Charlie's arrest, then the even more disturbing call an hour later saying the Indonesians were denying all knowledge of her.

Word of Charlie's disappearance had brought a chill to the newsroom, and to his heart. Through his mind flitted terrible visions of her bullet-riddled body lying in some godforsaken, mosquito-ridden jungle. But any guilt he felt for sending her out there had to be suppressed. It was *she* who'd demanded to go, he reminded himself. *She* who'd refused to come back when Paxton ordered her return.

Nonetheless, he was deeply worried. Uncertain what to do about it. Whether to announce on the news she was missing and get more front-page publicity for the Channel, or keep quiet about it for as long as possible in the hope she'd come up with an exclusive, all the more stunning because no one had known she was there.

Keith Copeland's arrival in the chamber of the House of Commons provoked a sustained murmur, more welcome, Sankey guessed, than the loud yawns with which the Honourable Members on the opposition benches frequently greeted him.

Copeland bowed to the speaker and took his seat. Environment Questions were just finishing. The beargarden of PMQs was about to begin. On the bench opposite, the weasel-eyed shadow spokesman for foreign affairs sat down and crossed his legs. The camera picked him out fixing Copeland with a glare that seemed to say *I'll see you in gaol.*

'*Questions to the Prime Minister!*' the speaker bellowed.

Sankey's secretary brought in a mug of coffee. He jabbed a finger at the point on the desk where he wanted it, then waved her quickly from the room.

Copeland rose to his feet to explain why he'd ordered the postponement of the aid statement. There was a note of apology in his voice.

'Madam Speaker, I have to express a certain degree of astonishment, not only at the question raised by the honourable member opposite, but also at the irresponsibility of certain outlets in the news media. I would remind the House that the life of one of its members is currently in grave jeopardy. Anything said or done by this government or the British media which could increase the danger to Stephen Bowen should in my judgement be avoided. That, madam speaker, is the reason I decided to postpone publication of the overseas aid statement. It does, as has been reported, focus on one aid project for Indonesia; nothing unusual in that. We've been giving aid to that country for many, many years. This House is of course entitled to ask as it has done before whether there is any connection between our overseas aid and the sale of armaments. The answer to that is an emphatic "no", but the proper time to discuss that issue is after Stephen Bowen has been safely returned to his family, not now.'

From behind him a murmur of support. From across the floor a jeer. The Opposition spokesman rose for his counter attack.

'Madam speaker, the prime minister has, as usual, missed the point. The essence of the report on the lunchtime news was that he has twice on this issue overridden the unanimous advice of his officials. Firstly in approving money for a power station on the island of Kutu – a project rejected by the Foreign Office as unsuitable for aid – and secondly in insisting on a delay in publication of the aid statement. The question is this; why is the Kutu power station project so important to the prime minister, and why is he so eager that it shouldn't be discussed at this time?'

Copeland's jaw set with increased determination.

'Madam speaker, I have already answered that question. I am not prepared to do or say anything which could impinge on the efforts being made to secure the release of Stephen Bowen. Madam speaker, there is a criminal investigation underway. To make comments on the matters being raised would be nothing short of irresponsible.'

He sat down and folded his arms.

'*The member for Nutley East,*' shouted the speaker.

'*Number two . . .*'

'*I refer the honourable member to the reply I gave some moments ago . . .*'

The MP for Nutley East was on Copeland's own back benches. Copeland half-turned as the member rose for his supplementary.

'*Madam speaker, there have been a number of comments in the media and elsewhere recently, implying that Minister of State for Foreign Affairs Stephen Bowen has retained a financial connection with the British company Metroc Minerals of which he was once a director and which has a one third stake in the Kutu mining project. Can the prime minister assure the House that this is not true?*'

A flicker of alarm spread across Copeland's face. Sankey leaned in towards the set.

'*I can assure the House that my government has no knowledge whatsoever of any financial connection between Stephen Bowen and Metroc Minerals.*'

He sat down again. The shadow spokesman leapt to his feet.

'*But what knowledge does he* personally *have?*'

Copeland flinched, like a man cut by a rapier tip.

'Fu-uck,' growled Sankey, convinced more than ever that the story had wings. Gordon's gut instinct had been right.

'*Madam speaker, I have no personal knowledge of such a connection.*'

Copeland stuck his chin out.

Sankey looked hard at Copeland's face. Defiant yet embattled. Arrogant yet guilt-ridden. Cocky, yet fearful. Yes, thought Sankey. He felt it now with utter conviction. The prime minister of Great Britain and Northern Ireland was lying to save his skin.

21

Kutu
Friday 03.30 hrs

A DARK BLUE minibus with windows of blackened glass and no registration plates turned out of the Kadama interrogation centre and headed for Piri. The night was inky and moonless, the road empty. Nobody to see the vehicle leave, nobody to watch its arrival at the isolated villa just half a kilometre away. Colonel Widodo was at the wheel, alone in the vehicle apart from his hooded passenger.

Charlie breathed in and out deeply, trying to steady her jerky heartbeat. Her wrists were cuffed to the metal tubing of the seat. She'd guessed it was Widodo from the groping feel of his hands as he'd half lifted, half pushed her into the vehicle. Also, there was now an overpowering smell of garlic in the air.

From the sacking that covered her head, another smell. Cloves. *Kretek* smoke from the last victim, she guessed. Her heart fluttered at the thought that whoever had worn this hood might have died in it. She hunched forward, her stomach spasming with terror and with emptiness. Under the hood she shut her eyes tight and pounded out desperate prayers. For her mother, for her father, for the people of Kutu, for Nick and for herself.

Dear God, I believed in you when I was young. Please. Please don't let me die.

A soldier had come to the cell fifteen minutes ago, not with the usual terrorising clamour, but silently while Teri and the other woman were asleep. Hustled her down to the courtyard. She'd made a token protest, asking again to speak to the British Embassy. The response was the bag over her head. Rough, black cloth with a hole for the nose.

She'd panicked, convinced they were about to shoot her. There in the yard. A firing squad. Pleaded shamelessly for her life, choking and sobbing. There'd been a chuckle, then the hands lifting her into the van, her shins scuffing against the step.

The vehicle swung abruptly to the left. Unable to support herself Charlie fell sideways and banged her head on the window. Then they stopped with a jerk, the engine off. In the silence of the night she heard the clinking of the radiator cooling. The door slid open. Fetid breath as the man freed her hands. Then she was outside, walking. Up a step. Into a building that smelled clean and fresh. Floor polish. Walking, walking, then a door closing behind her, a key in the lock. Footsteps going away. Rubber squeaking on polished parquet, then silence.

She listened. Just her own shaky breathing. Nobody else's. The hum of an air-conditioner. Then she smelled food.

'Hello?' she ventured. 'Anybody here?'

Silence. Why was she still hooded? With her freed hands she slid it off and straightened her greasy hair. Looked like a room in a private house. Two single beds with crisp white sheets, a sofa and a small, low table laid with mat, plate and cutlery. Beside it a bowl of the inevitable *nasi goreng* and a plate of fruit.

Disbelieving, she checked she was alone. There was a door open on the far side – a bathroom. Empty. She entered, ran the taps, then splashed water on her face. Soap. Clean towels. She gave a little snort. If this was a death cell, they meant her to die in comfort.

She flopped on to the sofa and spooned rice on to the plate. There was a Thermos jug of iced drinking water. She ate and drank carefully, feeling the food ease the knot in her stomach.

It helped her mind too. She began to think rationally again. They *weren't* going to kill her. *Deport* her more like. Softening her up with food and a bed so she wouldn't be too critical when she wrote about them . . .

When she'd eaten enough, she stood up and tried the door. Firmly locked. She knocked on it, then pressed her ear against the varnished wood. Nothing.

She knocked again, convinced she could hear voices.

'Hello,' she called, not very loudly. 'Could somebody please tell me what's going on?'

Major General Dino Sumoto didn't hear her. He stood by the open door to a veranda on the other side of the villa. The air was fresher than before, the result of the evening's rain that had beaten down like shot.

Sumoto's tall frame seemed to stoop, his shoulders sloping with defeat. More than twelve hours had passed since his oblique but chilling meeting with the president and he was still smarting from it. The ruler's hard, cold eyes had looked right through him.

The president was a lonely man, with dwindling authority and a family whose hunger for wealth was the reason he still clung to power. A power which was absolute and in Javan tradition could only be taken from him by force. Yet force would tear the country apart, which was why attempts at engineering change had failed. No one had had the guts to see it through before.

Sumoto had known this. Known his scheme had depended on building an irresistible head of pressure in the military. Weapons, money and promises should have been enough, if only the kidnap of Stephen Bowen had achieved what he'd planned for it.

The president had treated him with contempt that afternoon. Shown him no mercy. Most generals who'd dissented in the past had been bought off with ambassadorships. Sumoto had been offered nothing but his life – permission to go on living, just so long as what'd he'd done never became public.

How much the president knew, Sumoto had not been able to tell. The conversation had been oblique. A monologue about the undesirability of closer military links with China. No reference to Stephen Bowen, but from the ice crystals in the air Sumoto had known he was under suspicion.

The Australian Dugdale had been the first to be silenced. A loose tongue when drunk – and a foreigner. Throughout his interrogation the bar owner had sworn to Widodo he would never reveal Sumoto's secret. Sworn it until the end. But they couldn't take a chance with him. Now there were others to be dealt with.

Sumoto turned from the window. Still wearing the mud-green safari suit that was his second skin, he paced to the middle of the room. The villa had been furnished by his wife in the last months before their separation. Wide, soft armchairs and couches in ivory moquette, all bought at outrageous expense from a catalogue sent from America. Sumoto was a man of simple origins who'd never shaken off his peasant frugality. His wife's extravagance with his hard-won wealth was what had broken their marriage in the end. He loathed this house now; loathed it because it reminded him of her.

Colonel Widodo watched Sumoto from the corner of the room. It pained him to have backed the wrong horse, but it was too late to switch. Like with the general himself, what mattered now was self-preservation.

'You're certain you have left no trace of this Cavendish woman at Kadama?' Sumoto demanded.

'Certain. Her name's no longer on the register. I saw to it myself. And the guards are well drilled in not remembering faces.'

'What about Dugdale's woman? *She* saw her.'

'When we have finished with Teri she will be quite ready to deny seeing Miss Cavendish in Kadama,' Sumoto explained sullenly.

'And the other journalist? The man – Randall . . .'

'Still not found. Alive, we think. I'm almost certain the priest was bringing him to Santa Josef but got wind of my men waiting at the orphanage. Must have dropped him somewhere else.'

'How much did Dugdale say to Randall? Did he tell him about me?'

'No. Only what I'd ordered him to say – the rumour about Bowen being seen here. Nothing else. I'm sure of that.' Dugdale had been a weak man. Easy to break. If he'd said more he would have admitted it.

Sumoto paced back to the window. Who to trust, that was the question that pressed him so painfully. Widodo would stay loyal. And Sugeng. But the men on the boat? And Selina . . .? *She* had as much power as anyone to destroy him.

He held out his hands and examined the palms. In the sixties they'd been stained with communist blood, but he'd taken no pleasure from those killings. If blood was to be shed this time, he'd resolved that it could be done in his *name*, but not *by* him. A commander's prerogative, after all. There were plenty of other men who would take pleasure from it.

Selina. Unbearable to have to decide that she too must die.

'Where is Dugdale's body?' Sumoto checked, putting off the moment.

'In the morning, when the mist covers the foothills, they will fly it to Jiwa.'

'And Miss Cavendish too.'

'I . . . I think it better to wait until we have the two of them together,' Widodo suggested.

'Find him. Find Randall quickly,' Sumoto rambled, his mind on the decision that could be delayed no longer.

In the night would be best. While Selina slept. The guard in Menteng could do it.

'I would like to be alone,' he murmured. 'Come back at dawn. Miss Cavendish will not run away.'

Widodo got up, relieved. It was easy to fight for another man's success, harder to live with his failure.

Sumoto waited until he heard the minibus leave. Then he drifted from the living room to the hardwood-panelled, book-lined study that had also been chosen from a catalogue. He picked up the telephone and dialled his house in Jakarta. After an interminable ringing, the Sundanese houseboy answered, his voice dulled with despair at having to be the giver of bad news.

'*Bapak*, Selina Sakidin, she gone,' he whispered. 'Everybody gone. Run away. Only me here now.'

Very slowly Sumoto took the receiver from his ear and replaced it on its rest.

Defeat stared him in the face. He had let his heart rule his head and now he'd been betrayed.

But he still had a chance, he told himself quickly. Still had friends who could save him. Friends who could silence *her*, if he could get to them in time.

The Kutu Sea
06.05 hrs

The powerboat's wake lay on the water like a strip of lace. Dead astern the distant crater of Kutu's Mount Jiwa secured its position on the dawn horizon with a grey-white smudge of smoke.

Dedi had been unsurprised to learn Randall was a police officer – he was used to people not being what they claimed to be. Last night they'd left Piri harbour within minutes of Randall's call to Maxwell, jolted by his warning that Sumoto was now in Kutu on a killing spree. They'd crossed from the *Morning Glory* to the powerboat alongside, a fifteen-metre craft called *Timini* which Dugdale kept filled with fuel and tinned food. They'd upped anchor and puttered out of Piri Bay without lights.

During the night Dedi had talked to keep himself awake. Rambled about Kutuans he knew who'd been taken by the police and disappeared. And of mountain people seeing helicopters drop bodies into Jiwa's molten heart.

Myth or truth, Randall had been chilled by his words. *Charlie* was in the hands of these men. The minutes, the hours were ticking past. He hoped to God Maxwell had pulled his finger out in getting wheels turning on her behalf.

To reach Kutu from Bali, the ketch *Berkat Amanat* with the kidnapped minister on board would have to navigate a channel that had been carved through the large island of Manda by an earthquake in a previous millennium. A few hundred metres wide, it was a natural choke-point. And now it lay ahead of them. The ketch, they assumed, was still on the other side of it, heading their way.

Daylight had brought a feverishness to the Kutuan, a restlessness that verged on mania. Dedi sat hunched over the helm, staring into the

275

lightening haze, brooding about his sister's arrest, Brad's disappearance and his powerlessness to do anything about any of it.

Randall sat next to him on the bridge, locked in his own thoughts. He knew that the mission he'd been given defied common sense. A job for the marines, not a lone, unarmed copper. Saving Bowen would mean getting on board the *Berkat Amanat* unseen or unopposed, then surviving the attention of his captors. Madness, yet he'd been ordered to try.

'*You must judge,*' Maxwell had said. '*Up to you, old boy. But if it's possible, then do it.*'

'Nick!' Dedi jabbed a finger to port.

'What is it?' He saw the outline of a small ship about a mile off.

'*ABRI,*' Dedi growled fearfully. 'Gunboat.'

Pinisi *Berkat Amanat*

The British minister of state for foreign affairs lay on his side, left cheek on the floor sticky with sweat. The poison in his blood had taken hold and drained him of the strength to lift his head. The thrumming of the diesels throbbed through his jaw like an abscess. On the other side of his head, the stump of his ear burned beneath a stinking bandage.

For twelve hours he'd drifted in and out of consciousness as the fever took its grip. The scalpel they'd cut him with had been dirty and sepsis had infected his blood. His mouth was paper dry. They'd stopped bringing food or water. In moments of lucidity he knew they meant him to die.

His pulse pounded, his breath rasped. He wanted to scream at that devil Copeland who'd done nothing to save him. The bastard was letting him rot. Because of the money.

Bowen feared death. No solution for a gambler. There always had to be a way out. But not through the tiny bloody porthole that had been his only link with the outside world for the past nine days. The shaft of sun streaming in mocked him by dancing circles on the floor as the boat rolled and rocked.

For the first few days of his confinement – hands chained to his feet, feet chained to a ring on the floor – he'd believed they'd all been taken. General Sumoto, Selina too. Three of them. He'd worried about the abuse Selina's sweet, salty body might have been subjected to by these thugs. Then it had sunk in. He was *alone* on his prison ship. Just him and his guards. Slowly, a dripping tap of suspicion had led to the realisation it was Sumoto who had duped him – Sumoto who'd used his own whore to seduce him for some purpose that could only be guessed at.

Bowen watched the beam of light from the porthole brush back and forth on the floor in front of him as the boat ploughed purposely through the waters of the Pacific. Then a slight change of course swung it away from him so that it lit up the foot of something black and metal. The tripod. The video camera was still there.

It had been his enemy, that camera – an ogling witness to his pain. He focused his hate on the blurry blue of its lens. Then he softened as a thought came to him. A way in which he might yet win a trick.

He knew the odds on his survival were worsening by the minute, but if he was to go under, then it shouldn't be him alone. Keith Copeland should perish with him. If not in the flesh, then at least in reputation. The world would know by now of his own personal failings. What it didn't know, but should, was that the British prime minister was no better.

The camera.

In his mind a mist rolled in. He felt himself slip into sleep. He tried to hang on to his thread of thought. Some scheme to redress the balance . . . The camera. It could yet become his friend.

He summoned all his remaining strength to pull his body towards it, extending the links that chained him to the floor. In his delirium he imagined that if he could reach the switch, prop himself up and speak into the lens, his message might get out like it had before. In the confused swirl of his mind, the camera became a living being, a conversation partner.

He reached out. Nowhere near close enough. His heart thudded with the exertion. A few inches more.

Then he heard the key in the lock. He lay flat again.

The door opened. Feet in trainers close to his face. He knew the man was looking down at him, wondering. He cringed, expecting a kick. Then the feet turned away, hands snatching up the tripod like driftwood for a bonfire.

Bowen let the mists roll over him. In amongst them somewhere was Sally's face, smiling. Smiling at his plight.

★

The *Timini* had anchored halfway up the channel, thirty metres from the mangrove-choked northern shore. Randall sat on the canopied deck at the stern pretending to be fishing, a red baseball cap on his head, a plan of action cementing itself in his mind.

The naval patrol boat they'd seen had ignored them and motored on. They'd been half an hour at anchor already and only one craft had passed, the weekly Pelni Line ferry from Flores to Kutu.

The water was the colour of mud. There was a stench of decay from the mangroves covering the banks. Beyond, the land mass rose gently in a tangle of fig and scrub. Insects buzzed about his head and large, dark birds swooped over the stumpy growth.

He glanced up at the bridge. Dedi sat, chin on his fist, watching the ribbon of brown that stretched to the west, his brooding face like a threatening squall. Dedi was a worry – an unknown quantity. The risks in what Randall planned were huge. He *needed* the Kutuan. Needed him to be on his side one hundred per cent.

Randall rested the fishing rod on the stainless-steel guard rail and stood up. Last night, back in the dark of Piri harbour he'd explained the bones of his mission, but suspected it was Dedi's own fear of arrest that had spurred him into agreeing to help.

Randall stepped up to the bridge.

'How're you doing, Dedi?' he mumbled.

'Nothing. Not see nothing yet,' Dedi mumbled back, frowning. He looked Randall up and down as if expecting to see something about his person, but not finding it. He frowned again, then asked sharply, 'What ezactly we doin' here, mister?'

'Trying to save a man's life . . .'

'You got a gun, mister?' Dedi prodded.

'No,' Randall admitted, sensing his credibility with the Kutuan evaporate. Dedi stood up and pushed past, down into the main cabin.

Shit, thought Randall. He's giving up on me.

Suddenly from below there was a crash and a splintering of wood. Randall slid down the companion-way into the saloon. Dedi was on his knees, smashing open a locker with a hammer and a screwdriver.

'What the hell . . .?'

The Kutuan ignored him.

'Dedi, what the fuck are you up to?'

A corner of the door came away, but the rest held. Whatever its contents, the locker had been designed to keep it secure.

'You gonna need gun, mister,' Dedi grumbled, swinging at it with renewed vigour. He smashed the timber around the lock and levered the door open.

Inside was a hunting rifle.

'Brad keep for crocodiles,' Dedi explained with childlike seriousness, holding it out.

Randall took the weapon in his hands, a heavy calibre rifle of a type he didn't recognise, fitted with an optical sight. It changed things. For better and for worse. A gun meant more of a chance of boarding the ketch. But a gun also meant shooting and killing, and he'd not wanted it to be like Malaysia again.

'You know how to use?' Dedi asked over his shoulder as he swung up the companion-way to the bridge.

'I think I can work it out,' Randall snapped.

A few seconds later there was a shout from above. Dedi had binoculars to his eyes, pointing westwards. A masted vessel with a high prow was rounding a headland a few hundred metres away.

'*Pinisi!*' Dedi shouted, feverish with excitement.

'Can you read the name?' Randall breathed, pounding up to the bridge.

'Too far. But is *pinisi*-type boat.'

Randall took the binoculars and adjusted the eyepiece. The approaching craft was small and white, with a stumpy main mast forward of the hold, but no sails up despite a useful breeze from the north. Its bow churned the brown water into yellow froth.

'How fast can a boat like that go?'

'Maybe twelve knots.'

'And this one, the *Timini*?'

'Twenty-five.'

He raised the binoculars again. He could see lettering on the bow. Two words. First letter B. 'Shit! I think it's her!' He pushed the glasses back to Dedi.

Dedi looked hard. 'Mmmm. I don't think,' he cautioned. '*Berkat*, but not *Amanat*. Many boats called *Berkat* something.'

Deflated, Randall watched idly as the small ketch motored past, its decks stacked with baulks of reddish timber.

Dedi put down the binoculars. 'OK, mister. Maybe next time you lucky,' he declared earnestly.

Randall dropped back down to the saloon, leaving Dedi to keep watch. He'd seen a portable short-wave radio there. He took it to the stern and sat in the chair, spinning through the frequencies in search of the BBC.

It was thirty seconds past the hour when he found it. The news had just started.

Africa was the lead. Massacres, and refugees dying of starvation. Then a story on middle east peace.

Finally, a report on Bowen. Randall held the speaker to his ear. Soundbites from the House of Commons – the PM's credibility under pressure – allegations of key information being withheld about aid for some power station on Kutu. Then a brief line that stopped his heart.

Fears are growing for British journalist Charlotte Cavendish who has been reported missing on the island of Kutu, where she'd gone to investigate the kidnap of Minister Stephen Bowen. Reports that she was arrested by the Indonesian military are being strenuously denied by officials in Jakarta who maintain she had entered the country illegally and was last seen in a dangerous area where Kutuan resistance fighters are active.

Randall squeezed shut his eyes, the ambush as vivid to him now as if it had only just happened.

He knew what it meant. Sumoto had her.

Jakarta
08.05 hrs (01.05 hrs GMT)

The embassy chauffeur sat straight-backed and tense for the drive to police headquarters. In the rear slumped Harry Maxwell, his fawn suit in need of a press. Beside him, Selina Sakidin trim in her pink business suit but shaking with fear. He thought of holding her hand to comfort her, but suspected the gesture mightn't be welcome.

Last night after their talk in her car, he'd taken her to his own apartment for safety, before returning to the embassy to report. Several hours later, in the small hours of the morning, he'd gone home, his conscience heavy with the ambassador's orders to hand her to the police.

He'd broken it to her gently, explaining there was no alternative. She'd been involved in a crime and no British official could help her flee the country. Selina had sobbed pitiably, certain she would be killed. His avowal that Brigadier General Effendi was as honest a policeman as any in Indonesia had been of little comfort.

He'd given her his bed, but she'd not slept much. Maxwell had stayed up typing the dossier which he was to present to Effendi. The

280

ambassador's driver had collected a copy for Bruton to give to the minister of foreign affairs at nine.

Maxwell felt deeply uncomfortable. He had no idea how far Sumoto's web stretched and what side Effendi was on. If he *was* handing Selina to her executioner he would never forgive himself.

At POLRI headquarters they were expected. Maxwell had phoned Effendi at home at 6 a.m. A smartly uniformed guard glared in through the windscreen, then raised the security pole. At the entrance they were escorted to the sixth floor – the intelligence and security departments.

Brigadier Jenderal Effendi's round face smouldered with anger at the sight of Selina Sakidin. She wilted under his gaze, having to be helped to a chair.

'So,' Effendi began. 'What is it you want to tell me?'

Maxwell took a deep breath.

'Last night Miss Sakidin came to the British Embassy with information about the kidnapping of Stephen Bowen . . .' He spoke in a voice that contrived to sound calm and analytical. 'What she told us supported other information we had that implicated *Major General Sumoto* in the crime.'

He saw Effendi bristle. No policeman liked being told what to believe by a foreigner.

'The details are in here.' He laid a folder on the table. 'Miss Sakidin came to us instead of to you because she was afraid. She's been an intimate friend of General Sumoto for the past twelve months. She's afraid he will try to kill her. I assured her that you would guarantee her safety.'

Effendi blinked. Maxwell waited.

'You *do*, I take it?'

'Miss Sakidin has nothing to fear if she tells the truth,' Effendi answered chillingly.

Maxwell nodded. He knew it was the best he would get. He glanced at Selina. Her face had turned the colour of wet paper. Then he leaned forward and touched the folder.

'A copy of this dossier is about to be handed to your foreign minister by my ambassador. It provides proof that Stephen Bowen was kidnapped in Indonesia and that Indonesian citizens were the perpetrators. We are requesting that POLRI takes immediate steps to deal with General Sumoto in a way that's appropriate, and that it does all in its power to find Stephen Bowen, alive or dead. Oh, and on the matter of Miss Sakidin, we'll be making frequent enquiries to ensure she's being well cared for.'

Brigadier General Effendi smoothed the thin line of his moustache with a thumb and forefinger. His eyes burned. He reached for the folder and opened it.

'Oh. There's something else I need to bring to your attention,' Maxwell continued, heart in mouth. 'There are two British citizens currently in Kutu for whom we are seeking guarantees of safety. One, the journalist Charlotte Cavendish – we have reason to believe she *is* in official custody, despite the denials from ABRI. The other, Nick Randall, was in the same area of the jungle as Miss Cavendish when she was picked up by troops from KOPASSUS, but he escaped capture.'

'Mr Maxwell!' Effendi exploded. 'We only guarantee safety of foreigners in Kutu when they stay in place where foreigner allowed. If they break law by going to terrorist area, then . . .' He shrugged and spread his hands. 'Journalists – they not welcome in Kutu. They always break our law. They tell lies about us.'

'Nick Randall isn't a journalist,' Maxwell announced.

Effendi's eyes hardened into beads.

'He's a British police officer.'

Effendi's face drained of expression. The mask again. The impenetrable Javan mask.

'Well, well,' Effendi said after a long pause. 'You are man of surprises, Mr Maxwell.'

The Manda Channel

'Nick!'

The shout from the bridge jolted Randall back to the present. His mind had been filled with Charlie, her soft, brown eyes trusting him to keep her safe. If Maxwell's efforts failed, *he* would have to get her free. He propelled himself from his chair at the stern and scrambled up to the bridge.

Dedi pointed. Another *pinisi*, heading up the channel from the west.

Randall jammed binoculars to his eyes. He'd found a second pair in the saloon.

Berkat Am . . . Yes! Or was it? The last letters were obscured by a loose tarpaulin that flapped over the side.

Dedi steadied the glasses. The tarpaulin lifted. Randall heard a sharp intake of breath beside him.

'Yessir!' Dedi gulped. 'This it!'

Randall's heart leapt to his throat. Bowen's floating prison was motoring towards them. Amidships was a hold covered by the green canvas that had temporarily obscured the name. At the stern a pale awning gave shade to a square superstructure topped by a wheelhouse with a balcony each side. Inside it, the shapes of two men could be seen behind large rectangular windows.

'When they've passed, we up anchor and follow,' Nick snapped, scrambling back down to the deck.

'*Yes*, mister.'

Fighting back his fear, he pretended to fish again as the ketch neared, then rested the rod and focused his binoculars on the wheelhouse. One man emerged on to the bridge gallery. Big and burly, with a square, hard face, he put binoculars to his own eyes – watching Nick, watching him.

Ten minutes later the *Timini* sprinted from the Manda Channel at fifteen knots. The *Berkat Amanat* was half a mile in front, on an arrow-straight course for the distant smudge of Mount Jiwa. The ketch would make Kutu in four hours if they let it. Just two hours in the powerboat – once they'd got Stephen Bowen safely on board . . .

The sea was clear, the ABRI patrol boat nowhere in sight.

'OK. Let's go for it!' Randall snapped.

Dedi opened the throttle. The diesels churned the wake to cream as the *Timini* rose on the plane. The log on the console crept up to twenty-six knots. Randall steadied the binoculars against the buffeting of the boat. The thrumming of the diesels had a calming effect on his innards. Action at last.

Ahead, the haze was thickening, obscuring Kutu's volcano. They closed fast on the ketch, coming up on the left-hand side.

'Keep close in, eh Dedi? So we get a good look.' To try to see how many were on board and what they were armed with. The hunting rifle lay beside him on the floor of the bridge, a magazine of 7.62 clipped in place.

They came abreast with the ketch and swept past twenty metres off. The same square face he'd seen before pressed against the wheelhouse window. Behind him the second man stood rigid at the helm.

Just two men visible. No way of knowing if there were more below decks.

As they ploughed past, the ketch wallowed in their wake. Dedi held the wheel in a white-knuckle grip.

'Couple of minutes, then we stop,' Randall reminded him. As the ketch dropped behind, he snatched up the rifle and pushed off the safety catch.

Dedi cast an eye behind. Seeing the *Berkat Amanat* well astern he shunted the throttles to neutral and cut the fuel. The Yamahas shuddered and died. The hull settled back. Silence, apart from water slapping against fibreglass.

Then the Kutuan swung below like an orang-utan. Randall watched the ketch draw nearer again, suspecting Sumoto's men would see through his simple plan. He heard Dedi strike a match, then smelled the smoke – rags soaked in diesel, ignited in a bucket.

'Keep that extinguisher handy,' Randall growled. Last thing they wanted was a *real* fire.

The *Berkat Amanat* ploughed towards them, its bow swinging right to avoid a collision. By the rules of seamanship, seeing the smoke, the ketch should stop.

Chewing his lip, Randall moved out on to the open deck and waved furiously.

'They're watching,' he announced as Dedi emerged from below, spluttering from the smoke, his hands clutching an extinguisher. 'They've got the bins on us. Hey, squirt that damn thing.' Dedi sprayed a jet of gas into the saloon.

Randall saw square-face lower the glasses then, grim-faced, tuck his head back into the wheelhouse to give an order. The ketch swung away from them, sweeping by, its speed undiminished. The man watched them stonily, then raised a hand, but not to wave. The fingers were folded down – except the middle one, which he jerked upwards with a long, mocking sweep of his arm.

Dedi growled the word 'intel', dropped the extinguisher and propelled himself up to the bridge. He snatched the rifle from the deck and jammed the butt into his shoulder.

'Fuck! No!' Randall yelled, making to go after him. Suddenly a flame whooshed from the cabin below. The bucket had caught, spreading fire over the floor of the saloon. 'Shit!'

He grabbed the extinguisher, just as Dedi fired.

'Christ!' He spun towards the ketch. Square-face was clutching his chest, then his legs buckled.

'Christ! Christ!'

Thick, black smoke belched up towards him. Gripping the extinguisher, he blasted CO_2 into the flames.

Two more shots from above – heavy, urgent thuds. Then the crack-crack of automatic fire, and the zing of ricochets.

'Fuck, fuck, fuck!' he screamed. This was a total, fucking balls-up! He heard a wail from Dedi.

'You hit?' he yelled, choking on the smoke as he moved in towards the seat of the fire. If he didn't put it out they'd be finished.

No answer from Dedi. Just a rumble of the diesels starting up. Randall coughed and retched, crawling under the smoke to kill the last of the flames. The boat lurched and heeled. Dedi was making a run for it.

Shit! Randall ripped curtains from a flimsy track and threw them on the remains of the fire, stamping on them until there was no more smoke. A final squirt from the extinguisher, then he thundered up to the bridge.

Bullets had shattered the laminated glass spray-shield. Dedi hunched over the wheel, panic-stricken. The rifle lay on the deck. Randall picked it up and checked the magazine. Five rounds left.

'Any more below? More bullets?' he asked, trying to sound calm.

'No.'

So, every one had to count. Randall looked round. The ketch was astern, still heading east towards Kutu.

'Turn her round, Dedi,' he snapped.

'No mister.' Dedi seemed poleaxed by the immensity of what he'd done. He muttered to himself in incomprehensible Kutun.

'Dedi . . . get a grip.' Randall spoke gently but firmly.

'I got to hide, mister,' Dedi whispered, clinging to the wheel. 'I got to get away. Maybe go Australia. They come after me now . . .'

'No they won't – not if we go back and finish the job. We've got to stop that ketch, get the Englishman free then sink it, right? So nobody'll ever know . . .'

In his dreams, but they couldn't give up now.

'They got machine gun, mister.'

'An automatic, that's all. No better than this,' he lied, slapping the side of the hunting rifle.

He looked back at the ketch again, half a mile away. Now it would be twice as hard. Their only consolation – the opposition were one man down.

'Did you see who fired?' he asked urgently. 'Was it the guy on the helm?'

'No. I not see. Just this . . .' He pointed to the crazed holes in the screen. He looked at Randall's face, glanced at the gun in his hands, then eased the throttles, wavering. 'OK boss. What we do?' He swung the *Timini* into a slow turn.

'Good man.' Randall clapped him on the shoulder. 'We get round behind her. Come up her wake, weaving. Hopefully it's just that one bloke on the bridge, and by now he'll be in such a panic he won't know his arse from his elbow.' But if there were more of the buggers below decks it'd be a suicide run.

'OK, Dedi?'

'OK, mister.'

Five minutes later they were roaring up from behind the ketch, Randall spreadeagled in the bows, concealed behind a low gunwale. Rifle resting on the rim he squinted through the telescopic sight. Nothing. No sign of life. Just the squat stern of the ketch, a small radar antenna rotating above the superstructure.

Radar. No way of hiding from that.

As Dedi weaved the *Timini* from side to side, Randall kept the rifle-sight on the wheelhouse. Suddenly a face poked from an open window, saw them, dived back in, then re-emerged with an automatic.

Flashes from the muzzle. Firing wildly. Randall lined up the cross-hairs and squeezed. The rifle kicked hard against his cheek.

A dark mess puffed from the man's head. He saw the gun fall to the deck. A wave of nausea hit him, short and sharp. Malaysia, all over again.

Slowly the ketch began to veer right, out of control. Nick panned the sight, left then right. Not another soul. Maxwell had said two, and two it seemed to be.

They were getting unnervingly close. Dedi eased the throttles. Randall crawled back to the bridge.

'Get alongside and I'll jump on board,' he panted.

'Yes, mister.'

Randall ducked into the saloon to check the fire was fully out, then saw Charlie's camera bag on the seat. Yes, he thought. He slung the strap over his shoulder.

Port gunwale dipping low, the ketch ploughed on, it's speed steady, it's bridge devoid of life. Dedi powered the *Timini* to within a few feet of her.

'I'll try to cut her engines,' Randall yelled. 'When she's lost way, you tie up alongside.'

Dedi grunted.

Rifle in hand, Randall crouched by the *Timini*'s rail, alert for movement on the ketch as Dedi narrowed the gap. The *Berkat*'s exhaust belched from a vent on the water-line. A foot projecting beneath the canvas screen on the bridge wing showed the man Dedi shot hadn't moved.

The gunwales touched. Randall sprang across, grabbing the mast shrouds and spotting a small, sun-blistered door that led inside. Back pressed against the superstructure and gun in hand, he flicked it open and inched his face round the frame. A short, dingy passage ran the width of the boat. He stepped inside, listening. Two poky cabins to the left, steps up and down on the right.

He listened again, the ketch's engine pounding like a racing heart. Panels and fittings hummed and buzzed. He stopped by the corner of the companion-way, trying to see up into the wheelhouse. From above he heard a gurgling, like water in a half-blocked drain. He mounted the stairs, then gagged. The helmsman lay on the deck choking, his blood encircling him like a coulis.

Forcing himself to ignore him, Randall stepped across the body and grabbed the helm. He straightened the wheel then pulled the throttles to neutral. The ketch righted itself and lost way. Next to the wheel was the conical hood of the radar. To the left, two grey-painted radio sets, the handset for one of them swinging loose. The helmsman had sent a Mayday.

Gingerly, he stepped on to the wing where Dedi's victim lay, the man's eyes vacant and staring at the sky. Randall gave a wave astern to show he was in control. Dedi brought the *Timini* alongside again, warps ready on the deck.

Randall re-entered the wheelhouse. Now ... to find Stephen Bowen.

Down in the corridor below the bridge he checked the two rough cabins. Bare mattresses on the bunks and signs they'd been used by the two men above.

Down another deck. A second passageway and a smell of fried onions. Galley and mess to the left. His heart missed a beat. Maybe there was a cook ... He felt a bump. The *Timini* coming alongside. The ketch's idling engine rumbled somewhere close.

Beyond the galley, another door to the left. A blast of heat and oil smells as he opened and quickly closed it. Machine room. Then at the far end he saw it. A heavy hatch. Watertight seal. Steel clasps. Secured by a padlock ...

He inched forward, rifle in front of him. The key had been left in. He turned it, unhooked the lock and wrenched open the clips. The hatch creaked open.

'Christ!'

A foul stench of human wastes knocked him back. He pushed the door wider and forced himself to enter. Twice the size of the cabins above, sunlight streamed through a single porthole, illuminating a grubby heap in the centre of the floor. Her Majesty's minister for foreign affairs lay naked except for excreta-caked underpants, his head bound in a filthy bandage. Gagging at the stink, Randall crouched beside him.

'Mr Bowen . . .' he croaked, heart hammering his ribs. Daft to be so formal. 'Er . . . Stephen.'

No response. Only a rise and fall of the chest to show he wasn't dead. Randall recalled the face on the video. Big chin, peppery hair – hardly recognisable now. He laid the rifle and camera bag on the deck, then spotted the white pustules covering Bowen's shoulders and neck. The man was sick. Very sick.

He recoiled at first, nauseated, then felt Bowen's forehead. Skin hot and clammy. The bandage on his head was yellow with pus. He looked down. Hands and feet firmly chained to a ring bolted through the deck.

Bugger!

He lowered his head to Bowen's ear, just in case he could hear.

'Don't worry, we'll get you out of here.' Somehow . . . 'I'll find you some water.'

Suddenly the skin crawled on the back of his neck. There was someone else breathing. Not him. Not Bowen. A third person in the room. Dedi? He whipped round.

Hell! There *was* a cook. A squat, sweaty Chinaman in stained T-shirt and boxer shorts stood an arm's length away, hands raised above his head, clutching a meat cleaver, the sunlight glimmering on its polished blade. Randall lurched sideways as the knife swooped and thunked into the floor timbers.

'Uhhh!' the Chinaman grunted, his piggy eyes wide with fear.

Randall scrabbled for the rifle, not daring to take his eyes off his assailant. His fingers stabbed at empty spaces. The Chinaman's eyes flicked right and spotted the weapon. Randall lunged further as the cleaver slashed down again. He rolled aside, wincing as the blade nicked his shirt.

The gun still beyond reach, Randall scrambled to his feet but had his legs kicked from under him. The Chinaman towered over him, roaring like an animal, the cleaver raised for the kill. Arms up to protect his head, Randall hooked back his right foot and thumped it into the Chinaman's gut.

Air jetted from the man's rubbery mouth. He doubled up, swinging the knife wildly. Randall rolled clear. Fingers round the stock at last, he jerked the gun round and jabbed it into the soft cushion of the Chinaman's chest.

The crewman dropped the cleaver and pulled back, gibbering. He'd seen the carnage in the wheelhouse and didn't want to join it.

'*Air!*' Randall snapped, pointing down at Bowen. '*Air putih!*' Water. Purified water.

'*Ya!*'

Randall prodded him to the galley. From a cardboard box in a store locker the cook pulled out a plastic bottle. Randall marched him back to the cell.

'Give him some!' Hands shaking, the Chinaman ripped off the cap and poured water into Bowen's mouth. The minister gulped and stirred.

Randall dropped to his knees lifting Bowen's head.

'All right, Stephen?' Course he wasn't. Eyes flickered open then closed again. Randall looked up at the Chinaman and pointed at Bowen's chains.

'*Kunci?*' he snapped. He'd remembered the word for key.

'*Tidak! Tidak!*'

The Chinaman didn't have it. He jabbed a finger upwards.

'OK. You show me!' Randall assured the semi-conscious minister he would be right back, then prodded the cook into the corridor and up towards the bridge. '*Berapa laki-laki?*' How many of them were they?

'*Tiga. Tiga.*' Three.

True? Or was there an engineer or deck-hand lurking somewhere too?

Nick pointed up the companion-way. The cook nodded and climbed in front, hugging his head.

In the wheelhouse Randall panicked. No helmsman. His body was gone, the coulis of blood smeared in a long streak out to the bridge wing as if he'd come to life and dragged himself there.

He heard a splash. Then it clicked.

'Dedi!' Randall snapped. 'What've you done, you prat?' He pushed out on to the little balcony. Dedi turned round, a wild look in his eyes, the helmsman's assault rifle slung over his shoulder. The body of the other man was also gone.

'I give them to sharks,' Dedi retorted, glaring at the Chinaman.

Them and the keys to Bowen's shackles which were probably in one of their pockets.

'Shit!' Randall leaned over the rail. The sea was clear. They should be floating somewhere. 'Where are they?'

'They go to bottom. I make heavy so no one find.'

'Jeezus! When you fuck up, you don't half do it in spades . . .'

'I no understand . . .'

'Never mind. Keep an eye on this bugger,' Nick ordered. 'And don't hurt him.'

Dedi unslung the rifle and prodded the Chinaman with it. Heart

289

sinking, Randall searched the wheelhouse on the off-chance the keys would be hanging somewhere. Then he clattered below and turned over the two cabins. Nothing. On his way up to the wheelhouse again, he heard a shot and a scream.

'Christ almighty!' He rushed for the wing. The Chinaman was in the water, splashing feebly in his own little circle of crimson, his face submerging.

'If he live he tell intel 'bout me,' Dedi muttered, defensively. He'd become like a two-year-old, obsessive and beyond reason.

So matter-of-fact. Death as a way of life. But there was one life that could be saved, if they were quick.

'Come. We need tools, understand?'

No response from Dedi.

'The Englishman – he's down there, locked up. Have to break his chains. Come look.'

Two decks down, the smells of onions and faeces had combined in a gut-wrenching stink. Dedi wrinkled his face in disgust, then gaped at the now unconscious Stephen Bowen.

Randall pointed at the ankle shackles. 'Bolt cutters. We need bolt cutters. See?'

Dedi sucked his teeth. 'No. On *Timini* is nothing.' Then he saw the meat cleaver. He picked it up and looked at Randall. His eyes were questioning.

'Can't cut steel with tha . . .'

Then he realised what Dedi meant. Hack Bowen's foot off instead.

'No way!' The man was half-dead with septicaemia. An amputation like that would finish him.

The minister stirred. His eyes opened. He tried to raise his head, but gave up.

'Find something,' Randall ordered, crouching down. 'Must be something on board this tub. Something heavy enough to smash the links.'

The Kutuan held his look as if he'd not heard.

'Dedi?'

'Sure, mister. I go look.'

He shuffled out. As Randall cradled Bowen's head he heard the door to the machinery space open then close again and Dedi's feet going up to the next deck.

'Who . . . who are you?'

The croak startled him. Bowen was making an effort to focus his eyes.

'Nick Randall. I'm a detective sergeant with Scotland Yard Special Branch. Don't worry. We're going to get you out of here.'

Bowen's jaw worked, but no more words came. His eyes glazed over. Randall held the bottle to his quivering lips. The man was in such a state, it was hard to know how to help him.

'Keith wants me dead . . .'

Bowen's words tumbled out as he pushed the bottle aside with his manacled hands.

'Nobody wants you dead, Stephen.' The man was delirious. 'You'll be OK. You're safe now.' Far from it, but it was all he could think of to say.

Suddenly Bowen looked up at him with a fierce intensity.

'BBC?' he croaked. 'Are you the BBC?'

'No . . .' Randall frowned, puzzled. 'Police. From London. From home.'

'Something to tell you . . .' Bowen croaked. 'People have to know . . .'

Suddenly Randall realised what Bowen had just said. *Keith* wanted him dead.

'Listen,' Bowen hissed, 'you've got to know . . .'

Certain he was on the brink of some extraordinary revelation, Randall reached into the camera bag. If it was what he thought it was, he needed it on tape.

'What was that, Stephen?' he asked gently, switching on.

When he saw the video camera Bowen's eyes lit up.

'Is it on? Quick . . .'

'Yes. I'm recording,' Randall replied, steadying his voice. 'What is it you wanted to say, Stephen?'

'Keith wants me dead,' Bowen whispered, mouth set hard. 'Because of the money . . .'

His head dropped back, his eyelids flickering. His breath had the strength of a butterfly.

'Keith who, Stephen?' Randall pressed. He felt a door opening into another world.

Bowen mustered all his fading strength. '*Copeland!*' he hissed into the lens.

'The prime minister wants you dead?' Randall prompted gently.

'*Yes!* We had a deal . . .'

'What sort of deal?'

'A million for him and a million for me, if we got the money for the power station.'

Randall frowned. Mumbo-jumbo. Then he remembered the story on World Service.

'Million pounds?'

Bowen nodded, drawing breath.

'A million for *him* ... who did you mean by *him*?' Checking, checking. With dynamite you had to be absolutely sure.

'*Keith*. Copeland! Listen to me, you've got to listen.'

'I'm listening, I'm listening. You're saying you and the prime minister were each getting a million pounds in commission for the Kutu power station?'

Bowen was weakening. His eyelids drooped. A white curd of saliva dried on his lips.

'Yes. Sumoto arranged it ... Four-six-five-three-two-nine ...' His voice trailed away.

'What's that?' Randall reached forward with his spare hand to support Bowen's head. The man was fading.

'Züricher Bank ... Next month. Next month we get the money ...'

'What? An account number? Yours? Copeland's?'

But Bowen was gone. Unconscious again, his breath a rattle in his throat.

Shit! Evidence. Devastating evidence. But he needed Bowen to tell it in court. Camera off and into the bag. Bag on shoulder. Up on his feet. Where the hell was Dedi? Bowen needed medical help fast.

Out in the corridor he yelled up the companion-way to the bridge. 'Dedi!'

Nothing. He went back into the fetid cell. Bowen was motionless. Not even the rise and fall of his chest anymore.

'Don't die on me for fuck's sake,' Randall hissed. He dropped to one knee. The minister's face was in repose, devoid of pain.

'I don't believe it ...' Randall felt Bowen's neck for the carotid artery. No pulse.

For a moment he considered mouth-to-mouth resuscitation, but the thought of it made him gag. Anyway there'd be no point – the pustules all over him showed the man's body was a poison sack.

Suddenly feet clattered on the companion-way.

Dedi stuck his head round the door and beckoned frantically. 'We go now, mister. ABRI come!'

'What?' Randall ran behind him up the steps and out on to the deck.

Dedi pointed to the west. A few hundred metres away, bearing down on them fast was the sharp, grey prow of the navy patrol boat.

'Shit!'

What to do? Stick with Bowen? No point now. And anyway, there was no way to know whose side these navy boys were on.

They leapt the gunwales. Randall cast off while Dedi started up. Then they powered away, keeping the *Berkat Amanat* between them and the gunboat in the hope they'd not been identified. Dedi's survival would depend on it.

Randall looked back at the ketch wallowing in the swell like a drifting, wooden sarcophagus. His shoulders sagged. He felt numb. He'd just taken a man's life, but unlike in Malaysia, this time there'd been no life *saved* by which to justify it.

All he had to show was a statement on tape. An accusation of corruption at the highest level. Bowen's last desperate card.

Randall turned away from the *Berkat Amanat* and faced towards Kutu.

Back on the island, two hours or more away, another life was in jeopardy.

22

Kutu – east of Piri
13.40 hrs

THE COASTLINE WAS close, but no more than a blue shadow in the
haze. The heat blur which obscured it had helped cover their tracks.
They'd looped south before turning east again for Kutu and – so far as
they could tell – had avoided detection.

A mile from the coast Dedi throttled back, then cut the engines.
Shoulders hunched, he moved from the bridge to the bows and stood
listening. He was aiming for a bay east of Piri, familiar to him from
diving expeditions and seldom frequented by army patrols.

'Nothing?' Randall checked.

'Is quiet,' the Kutuan muttered. He turned back to the bridge,
restarted the engines and headed in. As they closed with the coast he
tried the mobile phone, desperate for news of his sister, but got no
connection. 'Piri too far 'way,' he explained, his face pained. A few
minutes later Randall tried, needing an urgent word with Maxwell. Still
no signal. Then the battery died.

He cursed. Absurd to have to rely on the World Service for updates
from London. On the journey back to Kutu he'd listened to the radio
every hour, but there'd been no change to the story saying there were
fears for Charlie's safety. He checked his watch, something he did
constantly now, fixated with the notion that every second that passed
was one less for her.

In the three hours since their escape from the patrol boat, he'd
quizzed Dedi about where prisoners were taken on Kutu. Kadama
would have been the first stop. But if Charlie was in Sumoto's hands she
could be almost anywhere. Then Dedi had snapped his fingers,
remembering the small private villa on the coast road between Kadama
and Piri, with flat ground behind for a helicopter to land. Sumoto had
had it built when he was commander on the island. Dedi had heard a

rumour once of a helicopter flying from there to the volcano. At a time when there'd been disappearances . . .

Sumoto still used the place occasionally, Dedi had said. He'd given Randall directions how to find it.

As they entered the bay, Nick scoured the shore line with the binoculars. Then, satisfied as he could be they weren't being watched, he tucked the glasses away in the grey holdall, which already held the compact assault rifle taken from the *Berkat Amanat* together with two magazines bound together with tape. Thirty-five rounds.

Randall knew he would be on his jack when they touched land – Dedi had his own life to save.

Two fishing boats bobbed at anchor in the bay. On one of them a man in denim shorts and shirt lay under an awning, sleeping away the hottest part of the day.

They dropped anchor well away from him, then lowered the inflatable, the sun beating down mercilessly as the outboard sped them to the shore. Dedi bowlined a long line round a tree root, then, once secure, crouched beside Randall in the shade of a fig tree.

The air was still, the foliage electric with crickets, the coast here rocky and barren. A battered truck piled with watermelons rattled towards Piri. Once it had passed, Dedi stood up and turned awkwardly to Randall. The time had come. His hands clenched and unclenched.

'Can't help you no more, mister,' he muttered, his flat face pinched and anxious. Survival for him meant going to ground. 'Got to go now.'

'I know. I understand.' Randall held out his hand. 'Thanks, friend. And if you ever come to London . . .' Stupid remark.

'Sure . . .' Dedi allowed himself a brief grin. Then he pointed up the road. 'Like I tell you, *bemo* come along here maybe every half hour.' He backed away, the look on his face saying Randall had to be insane to be going where he was going.

'Bye, Dedi.'

'Bye, mister Nick.'

The Kutuan marched off. Randall stared up the road praying it wouldn't *be* half an hour. Ten kilometres from town, it would take two hours to hoof it, with every chance of being picked up. And no Kutuan would risk giving a lift to a foreigner. So the bus it had to be. He twitched with frustration, trying to block his mind to what could be happening to Charlie in the meantime.

He had been responsible for her. No getting away from it. But it was more than a sense of duty driving him now. Charlie had got to him. She *had* penetrated his defences.

He checked the watch again. Just after two. Ringing Maxwell was his other priority. By rights he should make it number one – find a phone and tell them about Bowen. But the risk of being picked up that way was too great. Charlie had to come first.

Maxwell. How much should he tell him? *Not* about what Bowen had said. Too sensitive. And it could wait.

Another ten minutes passed before the bus came. On board three gnarled women sat with wicker baskets on their knees stuffed with squawking chickens.

The Kadama interrogation centre loomed on the right, impossible to miss just as Dedi had said – high, grey walls pock-marked with grilles. Randall took deep breaths to steady his pulse. The other *bemo* passengers kept their eyes averted.

Then he turned his head to look out for the brick depot Dedi had mentioned. Seeing it, he tacked twice on the overhead rail. The *bemo* stopped to let him out. As it drove off, he felt as alone as he had ever done. Alone and in the open. A white man on a black island clutching a holdall, strolling along a road where tourists had no business to be.

To his left the shore looked dirty and weed-clogged. It smelled of decay. To his right the terrain was stony and arid. Where there were trees, he ducked under them for shade and to hide from the occasional vehicle.

Then he saw the villa. Glazed green roof tiles glinting in the sun amidst a clump of vegetation, flat ground behind it. He crouched beneath a stumpy, thick-leaved tree. The house looked to be two hundred metres away. No sign of life when he scanned it with the glasses.

The villa was a bungalow, the side wall facing him comfortingly blank. Windows at the front overlooked the sea, and at the back a garden, surrounded by chain-link fencing and a dense hedge. A clump of eucalyptus grew by the roadside twenty metres short of the house. Minimal cover but all there was.

He unzipped the top of the bag so the gun was ready. His instinct was to run, to cross the open ground between him and the trees in the shortest possible time. But in this heat *nobody* ran. Mustn't attract attention. Heart battering his ribs, he started walking. He heard a vehicle coming up behind. It began to slow.

Please God not a patrol! With forced casualness he glanced round. A *bemo*, the fare collector leaning from the door with his arm like a scoop.

'Hey, mister!'

'No. *Tidak!*' Randall waved them on.

'Yes, mister! You want to go Piri! Yes, yes!'

'No. *Tidak! Tidak*,' Randall scowled. With a shrug and a grin the boy gave up and the *bemo* sped on, tootling its horn in a way guaranteed to attract a glance from a guard on watch.

'Fuck! Fuck!' Randall hissed, his eyes sweeping from one end of the villa's compound to the other. Nothing. Doubt crept in. Maybe this wasn't the place. Maybe Charlie was still at Kadama.

He reached the trees and stopped, crouching as if to tie a shoe lace. A stone's throw from the chain-link fence, he saw blue behind the hedge – a van parked in front of the house. There *was* someone here.

Then he froze. The terror of a rotor-beat. Coming from the direction of Mount Jiwa, pulsing towards him like a blast of icy air. Out of the hazy blue he saw a small, dark speck grow into the shape of a UH-1 and drop towards the landing strip behind the house. Motionless, he watched it disappear behind the hedge.

And he'd been seen. Bloody pilot had looked straight at him. Fifty metres between them, no more. Game up. The clock had stopped. Had to move before *they* did.

He grabbed the rifle, sprinted to the fence and searched for a break in the hedge that would let him see through. He found it.

Charlie. His heart stopped. Through the leaves of a hibiscus. Blindfolded and gagged, feet and hands bound, with two men in uniform, one on each side, dragging her to the helicopter. Next stop the volcano.

Randall fired. Single shot. High, to avoid Charlie. The head of the soldier nearest to him flicked sideways and seemed to burst, as his body crumpled. The second man, wearing an aviator's helmet, recoiled, let Charlie fall, then ducked and lurched forward, propelling himself back to his machine. Randall fired twice, dropping him before he reached a gate in the fence.

The rotors clattered, the engine pitch rose in panic. Randall's fevered brain said the chopper was a dragon that had to be slain. He darted to the end of the fence as it lifted, firing wildly, but the machine banked away unscathed.

By the open gate into the villa's grounds, he crouched, gun to his shoulder. The helicopter crewman lay just inside, a gaping wound in his flank. In the middle of the grass Charlie was on her knees, rigid with terror. One man dead to her left, his uniform clinging like a second skin.

Randall looked up to the villa. Open patio doors, two men crouching inside, pistols in their hands. They fired, then ducked further back. Randall loosed off two rounds, then crouched by Charlie.

'Charlie!' he barked. 'It's me!'

Tape across her mouth, a squeal from beneath it.

'Sit on your bum. I'll have to drag you backwards.' Gun in his right hand, he grabbed the collar of her bush shirt. 'Shove with your legs, understand?'

She nodded frantically, flopped on to her backside, then kicked with her bound feet as he pulled her towards the gate.

He felt it before he heard it. A thwack to his left shoulder, then the crack of a second shot that grazed his ear. His left hand lost all strength. He let go of Charlie's shirt. Dropping on to one knee, he fired twice into the open doors of the house, searching for where the shots had come from.

'Keep going!' he yelled to Charlie, diving sideways. Pain knifed through his shoulder. 'Straight back!' he screamed, flinching.

Another shot. He saw the flash this time. Not *inside* the house, but from a path at the side. He cracked back two rounds, then the gun died. A dead click on an empty chamber.

'Damn!'

Pinning the useless rifle under his weakened left arm, he grabbed Charlie's collar with his right hand and dragged her the last few metres through the gate as a bullet clanged off the metal post.

Hidden by the hedge now, they lay flat. Trying to stop his good hand shaking, he unclipped the rifle magazine, turned it over and slotted in the spare. Fifteen rounds left – each one had to count. How many was he up against? Two at least. Sumoto one of them, he guessed. Colonel Widodo the other? Both armed, both driven by the compelling need to eliminate anyone who knew their secrets.

They'd be coming for them. He jammed the barrel through the hedge, fired two rounds as cover, dragged Charlie back another few metres, then thrust a hand into his trouser pocket for the knife he'd put there earlier. Just enough feeling in his left hand to open the blade.

Had to free her legs before anything else. The cord was thin and parted easily. Then her hands. As the string frayed under the blade, Charlie wrenched them free, pushed off the blindfold and blinked at him in disbelief.

'Now we run. Like fuck!' he growled.

At a crouch, they sprinted for the eucalyptus trees, Charlie ripping the tape from her mouth. She gulped in air. She'd faced death for the past hour. Now she was glimpsing life again.

Two shots cracked over their heads.

'Down!' Randall screamed. 'Where are you now, you *bastards*?'

Grass and stones. Useless cover, but the trees were still too far. Rifle sight to his eye, raking round for a target, he saw a blur of green-brown – a uniformed arm reaching round the fence at the front of the house. He squeezed the trigger. One round. Had to ration them. The recoil shot through his frame to his injured shoulder. He winced. Then came the thud of a gun from behind.

'Back there!' Charlie croaked, pointing.

Randall swung the barrel and blatted off another single shot.

Without cover they'd soon be dead.

'Got to make it to those trees, understand?' he whispered. 'You first. Weave side to side. I'll cover . . .'

'Nick . . .'

'*Now!* Go!'

He elbowed her away, then fired twice, once in front, once behind at the spots in the fence where the targets had been a moment ago.

No response. No sign of uniforms now. Moving again. The buggers were moving, moving.

He scrambled up and sprinted after Charlie. Bullets cracked and zinged. Automatic fire now. Shit! The bastards had an arsenal in there. He dived to the ground, then rolled over twice to put a thin eucalyptus trunk between him and the guns, nearly blacking out from the pain.

'You all right?' Charlie gulped.

'Wonderful,' he croaked.

'They were going to *kill* me . . .' she choked, disbelief in her voice.

'Yep.' Still might, the way things were going.

Suddenly a motor roared to life. A patch of blue moving behind the hedge. The van backed out on to the verge.

Randall looked round at the road. Traffic backing away wildly. Not a healthy place to be.

The van swung towards them, creeping forward in low gear. The face behind the wheel was hard to see, as if the windscreen was opaque. But it was there.

Randall fired. Couldn't miss. But nothing happened. Crazing of the glass, nothing more. The face still there, teeth clenched with determination.

'Shit!' *Armoured glass!* 'It's a fucking tank . . .' he hissed.

They were staring at death. Motorised death. The passenger door opened as a shield. An automatic rifle poked round it. Bullets chipped bark from above their heads.

'No . . .!' Charlie screamed. To be rescued and then *both* of them die . . .

Randall aimed for the tyres. One exploded with a whoop. He'd lost count of the rounds. Five left. Five at the most.

Relentlessly the van crept towards them. Two options. Stay put, or run. Neither promising.

'Charlie . . .' Nick croaked, suddenly. 'I think we're stuffed.'

299

Then the van stopped. Nick cringed, expecting grenades. A bad way to die. He gritted his teeth, closed his eyes and waited.

Nothing. Instead of an explosion he heard the wap-wap of rotors. The flying hearse was back.

'Look!' Charlie moaned, pointing towards the beach.

Helicopters. Not Hueys this time. German-made Bo 105s. Four of them sweeping in from the sea, disgorging soldiers as they skimmed the sand.

Overkill. He reached out to Charlie. Wanted to say sorry, but his throat blocked up.

The troops ran from the beach, their rifles tut-tutting. Randall jammed his face to the earth. Bullets smacked against the wall of the villa. The *villa*? He lifted his head again to see the two men from the van running back to the house. One, taller and older than the other, raised a hand to protect himself, then toppled as a bullet caught him.

'Fu-uck! It's *them* they're shooting at, not us.'

He swung round and tossed the gun away. Best not to be seen with it.

'Sit up, quick,' he gabbled, scrabbling to his knees and ignoring the pain in his shoulder. 'Hands on your head.' Charlie couldn't move. 'It's OK. We're going to be OK.'

Suddenly the shooting stopped. Silence apart from the grind of the helicopters peeling back out to sea. Steel-helmeted commandos ran past them to secure the rear of the house. Then one stopped in front of them, berry-bright eyes in a tight, war-painted face, his rifle levelled at their heads.

'*Teman* . . .' Randall croaked. *Friend*. It was all he could think of to say.

Charlie gulped back tears, wiping her nose on her sleeve.

'W-what's happening?' she stammered.

'Don't know yet.'

With a jerk of his gun, the soldier bade them stand, while jabbering into a radio.

'Y-your arm,' Charlie choked, seeing the growing mess on Randall's shirt.

'It's OK,' he whispered, his eyes on the soldier. 'He wants us to walk.'

The soldier hurried them past the villa, towards a cluster of jeeps. Striding towards them in crisp camouflage and a shiny helmet that looked straight out of the box was a senior-looking officer, short of stature with a round, dark face and thin, black moustache.

'Mr Nick, Miss Charlotte?' His voice was snappy. Authoritative.

'Yes.'

'I am Brigadier General Effendi. *Police*. You are safe now. Come, please.'

The soldier trotted back to the house. Effendi hustled them to where a first aid tent was being pitched. He gabbled orders in Bahasa. Orderlies grabbed Randall and sat him in a canvas chair, cutting the bloodstained shirt from his shoulder.

'You hurt?' Effendi asked Charlie. His look was hard, as if angry at the trouble they'd caused him.

'No. Falling apart, that's all . . .' Tears filled her eyes.

More shouts in Bahasa, then another chair was produced for her.

Effendi crouched beside Randall. 'Mr Maxwell told me about you,' he said softly.

'Good.'

'Tell me please if you have seen Mr Bowen? You can speak free. These men have no English.'

Randall told him. Told him everything except Bowen's confession and the identity of the Kutuan who'd helped him. Charlie listened open-mouthed.

When he'd almost finished, they heard rubber-soled feet running towards them.

'My bag!' gasped Charlie, turning to look. She stood up.

A soldier carrying the grey holdall jogged to a halt in front of them. He saluted, then Effendi took it from him. Charlie touched her fingers to her mouth.

'It's mine,' she repeated feebly, her hand reaching out pointlessly.

Effendi searched the bag, pulling out the Handycam with a gleam of triumph. He looked it over then pressed the eject button, removing the tape and stuffing it into a breast pocket. Satisfied the bag now contained just binoculars and a water bottle, he gave it to Charlie.

'Thanks . . .' she murmured, taking it. 'But the er . . .'

'*Camera* not permitted in Kutu, Miss Charlotte,' Effendi told her, closing up the cassette mechanism and handing it to the soldier with a gesture that it should be put in his command vehicle.

'But you've taken the *tape*, why d'you need the camera?' she protested.

'Camera not permitted in Kutu,' he repeated icily.

The orderly cleaning Randall's wound stood to attention to report.

'He says it only small wound,' Effendi translated. 'You lucky the bullet miss the bone. In a minute they take you to hospital where they fix it. But first I see what happening.'

He left them, marching briskly down to the villa.

'Shit!' Charlie sat again, the bag on her lap, her fingers feeling inside it. Gone. The whole sodding lot. Camera, tapes. Not a frame of bloody picture. Or . . .?' She looked up at him, eyes wide, remembering the bag had a false bottom.

'Not now . . .' Randall warned out of the side of his mouth.

She flicked him a smile. The man was a saint. Not only saved her, he'd saved the tapes.

A few minutes later Effendi reappeared, his face drawn and tense.

'Sumoto?' Randall asked gently.

'The general is dead,' he answered curtly, as if it were none of Randall's business. 'And Colonel Widodo,' he added, relenting, 'And Captain Sugeng.'

A young officer hurried over from a nearby jeep bristling with aerials. Effendi followed him back, climbed inside and pressed a handset to his ear. Then he re-emerged and beckoned.

'It is Mr Maxwell on the line, Mr Randall,' he announced, his eyes smugly proud at the sophistication of his technology.

Astonished but relieved, Randall got to his feet.

'Who's Maxwell?' Charlie demanded.

'Oh . . . just the man at the embassy in Jakarta. I'll tell him to let your people know you're safe.'

Inside the jeep the handset he was given smelled of smoke.

'Harry?'

'*Nick. Thank God.*' Maxwell's voice, clear as a bell. '*What happened?*'

'Well, first thing, Bowen's dead. I was with him . . .'

'*Yes, Effendi just told me. Sad. But what about you?*'

'A graze. I'll live, and Charlie Cavendish is fine, but she's livid at having her camera and tape confiscated.' He said this loudly, for Effendi's benefit.

'*Ah. Now that's probably a good thing. But I'll come to that in a minute. First though, thank God you're safe. Look . . . he's OK, the brigadier. His troops are BRIMOB – the police mobile brigade. Three hundred of them flew into Kutu an hour ago. They've a list of Sumoto's men in KODAM Twelve. The place is going to be lively tonight. We want you out of there right away. In fact the Indonesians are demanding it. And demanding we never reveal we had a man there in the first place. This is an Indonesian op, OK? They cracked the case, right? And we're going to be bubbling over with gratitude even though they didn't manage to save our minister.*'

'Bloody typical,' Randall growled.

'*Yes, isn't it? Now look, when they recover Bowen's body it's going to be flown to Jakarta for an official hand-over to the ambassador, and Effendi will get you and Charlotte on the flight to Darwin this evening. But there's something you've got to do for us, Nick. The Indonesians are acutely*' *embarrassed that* we *had to tell them what was going on. And if Miss Cavendish blabs to the whole world about General Sumoto being behind the kidnap it could go really sour for us. Huge loss of trade – that sort of thing. Now, I don't know how much she knows . . . but get her to fudge it, will you? Something to the effect that it may never be clear who the kidnappers were exactly. That sort of thing. See what you can do, eh? Use your charms to make her tone it down . . . Tell her to keep Sumoto's name out of it. And for God's sake don't let her mention that you were there.'*

The minibus, borrowed from ABRI intel, had darkened windows.

Randall and Charlie sat alone in the back. His wound had been stitched and dressed at a military hospital. Now they were being driven to the airfield, rattling past the place where the night food stalls would begin business when darkness fell. Effendi had told them they were to be taken to a quiet corner of the field to await the Darwin flight. Their belongings were being collected from the Touristik Hotel and they'd be put on board ahead of the other passengers, with the small first class section to themselves. Keeping them isolated until they reached Australia was for their own protection, the police chief had explained. Mopping up Sumoto's supporters might take a while.

The vehicle entered through a security gate, turned left on to a perimeter road, drove for a minute and then stopped. The driver switched off the engine and lit a cigarette.

Charlotte looked across at Randall. The van had bench seats down each side in the back and they had one each. They'd spoken little on the journey after he'd passed on Maxwell's request for her to fudge her story – too much whirling around in their heads. The question of self-censorship for the sake of her country's national interest was not an issue she'd ever faced. She'd tried to imagine what Kate Adie would do in the circs. Then, slowly she'd realised it wasn't an issue she needed to address. The fact was she didn't *know* what Sumoto's role had been. And Nick had clammed up on her. So there was little to censor.

He looked pale, she thought. Shock and loss of blood. It was hot in the van despite the air-conditioning and his eyelids drooped. Must feel half dead after what he'd been through.

She'd thought about him endlessly in the past twenty-four hours. Fearing he was dead, telling herself he couldn't be, expecting him to get her free, cursing him when he didn't – a gamut of emotions. And now – when she wanted him to confide in her and he wouldn't – annoyance. Yet she *shouldn't* feel negative about him. If he hadn't turned up when he had, she'd be a cinder in Mount Jiwa by now. She owed her life to him . . . She looked across and felt a longing to touch him, to seal the bond which events had forged between them.

She frowned. What sort of bond? She hardly knew him really. Most things that mattered he'd kept to himself. She'd still not discovered the key to opening him up. But she knew she wanted to.

She felt disorientated, as if the nightmare of the past two days had been just that – a nightmare. She looked away from Nick, gazing through the dark glass windows, trying to make out where they were.

'Oh!' she exclaimed suddenly, sitting bolt upright. 'What's that?'

Randall shook off his drowsiness and turned to look through the glass behind him. They seemed to have stopped next to a park surrounded by a laurel hedge broken by an ornamental wrought-iron gateway. Beyond the entrance, raised on a dais, was a rectangular shrine covered with a tall, grass roof, its front and back open to the winds. In the middle of it stood a long wall of dark stone.

'Could be some sort of memorial,' Randall murmured.

'Of course!' Charlie exclaimed, leaning forward. 'War graves. The Jap prison camp that was here . . . Remember?' They'd been told about it by the man who'd driven them to the hotel when they arrived.

She reached for the door handle. Could it have been here . . .? No. But she had to see. She slid open the side door and jumped out before the BRIMOB driver could stop her.

'Leave her,' Randall told him in Malay.

He watched her step on to the dais and enter the shrine, curious about her trepidation. Then he remembered her father. She looked tiny under the towering roof, hugging herself as if scared of what she might find. He thought of getting out to be with her, but decided to leave her. Whatever she was going through, it was personal. And although a part of him wanted very much to get closer to her, he knew he must resist. The mission *here* was over. He was on his way home. Home to his mates at the Yard – home to Debbie.

Back also to a dilemma – what to do about Prime Minister Keith Copeland?

He looked down at the holdall lying on the floor of the van. The tape was still in it. Now was a good time to retrieve it, with Charlie outside and the driver not looking. He put the bag on his knee and felt for the concealed zip in the base. He pushed aside the tag and slipped his fingers into the hidden pocket, just large enough for two cassettes. He pulled them out. The one holding Bowen's confession he'd marked with an X. He pocketed it.

For a moment he held on to the other, trying to remember all that was on it. The ambush – the interviews with Kakadi and Bawi –

Charlie's arrest. Maxwell would doubtless prefer none of it got seen, for the benefit of *diplomacy*. But *justice* mattered too. It was wrong for the Kutuan rebels to be blackened by Bowen's kidnap and torture. He slipped the tape back into the bag.

Charlotte stood in front of the memorial wall, unable to rid herself of the weird feeling that some part of her had been here before. Not to this memorial, but to the *place*. The heat, the red-brown earth and the smell of sun-burned vegetation.

The black marble was engraved with names, over a hundred of them in neat gold lettering. Most seemed to be Indians, but amongst them were Dutch, Australians and a handful of English. As she stepped round the wall to see the other side, she looked out at an expanse of manicured grass laid out with rows of small plaques. A parade ground of the dead, of young lives wasted.

On the back of the wall were more names. She began to read.

Amin, Bandali, Bhatia, Cavendish, Chowdhary . . .

Cavendish.

Like stubbing her foot on a stone, the shock rippled through her. She reached out and touched the grooves of the lettering.

Second Lieutenant George Carmichael Cavendish.

Carmichael – her father's middle name.

'Can't be . . .' she mouthed.

Ambrose *had* had a brother – Uncle George who'd died in the war. Prayed for him each Armistice Day when she was a child. Killed on a bombing raid over Germany – or that's what they'd led her to believe . . .

Coincidence? Was this another George Carmichael Cavendish? Or had her parents lied to her? To conceal what had happened here . . . Had *both* brothers been imprisoned by the Japanese? One dying the other living? She felt a door had opened. A chink of light.

Must be a book lying around somewhere, telling the story of the prison camp. She glanced quickly at the end walls of the thatched-roofed shrine and realised they were covered with etched bronze plates. Head spinning, she stepped over to look. Sketches of what the camp had been like. Squat guards, skeletal prisoners.

And text. Words telling the story of the men whose forced labour had built and maintained the Japanese bomber base here on Kutu. She skim-read, moving from plate to plate. Then she found it. Heart in her mouth, she began to read more slowly, every word impacting in her mind like a dart.

The last of the prisoners to be killed was 2nd Lieutenant G.C. Cavendish, one of a pair of twins. Shortly before war end, the camp commandant suspected 2nd Lieutenants G.C. & A.C. Cavendish of trying to organize a mass escape. Both men were tortured but they revealed nothing. Then in an effort to break A.C. Cavendish, G.C. Cavendish was staked out in the middle of the parade ground for three days in the hot sun, while his brother watched. A.C. Cavendish stayed silent, but was forced to see his brother die.

'Oh God oh God!' Charlie choked, hands to her mouth. 'Oh Papa . . .'

She felt his pain as if it had been her own. Felt the acid burn of the guilt he could never expunge. If only he'd talked about it . . . To her, to Verity. A burden shared . . .

There was still time. Perhaps. If she hurried.

She turned back to the van with its blacked-out windows.

Darwin
Friday 17.05 hrs (07.35 hrs GMT)

The Premati Air Boeing 737 touched tarmac in Australia in a torrential downpour. For most of the flight Charlie had wept silently, her face turned away from Randall so he wouldn't see. She breathed in deeply. Time to pull herself together. In a little over an hour she had to be on air with her story.

She turned to Nick with a sigh and a forced smile.

'Civilisation,' she murmured.

'Mmm.'

His mind was elsewhere, she realised. As hers had been.

'Sorry I've not been very communicative,' she said.

He put his hand on hers and smiled. 'No matter.'

'You know, I'm not even sure I've said thank you . . .' she added, lowering her eyes, '. . . for saving my life.'

'Oh *that* . . .' he twinkled, squeezing her fingers. 'Think nothing of it, chuck. All part of the service. You pay your taxes . . .'

There was a tenseness in his humour that she didn't like. The sort of forced jollity people used before telling you something you wouldn't want to hear.

'I'm going to have to *run* when I get off this thing,' Charlie murmured, extricating her hand as the plane taxied in. 'Quick call to London from the terminal, then a cab and I *might* make the end of the Breakfast Show. You *will* come with me to the studios, won't you?' she asked, dreading his answer.

'I can't, Charlie.'

There was a leaden feeling in her stomach.

'Have to get back to London.'

'Oh,' she said softly. 'You're going *tonight*? What about your poor shoulder?'

'It'll be fine. I'll sleep all the way. There's a flight in two hours. The Met'll treat me to business class so I can stretch out.'

'Oh. Oh I see. Won't be so bad then.' She tried to conceal her disappointment. 'So . . . is this it? We say goodbye and that's the end?'

Yes, thought Randall. It had to be. For all sorts of reasons. One was that the tape in his pocket simply couldn't wait. A crime had been committed at the highest level. But just as important – if he stayed overnight in Darwin to keep her company, they'd end up in bed again. And this time it'd be different.

'Yep. I have to hand in a report. In person. Soon as poss,' he explained. 'No peace for the wicked, eh?'

He saw the pain on her face and almost had second thoughts.

'We were a good team, sweetheart,' he said, touching her hand again. 'You got me into Kutu, I got you out. But . . .' he added, trying to make a joke of it, 'sleeping with a journalist – that's not something a copper's meant to make a habit of.'

She blushed angrily. 'What makes you think you'd have got another opportunity . . .?'

She turned away. He annoyed her. Annoyed her because she never knew what he was really thinking. But not to be given the chance to find out – that wasn't fair.

'We must meet, then,' she said briskly, fumbling amongst her personal papers for a business card. 'I'll buy you a drink. It's the least I can do for saving me from Mount Jiwa.' She wrote her home phone number on the back of the card and gave it to him.

'Well . . . thanks.' He pocketed it quickly. Maybe in a week or two . . . When things were back to normal. Just for a chat.

They didn't speak again until they reached the baggage hall. Charlie made a lightning-fast call to the News Channel newsdesk and emerged from the booth glowing.

'I can just make it,' she gasped.

They hugged then parted.

'Good luck, chuck,' he murmured.

'You too.'

Then she was gone, running through customs control with her rucksack on her back to grab a taxi into town.

Randall watched her go, trying to pretend he didn't feel a sense of loss.

307

23

WHEN HE WALKED back into the Security Group Ops Room at Scotland Yard, Randall knew he'd returned to the fold.

'Nice tan,' muttered a colleague. 'Good holiday?'

'Get your leg over?' shouted another.

They knew where he'd been of course. Weren't supposed to, but when one of their own got a sunshine trip to the other side of the world envy pushed the word around.

Mostyn stood in the doorway of his office, hands on hips, impatient for a debrief before morning prayers.

The 747 had landed Randall back in London on Saturday morning. A Special Branch car had taken him to hospital for a change of dressing, then Debbie had collected him. A huge hug from her and he felt back on dry land. She'd wanted to whisk him home and mother him, but instead he'd persuaded her to drive him to a sports ground near Wormwood Scrubs to watch the final minutes of the Scotland Yard League match he should have been playing in. Special Branch were three goals down. *He*'d have saved them.

On the flight back from Darwin he'd thought long and hard about the taped confession in his bag and come to the unhappy conclusion it was legally worthless. Without other evidence or Bowen himself in the witness box repeating what he'd said about the million-pound commissions for him and Keith Copeland, there could be no case. Bowen was dead and so was Sumoto – Copeland's co-conspirators. If the only evidence against him was the taped word of a half-demented man close to death, the DPP would never press charges.

'Assistant Commissioner Stanley's chuffed to buggery,' Mostyn growled as he pulled out a chair for Randall to sit on. 'Says he'll be able to retire now with a great big grin on his face.'

Randall gave his account of Stephen Bowen's final hours. Mostyn listened with rapt attention. No mention of the confession. No mention of a tape. Randall had other plans for it.

Fifteen minutes later a Branch car dropped him by the gates to Downing Street. The PM had asked for a meeting – to thank him personally for trying to save Stephen Bowen.

South Devon

The woodland leaves had turned in the past week. The banks of the estuary were now a mottled yellow. Charlotte had wrapped herself in her mother's Barbour before setting out across the sandbanks in her wellies. A crisp wind whistled in from the sea. She felt cleansed by its purity.

She'd arrived back in London the previous morning, exhausted but aglow from the praise for her exclusive on what had happened in Kutu. The dramatic footage of her capture and the story of her escape from a gun battle between rival factions of the Indonesian armed forces had turned her into a national celebrity overnight.

Although keen to bask in her new-found fame, another priority had preoccupied her on arriving home. At Heathrow airport she'd discovered there was a flight to Plymouth in less than an hour. She'd phoned her mother to warn her, then taken it.

Verity had collected her at the airport and driven her to Sandpiper Cottage, shocked and a little angry that her daughter should have taken such risks for her work.

Charlie had sat alone with her father out on the terrace, wrapped up against the wind. As swans drifted by, she'd told him gently about the cemetery in Kutu and what she'd learned there. She'd assured him she understood, and begged him to talk about it at last. To open his heart. Eventually he had.

It had been terrible to watch him weep. Fifty years of grief and guilt flooding out from the dam which she had broken. Terrible too to learn later from her mother that she'd returned home last Thursday to find him sitting by the telephone with a revolver in his hand.

Charlie stood in the middle of the stream, the shallow water swirling round her boots. She looked back at the cottage, emotionally and physically drained, wondering if it was right for her to have done what she'd done. Wondering if her father *would* now find peace before he died.

There was a flight back to London after lunch. She'd decided to be on it. She needed to get her life back in order. To see her flat and her cat. To end her meaningless relationship with Jeremy. And above all to be with people. To tell them modestly of her exploits and to bask in the warmth of their admiration.

And, if he would let her, to talk it through with the only person in the world who would ever understand.

Downing Street

Nick Randall stepped from the door of Number 10, nodded at the man from the uniformed branch and headed down the pavement towards Whitehall.

From the moment he'd arrived, the PM had been jittery, as if expecting something. When Randall told him Bowen had accused him of putting his hands in the till, he'd feigned astonishment and outrage. But the charade had ended when Randall told him copies of the tape might soon find their way to the media.

Randall wasn't proud of what he'd done, but had convinced himself there'd been no alternative. If the courts couldn't dish out justice, there were times when others had to.

He sniffed deeply at the crisp autumn air, relieved that his confrontation with Copeland was over. Then, halfway towards the Downing Street gates, the rolling boom of an explosion stopped him dead in his tracks.

'Oh no . . .' he moaned.

The Revenue Men were saying 'welcome back'.

Without another thought he took the cell-phone from his pocket and called the Ops Room.

'Abingdon Green,' snapped Chris, the duty sergeant. 'Opposite parliament. Where the TV crews interview MPs. No warning and loads of casualties. Can you make it? I know you're meant to be off today . . .'

'On my way.'

TV crews. *Charlie.*

He ran through the gates, sprinted down Whitehall, weaved through the cars and buses jammed solid in Parliament Square and flashed his ID at a panicking constable trying to shoo away the crowds.

'Yeah, OK,' he said, pushing Randall through.

He heard the tinkle of glass falling from shattered windows. A woman screaming. The wail of sirens.

On the green opposite the St Stephen's entrance to the House, there were bodies everywhere. Some sitting, clamping handkerchiefs to bleeding faces, some lying flat, well beyond doing anything for themselves. Three or four tripods and cameras lay on the grass like toppled cranes.

'Anti-Terrorist Branch,' Randall puffed, showing his card to a uniformed inspector stumbling around in a state of shock.

'I was just over there.' The officer swung an arm towards parliament. 'We watch this lot like a hawk. Then a bomb went off in the middle of 'em. Out of thin air . . . TV people. And a couple of MPs.' A fresh burst of sirens distracted him. 'Bloody 'ell! Look at that . . .! Chaos!' He strode towards the road, yelling at his men to clear a way for more ambulances.

She *couldn't* be here, Randall told himself. Probably not even back in the country. But he looked, just to be sure.

Paramedics swarmed round the injured. A gaggle of nurses in blue ran from the Embankment to help. There was a hospital nearby and they'd come on foot.

Hell, thought Randall. Utter bloody carnage. He looked round for someone to talk to, to piece together what had happened. Then he saw a Branch car pull up and DCI Mostyn get out. He walked over to him.

'Je-esus!' Mostyn wheezed. 'Don't like this. The bastards are switching from businessmen to politicians. Talking of which . . .' He prodded Randall in the chest. 'Heard the news?'

'What?'

'PM's resigned. It was on the radio in the car. Just now.'

'Oh, really.'

Mostyn frowned at his lack of surprise.

'Suppose you got wind of this at your little *tête à tête* this morning.'

Randall pursed his lips.

'Anyway, don't just stand there, find us a prime witness so we can nail these bastards.'

Randall smiled fleetingly. He glanced round. So . . . his turn of special duties was over. He was back to the old routine, chipping away at the coal face, hoping for a glint of gold.

He walked to the end of the green where the injured looked more *compos mentis*. Striped plastic incident tape was being unrolled to seal off the site from the road. Suddenly, beyond it, an argument broke out. A young constable telling two TV newsmen to move their cameras back.

Randall stopped. The media were gathering in strength. He scanned the faces of the reporters – amongst them a young, blonde woman . . . No. Not her. He told himself to stop being daft.

He turned away, aiming for a likely witness. But his hand slipped into the pocket of his jacket to check that he still had Charlie's card.